G A
NIGH

Volume II

Also edited by Hugh Lamb in Futura:

GASLIT NIGHTMARES

G A S L I T
NIGHTMARES

Volume II

O

An Anthology of
Victorian Tales
of Terror

Edited by

HUGH LAMB

Futura

A Futura BOOK

First published in Great Britain in 1991 by
Futura Publications
A division of
Macdonald & Co (Publishers) Ltd
London & Sydney

Typeset in Bodoni by Leaper & Gard Ltd, Bristol, England
Made and printed in Great Britain by
BPCC Hazell Books
Aylesbury, Bucks, England
Member of BPCC Ltd.

ISBN 0 7088 4876 1

Futura Publications
A division of
Macdonald & Co (Publishers) Ltd
Orbit House
1 New Fetter Lane
London EC4A 1AR
A member of Maxwell Macmillan Pergamon Publishing Corporation

Acknowledgements

O

I must acknowledge, as usual, help received from Sutton Public Library who keep tracking the books down for me, and from Mike Ashley and Richard Dalby, who help with the background details when I've got hold of the books. And John Jarrold, who thought it was all a good idea.

Introduction

O

Readers of my previous Victorian anthologies will know by the title what this book contains. However, a word on the contents is necessary. GASLIT NIGHTMARES VOLUME II is my sixth Victorian anthology, but I've varied the format somewhat to include some equally worthy stories from later years than the usual closing date of 1901.

Thus the latest published story is 1927 (though that one was written in 1907) and we have a selection of tales ranging from 1901 through the 1910s up to the 1920s, as well as a splendid set of stories from the Victorian era itself. This is to try and give an airing to some other fine tales which might otherwise be disqualified by their date of publication. I hope you think the results worthwhile.

HUGH LAMB
Sutton, Surrey

Contents

O

THE STRANGE STORY
OF NORTHAVON PRIORY

O

Frank Frankfort Moore

What better way to start the book than this grand piece of Edwardian terror from one of the era's most prolific writers—who was also Bram Stoker's brother-in-law.

Frank Frankfort Moore (1855–1931) was born in Limerick and became a journalist when he was twenty. He travelled all over the world—India, the West Indies, South America and Africa—and in his spare time turned out fiction, plays and poetry.

His first book, the poetry collection FLYING FROM A SHADOW (1872) was published when he was seventeen but his first big success was the novel I FORBID THE BANNS (1893).

He published over eighty books, including novels, short story collections, verse, westerns, biographies (including books on Byron, Fanny Burney and Goldsmith), as well as books for the Christian Knowledge Society and even a book on collecting antique furniture! His last book, THE AWAKENING OF HELEN, was published in 1929.

Moore and Stoker were friends; both settled in London and they married the Balcombe sisters. Moore's wife Grace died in 1901.

Like Stoker, Moore tried his hand at the occasional ghost story and this one comes from his 1904 collection THE OTHER WORLD. *It certainly deserves a second chance but it warrants careful reading.*

FRANK FRANKFORT MOORE

O

The Strange Story
of Northavon Priory

WHEN Arthur Jephson wrote to me to join his Christmas party at Northavon Priory, I was set wondering where I had heard the name of this particular establishment. I felt certain that I had heard the name before, but I could not recollect for the moment whether I had come upon it in a newspaper report of a breach of promise of marriage or in a Blue-Book bearing upon Inland Fisheries: I rather inclined to the belief that it was in a Blue-Book of some sort. I had been devoting myself some years previously to an exhaustive study of this form of literature; for being very young, I had had a notion that a Blue-Book education was essential to any one with parliamentary aspirations. Yes, I had, I repeat, been very young at that time, and I had not found out that a Blue-Book is the *oubliette* of inconvenient facts.

It was not until I had promised Arthur to be with him on Christmas Eve that I recollected where I had read something about Northavon Priory, and in a moment I understood how it was I had acquired the notion that the name had appeared in an official document. I had read a good deal about this Priory in a curious manuscript which I had unearthed at Sir Dennis le Warden's place in

Norfolk, known as Marsh Towers. The document, which,
with many others, I found stowed away in a wall-
cupboard in the great library, purported to be a draft of
the evidence taken before one of the Commissions
appointed by King Henry VIII to inquire into the abuses
alleged to be associated with certain religious houses
throughout England. An ancestor of Sir Dennis's had, it
appeared, been a member of one of these Commissions,
and he had taken a note of the evidence which he had in
the course of his duties handed to the King.

The parchments had, I learned, been preserved in an
iron coffer with double padlocks, but the keys had been
lost at some remote period, and then the coffer had been
covered over with lumber in a room in the east tower
overlooking the moat, until an outbreak of fire had
resulted in an overturning of the rubbish and a discovery
of the coffer. A blacksmith had been employed to pick the
locks, which he did with a sledge-hammer; but it was
generally admitted that his energy had been wasted when
the contents of the box were made known. Sir Dennis
cared about nothing except the improvement of the breed
of horses through the agency of race meetings, so the
manuscripts of his painstaking ancestor were bundled
into one of the presses in the library, some, however,
being reserved by the intelligent housekeeper in the still-
room to make jam-pot covers—a purpose for which, as she
explained to me at considerable length, they were
extremely well adapted.

I had no great difficulty in deciphering those that
came under my hand, for I had had considerable experience of the tricks of early English writers; and as I read I
became greatly interested in all the original 'trustie and
well-beelou'd Sir Denice le Warden' had written. The
frankness of the evidence which he had collected on
certain points took away my breath, although I had been
long accustomed to the directness with which some of the
fifteenth-century people expressed themselves.

Northavon Priory was among the religious houses

whose practices had formed the subject of the inquiry, and it was the summary of Sir Denice's notes regarding the Black Masses alleged to have been celebrated within its walls that proved so absorbing to me. The bald account of the nature of these orgies would of itself have been sufficient, if substantiated, to bring about the dissolution of all the order in England. The Black Mass was a pagan revel, the details of which were unspeakable, though their nature was more than hinted at by the King's Commissioner. Anything so monstrously blasphemous could not be imagined by the mind of man, for with the pagan orgie there was mixed up the most solemn rite of the Mass. It was celebrated on the night of Christmas Eve, and at the hour of midnight the celebration culminated in an invocation to the devil, written so as to parody an office of the Church, and, according to the accounts of some witnesses, in a human sacrifice. Upon this latter point, however, Sir Denice admitted there was a diversity of opinion.

One of the witnesses examined was a man who had entered the Priory grounds from the river during a fearful tempest, on one Christmas Eve, and had, he said, witnessed the revel through a window to which he had climbed. He declared that at the hour of midnight the candles had been extinguished, but that a moment afterwards an awful red light had floated through the room, followed by the shrieks of a human being at the point of strangulation, and then by horrible yells of laughter. Another man who was examined had been a wood-cutter in the service of the Priory, and he had upon one occasion witnessed the celebration of a Black Mass; but he averred that no life was sacrificed, though he admitted that in the strange red light, which had flashed through the room, he had seen what appeared to be two men struggling on the floor. In the general particulars of the orgie there was, however, no diversity of opinion, and had the old Sir Denice le Warden been anything of a comparative mythologist, he could scarcely fail to have been greatly interested in being brought face to face with so striking an example of the survival of an ancient superstition within the walls of a holy building.

During a rainy week I amused myself among the parchments dealing with Northavon Priory, and although what I read impressed me greatly at the time, yet three years of pretty hard work in various parts of the world had so dulled my memory of any incident so unimportant as the deciphering of a mouldy document that, as I have already stated, it was not until I had posted my letter to Arthur Jephson agreeing to spend a day or two with his party, that I succeeded in recalling something of what I had read regarding Northavon Priory.

I had taken it for granted that the Priory had been demolished when Henry had superintended the dissolution of the religious establishments throughout the country: I did not think it likely that one with such a record as was embodied in the notes would be allowed to remain with a single stone on another. A moment's additional reflection admitted of my perceiving how extremely unlikely it was that, even if Northavon Priory had been spared by the King, it would still be available for visitors during the latter years of the nineteenth century. I had seen many red-brick 'abbeys' and 'priories' in various parts of the country, not more than ten years old, inhabited mostly by gentlemen who had made fortunes in iron, or perhaps lard, which constitutes, I understand, an excellent foundation for a fortune. There might be, for all I knew, a score of Northavon Priories in England. Arthur Jephson's father had made his money by the judicious advertising of a certain oriental rug manufactured in the Midlands, and I thought it very likely that he had built a mansion for himself which he had called Northavon Priory.

A letter which I received from Arthur set my mind at rest. He explained to me very fully that Northavon Priory was a hotel built within the walls of an ancient religious house. He had spent a delightful month fishing in the river during the summer—I had been fishing in the Amazon at that time—and had sojourned at the hotel, which he had found to be a marvel of comfort in spite of its picturesqueness. This was why, he said, he had thought how jolly it would be to entertain a party of his friends at the place during the Christmas week.

That explanation was quite good enough for me. I had a week or two to myself in England before going to India, and so soon as I recalled what I had read regarding Northavon Priory, I felt glad that my liking for Jephson had induced me to accept his invitation.

It was not until we were travelling together to the station nearest to the Priory that he mentioned to me, quite incidentally, that during the summer he had been fortunate enough to make the acquaintance of a young woman who resided in a spacious mansion within easy distance of the Priory Hotel, and who was, so far as he was capable of judging—and he considered that in such matters his judgment was worth something—the most charming girl in England.

'I see,' I remarked, before his preliminary panegyric had quite come to a legitimate conclusion—'I see all now: you haven't the courage—to be more exact, the impudence—to come down alone to the hotel—she has probably a brother who is a bit of an athlete—but you think that Tom Singleton and I will form a good enough excuse for an act on your part which parents and guardians can construe in one way only.'

'Well, perhaps—Hang it all, man, you needn't attribute to me any motives but those of the purest hospitality,' laughed my companion. 'Isn't the prospect of a genuine old English Christmas—the Yule log, and that sort of thing—good enough for you without going any further?'

'It's quite good enough for me,' I replied. 'I only regret that it is not good enough for you. You expect to see her every day?'

'Every day? Don't be a fool, Jim. If I see her more than four times in the course of the week—I think I should manage to see her four times—I will consider myself exceptionally lucky.'

'And if you see her less than four times you will reckon yourself uncommonly unlucky?'

'O, I think I have arranged for four times all right: I'll have to trust to luck for the rest.'

'What! You mean to say that the business has gone as far as that?'

'As what?'

'As making arrangements for meetings with her?'

My friend laughed complacently.

'Well, you see, old chap, I couldn't very well give you this treat without letting her know that I should be in the neighbourhood,' said he.

'Oh, indeed. I don't see, however, what the—'.

'Great heavens! You mean to say that you don't see— Oh, you will have your joke.'

'I hope I will have one eventually; I can't say that I perceive much chance of one at present, however. You'll not give us much of your interesting society during the week of our treat, as you call it.'

'I'll give you as much of it as I can spare—more than you'll be likely to relish, perhaps. A week's a long time, Jim.'

'"Time travels at divers paces with divers persons," my friend. I suppose she's as lovely as any of the others of past years?'

'As lovely! Jim, she's just the—'

'Don't trouble yourself over the description. I have a vivid recollection of the phrases you employed in regard to the others. There was Lily, and Gwen, and Bee, and— yes, by George! there was a fourth; her name was Nelly, or—'

'All flashes in the pan, my friend. I didn't know my own mind in those old days; but now, thank heaven!—Oh, you'll agree with me when you see her. This is the real thing and no mistake.'

He was good enough to give me a genuine lover's

description of the young woman, whose name was, he said, Sylvia St Leger; but it did not differ materially from the descriptions which had come from him in past days, of certainly four other girls for whom he had, he imagined, entertained a devotion strong as death itself. Alas! his devotion had not survived a single year in any case.

When we arrived at the hotel, after a drive of eight miles from the railway station, we found Tom Singleton waiting for us rather impatiently, and in a quarter of an hour we were facing an excellent dinner. We were the only guests at the hotel, for though it was picturesquely situated on the high bank of the river, and was doubtless a delightful place for a sojourn in summer, yet in winter it possessed few attractions to casual visitors.

After dinner I strolled over the house, and found, to my surprise, that the old walls of the Priory were practically intact. The kitchen was also unchanged, but the great refectory was now divided into four rooms. The apartments upstairs had plainly been divided in the same way by brick partitions; but the outer walls, pierced with narrow windows, were those of the original Priory.

In the morning I made further explorations, only outside the building, and came upon the ruins of the old Priory tower; and then I perceived that only a small portion of the original building had been utilised for the hotel. The landlord, who accompanied me, was certainly no antiquarian. He told me that he had been 'let in' so far as the hotel was concerned. He had been given to understand that the receipts for the summer months were sufficiently great to compensate for the absence of visitors during the winter; but his experience of one year had not confirmed this statement, made by the people from whom he had bought the place, and he had come to the conclusion that, as he had been taken in in the transaction, it was his duty to try to take in some one else in the same way.

'I only hope that I may succeed, sir,' he said, 'but I'm

doubtful about it. People are getting more suspicious every day.'

'You weren't suspicious, at any rate,' said I.

'That I weren't—more's the pity, sir,' said he. 'But it'll take me all my time to get the place off my hands, I know. Ah, yes; it's hard to get people to take your word for anything nowadays.'

For the next two days Tom Singleton and I were left a good deal together, the fact being that our friend Arthur parted from us after lunch and only returned in time for dinner, declaring upon each occasion that he had just passed the pleasantest day of his life. On Christmas Eve he came to us in high spirits, bearing with him an invitation from a lady who had attained distinction, through being the mother of Miss St Leger, for us to spend Christmas Day at her house—it had already been pointed out to us by Arthur: it was a fine Georgian country house, named The Grange.

'I've accepted for you both,' said Arthur. 'Mrs St Leger is a most charming woman, and her daughter—I don't know if I mentioned that she had a daughter—well, if I omitted, I am now in a position to assure you that her daughter—her name is Sylvia—is possibly the most beautiful—But there's no use trying to describe her; you'll see her for yourselves tomorrow, and judge if I've exaggerated in the least when I say that the world does not contain a more exquisite creature.'

'Yes, one hour with her will be quite sufficient to enable us to pronounce an opinion on that point,' laughed Tom.

We remained smoking in front of the log fire that blazed in the great hearth, until about eleven o'clock, and then went to our rooms upstairs, after some horse-play in the hall.

My room was a small one at the beginning of the corridor, Arthur Jephson's was alongside it, and at the very end of the corridor was Tom Singleton's. All had at one time been one apartment.

Having walked a good deal during the day, I was very tired, and had scarcely got into bed before I fell asleep.

When I awoke it was with a start and a consciousness that something was burning. A curious red light streamed into the room from outside. I sprang from my bed in a moment and ran to the window. But before I had reached it the room was in darkness once more, and there came a yell of laughter, apparently from the next room.

For a moment I was paralyzed. But the next instant I had recovered my presence of mind. I believed that Arthur and Tom had been playing some of their tricks upon me. They had burnt a red light outside my window, and were roaring with laughter as they heard me spring out of bed.

That was the explanation of what I had seen and heard which first suggested itself to me; and I was about to return to bed when my door was knocked at and then opened.

'What on earth have you been up to?' came the voice of Arthur Jephson. 'Have you set the bed-curtains on fire? If you have, that's nothing to laugh at.'

'Get out of this room with your larking,' said I. 'It's a very poor joke that of yours, Arthur. Go back to your bed.'

He struck a light—he had a match-box in his hand—and went to my candle without a word. In a moment the room was faintly illuminated.

'Do you mean to say that you hadn't a light here just now—a red light?' he cried.

'I had no light: a red light floated through the room, but it seemed to come from outside,' said I.

'And who was it laughed in that wild way?'

'I took it for granted that it was you and Tom who were about your usual larks.'

'Larks! No, I was about no larks, I can promise you. Good Lord! man, that laugh was something beyond a lark.' He seated himself on my bed. 'Do you fancy it may have been some of the servants going about the stables with a carriage-lamp?' he continued. 'There may have been a late arrival at the hotel, you know.'

'That's not at all unlikely,' said I. 'Yes, it may have been that, and the laughter may have been between the grooms.'

'I don't hear any sound of bustle through the house or outside,' said he.

'The stables are not at this angle of the building,' said I. 'We must merely have seen the light and heard that laughter as the carriage passed our angle. Anyhow, we'll only catch cold if we lounge about in our pyjamas like this. You'd best get back to bed and let me do the same.'

'I don't feel much inclined to sleep, but I'll not prevent your having your night's rest,' said he, resting. 'I wonder is it near morning?'

I held the candle before the dial of my watch that hung above my bed.

'It's exactly five minutes past twelve,' said I. 'We've slept barely an hour.'

'Then the sooner I clear out the better it will be for both of us,' said he.

He went away slowly, and I heard him strike a match in his own room. He evidently meant to light his candle.

Some hours had passed before I fell into an uneasy sleep, and once more I was awakened by Arthur Jephson, who stood by my bedside. The morning light was in the room.

'For God's sake, come into Tom's room!' he whispered. 'He's dead!—Tom is dead!'

I tried to realize his words. Some moments had elapsed before I succeeded in doing so. I sprang from my bed and ran down the corridor to the room occupied by Tom Singleton. The landlord and a couple of servants were already there. They had burst in the door.

It was but too true: our poor friend lay on his bed with his body bent and his arms twisted as though he had been struggling desperately with someone at his last moment. His face, too, was horribly contorted, and his eyes were wide open.

'A doctor,' I managed to say.

'He's already sent for, sir,' said the landlord.

In a few moments the doctor arrived.

'Cardiac attack,' said he. 'Was he alone in the room? No, he can't have been alone.'

'He was quite alone,' said Arthur. 'I knocked at the door a quarter of an hour ago, but getting no answer, I tried to force the lock. It was too strong for me; but the landlord and the man-servant who was bringing us our hot water burst in the door at my request.'

'And the window—was it fastened?' asked the doctor.

'It was secure, sir,' said the landlord.

'Ah, a sudden cardiac attack,' said the doctor.

There was, of course, an inquest, but as no evidence of foul play was forthcoming, the doctor's phrase 'cardiac attack' satisfied the jury, and a verdict of 'death from natural causes' was returned.

Before I went back to town I examined the room in which our poor friend had died. On the side of one of the window-shutters there were four curious burnt marks. They gave one the impression that the shutter had at one time been grasped by a man wearing a red-hot gauntlet.

I started for India before the end of the year and remained there for eight months. Then I thought I would pay a visit to a sister of mine in Queensland. On my return at the end of the year I meant to stop at Cairo for a few weeks. On entering Shepheard's Hotel I found myself face to face with Arthur Jephson and his wife—he called her Sylvia. They had been married in August, but their honeymoon seemed still to be in its first quarter. It was after Mrs Jephson had retired, and when Arthur was sitting with me enjoying the cool of the night by the aid of a pretty strong cigar or two, that we ventured to allude to the tragic occurrence which marked our last time of meeting.

'I wish to beg of you not to make any allusion to that awful business in the hearing of my wife,' said Arthur. 'In fact I must ask you not to allude to that fearful room in the Priory in any way.'

'I will be careful not to do so,' said I. 'You have your own reasons, I suppose, for giving me this warning.'

'I have the best of reasons, Jim. She too had her experience of that room, and it was as terrible as ours.'

'Good heavens! I heard nothing of that. She did not sleep in that room?'

'Thank God, she didn't. I arrived in time to save her.'

I need scarcely say that my interest was now fully aroused.

'Tell me what happened—if you dare tell it,' I said.

'You were abroad, and so you wouldn't be likely to hear of the fire at The Grange,' said my friend, after a pause.

'I heard nothing of it.'

'It took place only two days before last Christmas. I had been in the south of France, where I had spent a month or two with my mother—she cannot stand a winter at home—and I had promised Sylvia to return to The Grange for Christmas. When I got to Northavon I found her and her mother and their servants at the Priory Hotel. The fire had taken place the previous night, and they found the hotel very handy when they hadn't a roof of their own over their heads. Well, we dined together, and were as jolly as was possible under the circumstances until bedtime. I had actually said "Good night" to Sylvia before I recollected what had taken place the previous Christmas Eve in the same house. I rushed upstairs, and found Sylvia in the act of entering the room—that fatal room. When I implored of her to choose some other apartment, she only laughed at first, and assured me that she wasn't superstitious; but when she saw that I was serious—I was deadly serious, as you can believe, Jim—'

'I can—I can.'

'Well she agreed to sleep in her mother's room, and I went away relieved. So soon as I returned to the fire in the dining-room I began to think of poor Tom Singleton. I felt curiously excited, and I knew that it would be useless for me to go to bed—in fact, I made up my mind not to leave the dining-room for some hours, at any rate, and when the landlord came to turn out the lights I told him he might trust me to do that duty for him. He left me alone in the room about half-past eleven o'clock. When the sound of his feet upon the oaken stairs died away I felt as fearful as a child in the dark. I lit another cigar and walked about the room for some time. I went to the window that opened upon the old Priory ground, and, seeing that the night was a fine one, I opened the door and strolled out, hoping that the cool air would do me good. I had not gone many yards across the little patch of green before I turned and looked up at the house—at the last window, the window of that room. A fire had been lighted in the room early in the evening, and its glow shone through the white blind. Suddenly that faint glow increased to a terrific glare—a red glare, Jim—and then there came before my eyes for a moment the shadow of two figures upon the blind—one the figure of a woman, the other—God knows what it was. I rushed back to the room, but before I had reached the door I heard the horrible laughter once again. It seemed to come from that room and to pass on through the air into the distance across the river. I ran upstairs with a light, and found Sylvia and her mother standing together with wraps around them at the door of the room. "Thank God, you are safe!" I managed to cry. "I feared that you had returned to the room." "You heard it—that awful laughter?" she whispered. "You heard it, and you saw something—what was it?" I gently forced her and her mother back to their room, for the servants and the land-lord's family were now crowding into the corridor. They, too, had heard enough to alarm them.'

'You went to the room?'

'The scene of that dreadful morning was repeated. The door was locked on the inside. We broke it in and found a girl lying dead on the floor, her face contorted just as poor Singleton's was. She was Sylvia's maid, and it was thought that, on hearing that her mistress was not going to occupy the room, she had gone into it herself on account of the fire which had been lighted there.'

'And the doctor said—?'

'Cardiac attack—the same as before—singular coincidence! I need scarcely say that we never slept again under that accursed roof. Poor Sylvia! She was overwhelmed at the thought of how narrow her escape had been.'

'Did you notice anything remarkable about the room—about the shutters of the window?' I asked.

He looked at me curiously for a moment. Then he bent forward and said—

'On the edge of the shutter there were some curious marks where the wood had been charred.'

'As if a hand with a red-hot gauntlet had been laid upon it?'

'There were the marks of two such hands,' said my friend slowly.

We remained for an hour in the garden; then we threw away the ends of our cigars and went into the hotel without another word.

A TROPICAL HORROR

O

William Hope Hodgson

Few horror authors have been strong enough to lift a man over their head with one arm, but William Hope Hodgson (1877–1918) managed it. In addition to writing some of the most highly regarded works in this field, he was a physical fitness enthusiast and remarkable athlete.

Born in Weathersfield, Essex, Hodgson was the son of a clergyman and one of twelve children. Samuel Hodgson, his father, moved round the country a lot, even spending some time in Ireland, and friction between Hodgson and his father ended in William running away to sea in 1891 (it also left him a lifelong atheist). He joined the merchant navy, sailed round the world three times and won a medal from the Royal Humane Society for saving the life of a shipmate in New Zealand. He should have held on a bit longer, we now know; his father died the year after he left.

While in the merchant navy, Hodgson took up photography and body-building. He became an expert boxer into the bargain. His family, meanwhile, had fallen on hard times after Samuel's death, so William came home for good in 1899. The family had moved to Blackburn and here he set up a school of physical culture in 1901.

Around this time, he encountered Harry Houdini, the great magician and escapologist, who was then on a tour of northern theatres. Hodgson almost defeated the great man by challenging him to escape from a pair of handcuffs. It took Houdini an hour: he was not happy by all accounts!

Hodgson began his writing career in 1902, with a mixture of fitness articles and the short stories that would one day make his name. Very quickly, this led to him writing the brilliant novels that are now classics: THE BOATS OF THE GLEN CARRIG *(1907),* THE HOUSE ON THE BORDERLAND *(1908),* THE GHOST PIRATES *(1909) and* THE NIGHT LAND *(1912).*

Hodgson moved to London in 1910 and married Bessie Farnworth, a girl from his home town, in 1913. They moved to France but Hodgson's dreams of a quiet married life were rudely shattered the next year with the outbreak of the First World War.

He returned to Britain and joined the Royal Artillery as a lieutenant. An injury in training forced him out of the RA for a while but he could not stay away from the war and what he saw as his duty. He re-enlisted in 1917 and was sent to France.

On 19 April 1918, after fighting in the battle of Ypres, he was manning an observation post at Mont Kemmel in Belgium. A German shell landed straight on the post and Hodgson was blown apart.

It was as much a tragedy for those who enjoy his writings as it was for his family. We are left with a small output in book form and a steady uncovering, as years pass, of more of his short stories by diligent researchers.

Such a tale is 'A Tropical Horror'. It was first published in the Grand Magazine, June 1905, and never saw book form in Hodgson's lifetime. It was resurrected in an American edition of his stories in the mid-1970s but is still not widely known.

Hodgson enthusiasts will relish a little more of what they know to be Hodgson's speciality: horrors that come in the night for unfortunate seamen ...

WILLIAM HOPE HODGSON

O

A Tropical Horror

WE are a hundred and thirty days out from Melbourne, and for three weeks we have lain in this sweltering calm.

It is midnight, and our watch on deck until four a.m. I go out and sit on the hatch. A minute later, Joky, our youngest 'prentice, joins me for a chatter. Many are the hours we have sat thus and talked in the night watches; though, to be sure, it is Joky who does the talking. I am content to smoke and listen, giving an occasional grunt at seasons to show that I am attentive.

Joky has been silent for some time, his head bent in meditation. Suddenly he looks up, evidently with the intention of making some remark. As he does so, I see his face stiffen with a nameless horror. He crouches back, his eyes staring past me at some unseen fear. Then his mouth opens. He gives forth a strangulated cry and topples backwards off the hatch, striking his head against the deck. Fearing I know not what, I turn to look.

Great Heavens! Rising above the bulwarks, seen plainly in the bright moonlight, is a vast slobbering mouth a fathom across. From the huge dripping lips hang great tentacles. As I look the Thing comes further over the rail. It is rising, rising, higher and higher. There are no eyes visible; only that fearful slobbering mouth set on the tremendous trunk-like neck; which, even as I watch, is curling inboard with the stealthy celerity of an enormous eel. Over it comes in vast heaving folds. Will it never end? The ship gives a slow, sullen roll to starboard as she feels the weight. Then the tail, a broad, flat-shaped mass, slips over the teak rail and falls with a loud slump on to the deck.

For a few seconds the hideous creature lies heaped in writhing, slimy coils. Then, with quick darting movements, the monstrous head travels along the deck. Close by the mainmast stand the harness casks, and alongside of these a freshly opened cask of salt beef with the top loosely replaced. The smell of the meat seems to attract the monster, and I can hear it sniffing with a vast indrawing breath. Then those lips open, displaying four huge fangs; there is a quick forward motion of the head, a sudden crashing, crunching sound, and beef and barrel have disappeared. The noise brings one of the ordinary seamen out of the fo'cas'le. Coming into the night, he can see nothing for a moment. Then, as he gets further aft, he *sees*, and with horrified cries rushes forward. Too late! From the mouth of the Thing there flashes forth a long, broad blade of glistening white, set with fierce teeth. I avert my eyes, but cannot shut out the sickening 'Glut! Glut!' that follows.

The man on the 'look-out,' attracted by the disturbance, has witnessed the tragedy, and flies for refuge into the fo'cas'le, flinging to the heavy iron door after him.

The carpenter and sailmaker come running out from the half-deck in their drawers. Seeing the awful Thing, they rush aft to the cabin with shouts of fear. The second mate, after one glance over the break of the poop, runs down the companion-way with the helmsman after him. I can hear them barring the scuttle, and abruptly I realize that I am on the main deck alone.

So far I have forgotten my own danger. The past few minutes seem like a portion of an awful dream. Now, however, I comprehend my position and, shaking off the horror that has held me, turn to seek safety. As I do so my eyes fall upon Joky, lying huddled and senseless with fright where he has fallen. I cannot leave him there. Close by stands the empty half-deck—a little steel-built house with iron doors. The lee one is hooked open. Once inside I am safe.

Up to the present the Thing has seemed to be unconscious of my presence. Now, however, the huge barrel-like head sways in my direction; then comes a muffled bellow, and the great tongue flickers in and out as the brute turns and swirls aft to meet me. I know there is not a moment to lose, and, picking up the helpless lad, I make a run for the open door. It is only distant a few yards, but that awful shape is coming down the deck to me in great wreathing coils. I reach the house and tumble in with my burden; then out on deck again to unhook and close the door. Even as I do so something white curls round the end of the house. With a bound I am inside and the door is shut and bolted. Through the thick glass of the ports I see the Thing sweep round the house, in vain search for me.

Joky has not moved yet; so, kneeling down, I loosen his shirt collar and sprinkle some water from the breaker over his face. While I am doing this I hear Morgan shout something; then comes a great shriek of terror, and again that sickening 'Glut! Glut!'

Joky stirs uneasily, rubs his eyes, and sits up suddenly. 'Was that Morgan shouting—?' He breaks off with a cry. 'Where are we? I have had such awful dreams!'

At this instant there is a sound of running footsteps on the deck and I hear Morgan's voice at the door.

'Tom, open—!'

He stops abruptly and gives an awful cry of despair. Then I hear him rush forward. Through the porthole, I see him spring into the fore rigging and scramble madly aloft. Something steals up after him. It shows white in the moonlight. It wraps itself around his right ankle. Morgan stops dead, plucks out his sheath-knife, and hacks

fiercely at the fiendish thing. It lets go, and in a second he is
over the top and running for dear life up the t'gallant rigging.

A time of quietness follows, and presently I see that
the day is breaking. Not a sound can be heard save the
heavy gasping breathing of the Thing. As the sun rises
higher the creature stretches itself out along the deck and
seems to enjoy the warmth. Still no sound, either from the
men forward or the officers aft. I can only suppose that
they are afraid of attracting its attention. Yet, a little
later, I hear the report of a pistol away aft, and looking
out I see the serpent raise its huge head as though
listening. As it does so I get a good view of the fore part,
and in the daylight see what the night has hidden.

There, right about the mouth, is a pair of little pig-
eyes, that seem to twinkle with a diabolical intelligence. It
is swaying its head slowly from side to side; then, without
warning, it turns quickly and looks right in through the
port. I dodge out of sight; but not soon enough. It has
seen me, and brings its great mouth up against the glass.

I hold my breath. My God! If it breaks the glass! I
cower, horrified. From the direction of the port there
comes a loud, harsh, scraping sound. I shiver. Then I
remember that there are little iron doors to shut over the
ports in bad weather. Without a moment's waste of time I
rise to my feet and slam to the door over the port. Then I
go round to the others and do the same. We are now in
darkness, and I tell Joky in a whisper to light the lamp,
which, after some fumbling, he does.

About an hour before midnight I fall asleep. I am
awakened suddenly some hours later by a scream of
agony and the rattle of a water-dipper. There is a slight
scuffling sound; then that soul-revolting 'Glut! Glut!'

I guess what has happened. One of the men forrad has
slipped out of the fo'cas'le to try and get a little water.
Evidently he has trusted to the darkness to hide his
movements. Poor beggar! He has paid for his attempt with
his life!

After this I cannot sleep, though the rest of the night

passes quietly enough. Towards morning I doze a bit, but wake every few minutes with a start. Joky is sleeping peacefully; indeed, he seems worn out with the terrible strain of the past twenty-four hours. About eight a.m. I call him, and we make a light breakfast off the dry ship's biscuit and water. Of the latter happily we have a good supply. Joky seems more himself, and starts to talk a little—possibly somewhat louder than is safe; for, as he chatters on, wondering how it will end, there comes a tremendous blow against the side of the house, making it ring again. After this Joky is very silent. As we sit there I cannot but wonder what all the rest are doing, and how the poor beggars forrad are faring, cooped up without water, as the tragedy of the night has proved.

Towards noon, I hear a loud bang, followed by a terrific bellowing. Then comes a great smashing of woodwork, and the cries of men in pain. Vainly I ask myself what has happened. I begin to reason. By the sound of the report it was evidently something much heavier than a rifle or pistol, and judging from the mad roaring of the Thing, the shot must have done some execution. On thinking it over further, I become convinced that, by some means, those aft have got hold of the small signal cannon we carry, and though I know that some have been hurt, perhaps killed, yet a feeling of exultation seizes me as I listen to the roars of the Thing, and realize that it is badly wounded, perhaps mortally. After a while, however, the bellowing dies away, and only an occasional roar, denoting more of anger than aught else, is heard.

Presently I become aware, by the ship's canting over to starboard, that the creature has gone over to that side, and a great hope springs up within me that possibly it has had enough of us and is going over the rail into the sea. For a time all is silent and my hope grows stronger. I lean across and nudge Joky, who is sleeping with his head on the table. He starts up sharply with a loud cry.

'Hush!' I whisper hoarsely. 'I'm not certain, but I do believe it's gone.'

Joky's face brightens wonderfully, and he questions me eagerly. We wait another hour or so, with hope ever rising. Our confidence is returning fast. Not a sound can we hear, not even the breathing of the Beast. I get out some biscuits, and Joky, after rummaging in the locker, produces a small piece of pork and a bottle of ship's vinegar. We fall to with a relish. After our long abstinence from food the meal acts on us like wine, and what must Joky do but insist on opening the door, to make sure the Thing has gone. This I will not allow, telling him that at least it will be safer to open the iron port-covers first and have a look out. Joky argues, but I am immovable. He becomes excited. I believe the youngster is light-headed. Then, as I turn to unscrew one of the after-covers, Joky makes a dash at the door. Before he can undo the bolts I have him, and after a short struggle lead him back to the table. Even as I endeavour to quieten him there comes at the starboard door—the door that Joky has tried to open—a sharp, loud sniff, sniff, followed immediately by a thunderous grunting howl and a foul stench of putrid breath sweeps in under the door. A great trembling takes me, and were it not for the carpenter's tool-box I should fall. Joky turns very white and is violently sick, after which he is seized by a hopeless fit of sobbing.

Hour after hour passes, and, weary to death, I lie down on the chest upon which I have been sitting, and try to rest.

It must be about half past two in the morning, after a somewhat longer doze, that I am suddenly awakened by a most tremendous uproar away forrad—men's voices shrieking, cursing, praying; but in spite of the terror expressed, so weak and feeble; while in the midst, and at times broken off short with that hellishly suggestive 'Glut! Glut!', is the unearthly bellowing of the Thing. Fear incarnate seizes me, and I can only fall on my knees and pray. Too well I know what is happening.

Joky has slept through it all, and I am thankful.

Presently, under the door there steals a narrow ribbon

of light, and I know that the day has broken on the
second morning of our imprisonment. I let Joky sleep on.
I will let him have peace while he may. Time passes, but I
take little notice. The Thing is quiet, probably sleeping.
About midday I eat a little biscuit and drink some of the
water. Joky still sleeps. It is best so.

A sound breaks the stillness. The ship gives a slight
heave, and I know that once more the Thing is awake.
Round the deck it moves, causing the ship to roll perceptibly. Once it goes forrad—I fancy to explore the fo'cas'le.
Evidently it finds nothing, for it returns almost immediately. It pauses a moment at the house, then goes on
further aft. Up aloft, somewhere in the fore-rigging, there
rings out a peal of wild laughter, though sounding very
faint and far away. The Horror stops suddenly. I listen
intently, but hear nothing save a sharp creaking beyond
the after end of the house, as though a strain had come
upon the rigging.

A minute later I hear a cry aloft, followed almost
instantly by a loud crash on deck that seems to shake the
ship. I wait in anxious fear. What is happening? The
minutes pass slowly. Then comes another frightened
shout. It ceases suddenly. The suspense has become
terrible, and I am no longer able to bear it. Very
cautiously I open one of the after port-covers, and peep
out to see a fearful sight. There, with its tail upon the
deck and its vast body curled round the mainmast, is the
monster, its head above the topsail yard, and its great
claw-armed tentacle waving in the air. It is the first
proper sight that I have had of the Thing. Good Heavens!
It must weigh a hundred tons! Knowing that I shall have
time, I open the port itself, then crane my head out and
look up. There on the extreme end of the lower topsail
yard I see one of the able seamen. Even down here I note
the staring horror of his face. At this moment he sees me
and gives a weak, hoarse cry for help. I can do nothing for
him. As I look the great tongue shoots out and licks him
off the yard, much as might a dog a fly off the window-pane.

Higher still, but happily out of reach, are two more of the men. As far as I can judge they are lashed to the mast above the royal yard. The Thing attempts to reach them, but after a futile effort it ceases, and starts to slide down, coil on coil, to the deck. While doing this I notice a great gaping wound on its body some twenty feet above the tail.

I drop my gaze from aloft and look aft. The cabin door is torn from its hinges, and the bulkhead—which, unlike the half-deck, is of teak wood—is partly broken down. With a shudder I realize the cause of those cries after the cannon-shot. Turning I screw my head round and try to see the foremast, but cannot. The sun, I notice, is low, and the night is near. Then I draw in my head and fasten up both port and cover.

How will it end? Oh! how will it end?

After a while Joky wakes up. He is very restless, yet though he has eaten nothing during the day I cannot get him to touch anything.

Night draws on. We are too weary—too dispirited to talk. I lie down, but not to sleep … Time passes.

A ventilator rattles violently somewhere on the main deck, and there sounds constantly that slurring, gritty noise. Later I hear a cat's agonized howl, and then again all is quiet. Some time after comes a great splash alongside. Then, for some hours, all is silent as the grave. Occasionally I sit up on the chest and listen, yet never a whisper of noise comes to me. There is an absolute silence, even the monotonous creak of the gear has died away entirely, and at last a real hope is springing up within me. That splash, this silence—surely I am justified in hoping. I do not wake Joky this time. I will prove first for myself that all is safe. Still I wait. I will run no unnecessary risks. After a time I creep to the after-port and will listen; but there is no sound. I put up my hand and feel at the screw, then again I hesitate, yet not for long. Noiselessly I begin to unscrew the fastening of the heavy shield. It swings loose on its hinge, and I pull it back and peer out. My heart is beating madly. Everything seems strangely dark outside. Perhaps the moon has gone behind a cloud. Suddenly a beam of moonlight enters through the port, and goes as quickly. I stare out. Something moves. Again the light streams in, and now I seem to be looking into a great cavern, at the bottom of which quivers and curls something palely white.

My heart seems to stand still! It is the Horror! I start back and seize the iron port-flap to slam it to. As I do so, something strikes the glass like a steam ram, shatters it to atoms, and flicks past me into the berth. I scream and spring away. The port is quite filled with it. The lamp shows it dimly. It is curling and twisting here and there. It is as thick as a tree, and covered with a smooth slimy skin. At the end is a great claw, like a lobster's, only a thousand times larger. I cower down into the farthest corner.... It has broken the tool-chest to pieces with one click of those frightful mandibles. Joky has crawled under a bunk. The Thing sweeps round in my direction. I feel a drop of sweat trickle slowly down my face—it tastes salty. Nearer comes that awful death ... Crash! I roll over backwards. It has crushed the water breaker against which I leant, and I am rolling in the water across the floor. The claw drives up, then down, with a quick uncertain movement, striking the deck a dull, heavy blow, a foot from my head. Joky gives a little gasp of horror. Slowly the Thing rises and starts feeling its way round the berth. It plunges into a bunk and pulls out a bolster, nips it in half and drops it, then moves on. It is feeling along the deck. As it does so it comes across a half of the bolster. It seems to toy with it, then picks it up and takes it out through the port....

A wave of putrid air fills the berth. There is a grating sound, and something enters the port again—something white and tapering and set with teeth. Hither and thither it curls, rasping over the bunks, ceiling, and deck, with a noise like that of a great saw at work. Twice it flickers above my head, and I close my eyes. Then off it goes

again. It sounds now on the opposite side of the berth and
nearer to Joky. Suddenly the harsh, raspy noise becomes
muffled, as though the teeth were passing across some
soft substance. Joky gives a horrid little scream, that
breaks off into a bubbling, whistling sound. I open my
eyes. The tip of the vast tongue is curled tightly round
something that drips, then is quickly withdrawn, allowing
the moonbeams to steal again into the berth. I rise to my
feet. Looking round, I note in a mechanical sort of way
the wrecked state of the berth–the shattered chests,
dismantled bunks, and something else–

'Joky!' I cry, and tingle all over.

There is that awful Thing again at the port. I glance
round for a weapon. I will revenge Joky. Ah! there, right
under the lamp, where the wreck of the carpenter's chest
strews the floor, lies a small hatchet. I spring forward and
seize it. It is small, but so keen–so keen! I feel its razor
edge lovingly. Then I am back at the port. I stand to one
side and raise my weapon. The great tongue is feeling its
way to those fearsome remains. It reaches them. As it does
so, with a scream of 'Joky! Joky!' I strike savagely again
and again and again, gasping as I strike; once more, and
the monstrous mass falls to the deck, writhing like a
hideous eel. A vast, warm flood rushes in through the
porthole. There is a sound of breaking steel and an enormous bellowing. A singing comes in my ears and grows
louder–louder. Then the berth grows indistinct and
suddenly dark.

Extract from the log of the steamship *Hispaniola*.

June 24.–Lat.–N. Long.–W. 11 a.m.–Sighted four-
masted barque about four points on the port bow, flying
signal of distress. Ran down to her and sent a boat aboard.
She proved to be the *Glen Doon*, homeward bound from
Melbourne to London. Found things in a terrible state.
Decks covered with blood and slime. Steel deck-house
stove in. Broke open door, and discovered youth of about
nineteen in last stage of inanition, also part remains of

boy about fourteen years of age. There was a great quantity of blood in the place, and a huge curled-up mass of whitish flesh, weighing about half a ton, one end of which appeared to have been hacked through with a sharp instrument. Found forecastle door open and hanging from one hinge. Doorway bulged, as though something had been forced through. Went inside. Terrible state of affairs, blood everywhere, broken chests, smashed bunks, but no men nor remains. Went aft again and found youth showing signs of recovery. When he came round, gave the name of Thompson. Said they had been attacked by a huge serpent—thought it must have been sea-serpent. He was too weak to say much, but told us there were some men up the mainmast. Sent a hand aloft, who reported them lashed to the royal mast, and quite dead. Went aft to the cabin. Here we found the bulkhead smashed to pieces, and the cabin-door lying on the deck near the after-hatch. Found body of captain down lazarette, but no officers. Noticed amongst the wreckage part of the carriage of a small cannon. Came aboard again.

Have sent the second mate with six men to work her into port. Thompson is with us. He has written out his version of the affair. We certainly consider that the state of the ship, as we found her, bears out in every respect his story. (Signed)

William Norton (Master).
Tom Briggs (1st Mate).

NIGHTMARE-TOUCH

O

Lafcadio Hearn

Many authors at the turn of the century felt the pull of the Orient; however, precious few plunged into the Eastern cauldron with the fervour of Lafcadio Hearn (1850–1904), who spent the last years of his life as a Japanese citizen.

Hearn came from a tangled line of descent: born in Greece of a Greek mother and Irish father, he was raised in England and Ireland and ended up in America at the age of twenty.

He started work as a newspaper reporter, and by all accounts not a well-paid one, as he is widely described as having slept on the streets of New York for a while. He gained a fearsome reputation in America for digging up and writing the most lurid and repellent stories (something he continued to do when in Japan).

In 1890 he was sent to Japan on an assignment, fell in love with the country and stayed there for good. He delved into Japanese culture and literature, and wrote several books of stories and articles about the country and its folklore. Prominent among them are IN GHOSTLY JAPAN (1899), A JAPANESE MISCELLANY (1901) and a really odd volume, SHADOWINGS (1900).

When he died, Hearn had risen to become a lecturer in *English literature at the Imperial University, Tokyo. His students must have found him an odd customer, especially if he spent his lessons musing on subjects like that of 'Nightmare-Touch'. This essay, taken from SHADOW-INGS, deals with a little-considered but nonetheless very true aspect of the fear of ghosts.*

LAFCADIO HEARN

O

Nightmare-Touch

I

WHAT *is* the fear of ghosts among those who believe in ghosts?

All fear is the result of experience–experience of the individual or of the race–experience either of the present life or of lives forgotten. Even the fear of the unknown can have no other origin. And the fear of ghosts must be a product of past pain.

Probably the fear of ghosts, as well as the belief in them, had its beginning in dreams. It is a peculiar fear. No other fear is so intense; yet none is so vague. Feelings thus voluminous and dim are super-individual mostly–feelings inherited–feelings made within us by the experience of the dead.

What experience?

Nowhere do I remember reading a plain statement of the reason why ghosts are feared. Ask any ten intelligent persons of your acquaintance, who remember having once been afraid of ghosts, to tell you exactly why they were afraid–to define the fancy behind the fear–and I doubt whether even one will be able to answer the question. The literature of folklore–oral and written–throws no clear light upon the subject. We find, indeed, various legends of men torn asunder by phantoms; but such gross imaginings could not explain the peculiar quality of ghostly fear. It is not a fear of bodily violence. It is not even a reasoning fear—not a fear that can readily explain itself—which would not be the case if it were founded upon definite ideas of physical danger. Furthermore, although primitive ghosts may have been imagined as capable of tearing and devouring, the common idea of a ghost is certainly that of a being intangible and imponderable.*

Now I venture to state boldly that the common fear of ghosts is *the fear of being touched by ghosts*—or, in other words, that the imagined Supernatural is dreaded mainly because of its imagined power to touch. Only to *touch*, remember!—not to wound or to kill.

But this dread of the touch would itself be the result of experience—chiefly, I think, of prenatal experience stored up in the individual by inheritance, like the child's fear of darkness. And who can ever have had the sensation of being touched by ghosts? The answer is simple:—*Everybody who has been seized by phantoms in a dream.*

Elements of primeval fears—fears older than humanity—doubtless enter into the child-terror of darkness. But the more definite fears of ghosts may very possibly be composed with inherited results of dream-pain—ancestral experience of nightmare. And the intuitive terror of supernatural touch can thus be evolutionally explained.

Let me now try to illustrate my theory by relating some typical experiences.

---

*I may remark there that in many old Japanese legends and ballads, ghosts are represented as having power to *pull off* people's heads. But so far as the origin of the fear of ghosts is concerned, such stories explain nothing—since the experiences that evolved the fear must have been real, not imaginary, experiences.

II

When about five years old I was condemned to sleep by
myself in a certain isolated room, thereafter always called
the Child's Room. (At that time I was scarcely ever
mentioned by name, but only referred to as 'the Child.')
The room was narrow, but very high, and, in spite of one
tall window, very gloomy. It contained a fire-place
wherein no fire was ever kindled; and the Child suspected
that the chimney was haunted.

A law was made that no light should be left in the
Child's Room at night—simply because the Child was
afraid of the dark. His fear of the dark was judged to be a
mental disorder requiring severe treatment. But the treatment aggravated the disorder. Previously I had been
accustomed to sleep in a well-lighted room, with a nurse
to take care of me. I thought that I should die of fright
when sentenced to lie alone in the dark, and—what
seemed to me then abominably cruel—actually *locked*
into my room, the most dismal room of the house. Night
after night when I had been warmly tucked into bed, the
lamp was removed; the key clicked in the lock; the
protecting light and the footsteps of my guardian receded
together. Then an agony of fear would come upon me.
Something in the black air would seem to gather and
grow—(I thought that I could even *hear* it grow)—till I had
to scream. Screaming regularly brought punishment; but
it also brought back the light, which more than consoled
for the punishment. This fact being at last found out,
orders were given to pay no further heed to the screams
of the Child.

Why was I thus insanely afraid? Partly because the dark
had always been peopled for me with shapes of terror. So
far back as memory extended, I had suffered from ugly
dreams; and when aroused from them I could always *see*
the forms dreamed of, lurking in the shadows of the
room. They would soon fade out; but for several moments

they would appear like tangible realities. And they were
always the same figures ... Sometimes, without any
preface of dreams, I used to see them at twilight-time—
following me about from room to room, or reaching long
dim hands after me, from storey to storey, up through the
interspaces of the deep stairways.

I had complained of these haunters only to be told that
I must never speak of them, and that they did not exist. I
had complained to everybody in the house; and everybody in the house had told me the very same thing. But
there was the evidence of my eyes! The denial of that evidence I could explain only in two ways:— Either the shapes
were afraid of big people, and showed themselves to me
alone, because I was little and weak; or else the entire
household had agreed, for some ghastly reason, to say
what was not true. This latter theory seemed to me the
more probable one, because I had several times perceived
the shapes when I was not unattended;—and the conse-
quent appearance of secrecy frightened me scarcely less
than the visions did. Why was I forbidden to talk about
what I saw, and even heard—on creaking stairways—
behind waving curtains?

'Nothing will hurt you,'—this was the merciless answer
to all my pleadings not to be left alone at night. But the
haunters *did* hurt me. Only—they would wait until after I
had fallen asleep, and so into their power—for they
possessed occult means of preventing me from rising or
moving or crying out.

Needless to comment upon the policy of locking me up
alone with these fears in a black room. Unutterably was I
tormented in that room—for years! Therefore I felt relat-
ively happy when sent away at at last to a children's
boarding-school, where the haunters very seldom
ventured to show themselves.

They were not like any people that I had ever known.
They were shadowy dark-robed figures, capable of atrocious self-distortion—capable, for instance, of growing up

to the ceiling, and then across it, and then lengthening themselves, head-downwards, along the opposite wall. Only their faces were distinct; and I tried not to look at their faces. I tried also in my dreams—or thought that I tried—to awaken myself from the sight of them by pulling at my eyelids with my fingers; but the eyelids would remain closed, as if sealed.... Many years afterwards, the frightful plates in Orfila's *Traité des Exhumés*, beheld for the first time, recalled to me with a sickening start the dream-terrors of childhood. But to understand the Child's experience, you must imagine Orfila's drawings intensely alive, and continually elongating or distorting, as in some monstrous anamorphosis.

Nevertheless the mere sight of those nightmare-faces was not the worst of the experiences in the Child's Room. The dreams always began with a suspicion, or sensation of something heavy in the air—slowly quenching will,—slowly numbing my power to move. At such times I usually found myself alone in a large unlighted apartment; and, almost simultaneously with the first sensation of fear, the atmosphere of the room would become suffused, half-way to the ceiling, with a sombre-yellowish glow, making objects dimly visible—though the ceiling itself remained pitch-black. This was not a true appearance of light: rather it seemed as if the black air were changing colour from beneath.... Certain terrible aspects of sunset, on the eve of storm, offer like effects of sinister colour.... Forthwith I would try to escape—(feeling at every step a sensation *as of wading*)—and would sometimes succeed in struggling half-way across the room;—but there I would always find myself brought to a standstill—paralyzed by some innominable opposition. Happy voices I could hear in the next room—I could see light through the transom over the door that I had vainly endeavoured to reach—I knew that one loud cry would save me. But not even by the most frantic effort could I raise my voice above a whisper.... And all this signified only that the Nameless was coming—was nearing—was

mounting the stairs. I could hear the step–booming like
the sound of a muffled drum–and I wondered why
nobody else heard it. A long, long time the haunter would
take to come–malevolently pausing after each ghastly
footfall. Then, without a creak, the bolted door would
open–slowly, slowly–and the thing would enter,
gibbering soundlessly–and put out hands–and clutch
me–and toss me to the black ceiling–and catch me
descending to toss me up again, and again, and again....
In those moments the feeling was not fear: fear itself had
been torpified by the first seizure. It was a sensation that
has no name in the language of the living. For every
touch brought a shock of something infinitely worse than
pain–something that thrilled into the innermost secret
being of me–a sort of abominable electricity, discovering
unimagined capacities of suffering in totally unfamiliar
regions of sentiency.... This was commonly the work of a
single tormentor; but I can also remember having been
caught by a group, and tossed from one to another–seemingly for a time of many minutes.

III

Whence the fancy of those shapes? I do not know.
Possibly from some impression of fear in earliest infancy;
possibly from some experience of fear in other lives than
mine. That mystery is forever insoluble. But the mystery
of the shock of the touch admits of a definite hypothesis.

First, allow me to observe that the experience of the
sensation itself cannot be dismissed as 'mere imagination.' Imagination means cerebral activity: its pains and
its pleasures are alike inseparable from nervous oper-
ation, and their physical importance is sufficiently
proved by their physiological effects. Dream-fear may kill
as well as other fear; and no emotion thus powerful can
be reasonably deemed undeserving of study.

One remarkable fact in the problem to be considered

is that the sensation of seizure in dreams differs totally
from all sensations familiar to ordinary waking life. Why
this differentiation? How interpret the extraordinary
massiveness and depth of the thrill?

I have already suggested that the dreamer's fear is
most probably not a reflection of relative experience, but
represents the incalculable total of ancestral experience
of dream-fear. If the sum of the experience of active life
be transmitted by inheritance, so must likewise be transmitted the summed experience of the life of sleep. And in
normal heredity either class of transmissions would
probably remain distinct.

Now, granting this hypothesis, the sensation of dream-
seizure would have had its beginnings in the earliest
phases of dream-consciousness—long prior to the apparition of man. The first creatures capable of thought and
fear must often have dreamed of being caught by their
natural enemies. There could not have been much
imagining of pain in these primal dreams. But higher
nervous development in later forms of being would have
been accompanied with larger susceptibility to dream-
pain. Still later, with the growth of reasoning-power, ideas
of the supernatural would have changed and intensified
the character of dream-fear. Furthermore, through all the
course of evolution, heredity would have been accumulating the experience of such feeling. Under those forms
of imaginative pain evolved through reaction of religious
beliefs, there would persist some dim survival of savage
primitive fears, and again, under this, a dimmer but
incomparably deeper substratum of ancient animal-
terrors. In the dreams of the modern child all these
latencies might quicken—one below another—unfathom-
ably-with the coming and the growing of nightmare.

It may be doubted whether the phantasms of any particular nightmare have a history older than the brain in
which they move. But the shock of the touch would seem
to indicate *some point of dream-contact with the total
race-experience of shadowy seizure*. It may be that

profundities of Self—abysses never reached by any ray
from the life of sun—are strangely stirred in slumber, and
that out of their blackness immediately responds a shuddering of memory, measureless even by millions of years.

THE PHANTOM RIDERS

O

E.R. Suffling

While Lafcadio Hearn wandered far and abroad, Ernest Richard Suffling appeared to stay very close to home on the Norfolk Broads. He was a local expert on the Broads and boating generally and published eighteen books on an impressive variety of subjects. They include his first, THE LAND OF THE BROADS *(1885);* ENGLISH CHURCH BRASSES *(1910);* EPITAPHIA *(1909), a book of British epitaphs; books on stained glass and glass painting; boating on the Broads and abroad, in* A CRUISE ON THE FRIESLAND MERES *(1894); and a work on church festival decorations.*

Of interest to readers in this genre is his book of short stories THE STORY HUNTER: TALES OF THE WEIRD AND WILD *(1896). These are the adventures of a hypnotist who roams the countryside gaining his tales from various folk whom he places into a trance if they look like they have a good yarn to pass on. It may be somewhat unconventional but it certainly worked; Suffling followed this up with another book in the same vein,* THE DECAMERON OF A HYPNOTIST *(1898).*

In the main, Suffling's stories as told to his hypnotist were somewhat feeble, but he managed to tweak an occasional eerie nerve, as in the following tale from THE STORY HUNTER.

E.R. SUFFLING

O

The Phantom Riders

STRANGE to say, amid the scores of stories which I heard in all parts of England, but few of them were connected with ghosts, visions, or apparitions, and from this paucity of tales of the supernatural, I have come to the conclusion that the majority of such stories are somewhat mythical and usually mere hearsay, not even second-hand versions of something that has really happened, but stories told by the fireside in the first place, and afterwards handed from mouth to mouth with numerous additions and alterations to suit places and individuals, until at length they become so changed and distorted that their inventors would not recognize the offspring of their own imagination, should they at any subsequent period listen to their recital.

Usually, after a story had been told, if I put the question, 'Did you see this?', the answer would be, 'Oh, no; John Williams told me about it, and I believe he heard it from Tom Smith.' A search for Tom Smith would only result in the fact that he had heard it from Harry Jones, etc., so that, strive as one might, the actual participator in the gruesome adventure one wished to fathom could never be discovered.

One very cold December day I happened to be passing through North Somersetshire, and whilst in the vicinity of Minehead, made the acquaintance of a farmer who was also a blacksmith. My caravan's stove had broken down, and one or two odd jobs of ironwork required to be done, so I procured the services of my new acquaintance, and when the various little repairs had been finished, invited him to share my evening meal, and join me in a pipe and hand at cards.

He was nothing loath, and stayed. Of course my usual ghoulish thirst for a story possessed me, and I endeavoured to obtain one from my guest, but he affirmed that he could no more tell a story than I could put him to sleep. Nothing memorable, he averred, had ever occurred during his life, so how could he tell of what had never happened?

Then we fell to speaking of farming and crops, horses and fields, and among other items he mentioned that his best crops were obtained from the field in which my van was then located, called the Haunted Field.

'What,' thought I, 'the haunted field! This must be seen into.'

And see into it I did, for five minutes later my guest was in a hypnotic trance, and from his lips I gathered the following very Christmassy story.

'Once upon a time' might fittingly be the initial words of this story, for the terrible events of which it is a narration took place long, long years ago; in fact, at the end of the seventeenth century.

To be precise, the day on which the stirring narrative commences was the 23rd of December, 1695, two hundred years ago this very Christmas, but heaven protect us from such a dreadful Christmastide as that.

The old Manor House at Minehead, in Somersetshire, no longer exists, for the legends attached to it were of such a terrifying nature that no one dare rent it after the death of John Simmonds in 1696, so that being uncared

for, the old house lingered and decayed till it looked an
ideal picture of 'desolation.'

Haunted or no, there was something so uncanny in the
appearance of the old gables, fast tottering to ruin, that
even in the crepuscular light of early evening, persons
would hurry by it with a shudder, while later at night,
many would go a long way round rather than pass its
weather-worn walls. The very air that blew past the ruin
seemed to gather a deathly fragrance, which was doubtless due to the fast-rotting timbers of the floors and ceil-
ings.

Be that as it may, the evil repute of the old house grew
so great, and such dreadful stories were current
concerning its sights and sounds, that it was some years
ago pulled down, the ground ploughed up, and crops now
flourish where, for generations, owls and bats held their
habitation undisturbed.

Minehead Manor House was an Elizabethan red-brick
structure, with tall twisted chimneys, curved gables, and
dormer windows peeping out from the red clay tiles. Its
grounds were extensive, its gardens prim, and its fish-
pond well stocked with carp, eel, and pike; for John
Simmonds, the owner, was fond of wandering about and
improving his domain. His gardens and fish-pond were
his hobbies, and so fully occupied his entire time that he
was seldom seen in the village, where he was greatly
respected and admired for his kindness to the poor, while
his grand old English appearance had all the stateliness
of a typical country squire.

He had an only daughter, Julia, an accomplished
young lady as accomplishments went in those days. She
could sing and accompany herself upon the spinet, could
embroider beautifully, spin, and generally comport
herself as a young lady of twenty-three should, who has a
whole household on her shoulders.

Of lady friends she had few, and her gentlemen friends
were even still more scarce. One young gentleman,
Wynne Clarge (a distant relative), who lived near,

assumed, probably because of the non-existence of any rival, that he should some day claim her for his wife, but he was very apathetic in the matter. There was little real *love* between them; they were passable friends, and that was all; he looked upon Julia as he did upon his horse—they were both nice in their way, and ministered to his wants; for the rest he took everything as a matter of course, simply because he had no rival.

Things were running in their usual groove, when one day, early in December, a gentleman was announced, who had called to pay his respects to Mr Simmonds.

It was soon explained that he was Charles Benwell, the son of Mr Simmonds' sister, who had for many years resided in Virginia.

The cousins (for Charles was invited to stay at the Manor House for a few weeks) fell in love with each other at first sight, and the love was so sincere and intense, that ere three weeks had passed Mr Simmonds was solicited for Julia's hand.

'Quick work, my boy,' quoth the genial old man. 'Why, you have scarcely had time to know each other yet. It puts me in mind of Julius Cæsar, does this visit of yours, "He came, he saw, he conquered," and so have you, apparently. Well, well, we shall see. But you must not expect a fat dowry with her, for she can sing, "My face is my fortune," like the maid in the song; but still she will not be penniless—no, no! I will see that she has a suitable maintenance.'

'As to that, Mr Simmonds, you know I am over here for the purpose of selling the property which my poor mother—your sister—has left me. There are three estates of considerable size, amounting in the aggregate to something like twelve hundred acres, besides several houses, the documents appertaining to which I have left at the solicitor's at Dulverton.

'Now, Mr Simmonds, tell me, have you any objection to my looking upon your daughter as my affianced bride?'

Mr Simmonds had no objection, but being a very

cautious, business man, would like just a glance at the documents empowering Charles to sell his late mother's estates, simply as a matter of precaution, and to ascertain if there were a flaw anywhere that might cause any delay in the disposal of the property.

'As to that,' rapturously vociferated Benwell, 'the papers shall be in your hands by this time to-morrow, so that you may search them through, and then on glorious Christmas Eve give your sanction and blessing to our engagement.'

'Only fancy being engaged on Christmas Eve, Julia!' exclaimed Charles. 'How romantic! It is like the beginning of a story-book.'

From the day of Benwell's arrival, Wynne Clarge had roamed about the house and grounds, snarling at every one and everything. He had treated Julia very rudely, and one day suddenly asked her—

'What is that fellow dangling about after you for? I will not have it, Julia.'

'But, Wynne,' his fair cousin replied, 'it can surely be no business of yours if he wishes to pay me attention; he is my cousin, and who knows but he may make me a proposal before he leaves Minehead?'

All this was said coquettishly, but looking up at Wynne she was frightened at the look of hatred she perceived on his face.

'A proposal he *may* make, but your husband he shall never be while I wear this by my side,' and he touched the hilt of his rapier significantly, as he strode off down the garden path.

From that day he sought to quarrel with young Benwell, and his relations with Mr Simmonds became so strained, that the old gentleman grew alarmed at his manner, and quietly but firmly forbade him the house.

'It is not your house or lands I want,' exclaimed the irate Wynne; 'but hark ye, old man, Julia shall be my wife and no other's; willy-nilly she *shall* be mine. I have waited for years, and will not be baulked by this sallow-faced American loon! Let him have his holiday, and go as he came, and leave Julia in my hands, or—I will know the reason why!'

It was Christmas Eve, and Squire Simmonds had invited a few of the neighbouring gentry to spend the evening sociably together under his roof. Wynne had been invited with the rest for at Christmastide the squire could not be at variance with any man; but in the evening no Wynne appeared. This gave rise to some little comments among the guests, who good-naturedly twitted pretty Julia with having two strings to her bow.

She blushed and bore it, only looking anxiously now and again at the face of the old clock at the end of the dining-room, for it was past the hour when Charley had promised he would return; for he had gone over to Dulverton in the morning to fetch the required documents. He had promised to be back by six o'clock, and it was now eight, and both Julia and her father began to exchange glances of alarm.

At nine o'clock the guests also became anxious, and Mr Simmonds tried to persuade both himself and those present that all was right.

'You see, it is fifteen miles from here to Dulverton,' said Mr Simmonds. 'Possibly he did not start till six o'clock; then he had to make a *détour*, so as to call at Stoke-Pero and deliver a message to one of Julia's friends, and that would make his homeward journey eighteen or twenty miles, and thirty-five miles there and back is a longish ride. Besides, his horse, Old Maggy, is none too good for a long trot over this hilly country. Fill up, my friends! Here's to our future squire, Charles Benwell!'

He raised the goblet to his lips, but had not commenced to quaff, when looking towards the door, he saw the absent Charley advancing towards the table, looking extremely pale. All in the room rose in greeting, but he turned from them, and unbuckling the clasp of his

riding-cloak, walked to an alcove, formerly an immense
fire-place, but now used as a closet for hanging outdoor
coats, wraps, and accoutrements, a curtain being drawn
across it.

To their surprise, every one present noticed, as he
turned, that his deep white collar (which was the fashion
of those days) was saturated with blood, and as they noted
this, and had the words on their lips to speak to him
about it, he disappeared into the alcove by walking, as it
seemed, *right through the curtain*, and not drawing it
aside in the usual way!

The assembled guests stood aghast.

What could it mean?

For a long time not a man stirred. But at length the
spell was broken by a young fellow named William
Rayner advancing to the curtain sword in hand: he
snatched it suddenly aside.

The recess was empty!

Charles Benwell had apparently vanished through the
solid wall!

The curtain fell from Rayner's grasp as he stood
immovable with amazement. Then came another long
pause; a consultation; a replenishment of glasses; and
finally the conclusion was arrived at that it was the
apparition of Julia's lover they had seen.

Fear now settled on them all, and as they sat, talking
in hushed tones and glancing nervously about, the
curtain guarding the alcove was seen to move.

It bulged out slightly as if caught by a draught of air,
and then again its long, sombre folds trailed upon the
floor and were still again.

No one moved from the spot where he happened to be
sitting or standing, but all eyes were fixed in horror on
the agitated tapestry.

Again it swayed.

This time the bold Will Rayner rose, and drawing his
sword, was joined by some of the others, also sword in
hand. Rapidly they advanced across the intervening

space, and Rayner, plucking hold of the fabric with his left hand, drew it aside with a quick jerk.

Wonder of wonders, in place of the white-faced Benwell there stood his scowling rival, Wynne Clarge.

His right wrist was bared, and his sword point, which was advanced towards the spectators, was seen to be covered with blood.

As they looked with startled eyes, the blood slowly dripped to the floor, drip–drip–drip!

'How now, Master Clarge, think you to frighten us with such tomfoolery?' exclaimed Will Rayner. 'Get thee gone with thy mummery, or my sword shall teach thee a lesson not to make fools of thy betters.'

Then, rushing forward, he attempted to beat the sword out of Wynne's hand with his own, but to his amazement no clang of steel sounded as their weapons met.

'Here's at thee, Wynne,' cried the now enraged man; and suiting the action to the word, he made a deadly thrust at his opponent's breast: the blade pierced the figure without any resistance, and struck the wall so violently that it was knocked out of his hand and rolled clattering on the floor.

At the attack and thrust Wynne looked straight at his assailant, smiled sardonically, and–*slowly melted away*.

The guests stayed all night, sleeping where they best could, at least those whose eyelids had the power to close; while the more nervous scarce dare move from the room for fear of encountering one or other of their ghostly visitors.

It was useless trying to search the wild country between Minehead and Dulverton while it was yet dark, but with the first grey light of a dull morning–Christmas Day–a party of eight gentlemen rode off in search of the missing Charles Benwell.

Through Selworthy they silently rode, and turning to the left entered the lovely woods of Korner. Hills rose to a great height on either side of the valley up which they travelled; hills that seemed to touch—aye, and really did touch—the low-lying dun-coloured snowclouds. There was a rough kind of path, which ran beside the brook—now swollen to a mountain torrent—but at best it was a mere cattle track, and was now fast becoming obliterated by the silently falling snow.

The men rode on, scarcely speaking a word; the only sound that was heard was the roar of the turbulent torrent as it tore through its rocky bed on its way to the sea at Porlock.

Presently they heard a horse neigh, and making at once towards the sound, quickly found poor Old Maggie grazing at the foot of Dunkery Beacon near the village of Stoke Pero.

The snow was now falling so fast that not the sharpest eye could perceive the summit of the Beacon, which towered sixteen hundred feet above them.

'Coup! coup! Maggie,' coaxingly cried Will Rayner, and the mare, whinnying, trotted to him. She was still saddled, and they found, as they feared to find, both upon the saddle and back, stains of blood.

'Follow up, friends,' said Will, 'as rapidly as possible, for if I mistake not, our poor friend lies not far away, and if we make not the best of our way, the snow may hide from us that which we seek.'

They accordingly travelled on much quicker, and as they turned to cross the rustic bridge, at the foot of the hill from which Stoke Pero looks dreamily down, they found poor Benwell, lying on his face, dead, frozen stark and stiff, and partly covered with snow as with a winding-sheet.

They dismounted, and examined the murdered man, discovering to their amazement and horror that he had been run through the base of the neck from *behind*, by some cowardly hand.

The body was laid over the back of a horse, and four of the gentlemen returned with it to the Manor House, while Will and the other three friends prosecuted their search for Wynne Clarge.

This search, however, was in vain; no signs of him could be found, and after wandering about in the snow for a long time they returned to Minehead.

It was indeed a sad Christmas Day for the good folks of the Manor House, which instead of being a place of rejoicing was now a house of the deepest sorrow.

Poor Julia was inconsolable.

No papers relating to the property were found on the body, and this gave some clue to Wynne's reason for waylaying the poor young fellow.

Benwell was buried in the churchyard which lies high upon the hill, a churchyard surrounded by walls that look out over the quiet town like the ramparts of a fortress dominating a city.

A week later, a great commotion was caused by the news being brought, that Wynne's body had been discovered in the trout pool, which lies nearly hidden under the great hill near Stoke Pero.

True it was, and for him too—murderer as well as murdered—a resting-place was found in the quiet hill-top churchyard.

The missing papers could not be discovered, although the woods had been searched in all directions, and as the unusually cold winter gave place to the genial early spring, people began to look upon the tragedy as a thing of the past, and talked no more of it.

Poor Julia drooped and faded; but with the advent of the lovely warm May days she revived, and, by and by, became her own sweet self again; not quite so tuneful in her songs as of yore, but still her father's own little warbling bird, for he delighted in music and in singing, particularly the songs his daughter sang to him of an evening.

Summer came with its flowers and autumn with its grain and fruit, and then—then came cold dreary winter once more.

Christmas approached, but this year, instead of the

usual jovial party at the Manor House, Julia and her
father accepted an invitation to spend a few days with the
sporting rector of Stoke Pero. They arrived at the Rectory
on the 22nd of December (a Monday), and were invited to
stay over Christmas Day, which was on the Thursday.

Julia was not at all in good spirits, and was evidently
thinking of the dreadful Christmas a year ago and her
lost love. She brooded so that, as Christmas Eve
approached, she was positively unable to hide her state of
intense nervousness and melancholy, and at noon on the
24th she felt herself so unwell that she implored her
father to take her home.

Mr Simmonds and the worthy parson took counsel
together, and as Julia appeared in a high state of nervous
excitement bordering on fever, they gave her a sleeping
draught, placing her in the chimney corner in the
Rector's great arm-chair. There she slept for three hours,
but when she awoke, again implored her father to take
her home, as she felt so ill and did not wish to give her
kind hosts trouble.

There was no resisting this second appeal, so after a
little delay in getting ready, they mounted their horses,
and with a boy riding a pony and carrying a lantern in
advance, they set off on their journey homeward.

The snow lay thick on hill and tree, and they made but
slow progress. The lantern gave but little light; it bobbed
about hither and thither like an *ignis fatuus*, and finally
the boy's pony stumbled, and boy, pony, and lantern were
buried in a deep snow-drift. The boy scrambled out
quickly, but by the squire's orders did not light his lantern
again. They crossed the bridge and picked their uncertain
way along the snow-covered path by the torrent's brink.

Suddenly the squire drew rein as a man rode quickly
and silently past them, over the snow, going in the same
direction as themselves.

'How like Old Maggie', said the squire half aloud; 'and
if I did not know to the contrary, I could have sworn that
the rider was poor Benwell!'

The squire supported Julia with his left arm as she rode by his side, cheering her as best he could.

'Who was that, father?' she asked. 'How strange he did not speak as he passed us by.'

'It was indeed, my dear,' he rejoined; 'but probably he was a stranger, and unaccustomed to our hearty West Country greetings. But see, he has stopped and dismounted.'

They beheld him in the moonlight standing by his horse's side, but for some reason the squire's horse and his daughter's both stopped of their own accord, while the boy's pony wheeled round and dashed back towards Stoke.

The strange horseman patted his steed's neck, tightened the saddle-girth, and was about to remount, when another man suddenly bounded forward, with a drawn sword, and making a lunge at the unfortunate traveller, thrust him, from behind, right through the neck.

Then the murderer searched the dying man, taking a large bundle of papers from the saddle-bags, and transferring them to his own pockets.

Turning once more to his victim, who was not dead, but feebly struggling in the snow to regain his feet, he again stabbed him, this time clean through the heart. Then, with a malignant smile he turned away, strode to his own horse, which was tethered to a tree hard by, mounted, and in a trice galloped close past the spellbound onlookers.

As he galloped silently by, the squire beheld, to his astonishment, the features of Wynne Clarge!

Thus was re-enacted, in phantom-vision, the murder of Charles Benwell, as it took place twelve months before.

Trembling in every limb, Mr Simmonds turned to his daughter. But Julia was no more, *his arm encircled her lifeless clay.*

An old man and feeble was John Simmonds, when two months after the above events, he left his bed, slowly recovering from brain-fever; but although he was able occasionally to wander listlessly in his garden in the warm days of the summer, he lingered only till the first days of autumn tinged the foliage with gold and red, then drooped like the flowers, and like the flowers he died.

By his daughter's side, upon that hillside in the west, the old man sleeps, and to this day their tombs are pointed out; the one known as 'the Good Squire's Tomb,' and the other is called 'Julia's Grave.'

When the next Christmas Eve came round, bold Will Rayner organized a little party to watch the spot where the murder took place. They did not keep their dread vigil in vain, for a little after darkness set in they all saw the phantom horseman ride up, dismount to tighten his saddle-girth, and pat his tired horse on the neck. They saw the dastardly rush of his rival: they saw the deed enacted before their eyes, as Mr Simmonds and Julia had seen it in a marvellous manner, and Will had difficulty in restraining his comrades from rushing upon the murderous Wynne, although they knew him to be but the phantasm of a man.

Their purpose, however, in watching was to *follow* the ghost, and as it mounted its shadowy horse they all gave chase.

It was a wild sight to see these young men following the apparition, who pursued his course through the wild woods apparently unconscious that he was being followed.

For three miles he rode, and then drew rein by a low cliff which overhung the stream. He dismounted, took the bundle of papers from under his cloak, and hid them beneath the stump of a tree, whose roots flung themselves in fantastic shapes from the side of the cliff. Then he mounted his horse again, with a smile of triumph on his ghastly face, rode up the precipitous bank, and had nearly gained the brink, when his horse missed its footing, rolled over backwards with its rider, and both disappeared into the turbid water below.

The ghostly horse quickly emerged and galloped away, but the shade of Wynne Clarge, its rider, rose no more.

A search was made in the low cliff for the missing documents relating to the Benwell estate, and they were easily found; but having laid in a damp cavity impregnated with lime for two years, they fell to pieces as Rayner grasped them, and all that remained in his hand was an undecipherable pulp.

UN PEU D'AMOUR

○

Robert W. Chambers

Like many of the writers in this book, Robert W. Chambers (1865–1933) stumbled on his writing talent by accident and made his living at it thereafter.

Born in New York, he trained to be an artist and went to Paris to study art in 1886, with his friend the portrait painter Charles Dana Gibson. He studied and exhibited in Paris for seven years, but, on his return to New York in 1893, found it hard to get decent work. He did some magazine illustrations but at the same time tried writing a book based on his Paris experiences. The book, IN THE QUARTER (1894), was published, perhaps much to his surprise, and he followed it up with an even more successful work, THE KING IN YELLOW (1895).

Chambers is remembered by macabre fiction enthusiasts for that second book. It has been reprinted steadily over the years and remains one of the finest, if somewhat erratic in quality, works in this genre. One story in particular, 'The Yellow Sign', has been rightly included in many anthologies.

Sadly, Chambers only seldom returned to the macabre vein he had so richly mined in THE KING IN YELLOW. Throughout his writing career, which spanned 40 years and encompassed over 70 books, he concentrated on detective and thriller novels, and society comedies and dramas. Just occasionally he wrote some more creepy stuff. There was a novel, THE SLAYER OF SOULS (1920) and some items in later books of short stories.

Happily, this one seems to have escaped reprinting since its original appearance. It comes from Chambers' 1915 book POLICE!, a semi-humorous collection of fantasies, described by the author as 'a few deathless truths concerning several mysteries recently and scientifically unravelled by a modest servant of science.' Perhaps fittingly, it deals with an artist, though the problems encountered by this poor painter would be enough to deter the entire Royal Academy.

ROBERT W. CHAMBERS

O

Un Peu d'Amour

WHEN I returned to the plateau from my investigation of the crater, I realized that I had descended the grassy pit as far as any human being could descend. No living creature could pass that barrier of flame and vapour. Of that I was convinced.

Now, not only the crater but its steaming effluvia were utterly unlike anything I had ever before held. There was no trace of lava to be seen, or of pumice, ashes, or of volcanic rejecta in any form whatever. There were no sulphuric odours, no pungent fumes, nothing to teach the olfactory nerves what might be the nature of the silvery steam rising from the crater incessantly in a vast circle, ringing its circumference halfway down the slope.

Under this thin curtain of steam a ring of pale yellow flames played and sparkled, completely encircling the slope.

The crater was about half a mile deep; the sides sloped gently to the bottom.

But the odd feature of the entire phenomenon was this: the bottom of the crater seemed to be entirely free from fire and vapour. It was disk-shaped, sandy, and flat, about a quarter of a mile in diameter. Through my field-glasses I could see patches of grass and wild flowers growing in the sand here and there, and the sparkle of water, and a crow or two, feeding and walking about.

I looked at the girl who was standing beside me, then cast a glance around at the very unusual landscape.

We were standing on the summit of a mountain some two thousand feet high, looking into a cup-shaped depression or crater, on the edges of which we stood.

This low, flat-topped mountain, as I say, was grassy and quite treeless, although it rose like a truncated sugar-cone out of a wilderness of trees which stretched for miles below us, north, south, east, and west, bordered on the horizon by towering blue mountains, their distant ranges enclosing the forests as in a vast amphitheatre.

From the centre of this enormous green floor of foliage rose our grassy hill, and it appeared to be the only irregularity which broke the level wilderness as far as the base of the dim blue ranges encircling the horizon.

Except for the log bungalow of Mr Blythe on the eastern edge of this grassy plateau, there was not a human habitation in sight, nor a trace of man's devastating presence in the wilderness around us.

Again I looked questioningly at the girl beside me and she looked back at me rather seriously.

'Shall we seat ourselves here in the sun?' she asked.

I nodded.

Very gravely we settled down side by side on the thick green grass.

'Now,' she said, 'I shall tell you why I wrote you to come out here. Shall I?'

'By all means, Miss Blythe.'

Sitting cross-legged, she gathered her ankles into her hands, settling herself as snugly on the grass as a bird settles on its nest.

'The phenomena of nature,' she said, 'have always interested me intensely, not only from the artistic angle but from the scientific point of view.

'It is different with Father. He is a painter; he cares only for the artistic aspects of nature. Phenomena of a scientific nature bore him. Also, you may have noticed that he is of a—a slightly impatient disposition.'

I had noticed it. He had been anything but civil to me when I arrived the night before, after a five-hundred mile trip on a mule, from the nearest railroad—a journey performed entirely alone and by compass, there being no trail after the first fifty miles.

To characterize Blythe as slightly impatient was letting him down easy. He was a selfish, bad-tempered old pig.

'Yes,' I said, answering her, 'I did notice a negligible trace of impatience about your father.'

She flushed.

'You see I did not inform my father that I had written to you. He doesn't like strangers; he doesn't like scientists. I did not dare tell him that I had asked you to come out here. It was entirely my own idea. I felt that I *must* write you because I am positive that what is happening in this wilderness is of vital scientific importance.'

'How did you get a letter out of this distant and desolate place?' I asked.

'Every two months the storekeeper at Windflower Station sends in a man and a string of mules with staples for us. The man takes our further orders and our letters back to civilization.'

I nodded.

'He took my letter to you—among one or two others I sent—'

A charming colour came into her cheeks. She was really extremely pretty. I liked that girl. When a girl blushes when she speaks to a man he immediately accepts her heightened colour as a personal tribute. This is not vanity: it is merely a proper sense of personal worthiness.

She said thoughtfully:

'The mail bag which that man brought to us last week contained a letter which, had I received it earlier, would have made my invitation to you unnecessary. I'm sorry I disturbed you.'

'*I* am not,' said I, looking into her beautiful eyes.

I twisted my mustache into two attractive points, shot my cuffs, and glanced at her again, receptively.

She had a far-away expression in her eyes. I straightened my necktie. A man, without being vain, ought to be conscious of his own worth.

'And now,' she continued, 'I am going to tell you the various reasons why I asked so celebrated a scientist as yourself to come here.'

I thanked her for her encomium.

'Ever since my father retired from Boston to purchase this hill and the wilderness surrounding it,' she went on, 'ever since he came here to live a hermit's life—a life devoted solely to painting landscapes—I also have lived here all alone with him.

'That is three years, now. And from the very beginning—from the very first day of our arrival, somehow or other I was conscious that there was something abnormal about this corner of the world.'

She bent forward, lowering her voice a trifle:

'Have you noticed,' she asked, 'that so many things seem to be *circular* out here?'

'Circular?' I repeated, surprised.

'Yes. That crater is circular; so is the bottom of it; so is this plateau, and the hill; and the forests surrounding us; and the mountain ranges on the horizon.'

'But all this is natural.'

'Perhaps. But in those woods, down there, there are, here and there, great circles of crumbling soil—*perfect* circles a mile in diameter.'

'Mounds built by prehistoric man, no doubt.'

She shook her head:

'These are not prehistoric mounds.'

'Why not?'

'Because they have been freshly made.'

'How do you know?'

'The earth is freshly upheaved; great trees, partly uprooted, slant at every angle from the sides of the enormous piles of newly upturned earth; sand and stones are still sliding from the raw ridges.'

She leaned nearer and dropped her voice still lower:

'More than that,' she said, 'my father and I both have seen one of these huge circles *in the making!*'

'What!' I exclaimed, incredulously.

'It is true. We have seen several. And it enrages Father.'

'Enrages?'

'Yes, because it upsets the trees where he is painting landscapes, and tilts them in every direction. Which, of course, ruins his picture; and he is obliged to start another, which vexes him dreadfully.'

I think I must have gaped at her in sheer astonishment.

'But there is something more singular than that for you to investigate,' she said calmly. 'Look down at that circle of steam which makes a perfect ring around the bowl of the crater, halfway down. Do you see the flicker of fire under the vapour?'

'Yes.'

She leaned so near and spoke in such a low voice that her fragrant breath fell upon my cheek:

'In the fire, under the vapours, there are little animals.'

'What!'

'Little beasts live in the fire—slim, furry creatures, smaller than a weasel. I've seen them peep out of the fire and scurry back into it.... *Now* are you sorry that I wrote you to come? And will you forgive me for bringing you out here?'

An indescribable excitement seized me, endowing me with a fluency and eloquence unusual:

'I thank you from the bottom of my heart!' I cried; '–from the depths of a heart the emotions of which are entirely and exclusively of scientific origin!'

In the impulse of the moment I held out my hand; she laid hers in it with charming diffidence.

'Yours is the discovery,' I said. 'Yours shall be the glory. Fame shall crown you; and perhaps if there remains any reflected light in the form of a by-product, some modest and negligible little ray may chance to illuminate me.'

Surprised and deeply moved by my eloquence, I bent over her hand and saluted it with my lips.

She thanked me. Her pretty face was rosy.

It appeared that she had three cows to milk, new-laid eggs to gather, and the construction of some fresh butter to be accomplished.

At the bars of the grassy pasture slope she dropped me a curtsey, declining very shyly to let me carry her lacteal paraphernalia.

So I continued on to the bungalow garden, where Blythe sat on a camp stool under a green umbrella, painting a picture of something or other.

'Mr Blythe!' I cried, striving to subdue my enthusiasm. 'The eyes of the scientific world are now open upon this house! The searchlight of Fame is about to be turned upon you–'

'I prefer privacy,' he interrupted. 'That's why I came here. I'll be obliged if you'll turn off that searchlight.'

'But, my dear Mr Blythe–'

'I want to be let alone,' he repeated irritably. 'I came out here to paint and to enjoy privately my own paintings.'

If what stood on his easel was a sample of his pictures, nobody was likely to share his enjoyment.

'Your work,' said I, politely, 'is–is–'

'Is what!' he snapped. '*What* is it–if you think you know?'

'It is entirely, so to speak, *per se*–by itself–'

'What the devil do you mean by that?'

I looked at his picture, appalled. The entire canvas was one monotonous vermilion conflagration. I examined it with my head on one side, then on the other side; I made a funnel with both hands and peered intently through it at the picture. A menacing murmuring sound came from him.

'Satisfying—exquisitely satisfying,' I concluded. 'I have often seen such sunsets—'

'What!'

'I mean such prairie fires—'

'Damnation!' he exclaimed. 'I'm painting a bowl of nasturtiums!'

'I was speaking purely in metaphor,' said I with a sickly smile. 'To me a nasturtium by the river brink is more than a simple flower. It is a broader, grander, more magnificent, more stupendous symbol. It may mean anything, everything—such as sunsets and conflagrations and Götterdämmerungs! Or—' and my voice was subtly modulated to an appealing and persuasive softness—'it may mean nothing at all—chaos, void, vacuum, negation, the exquisite annihilation of what has never even existed.'

He glared at me over his shoulder. If he was infected by Cubist tendencies he evidently had not understood what I said.

'If you won't talk about my pictures I don't mind your investigating this district,' he grunted, dabbing at his palette and plastering a wad of vermilion upon his canvas; 'but I object to any public invasion of my artistic privacy until I am ready for it.'

'When will that be?'

He pointed with one vermilion-soaked brush towards a long, low, log building.

'In that structure,' he said, 'are packed one thousand and ninety-five paintings—all signed by me. I have executed one or two every day since I came here. When I have painted exactly ten thousand pictures, no more, no less, I shall erect here a gallery large enough to contain them all.

'Only real lovers of art will ever come here to study them. It is five hundred miles from the railroad. Therefore, I shall never have to endure the praises of the dilettante, the patronage of the idler, the vapid rhapsodies of the vulgar. Only those who understand will care to make the pilgrimage.'

He waved his brushes at me:

'The conservation of national resources is all well enough—the setting aside of timber reserves, game preserves, bird refuges, all these projects are very good in a way. But I have dedicated this wilderness as a last and only refuge in all the world for true Art! Because true Art, except for my pictures, is, I believe, now practically extinct! ... You're in my way. Would you mind getting out?'

I had sidled around between him and his bowl of nasturtiums, and I hastily stepped aside. He squinted at the flowers, fixed up a flamboyant mess of colour on his palette, and daubed away with unfeigned satisfaction, no longer noticing me until I started to go. Then:

'What is it you're here for, anyway?' he demanded abruptly. I said with dignity:

'I am here to investigate those huge rings of earth thrown up in the forest as by a gigantic mole.' He continued to paint for a few moments: 'Well, go and investigate 'em,' he snapped. 'I'm not infatuated with your society.'

'What do you think they are?' I asked, mildly ignoring his wretched manners.

'I don't know and I don't care, except, that sometimes when I begin to paint several trees, the very trees I'm painting are suddenly heaved up and tilted in every direction, and all my work goes for nothing. *That* makes me mad! Otherwise, the matter has no interest for me.'

'But what in the world could cause—'

'I don't know and I don't care!' he shouted, waving palette and brushes angrily. 'Maybe it's an army of moles working all together under the ground; maybe it's some species of circular earthquake. I don't know! I don't care! But it annoys me. And if you can devise any scientific means to stop it, I'll be much obliged to you. Otherwise, to be perfectly frank, you bore me.'

'The mission of Science,' said I solemnly, 'is to alleviate the inconveniences of mundane existence. Science, therefore, shall extend a helping hand to her frailer sister, Art–'

'Science can't patronize Art while I'm around!' he retorted. 'I won't have it!'

'But, my dear Mr Blythe–'

'I won't dispute with you, either! I don't like to dispute!' he shouted. 'Don't try to make me. Don't attempt to inveigle me into discussion! I know all I want to know. I don't want to know anything you want me to know, either!'

I looked at the old pig in haughty silence, nauseated by his conceit.

After he had plastered a few more tubes of vermilion over his canvas he quieted down, and presently gave me an oblique glance over his shoulder.

'Well,' he said, 'what else are you intending to investigate?'

'Those little animals that live in the crater fires,' I said bluntly.

'Yes,' he nodded, indifferently, 'there are creatures that live somewhere in the fires of that crater.'

'Do you realize what an astounding statement you are making?' I asked.

'It doesn't astound *me*. What do I care whether it astounds you or anybody else? Nothing interests me except Art.'

'But–'

'I tell you nothing interests me except Art!' he yelled. 'Don't dispute it! Don't answer me! Don't irritate me! I don't care whether anything lives in the fire or not! Let it live there!'

'But have you actually seen live creatures in the flames?'

'Plenty! *Plenty!* What of it? What about it? Let 'em live there, for all I care. I've painted pictures of 'em, too. That's all that interests me.'

'What do they look like, Mr Blythe?'

'Look like? I don't know! They look like weasels or rats

or bats or cats or—stop asking me questions! It irritates me! It depresses me! Don't ask any more ! Why don't you go in to lunch? And—tell my daughter to bring me a bowl of salad out here. *I've* no time to stuff myself. Some people have. I haven't. You'd better go in to lunch.... And tell my daughter to bring me seven tubes of Chinese vermilion with my salad!'

'You don't mean to mix–' I began, then checked myself before his fury.

'I'd rather eat vermilion paint on my salad than sit here talking to *you*!' he shouted.

I cast a pitying glance at this impossible man, and went into the house. After all, he was *her* father. I *had* to endure him.

After Miss Blythe had carried to her father a large bucket of lettuce leaves, she returned to the veranda of the bungalow.

A delightful luncheon awaited us; I seated her, then took the chair opposite.

A delicious omelette, fresh biscuit, salad, and strawberry preserves, and a tall tumbler of iced tea imbued me with a sort of mild exhilaration.

Out of the corner of my eye I could see Blythe down in the garden, munching his lettuce leaves like an ill-tempered rabbit, and daubing away at his picture while he munched.

'Your father,' said I politely, 'is something of a genius.'

'I am so glad you think so,' she said gratefully. 'But don't tell him so. He has been surfeited with praise in Boston. That is why we came out here.'

'Art,' said I, 'is like Science, or tobacco, or toothwash. Every man to his own brand. Personally, I don't care for his kind. But who can say which is the best kind of anything? Only the consumer. Your father is his own consumer. He is the best judge of what he likes. And that is the only true test of art, or anything else.'

'How delightfully you reason!' she said. 'How logically, how generously!'

'Reason is the handmaid of Science, Miss Blythe.'

She seemed to understand me. Her quick intelligence surprised me, because I myself was not perfectly sure whether I had emitted piffle or an epigram.

As we ate our strawberry preserves we discussed ways and means of capturing a specimen of the little fire creatures which, as she explained, so frequently peeped out at her from the crater fires, and, at her slightest movement, scurried back again into the flames. Of course I believed that this was only her imagination. Yet, for years I had entertained a theory that fire supported certain unknown forms of life.

'I have long believed,' said I, 'that fire is inhabited by living organisms which require the elements and temperature of active combustion for their existence—micro-organisms, but not,' I added smilingly, 'any higher type of life.'

'In the fireplace,' she ventured diffidently, 'I sometimes see curious things—dragons and snakes and creatures of grotesque and peculiar shapes.'

I smiled indulgently, charmed by this innocently offered contribution to science. Then she rose, and I rose and took her hand in mine, and we wandered over the grass towards the crater, while I explained to her the difference between what we imagine we see in the glowing coals of a grate fire and my own theory that fire is the abode of living animalculae.

On the grassy edge of the crater we paused and looked down the slope, where the circle of steam rose, partly veiling the pale flash of fire underneath.

'How near can we go?' I inquired.

'Quite near. Come; I'll guide you.'

Leading me by the hand, she stepped over the brink and we began to descend the easy grass slope together.

There was no difficulty about it at all. Down we went, nearer and nearer to the wall of steam, until at last, when but fifteen feet away from it, I felt the heat from the flames which sparkled below the wall of vapour.

Here we seated ourselves upon the grass, and I knitted my brows and fixed my eyes upon this curious phenomenon, striving to discover some reason for it.

Except for the vapour and the fires, there was nothing whatever volcanic about this spectacle, or in the surroundings.

From where I sat I could see that the bed of fire which encircled the crater, and the wall of vapour which crowned the flames, were about three hundred feet wide. Of course this barrier was absolutely impassable. There was no way of getting through it into the bottom of the crater.

A slight pressure from Miss Blythe's fingers engaged my attention; I turned towards her, and she said:

'There is one more thing about which I have not told you. I feel a little guilty, because *that* is the real reason I asked you to come here.'

'What is it?'

'I think there are emeralds on the floor of that crater.'

'Emeralds!'

'I *think* so.' She felt in the ruffled pocket of her apron, drew out a fragment of mineral, and passed it to me.

I screwed a jeweller's glass into my eye and examined it in astonished silence. It was an emerald; a fine, large, immensely valuable stone, if my experience counted for anything. One side of it was thickly coated with vermilion paint.

'Where did this come from?' I asked in an agitated voice.

'From the floor of the crater. Is it *really* an emerald?'

I lifted my head and stared at the girl incredulously.

'It happened this way,' she said excitedly. 'Father was painting a picture up there by the edge of the crater. He left his palette on the grass to go to the bungalow for some more tubes of colour. While he was in the house, hunting for the colours which he wanted, I stepped out on the veranda, and I saw some crows alight near the palette and begin to stalk about in the grass. One bird walked right over his wet palette; I stepped out and waved my sun-bonnet to frighten him off, but he had both feet in a sticky mass of Chinese vermilion, and for a moment was unable to free himself.

'I almost caught him, but he flapped away over the edge of the crater, high above the wall of vapour, sailed down onto the crater floor, and alighted.

'But his feet bothered him; he kept hopping about on the bottom of the crater, half running, half flying; and finally he took wing and rose up over the hill.

'As he flew above me, and while I was looking up at his vermilion feet, something dropped from his claws and nearly struck me. It was that emerald.'

When I had recovered sufficient composure to speak steadily, I took her beautiful little hand in mine.

'This,' said I, 'is the most exciting locality I have ever visited for purposes of scientific research. Within this crater may lie millions of value in emeralds. You are probably, today, the wealthiest heiress upon the face of the globe!'

I gave her a winning glance. She smiled, shyly, and blushingly withdrew her hand.

For several exquisite minutes I sat there beside her in a sort of heavenly trance. How beautiful she was! How engaging—how sweet—how modestly appreciative of the man beside her, who had little beside his scientific learning, his fame, and a kind heart to appeal to such youth and loveliness as hers!

There was something about her that delicately appealed to me. Sometimes I pondered what this might be; sometimes I wondered how many emeralds lay on that floor of sandy gravel below us.

Yes, I loved her. I realized it now. I could even endure her father for her sake. I should make a good husband. I was quite certain of that.

I turned and gazed upon her, meltingly. But I did not wish to startle her, so I remained silent, permitting the chaste language of my eyes to interpret for her what my lips had not yet murmured. It was a brief but beautiful moment in my life.

'The way to do,' said I, 'is to trap several dozen crows, smear their feet with glue, tie a ball of Indian twine to the ankle of every bird, then liberate them. Some are certain to fly into the crater and try to scrape the glue off in the sand. Then,' I added, triumphantly, 'all we have to do is to haul in our birds and detach the wealth of Midas from their sticky claws!'

'That is an excellent suggestion,' she said gratefully, 'but I can do that after you have gone. All I wanted you to tell me was whether the stone is a genuine emerald.'

I gazed at her blankly.

'You are here for purposes of scientific investigation,' she added, sweetly. 'I should not think of taking your time for the mere sake of accumulating wealth for my father and me.'

There didn't seem to be anything for me to say at that moment. Chilled, I gazed at the flashing ring of fire.

And, as I gazed, suddenly I became aware of a little, pointed muzzle, two pricked-up ears, and two ruby-red eyes gazing intently out at me from the mass of flames.

The girl beside me saw it, too.

'Don't move!' she whispered. 'That is one of the flame creatures. It may venture out if you keep perfectly still.'

Rigid with amazement, I sat like a stone image, staring at the most astonishing sight I had ever beheld.

For several minutes the ferret-like creature never stirred from where it crouched in the crater fire; the alert head remained pointed towards us; I could even see that its thick fur must have possessed the qualities of asbestos, because here and there a hair or two glimmered incandescent; and its eyes, nose, and whiskers glowed and glowed as the flames pulsuated around it.

After a long while it began to move out of the fire, slowly, cautiously, cunning eyes fixed on us—a small, slim, wiry, weasel-like creature on which the sunlight fell with a vitreous glitter as it crept forward into the grass.

Then, from the fire behind, another creature of the same sort appeared, another, others, then dozens of eager, lithe, little animals appeared everywhere from the flames and began to frisk and play and run about in the grass and nibble the fresh, green, succulent herbage with a snipping sound quite audible to us.

One came so near my feet that I could examine it minutely.

Its fur and whiskers seemed heavy and dense and like asbestos fibre, yet so fine as to appear silky. Its eyes, nose, and claws were scarlet, and seemed to possess a glassy surface.

I waited my opportunity, and when the little thing came nosing along within reach, I seized it.

Instantly it emitted a bewildering series of whistling shrieks, and twisted around to bite me. Its body was icy.

'Don't let it bite!' cried the girl. 'Be careful, Mr Smith!'

But its jaws were toothless; only soft, cold gums pinched me, and I held it twisting and writhing, while the icy temperature of its body began to benumb my fingers and creep up my wrist, paralyzing my arm; and its incessant and piercing shrieks deafened me.

In vain I transferred it to the other hand, and then passed it from one hand to the other, as one shifts a lump of ice or a hot potato, in an attempt to endure the temperature: it shrieked and squirmed and doubled, and finally wriggled out of my stiffened and useless hands, and scuttled away into the fire.

It was an overwhelming disappointment. For a moment it seemed unendurable.

'Never mind,' I said, huskily, 'if I caught one in my hands, I can surely catch another in a trap.'

'I am so sorry for your disappointment,' she said, pitifully.

'Do *you* care, Miss Blythe?' I asked.

She blushed.

'Of course I care,' she murmured.

My hands were too badly frost-nipped to become

eloquent. I merely sighed and thrust them into my pockets. Even my arm was too stiff to encircle her shapeful waist. Devotion to Science had temporarily crippled me. Love must wait. But, as we ascended the grassy slope together, I promised myself that I would make her a good husband, and that I should spend at least part of every day of my life in trapping crows and smearing their claws with glue.

That evening I was seated on the veranda beside Wilna—Miss Blythe's name was Wilna—and what with gazing at her and fitting together some of the folding box-traps which I always carried with me—and what with trying to realize the pecuniary magnificence of our future existence together, I was exceedingly busy when Blythe came in to display, as I supposed, his most recent daub to me.

The canvas he carried presented a series of crimson speckles, out of which burst an eruption of green streaks—and it made me think of stepping on a caterpillar.

My instinct was to placate this impossible man. He was *her* father. I meant to honour him if I had to assault him to do it.

'Supremely satisfying!' I nodded, chary of naming the subject. 'It is a stride beyond the art of the future: it is a flying leap out of the Not Yet into the Possibly Perhaps! I thank you for enlightening me, Mr Blythe. I am your debtor.'

He fairly snarled at me:

'What are *you* talking about!' he demanded.

I remained modestly mute.

To Wilna he said, pointing passionately at his canvas:

'The crows have been walking all over it again! I'm going to paint in the woods after this, earthquakes or no earthquakes. Have the trees been heaved up anywhere recently?'

'Not since last week,' she said soothingly. 'It usually happens after a rain.'

'I think I'll risk it then—although it did rain early this morning. I'll do a moonlight down there this evening.' And, turning to me: 'If you know as much about science as you do about art you won't have to remain here long—I trust.'

'What?' said I, very red.

He laughed a highly disagreeable laugh, and marched into the house. Presently he bawled for dinner, and Wilna went away. For her sake I had remained calm and dignified, but presently I went out and kicked up the turf two or three times; and, having foozled my wrath, I went back to dinner, realizing that I might as well begin to accustom myself to my future father-in-law.

It seemed that he had a mania for prunes, and that's all he permitted anybody to have for dinner.

Disgusted, I attempted to swallow the loathly stewed fruit, watching Blythe askance as he hurriedly stuffed himself, using a tablespoon, with every symptom of relish.

'Now,' he cried, shoving back his chair, 'I'm going to paint a moonlight by moonlight. Wilna, if Billy arrives, make him comfortable, and tell him I'll return by midnight.' And without taking the trouble to notice me at all he strode away towards the veranda, chewing vigorously upon his last prune.

'Your father,' said I, 'is eccentric. Genius usually is. But he is a most interesting and estimable man. I revere him.'

'It is kind of you to say so,' said the girl, in a low voice.

I thought deeply for a few moments, then:

'Who is "Billy?"' I inquired, casually.

I couldn't tell whether it was a sudden gleam of sunset light on her face, or whether she blushed.

'Billy,' she said softly, 'is a friend of Father's. His name is William Green.'

'Oh.'

'He is coming out here to visit—Father—I believe.'

'Oh. An artist; and doubtless of mature years.'

'He is a mineralogist by profession,' she said, '—and somewhat young.'

'Oh.'

'Twenty-four years old,' she added. Upon her pretty face was an absent expression, vaguely pleasant. Her blue eyes became dreamy and exquisitely remote.

I pondered deeply for a while:

'Wilna?' I said.

'Yes, Mr Smith?' as though aroused from agreeable meditation.

But I didn't know exactly what to say, and I remained uneasily silent, thinking about that man Green and his twenty-four years, and his profession, and the bottom of the crater, and Wilna—and striving to satisfy myself that there was no logical connection between any of these.

'I think,' said I, 'that I'll take a bucket of salad to your father.'

Why I should have so suddenly determined to ingratiate myself with the old grouch I scarcely understood: for the construction of a salad was my very best accomplishment.

Wilna looked at me in a peculiar manner, almost as though she were controlling a sudden and not unpleasant inward desire to laugh.

Evidently the finer and more delicate instincts of a woman were divining my motive and sympathizing with my mental and sentimental perplexity.

So when she said: 'I don't think you had better go near my father,' I was convinced of her gentle solicitude in my behalf.

'With a bucket of salad,' I whispered softly, 'much may be accomplished, Wilna.' And I took her little hand and pressed it gently and respectfully. 'Trust all to me,' I murmured.

She stood with her head turned away from me, her slim hand resting limply in mine. From the slight tremor of her shoulders I became aware how deeply her emotion was now swaying her. Evidently she was nearly ready to become mine.

But I remained calm and alert. The time was not yet.

Her father had had his prunes, in which he delighted. And when pleasantly approached with a bucket of salad he could not listen otherwise than politely to what I had to say to him. Quick action was necessary—quick but diplomatic action—in view of the imminence of this young man Green, who evidently was *persona grata* at the bungalow of this irritable old dodo.

Tenderly pressing the pretty hand which I held, and saluting the finger-tips with a gesture which was, perhaps, not wholly ungraceful, I stepped into the kitchen, washed out several heads of lettuce, deftly chopped up some youthful onions, constructed a seductive French dressing, and, stirring together the crisp ingredients, set the savoury masterpiece away in the ice-box, after tasting it. It was delicious enough to draw sobs from any pig.

When I went to the veranda, Wilna had disappeared. So I unfolded and set up some more box-traps, determined to lose no time.

Sunset still lingered beyond the chain of western mountains as I went out across the grassy plateau to the cornfield.

Here I set and baited several dozen aluminium crow-traps, padding the jaws so that no injury could be done to the birds when the springs snapped on their legs.

Then I went over to the crater and descended its gentle, grassy slope. And there, all along the borders of the vapoury wall, I set box-traps for the lithe little denizens of the fire, baiting every trap with a handful of fresh, sweet clover which I had pulled up from the pasture beyond the cornfield.

My task ended, I ascended the slope again, and for a while stood there immersed in pleasurable premonitions.

Everything had been accomplished swiftly and methodically within the few hours in which I had first set eyes upon this extraordinary place—everything!—love at first sight, the delightfully lightning-like wooing and winning of an incomparable maiden and heiress; the discovery of the fire creatures; the solving of the emerald problem.

And now everything was ready, crow-traps, fire-traps, a bucket of irresistible salad for Blythe, a modest and tremulous avowal for Wilna as soon as her father tasted the salad and I had pleasantly notified him of my intentions concerning his lovely offspring.

Daylight faded from rose to lilac; already the mountains were growing fairy-like under that vague, diffuse lustre which heralds the rise of the full moon. It rose, enormous, yellow, unreal, becoming imperceptibly silvery as it climbed the sky and hung aloft like a stupendous arc-light flooding the world with a radiance so white and clear that I could very easily have written verses by it, if I wrote verses.

Down on the edge of the forest I could see Blythe on his camp-stool, madly besmearing his moonlit canvas, but I could not see Wilna anywhere. Maybe she had shyly retired somewhere by herself to think of me.

So I went back to the house, filled a bucket with my salad, and started towards the edge of the woods, singing happily on feet so light and frolicsome that they seemed to skim the ground. How wonderful is the power of love!

When I approached Blythe he heard me coming and turned around.

'What the devil do *you* want?' he asked with characteristic civility.

'I have brought you,' said I gaily, 'a bucket of salad.'

'I don't want any salad!'

'W-what?'

'I never eat it at night.'

I said confidently:

'Mr Blythe, if you will taste this salad I am sure you will not regret it.' And with hideous cunning I set the bucket beside him on the grass and seated myself near it. The old dodo grunted and continued to daub the canvas; but presently, as though forgetfully, and from sheer instinct, he reached down into the bucket, pulled out a leaf of lettuce, and shoved it into his mouth.

My heart leaped exultantly. I had him!

'Mr Blythe,' I began in a winningly modulated voice, and, at the same instant, he sprang from his camp-chair, his face distorted.

'There are onions in this salad!' he yelled. 'What the devil do you mean! Are you trying to poison me! What are you following me about for, anyway? Why are you running about under foot every minute?'

'My dear Mr Blythe,' I protested—but he barked at me, kicked over the bucket of salad, and began to dance with rage.

'What's the matter with you, anyway!' he bawled. 'Why are you trying to feed me? What do you mean by trying to be attentive to me!'

'I—I admire and revere you—'

'No you don't!' he shouted. 'I don't want you to admire me! I don't desire to be revered! I don't like attention and politeness! Do you hear! It's artificial—out of date—ridiculous! The only thing that recommends a man to me is his bad manners, bad temper, and violent habits. There's some meaning to such a man, none at all to men like you!'

He ran at the salad bucket and kicked it again.

'They all fawned on me in Boston!' he panted. 'They ran about under foot! They bought my pictures! And they made me sick! I came out here to be rid of 'em!'

I rose from the grass, pale and determined.

'You listen to me, you old grouch!' I hissed. 'I'll go. But before I go I'll tell you why I've been civil to you. There's only one reason in the world: I want to marry your daughter! And I'm going to do it!'

I stepped nearer him, menacing him with outstretched hand:

'As for you, you pitiable old dodo, with your bad manners and your worse pictures, and your degraded mania for prunes, you are a necessary evil, that's all, and I haven't the slightest respect for either you or your art!'

'Is that true?' he said in an altered voice.

'True?' I laughed bitterly. 'Of course it's true, you miserable dauber!'

'D-dauber!' he stammered.

'Certainly! I said "dauber," and I mean it. Why, your work would shame the pictures on a child's slate!'

'Smith,' he said unsteadily, 'I believe I have utterly misjudged you. I believe you are a good deal of man, after all–'

'I'm man enough,' said I, fiercely, 'to go back, saddle my mule, kidnap your daughter, and start for home. And I'm going to do it!'

'Wait!' he cried. 'I don't want you to go. If you'll remain I'll be very glad. I'll do anything you like. I'll quarrel with you, and you can insult my pictures. It will agreeably stimulate us both. Don't go, Smith–'

'If I stay, may I marry Wilna?'

'If you ask me I won't let you!'

'Very well!' I retorted, angrily. 'Then I'll marry her anyway!'

'That's the way to talk! Don't go, Smith. I'm really beginning to like you. And when Billy Green arrives you and he will have a delightfully violent scene–'

'What!'

He rubbed his hands gleefully.

'He's in love with Wilna. You and he won't get on. It is going to be very stimulating for me–I can see that! You and he are going to behave most disagreeably to each other. And I shall be exceedingly unpleasant to you both! Come, Smith, promise me that you'll stay!'

Profoundly worried, I stood staring at him in the moonlight, gnawing my mustache.

'Very well,' I said, 'I'll remain if–'

Something checked me, I did not quite know what for a moment. Blythe, too, was staring at me in an odd, apprehensive way. Suddenly I realized that under my feet the ground was stirring.

'Look out!' I cried; but speech froze on my lips as

beneath me the solid earth began to rock and crack and
billow up into a high, crumbling ridge, moving continually, as the sod cracks, heaves up, and crumbles above the
subterranean progress of a mole.

Up into the air we were slowly pushed on the ever-
growing ridge; and with us were carried rocks and bushes
and sod, and even forest trees.

I could hear their tap-roots part with pistol-like
reports; see great pines and hemlocks and oaks moving,
slanting, settling, tilting crazily in every direction as they
were heaved upward in this gigantic disturbance.

Blythe caught me by the arm; we clutched each other,
balancing on the crest of the steadily rising mound.

'W-what is it?' he stammered. 'Look! It's circular. The
woods are rising in a huge circle. What's happening? Do
you know?'

Over me crept a horrible certainty that *something
living* was moving under us through the depths of the
earth—something that, as it progressed, was heaping up
the surface of the world above its unseen and burrowing
course—something dreadful, enormous, sinister, and
alive!

'Look out!' screamed Blythe; and at the same instant
the crumbling summit of the ridge opened under our feet
and a fissure hundreds of yards long yawned ahead of us.

And along it, shining slimily in the moonlight, a vast,
viscous, ringed surface was moving, retracting, undulating, elongating, writhing, squirming, shuddering.

'It's a worm!' shrieked Blythe. 'Oh, God! It's a mile
long!'

As in a nightmare we clutched each other, struggling
frantically to avoid the fissure; but the soft earth slid and
gave way under us, and we fell heavily upon that ghastly,
living surface.

Instantly a violent convulsion hurled us upwards; we
fell on it again, rebounding from the rubbery thing,
strove to regain our feet and scramble up the edges of the
fissure, strove madly while the mammoth worm slid more

rapidly through the rocking forests, carrying us forward with a speed increasing.

Through the forest we tore, reeling about on the slippery back of the thing, as though riding on a ploughshare, while trees clashed and tilted and fell from the enormous furrow on every side; then, suddenly out of the woods into the moonlight, far ahead of us we could see the grassy upland heave up, cake, break, and crumble above the burrowing course of the monster.

'It's making for the crater!' gasped Blythe; and horror spurred us on, and we scrambled and slipped and clawed the billowing sides of the furrow until we gained the heaving top of it.

As one runs in a bad dream, heavily, half-paralyzed, so ran Blythe and I, toiling over the undulating, tumbling upheaval until, half-fainting, we fell and rolled down the shifting slope onto solid and unvexed sod on the very edges of the crater.

Below us we saw, with sickened eyes, the entire circumference of the crater agitated, saw it rise and fall as avalanches of rock and earth slid into it, tons and thousands of tons rushing down the slope, blotting from our sight the flickering ring of flame, and extinguishing the last filmy jet of vapour.

Suddenly the entire crater caved in and filled up under my anguished eyes, quenching for all eternity the vapour wall, the fire, and burying the little denizens of the flames, and perhaps a billion dollars' worth of emeralds under as many billion tons of earth.

Quieter and quieter grew the earth as the gigantic worm bored straight down into depths immeasurable. And at last the moon shone upon a world that lay without a tremor in its milky lustre.

'I shall name it *Verma gigantica*.' said I, with a hysterical sob; 'but nobody will ever believe me when I tell this story!'

Still terribly shaken, we turned towards the house. And, as we approached the lamplit veranda, I saw a horse standing there and a young man hastily dismounting.

And then a terrible thing occurred; for, before I could even shriek, Wilna had put both arms around that young man's neck, and both of his arms were clasping her waist.

Blythe was kind to me. He took me around the back way and put me to bed.

And there I lay through the most awful night I ever experienced, listening to the piano below, where Wilna and William Green were singing *Un Peu d'Amour.*

THE SPIRIT OF THE FJORD

O

John C. Shannon

John C. Shannon, alas, is shrouded in mystery. All that is known about him is that he lived in Walsall, where he published several stories in the Walsall Advertiser in the 1890s, and later collected them into two volumes, WHO SHALL CONDEMN (1894), published in Walsall, and the later ZYLGRAHOF (1901).

He also published a novel, D'AUBISE (1900) and that seems to have been his total output. He never made enough of a mark to have been included in any directory of the day, so who he was and what he did for a living remains a puzzle.

'The Spirit of the Fjord' comes from ZYLGRAHOF and is a neat little story in an unusual locale. Curiously, it covers the same territory as Jerome K. Jerome's story later in this book, and stands up well to the obvious comparisons.

JOHN C. SHANNON

O

The Spirit of the Fjord

THE SS *Valda* was steaming slowly over the broad expanse of one of the largest of the Norwegian Fjords. So slow was her progress that the lazy parting of the water at her prow was almost invisible.

Dinner was just over. Her passengers were seated in small groups about her spacious deck. Some talked, their conversation punctuated by frequent laughter; others passed the time indulging in the various amusements available on such a trip. Two or three of the men were pacing the deck arm-in-arm, smoking.

The sun was setting, flooding the water with dazzling glory. On the horizon the hills lay low and black. Nearer were a few solitary islands, their every detail clearly visible in the departing blaze. Afar was a solitary, tiny sail—the only sign of life, except the graceful steamship *Valda*, whose masts and rigging shewed blackly-delicate against the golden sky.

The sun sank swiftly till its lower edge disappeared behind the hills, and the distant mountains glowed blood-red. The light crept stealthily over the water, enveloped the vessel, passed over it, and finally outlined the lonely islands with a band of liquid fire. Then there succeeded that mysterious, purple twilight peculiar to those latitudes.

As the sun disappeared, a young man, who had been leaning alone over the vessel's stern contemplating the scene, turned from the rail and walked along the deck into the smoking-room. He was tall, well-proportioned, had a well-knit, athletic figure, and handsome, debonair face.

During the few days he had been aboard the *Valda*, Gilbert Amyn had succeeded in making himself extremely popular. Of a sunny disposition, prone to see the ludicrous side of most things, he was an ideal shipmate. Ever willing to join in any amusement, he was in universal request, and his appearance was hailed with delight. Immediately half-a-dozen voices invited him to join in one or other of the various games in progress.

Soon, as the deck became deserted, cards were abandoned, and the men strolled out to seat themselves in the vacated deck-chairs for a final smoke in the cool night air before going below.

As they smoked, the Captain joined the circle. Wishing his passengers 'Good evening,' he sat down and lighted a cigar.

Taking advantage of a lull in the conversation, Amyn addressed the company in general.

'As I was leaning over the stern about an hour ago,' he remarked, 'a most extraordinary thing happened. I don't know whether it was what you would call an optical illusion or not. At any rate, it has puzzled me considerably. If it won't bore you, I will tell you what I saw. Perhaps between us we may evolve a solution of the mystery.'

It is curious how small a thing awakens interest aboard ship. The men gathered on the *Valda*'s deck immediately evinced their eagerness to hear what Amyn had to say. The Doctor, acting as spokesman, and lighting a fresh cigar, replied for all:—

'Fire away, Amyn, by all means let us hear your experience.'

Thus adjured, Amyn told his story:—

'I was watching the sunset from the stern of the vessel. I confess to a weakness for sunsets, and this evening's was passing beautiful. Over yonder the hills were intensely black, presenting a vivid contrast to the luminous yellow radiance cast by the setting sun. Overhead the sky was a beautiful tinge midway between crimson and gold. The whole scene was lovely in the extreme. I was watching more particularly the long trail made by our propellor, noting the varied tints the foam assumed as it danced in the brilliant light, when suddenly, a short distance away, I saw a skiff. Now, I can swear that a moment before the Fjord was absolutely deserted, except for our own vessel and a solitary fishing-boat over by the distant mountains. Whence, then, came the skiff?

'As I watched it drew swiftly nearer, and I saw that it was occupied by a girl. She was quite alone, standing erect in the boat, her hands loosely clasped before her. The skiff moved rapidly towards me, though the girl had no oar, and did not appear, so far as I could see, to make any movement which would account for its progress. How it advanced, therefore, was as much a mystery as it coming.

'These questions, however, faded into insignificance beside the amazing beauty of the girl. I have seen many beautiful women, but never so lovely a face.

'Its colouring was fresh and delicate. The skin was tinged with a dainty rose-flush. The mouth was small; the eyes large and blue, their half-shy, half-tender, wholly trusting glance making them dangerously fascinating. But her hair was her crowning glory. It fell around her in rich, wavy masses, completely enveloping the upper part of her form. The colour of molten gold, it flamed about her like some gorgeous aureole as the waning sunlight kissed it.

'Clad in white from head to foot, her simple robe was exquisitely broidered, and was confined at her waist by a curiously wrought silver girdle. The skiff in which she stood was of ancient shape and very small.

'Such was the vision. To say that I was astonished is but feebly to express my feelings. Whither the girl and the boat had come was beyond my power to fathom.

'As she approached I obtained a clearer view of her, but the nearer she came the more beautiful she seemed. It was the type of face for love of which men commit crimes; the dangerous beauty of a Circe; the witching countenance of a Siren.

'Soon she drew abreast of our vessel, but as she came within a stone's throw the skiff turned aside and shot away towards the mountains. As it receded I strained my eyes in my eagerness to catch the last glimpse of that lovely form. When some little distance away she turned her head and smiled at me; and, smiling, I think she looked more beautiful than before. Then, as I watched, though I am not conscious of having removed my eyes for a moment, she vanished. It was most mysterious.'

'A very curious occurrence altogether, Amyn. You are quite sure, old fellow, that you were not enjoying an afternoon siesta?' laughingly remarked the Doctor.

'Spare me your chaff, if you please, Doctor. I was most certainly not asleep, though I was almost tempted to think I was the victim of a waking dream.'

'I think I can give Mr Amyn some explanation of the phenomenon,' interjected the Captain.

Every man settled himself to listen. Amyn's story had evidently excited their imaginations.

'First of all, are you superstitious?'

'Not the least,' replied Amyn, somewhat surprised.

'I only ask because if you are, what I am about to say may affect your nerves and considerably startle you. In short, are you a believer in omens or presentiments?'

'No, Captain, I'm not,' answered Amyn, emphatically.

'Good. Then I'll tell you as briefly as possible the story of the "Spirit of the Fjord."'

Clearing his throat, and flicking the ash from his cigar, the Captain related the following legend:—

'Many years ago there stood on the brow of a cliff over

yonder,' pointing to the distant mountains, 'a Castle. It was strongly fortified, and occupied a position practically impregnable.

'It was the home of a warrior Norseman, of whose life-history the legend does not speak. He does not seem to have been of the slightest importance to the story.

'He had a beautiful wife, but unfortunately, up to a certain point in their lives, children had been denied them. Sorely troubled, the woman prayed to the Norwegian Fates to give her a child, Pitying her, they promised that she should have a daughter. In process of time the child was born, and the mother's heart rejoiced.

'Norwa grew and throve as the years passed, ever increasing in beauty. Gradually, however, the mother forgot the kindness of the Norns. Her heart grew arrogant because of the loveliness which had been entrusted to her, till at last her pride became so great that it burst all bounds. She openly boasted to her kinsfolk concerning the exceeding beauty of her child, asserting that nothing could surpass it. In extravagant language she eulogized it, saying that to her, and to her only, had been born one so lovely. The Fates grew angry at the vain-glorious boasting of the woman, and one night, as she slept, they appeared to her in a dream to upbraid her for her folly.

'In fear, the mother prayed to be forgiven. Willingly the Norns extended their forgiveness, but as the penalty of her boasting they decreed that henceforth the child's beauty should be accursed and the death of many. Humbly the mother pleaded, but they would not relent, and as the morning broke they left her weeping.

'Years passed. Norwa's beauty increased exceedingly, till the fame of it spread throughout the length and breadth of Norway. From far and near came knights and warriors eager to win her hand. The mother's heart was heavy as she saw these things, for the words of the Fates echoed continually in her memory.

'Men of noble blood, of mighty deeds—the greatest the land could boast—sought Norwa's love. But the girl's heart seemed formed of ice. She laughed at their words, sending them away sorrowing or gnashing their teeth at the bitterness of her speech. Then came the fulfilment of the curse the Norns had laid upon her. Of all those who came, confident of success, few were heard of more. Many vanished as though the earth had opened and swallowed them. Others were found dead on the path leading to the Castle gate, a look of nameless terror on their faces. Others, missing their way in the darkness, fell over the precipice and were either drowned in the sea or dashed to pieces on the rocks below.

'Awesome tales began to be whispered concerning these things, and Frelda, Norwa's mother, sorrowed over the terrible thing her folly had brought to pass. As for the beautiful Norwa, she did but laugh, singing softly to herself as she stood by the edge of the cliff looking out over the sea. What were the lives of men to her? Of their own free will they sought her. If her beauty slew them, what mattered it?

'So time passed, till the Castle of Geiranger came to be regarded as a haunted place, and dark stories were recounted concerning Norwa, Maiden of the Ice Heart.

'Then came a noble knight. His manner was winsome, his words pleasing. He had come, he said, to woo and win the lady Norwa, and for many days he sojourned at the Castle.

'At this time, Frelda, Norwa's mother, wearied by much sorrow, died, and was buried by the edge of the cliff, in sight of the great Fjord, whose constant murmur sighed plaintively above her grave.

'At last the knight told his love to Norwa. With a radiant smile she listened to his impassioned words. As he ceased, she laughed in his face, a silvery, rippling laugh which maddened him. Fiercely he demanded if she loved him. Gaily the maiden answered "Nay," and laughed again.

'In silence he turned on his heel and left her. His face was not good to see. He strode to the brow of the preci-

pice, and descending a steep and dangerous path reached
the shore. There he entered a boat and rowed out over the
waters of the Fjord.

'Dark clouds gathered, lightning flashed, thunder
rolled; great waves rose and threatened to engulf the
slender craft in which he rode.

'Seeing from the Castle battlements the peril her
knight endured, love came into the Ice Heart of the
maiden. With a wild cry she dashed down the path to the
shore and, entering her own tiny skiff, followed her lover
out into the storm. Nearer, nearer she approached, till at
last, when only a few boat-lengths separated them, a huge
wave swept over his craft and he sank from sight. A
blinding flash of lightning split the heavens; a deafening
crash of thunder rent the air; darkness covered the sea.
Again the lightning blazed forth. The maiden and her
craft had also vanished. Afar on the cliff the Castle, struck
by the electric fluid, was burning fiercely.

'Such gentlemen, is the legend of the "Spirit of the
Fjord." It is a typical Norwegian myth, but at the same
time one little known. Now comes the most extraordinary
part of the story. The spirit of Norwa is still supposed to
haunt the Fjords, and so the legend runs, whoever sees
her dies suddenly within a short time. Now, I hope what I
have just said does not make you feel uneasy.'

'Not the least,' answered Amyn, nonchalantly, 'it would
require considerably more than an old legend of that
description to affect me. Nevertheless, it is all very interesting. I am infinitely obliged to you. Of course I
presume, after what I have just heard, that I have actually
seen Norwa, "Spirit of the Fjord."'

'Don't you think, Captain, that it is most ludicrous to
hear members of the civilization of the twentieth century
gravely discussing the ghosts of people who lived so long
ago?' asked one of the men present.

'It certainly does,' replied the Captain, 'but I am a
superstitious man, and must confess, though you may laugh,
that I fully believe Amyn has seen the "Spirit of the Fjord."'

Silence fell on the group as the Captain ceased speaking. Presently he remarked:–

'I don't wish to appear a "croaker," or in any way to alarm you, but I happen to have had aboard the *Valda* three other passengers who have, at various times and under similar circumstances to those Mr Amyn has just described, seen the "Spirit of the Fjord." One, going ashore, fell between the companion-ladder and the launch. Striking his head violently, he became unconscious, and never came to the surface again. The second was thrown from a *stolkjaerre* over a precipice and instantly killed. The third died suddenly in the smoking-room whilst playing cards. Of course, these may simply have been startling coincidences, but to a superstitious man like myself they appeal strongly.'

'It is, indeed, strange,' commented Amyn, 'that such things should have happened at such times, but after all, one often hears of similar coincidences. You will pardon me saying so, but personally, I attach no importance whatever to facts like these.'

The Captain's other listeners seemed far more impressed than Amyn.

Two days afterwards a fellow-passenger was pacing the deck with him. The two men were smoking and chatting confidentially.

Again the sun was setting, lighting up the scene with golden glory. Suddenly Amyn gripped his companion tightly by the arm. Pointing out over the water, he exclaimed, excitedly:–

'There is precisely what I saw the other evening. The "Spirit of the Fjord" the Captain calls her. Can't you see her—yonder in that skiff?'

His friend looked in the direction indicated, but could see nothing.

'That is very strange,' said Amyn, thoughtfully, 'I certainly saw her a moment ago, but now she has vanished.'

Three days afterwards, in the evening, it being somewhat cold, the male section of the passengers was in the smoking-room. Presently the Captain joined them. Someone introduced the subject of the legend he had told them a night or two previously. As he answered he glanced quickly round the room.

'By the way,' he asked, 'where is our friend Amyn?'

Scarcely were the words spoken than the door opened and the scared face of the man who had been walking with Amyn appeared.

'Will you come with me at once, Doctor?' he asked, directly addressing that gentleman. 'Something very serious has happened.'

The Doctor immediately complied with the request. The Captain, signing to the others, remained seated to await his report.

The two men soon reappeared. Their faces wore a grave, awe-stricken expression. The Doctor addressed the Captain:–

'Sir,' said he, 'it is my painful duty to inform you that an hour ago Mr Amyn died very suddenly.' His words created a profound sensation. 'Of course I shall have to make a post-mortem examination, but at present his death is a mystery. Mr Winterton, will you please explain to the Captain under what circumstances you found Mr Amyn?'

'Not feeling very well, I did not go down to dinner this evening, thinking that a walk would relieve the headache and depression from which I was suffering. I had taken three or four turns up and down the deck when I noticed that someone was leaning over the stern-rail. Seeing that it was neither one of the crew, nor yet an officer, I was curious to know who was omitting dinner from the day's programme.

'I walked aft. As I approached I recognized poor Amyn. He was standing in an attitude of strained attention, evidently watching something intently. I might say that last evening I was walking with him when, pointing over the water he asked me if I could see a girl in a skiff.

Thinking he was again under the impression that he saw the vision, I went up to him and laughingly remarked, "Are you receiving another visit from the Spirit of the Fjord, Amyn?"

'He did not answer, nor, indeed, did he appear to have heard me. Going nearer I said, "You seem very much absorbed in your dreams, old fellow. Are you not going down to dinner?"

'Still he took no notice. I saw that his eyes were staring fixedly out over the water, that his face was pale as though from intense excitement. For a minute or two I looked at him in silence. Then a curious feeling came over me–a feeling of dread I never wish to experience again. I tapped him on the shoulder. My touch disturbed the perfect balance of his body. He fell full length upon the deck. He was quite dead.'

An ejaculation of horror escaped Winterton's listeners. After a moment, he added:–

'For a minute or two I was too overcome to move. I did not wish to make a scene during dinner, or unnecessarily to alarm the other passengers, so obtaining assistance, we carried him down to his cabin and laid him in his bunk. Then I sat by him, dazed and horror-stricken, till I came up here to ask the Doctor to come and see him. I tell you, gentlemen, the shock was very terrible.'

The Captain listened in silence, then beckoning to the Doctor and muttering some words under his breath, he rose and, followed by his brother-officer, left the room.

For some time after he had gone no one spoke. Winterton, who had been sitting next to the Captain, broke the silence.

'Did any of you hear what the Captain said just before he went out?' he asked.

No one had.

'My God, the Spirit of the Fjord again,' repeated Winterton, gravely.

MUSTAPHA

O

S. Baring-Gould

There are few writers of books on werewolves who can also boast of having their work regularly performed by the massed choirs of the Salvation Army. Sabine Baring-Gould (1834–1924) is one. This prolific author–he published over a hundred books on all kinds of subjects– found time between his writing on mythology, folklore, theology, history and topography, to write some of the most famous hymns still sung today, including 'Now the Day is Over', 'Through the Night of Doubt and Sorrow' and 'Onward Christian Soldiers'. The latter being performed by the Salvation Army, tambourines flying, is a spectacle that would probably have gladdened the author's heart.

S. Baring-Gould was a Devon man, born and bred, and in 1881 he inherited the estate of Lew Trenchard, Devon, of which he became squire-parson (he stayed there until he died). With the leisure and lifestyle at his disposal, he started to research all kinds of topics, as some of his books reveal. As well as THE BOOK OF WEREWOLVES (1865), he wrote CURIOUS MYTHS OF THE MIDDLE AGES (1866), the fantasy novel THE CROCK OF GOLD (1889) and the historical novel PABO THE PRIEST

(1899). He spent many years delving into the Nordic languages, particularly those of Iceland and Denmark, using the knowledge gained to translate the thirteenth century saga GRETTIR THE OUTLAW (1889).

There are one or two Nordic tales in his much-prized volume of ghost stories A BOOK OF GHOSTS (1904), garnered from over fifty years of writing. This story, however, is set faraway from the Nordic snows and cold. Its background is an exotic location much favoured by E.F. Benson in his ghost stories—Egypt.

S. BARING GOULD

O

Mustapha

I

AMONG the many hangers-on at the Hotel de l'Europe at Luxor—donkey-boys, porters, guides, antiquity dealers—was one, a young man named Mustapha, who proved a general favourite.

I spent three winters at Luxor, partly for my health, partly for pleasure, mainly to make artistic studies, as I am by profession a painter. So I came to know Mustapha fairly well in three stages, during those three winters.

When first I made his acquaintance he was in the transition condition from boyhood to manhood. He had an intelligent face, with bright eyes, a skin soft as brown silk, with a velvety hue on it. His features were regular, and if his face was a little too round to quite satisfy an English artistic eye, yet this was a peculiarity to which one soon became accustomed. He was unflaggingly good-natured and obliging. A mongrel, no doubt, he was; Arab and native Egyptian blood were mingled in his veins. But the result was happy; he combined the patience and gentleness of the child of Mizraim with the energy and pluck of the son of the desert.

Mustapha had been a donkey-boy, but had risen a
stage higher, and looked, as the object of his supreme
ambition, to become some day a dragoman, and blaze like
one of these gilded beetles in lace and chains, rings and
weapons. To become a dragoman—one of the most obseq-
uious of men till engaged, one of the veriest tyrants when
engaged—to what higher could an Egyptian boy aspire?

To become a dragoman means to go in broadcloth and
with gold chains when his fellows are half naked; to
lounge and twist the moustache when his kinsfolk are
toiling under the water-buckets; to be able to extort backsheesh from all the tradesmen to whom he can introduce
a master; to do nothing himself and make others work for
him; to be able to look to purchase two, three, even four
wives when his father contented himself with one; to soar
out of the region of native virtues into that of foreign
vices; to be superior to all instilled prejudices against
spirits and wine—that is the ideal set before young Egypt
through contact with the English and the American
tourist.

We all liked Mustapha. No one had a bad word to say
of him. Some pious individuals rejoiced to see that he had
broken with the Koran, as if this were a first step towards
taking up with the Bible. A free-thinking professor was
glad to find that Mustapha had emancipated himself from
some of those shackles which religion places on august,
divine humanity, and that by getting drunk he gave
pledge that he had risen into a sphere of pure emancipa-
tion, which eventuates in ideal perfection.

As I made my studies I engaged Mustapha to carry my
easel and canvas, or camp-stool. I was glad to have him as
a study, to make him stand by a wall or sit on a pillar that
was prostrate, as artistic exigencies required. He was
always ready to accompany me. There was an understanding between us that when a drove of tourists came to
Luxor he might leave me for the day to pick up what he
could then from the natural prey; but I found him not
always keen to be off duty to me. Though he could get

more from the occasional visitor than from me, he was above the ravenous appetite for backsheesh which consumed his fellows.

He who has much to do with the native Egyptian will have discovered that there are in him a fund of kindliness and a treasure of good qualities. He is delighted to be treated with humanity, pleased to be noticed, and ready to repay attention with touching gratitude. He is by no means as rapacious for backsheesh as the passing traveller supposes; he is shrewd to distinguish between man and man; likes this one, and will do anything for him unrewarded, and will do naught for another for any bribe.

The Egyptian is now in a transitional state. If it be quite true that the touch of England is restoring life to his crippled limbs, and the voice of England bidding him rise up and walk, there are occasions on which association with Englishmen is a disadvantage to him. Such an instance is that of poor, good Mustapha.

It was not my place to caution Mustapha against the pernicious influences to which he was subjected, and, to speak plainly, I did not know what line to adopt, on what ground to take my stand, if I did. He was breaking with the old life, and taking up with what was new, retaining of the old only what was bad in it, and acquiring of the new none of its good parts. Civilization—European civilization—is excellent, but cannot be swallowed at a gulp, nor does it wholly suit the oriental digestion.

That which impelled Mustapha still further in his course was the attitude assumed towards him by his own relatives and the natives of his own village. They were strict Moslems, and they regarded him as one on the highway to becoming a renegade. They treated him with mistrust, showed him aversion, and loaded him with reproaches. Mustapha had a high spirit, and he resented rebuke. Let his fellows grumble and objurgate, said he; they would cringe to him when he became a dragoman, with his pockets stuffed with piastres.

There was in our hotel, the second winter, a young
fellow of the name of Jameson, a man with plenty of
money, superficial good nature, little intellect, very con-
ceited and egotistic, and this fellow was Mustapha's evil
genius. It was Jameson's delight to encourage Mustapha in
drinking and gambling. Time hung heavy on his hands. He
cared nothing for hieroglyphics, scenery bored him,
antiquities and art had no charm for him. Natural history
presented to him no attraction, and the only amusement
level with his mental faculties was that of hoaxing natives,
or breaking down their religious prejudices.

Matters were in this condition as regarded Mustapha,
when an incident occurred during my second winter at
Luxor that completely altered the tenor of Mustapha's
life.

One night a fire broke out in the nearest village. It
originated in a mud hovel belonging to a fellah; his wife
had spilled some oil on the hearth, and the flames
leaping up had caught the low thatch, which immediately
burst into a blaze. A wind was blowing from the direction
of the Arabian desert, and it carried the flames and
ignited the thatch before it on other roofs; the conflagration spread and the whole village was menaced with
destruction. The greatest excitement and alarm prevailed.
The inhabitants lost their heads. Men ran about rescuing
from their hovels their only treasures—old sardine tins
and empty marmalade pots; women wailed, children
sobbed; no one made any attempt to stay the fire; and,
above all, were heard the screams of the woman whose
incaution had caused the mischief, and who was being
beaten unmercifully by her husband.

The few English in the hotel came on the scene, and
with their instinctive energy and system set to work to
organize a corps and subdue the flames. The women and
girls who were rescued from the menaced hovels, or
plucked out of those already on fire, were in many cases
unveiled, and so it came to pass that Mustapha, who,
under English direction, was ablest and most vigorous in

his efforts to stop the conflagration, met his fate in the shape of the daughter of Ibraim the Farrier.

By the light of the flames he saw her, and at once resolved to make that fair girl his wife.

No reasonable obstacle intervened, so thought Mustapha. He had amassed a sufficient sum to entitle him to buy a wife and set up a household of his own. A house consists of four mud walls and a low thatch, and house-keeping in an Egyptian house is as elementary and economical as the domestic architecture. The maintenance of a wife and family is not costly after the first outlay, which consists in indemnifying the father for the expense to which he has been put in rearing a daughter.

The ceremony of courting is also elementary, and the addresses of the suitor are not paid to the bride, but to her father, and not in person by the candidate, but by an intermediary.

Mustapha negotiated with a friend, a fellow hanger-on at the hotel, to open proceedings with the farrier. He was to represent to the worthy man that the suitor entertained the most ardent admiration for the virtues of Ibraim personally, that he was inspired with but one ambition, which was alliance with so distinguished a family as his. He was to assure the father of the damsel that Mustapha undertook to proclaim through Upper and Lower Egypt, in the ears of Egyptians, Arabs, and Europeans, that Ibraim was the most remarkable man that ever existed for solidity of judgement, excellence of parts, uprightness of dealing, nobility of sentiment, strictness in observance of the precepts of the Koran, and that finally Mustapha was anxious to indemnify this same paragon of genius and virtue for his condescension in having cared to breed and clothe and feed for several years a certain girl, his daughter, if Mustapha might have that daughter as his wife. Not that he cared for the daughter in herself, but as a means whereby he might have the honour of entering into alliance with one so distinguished and so esteemed of Allah as Ibraim the Farrier.

To the infinite surprise of the intermediary, and to the no less surprise and mortification of the suitor, Mustapha was refused. He was a bad Moslem. Ibraim would have no alliance with one who had turned his back on the Prophet and drunk bottled beer.

Till this moment Mustapha had not realized how great was the alienation between his fellows and himself—what a barrier he had set up between himself and the men of his own blood. The refusal of his suit struck the young man to the quick. He had known and played with the farrier's daughter in childhood, till she had come of age to veil her face; now that he had seen her in her ripe charms, his heart was deeply stirred and engaged. He entered into himself, and going to the mosque he there made a solemn vow that if he ever touched wine, ale or spirits again he would cut his throat, and he sent word to Ibraim that he had done so, and begged that he would not dispose of his daughter and finally reject him till he had seen how that he, who had turned in thought and manner of life from the Prophet, would return with firm resolution to the right way.

II

From this time Mustapha changed his conduct. He was obliging and attentive as before, ready to exert himself to do for me what I wanted, ready also to extort money from the ordinary tourist for doing nothing, to go with me and carry my tools when I went forth painting, and to joke and laugh with Jameson; but, unless he were unavoidably detained, he said his prayers five times daily in the mosque, and no inducement whatever would make him touch anything save sherbet, milk, or water.

Mustapha had no easy time of it. The strict Mohammedans mistrusted this sudden conversion, and believed that he was playing a part. Ibraim gave him no encouragement. His relatives maintained their reserve and stiffness towards him.

His companions, moreover, who were in the transitional stage, and those who had completely shaken off all faith in Allah and trust in the Prophet and respect for the Koran, were incensed at his desertion. He was ridiculed, insulted; he was waylaid and beaten. The young fellows mimicked him, the elder scoffed at him.

Jameson took his change to heart, and laid himself out to bring him out of his pot of scruples.

'Mustapha ain't any sport at all now,' said he. 'I'm hanged if he has another para from me.' He offered him bribes in gold, he united with the others in ridicule, he turned his back on him, and refused to employ him. Nothing availed. Mustapha was respectful, courteous, obliging as before, but he had returned, he said, to the faith and rule of life in which he had been brought up, and he would never again leave it.

'I have sworn,' said he, 'that if I do I will cut my throat.'

I had been, perhaps, negligent in cautioning the young fellow the first winter that I knew him against the harm likely to be done him by taking up with European habits contrary to his law and the feelings and prejudices of his people. Now, however, I had no hesitation in expressing to him the satisfaction I felt at the courageous and determined manner in which he had broken with acquired habits that could do him no good. For one thing, we were now better acquaintances, and I felt that as one who had known him for more than a few months in the winter, I had a good right to speak. And, again, it is always easier or pleasanter to praise than to reprimand.

One day when sketching I cut my pencil with a pruning-knife I happened to have in my pocket; my proper knife of many blades had been left behind by misadventure.

Mustapha noticed the knife and admired it, and asked if it had cost a great sum.

'Not at all,' I answered. 'I did not even buy it. It was given me. I ordered some flower seeds from a seedsman, and when he sent me the consignment he included this knife in the case as a present. It is not worth more than a shilling in England.'

He turned it about, with looks of admiration.

'It is just the sort that would suit me,' he said. 'I know your other knife with many blades. It is very fine, but it is too small. I do not want to cut pencils. It has other things in it, a hook for taking stones from a horse's hoof, a pair of tweezers for removing hairs. I do not want such, but a knife such as this, with such a curve, is just the thing.'

'Then you shall have it,' said I. 'You are welcome. It was for rough work only that I brought the knife to Egypt with me.'

I finished a painting that winter that gave me real satisfaction. It was of the great court of the temple of Luxor by evening light, with the last red glare of the sun over the distant desert hills, and the eastern sky above of a purple depth. What colours I used! the intensest on my palette, and yet fell short of the effect.

The picture was in the Academy, was well hung, abominably represented in one of the illustrated guides to the galleries, as a blotch, by some sort of photographic process on gelatine; my picture sold, which concerned me most of all, and not only did it sell at a respectable figure, but it also brought me two or three orders for Egyptian pictures. So many English and Americans go up the Nile, and carry away with them pleasant reminscences of the Land of the Pharoahs, that when in England they are fain to buy pictures which shall remind them of scenes in that land.

I returned to my hotel at Luxor in November, to spend there a third winter. The fellaheen about there saluted me as a friend with an affectionate delight, which I am quite certain was not assumed, as they got nothing out of me save kindly salutations. I had the Egyptian fever on me, which, when once acquired, is not to be shaken off— an enthusiasm for everything Egyptian, the antiquities, the history of the Pharoahs, the very desert, the brown Nile, the desolate hill ranges, the ever-blue sky, the marvellous colorations at rise and set of sun, and last, but not least, the prosperity of the poor peasants.

I am quite certain that the very warmest welcome accorded to me was from Mustapha, and almost the first words he said to me on my meeting him again were: 'I have been very good. I say my prayers. I drink no wine, and Ibraim will give me his daughter in the second Iomada—what you call January.'

'Not before, Mustapha?'

'No, sir; he says I must be tried for one whole year, and he is right.'

'Then soon after Christmas you will be happy!'

'I have got a house and made it ready. Yes. After Christmas there will be one very happy man—one very, very happy man in Egypt, and that will be your humble servant, Mustapha.'

III

We were a pleasant party at Luxor, this third winter, not numerous, but for the most part of congenial tastes. For the most part we were keen on hieroglyphics, we admired Queen Hatasou and we hated Rameses II. We could distinguish the artistic work of one dynasty from that of another. We were learned on cartouches, and flourished our knowledge before the tourists dropping in.

One of those staying in the hotel was an Oxford don, very good company, interested in everything, and able to talk well on everything—I mean everything more or less remotely connected with Egypt. Another was a young fellow who had been an attaché at Berlin, but was out of health—nothing organic the matter with his lungs, but they were weak. He was keen on the political situation, and very anti-Gallican, as every man who has been in Egypt naturally is, who is not a Frenchman.

There was also staying in the hotel an American lady, fresh and delightful, whose mind and conversation twinkled like frost crystals in the sun, a woman full of good-humour, of the most generous sympathies, and so droll that she kept us ever amused.

And, alas! Jameson was back again, not entering into any of our pursuits, not understanding our little jokes, not at all content to be there. He grumbled at the food— and, indeed, that might have been better; at the monotony of the life at Luxor; at his London doctor for putting the veto on Cairo because of its drainage, or rather the absence of all drainage. I really think we did our utmost to draw Jameson into our circle, to amuse him, to interest him in something; but one by one we gave him up, and the last to do this was the little American lady.

From the outset he had attacked Mustapha, and endeavoured to persuade him to shake off his 'squeamish nonsense,' as Jameson called his resolve. 'I'll tell you what it is, old fellow,' he said, 'life isn't worth living without good liquor, and as for that blessed Prophet of yours, he showed he was a fool when he put a bar on drinks.'

But as Mustapha was not pliable he gave him up. 'He's become just as great a bore as that old Rameses,' said he. 'I'm sick of the whole concern, and I don't think anything of fresh dates, that you fellows make such a fuss about. As for that stupid old Nile—there ain't a fish worth eating comes out of it. And those old Egyptians were arrant humbugs. I haven't seen a lotus since I came here, and they made such a fuss about them too.'

The little American lady was not weary of asking questions relative to English home life, and especially to country-house living and amusements.

'Oh, my dear!' said she, 'I would give my ears to spend a Christmas in the fine old fashion in a good ancient manor-house in the country.'

'There is nothing remarkable in that,' said an English lady.

'Not to you, maybe; but there would be to us. What we read of and make pictures of in our fancies, that is what you live. Your facts are our fairy tales. Look at your hunting.'

'That, if you like, is fun,' threw in Jameson. 'But I don't myself think anything save Luxor can be a bigger bore than country-house life at Christmas time—when all the boys are back from school.'

'With us,' said the little American, 'our sportsmen dress in pink like yours—the whole thing—and canter after a bag of anise seed that is trailed before them.'

'Why do they not import foxes?'

'Because a fox would not keep to the road. Our farmers object pretty freely to trespass; so the hunting must of necessity be done on the highway, and the game is but a bag of anise seed. I would like to see an English meet and a run.'

This subject was thrashed out after having been prolonged unduly for the sake of Jameson.

'Oh, dear me!' said the Yankee lady. 'If but that chef could be persuaded to give us plum-puddings for Christmas, I would try to think I was in England.'

'Plum-pudding is exploded,' said Jameson. 'Only children ask for it now. A good trifle or a tipsy-cake is much more to my taste; but this hanged cook here can give us nothing but his blooming custard pudding and burnt sugar.'

'I do not think it would be wise to let him attempt a plum-pudding,' said the English lady. 'But if we can persuade him to permit me I will mix and make the pudding, and then he cannot go far wrong in the boiling and dishing up.'

'That is the only thing wanting to make me perfectly happy,' said the American. 'I'll confront monsieur. I am sure I can talk him into a good humour, and we shall have our plum-pudding.'

No one has yet been found, I do believe, who could resist that little woman. She carried everything before her. The cook placed himself and all his culinary apparatus at her feet. We took part in the stoning of the raisins, and the washing of the currants, even the chopping of the suet; we stirred the pudding, threw in sixpence apiece, and a ring, and then it was tied up in a cloth, and set aside to be boiled. Christmas Day came, and the English chaplain preached us a practical sermon on 'Goodwill towards men.' That was his text, and his sermon was but a swelling out of the words just as rice is swelled to thrice its size by boiling.

We dined. There was an attempt at roast beef—it was more like baked leather. The event of the dinner was to be the bringing in and eating of the plum-pudding.

Surely all would be perfect. We could answer for the materials and the mixing. The English lady could guarantee the boiling. She had seen the plum-pudding 'on the boil,' and had given strict injunctions as to the length of time during which it was to boil.

But, alas! the pudding was not right when brought on the table. It was not enveloped in lambent blue flame—it was not crackling in the burning brandy. It was sent in dry, and the brandy arrived separate in a white sauce-boat, hot indeed, and sugared, but not on fire.

There ensued outcries of disappointment. Attempts were made to redress the mistake by setting fire to the brandy in a spoon, but the spoon was cold. The flame would not catch, and finally, with a sigh, we had to take our plum-pudding as served.

'I say, chaplain!' exclaimed Jameson, 'practice is better than precept, is it not?'

'To be sure it is.'

'You gave us a deuced good sermon. It was short, as it ought to be; but I'll go better on it, I'll practise where you preached, and have larks, too!'

Then Jameson started from the table with a plate of plum-pudding in one hand and the sauce-boat in the other. 'By Jove!' he said, 'I'll teach these fellows to open their eyes. I'll show them that we know how to feed. We can't turn out scarabs and cartouches in England, that are no good to anyone, but we can produce the finest roast beef in the world, and do a thing or two in puddings.'

And he left the room.

We paid no heed to anything Jameson said or did. We were rather relieved that he was out of the room, and did not concern ourselves about the 'larks' he promised himself, and which we were quite certain would be as insipid as were the quails of the Israelites.

In ten minutes he was back, laughing and red in the face.

'I've had splitting fun,' he said. 'You should have been there.'

'Where, Jameson?'

'Why, outside. There were a lot of old moolahs and other hoky-pokies sitting and contemplating the setting sun and all that sort of thing, and I gave Mustapha the pudding. I told him I wished him to try our great national English dish, on which her Majesty the Queen dines daily. Well, he ate and enjoyed it, by George. Then I said, "Old fellow, it's uncommonly dry, so you must take the sauce to it." He asked if it was only sauce—flour and water. "It's sauce, by Jove," said I, "a little sugar to it; no bar on the sugar, Musty." So I put the boat to his lips and gave him a pull. By George, you should have seen his face! It was just thundering fun. "I've done you at last, old Musty," I said. "It is best cognac." He gave me such a look! He'd have eaten me, I believe—and he walked away. It was just splitting fun. I wish you had been there to see it.'

I went out after dinner, to take my usual stroll along the river-bank, and to watch the evening lights die away on the columns and obelisk. On my return I saw at once that something had happened which had produced commotion among the servants of the hotel. I had reached the salon before I inquired what was the matter.

The boy who was taking coffee round said: 'Mustapha is dead. He cut his throat at the door of the mosque. He could not help himself. He had broken his vow.'

I looked at Jameson without a word. Indeed, I could not speak; I was choking. The little American lady was trembling, the English lady crying. The gentlemen stood silent in the windows, not speaking a word.

Jameson's colour changed. He was honestly distressed, uneasy, and tried to cover his confusion with bravado and a jest.

'After all,' he said, 'it is only a nigger the less.'

'Nigger!' said the American lady. 'He was no nigger, but an Egyptian.'

'Oh! I don't pretend to distinguish between your blacks and whity-browns any more than I do between your cartouches,' returned Jameson.

'He was no black,' said the American lady, standing up. 'But I do mean to say that I consider you an utterly unredeemed black—'

'My dear, don't,' said the Englishwoman, drawing the other down. 'It's no good. The thing is done. He meant no harm.'

IV

I could not sleep. My blood was in a boil. I felt that I could not speak to Jameson again. He would have to leave Luxor. That was tacitly understood among us. Coventry was the place to which he would be consigned.

I tried to finish in a little sketch I had made in my notebook when I was in my room, but my hand shook, and I was constrained to lay my pencil aside. Then I took up an Egyptian grammar, but could not fix my mind on study. The hotel was very still. Everyone had gone to bed at an early hour that night, disinclined for conversation. No one was moving. There was a lamp in the passage; it was partly turned down. Jameson's room was next to mine. I heard him stir as he undressed, and talk to himself. Then he was quiet. I wound up my watch and emptying my pocket, put my purse under the pillow. I was not in the least heavy with sleep. If I did go to bed I should not be able to close my eyes. But then—if I sat up I could do nothing.

I was about leisurely to undress, when I heard a sharp cry, or exclamation of mingled pain and alarm, from the adjoining room. In another moment there was a rap at my door. I opened, and Jameson came in. He was in his nightshirt, and looking agitated and frightened.

'Look here, old fellow,' said he in a shaking voice, 'there is Musty in my room. He has been hiding there, and just as I dropped asleep he ran that knife of yours into my throat.'

'My knife?'

'Yes—that pruning knife you gave him, you know. Look here—I must have the place sewn up. Do go for a doctor, there's a good chap.'

'Where is the place?'

'Here on my right gill.'

Jameson turned his head to the left, and I raised the lamp. There was no wound of any sort there.

I told him so.

'Oh, yes! That's fine—I tell you I felt his knife go in.'

'Nonsense, you were dreaming.'

'Dreaming! Not I. I saw Musty as distinctly as I now see you.'

'This is a delusion, Jameson,' I replied. 'The poor fellow is dead.'

'Oh, that's very fine,' said Jameson. 'It is not the first of April, and I don't believe the yarns that you've been spinning. You tried to make believe he was dead, but I know he is not. He has got into my room, and he made a dig at my throat with your pruning-knife.'

'I'll go into your room with you.'

'Do so. But he's gone by this time. Trust him to cut and run.'

I followed Jameson, and looked about. There was no trace of anyone beside himself having been in the room. Moreover, there was no place but the nut-wood wardrobe in the bedroom in which anyone could have secreted himself. I opened this and showed that it was empty.

After a while I pacified Jameson, and induced him to go to bed again, and then I left his room. I did not now attempt to court sleep. I wrote letters with a hand not the steadiest, and did my accounts.

As the hour approached midnight I was again startled by a cry from the adjoining room, and in another moment Jameson was at my door.

'That blooming fellow Musty is in my room still,' said he. 'He has been at my throat again.'

'Nonsense,' I said. 'You are labouring under hallucinations. You locked your door.'

'Oh, by Jove, yes—of course I did; but, hang it, in this hole, neither doors nor windows fit, and the locks are no good, and the bolts nowhere. He got in again somehow, and if I had not started up the moment I felt the knife, he'd have done for me. He would, by George. I wish I had a revolver.'

I went into Jameson's room. Again he insisted on my looking at his throat.

'It's very good of you to say there is no wound,' said he. 'But you won't gull me with words. I felt his knife in my windpipe, and if I had not jumped out of bed—'

'You locked your door. No one could enter. Look in the glass, there is not even a scratch. This is pure imagination.'

'I'll tell you what, old fellow, I won't sleep in that room again. Change with me, there's a charitable buffer. If you don't believe in Musty, Musty won't hurt you, maybe—anyhow you can try if he's solid or a phantom. Blow me if the knife felt like a phantom.'

'I do not quite see my way to changing rooms,' I replied; 'but this I will do for you. If you like to go to bed again in your own apartment, I will sit up with you till morning.'

'All right,' answered Jameson. 'And if Musty comes in again, let out at him and do not spare him. Swear that.'

I accompanied Jameson once more to his bedroom. Little as I liked the man, I could not deny him my presence and assistance at this time. It was obvious that his nerves were shaken by what had occurred, and he felt his relation to Mustapha much more than he cared to show. The thought that he had been the cause of the poor fellow's death preyed on his mind, never strong, and now it was upset with imaginary terrors.

I gave up letter-writing, and brought my Baedeker's *Upper Egypt* into Jameson's room, one of the best of all guide-books, and one crammed with information. I seated myself near the light, and with my back to the bed, on which the young man had once more flung himself.

'I say,' said Jameson, raising his head, 'is it too late for a brandy-and-soda?'

'Everyone is in bed.'

'What lazy dogs they are. One can never get anything one wants here.'

'Well, try to go to sleep.'

He tossed from side to side for some time, but after a while, either he was quiet, or I was engrossed in my Baedeker, and I heard nothing till a clock struck twelve. At the last stroke I heard a snort and then a gasp and a cry from the bed. I started up, and looked round. Jameson was slipping out with his feet onto the floor.

'Confound you!' said he angrily, 'you are a fine watch, you are, to let Mustapha steal in on tiptoe whilst you are cartouching and all that sort of rubbish. He was at me again, and if I had not been sharp he'd have cut my throat. I won't go to bed any more!'

'Well, sit up. But I assure you no one has been here.'

'That's fine. How can you tell? You had your back to me, and these devils of fellows steal about like cats. You can't hear them till they are at you.'

It was no use arguing with Jameson, so I let him have his way.

'I can feel all the three places in my throat where he ran the knife in,' said he. 'And–don't you notice?–I speak with difficulty.'

So we sat up together the rest of the night. He became more reasonable as dawn came on, and inclined to admit that he had been a prey to fancies.

The day passed very much as did others–Jameson was dull and sulky. After *déjeuner* he sat on at table when the ladies had risen and retired, and the gentlemen had formed in knots at the window, discussing what was to be done in the afternoon.

Suddenly, Jameson, whose head had begun to nod, started up with an oath and threw down his chair.

'You fellows!' he said, 'you are all in league against me. You let that Mustapha come in without a word, and try to stick his knife into me.'

'He has not been here.'

'It's a plant. You are combined to bully me and drive me away. You don't like me. You have engaged Mustapha to murder me. This is the fourth time he has tried to cut my throat, and in the *salle à manger*, too, with you all standing round. You ought to be ashamed to call your-selves Englishmen. I'll go to Cairo. I'll complain.'

It really seemed that the feeble brain of Jameson was affected. The Oxford don undertook to sit up in the room the following night.

The young man was fagged and sleep-weary, but no sooner did his eyes close, and clouds form about his head, than he was brought to wakefulness again by the same fancy or dream. The Oxford don had more trouble with him on the second night than I had on the first, for his lapses into sleep were more frequent, and each such lapse was succeeded by a start and a panic.

The next day he was worse, and we felt that he could no longer be left alone. The third night the attaché sat up to watch him.

Jameson had now sunk into a sullen mood. He would not speak, except to himself, and then only to grumble.

During the night, without being aware of it, the young attaché, who had taken a couple of magazines with him to read, fell asleep. When he went off he did not know. He woke just before dawn, and in a spasm of terror and self-reproach saw that Jameson's chair was empty.

Jameson was not on his bed. He could not be found in the hotel.

At dawn he was found—dead, at the door of the mosque, with his throat cut.

MARCEAU'S PRISONER

O

Alexandre Dumas

*The name Dumas is not generally associated with the tale
of terror; it more usually signifies dashing historical
romance and adventure like his famous THE THREE
MUSKETEERS (1844) or THE COUNT OF MONTE
CRISTO (1844). However, Alexandre Dumas the elder
(1802–1870) wrote so extensively, producing something
like 800 books or plays, that occasional forays into the
macabre were almost inevitable. Here is one of them, in
perhaps its first ever book publication, and certainly its
first appearance in this kind of anthology.*

*Alexandre Dumas was born in Villers-Cotterets, Aisne,
the son of a Napoleonic general and the grandson of a
Caribbean negress. Declining family fortunes drove the
young Dumas to Paris and the hope of a legal career, but
once there, he was drawn into the world of the theatre. He
started writing plays and in 1828 his first drama to be
staged was an instant success. It was a foretaste of what
would make his name: HENRY III, a Renaissance adventure, full of historical intrigue and passion. Dumas has
been shown to be not so keen on historical accuracy, but
more interested in a good story with plenty of action,
preferably set in the sixteenth or seventeenth century. It
proved to be what the customers wanted.*

Dumas himself was a better writer than businessman. His books and plays brought him great wealth, which he threw away as fast as he got it, to the extent he had to write with both hands and feet to keep up with the bills. Later in his life, he was reduced to even odder ways of augmenting his income, as his annual average of fifty books started to tail off. He is reported as having written shopkeepers' advertisements, and when that proved insufficient, exhibiting himself in shop-windows. It is hard to see Stephen King doing the same!

His son, Alexandre the younger, never gained his father's reputation or approached his colossal output.

His father's works were scattered liberally throughout journals and magazines through the entire Victorian era, often with scant regard for copyright. 'Marceau's Prisoner' appeared in Britain in the Strand Magazine, July 1892, and has not seen the light of day since, I believe. It is what the French call a conte cruel *(see my note on Maurice Level later in this book) and is among the first of this type. It has a satisfying historical background—the French revolution and the reign of terror—but don't let the colours fool you. Dumas lowers his boom with a nasty bang at the end.*

ALEXANDRE DUMAS

O

Marceau's Prisoner

On the evening of the 15th of December, 1793, a traveller, pausing on the summit of the mountain at the foot of which rolls the river Moine, near the village of Saint-Crépin, would have looked down upon a strange spectacle.

He would have perceived thick volumes of smoke rising from the roofs and windows of cottages, succeeded by fierce tongues of flame, and in the crimson glare of the increasing conflagration, the glitter of arms. A Republican brigade of twelve or fifteen hundred men had found the village of Saint-Crépin abandoned, and had set it in a blaze. Apart from the rest stood a cottage, which had been left untouched by the flames. At the door were stationed two sentinels. Inside, sitting at a table, was a young man, who appeared to be from twenty to twenty-two years old. His long, fair hair waved round his clear-cut features, and his blue mantle, but half concealing his figure, left revealed the epaulettes of a general. He was tracing on a map by the light of a lamp the route his soldiers must follow. This man was General Marceau.

'Alexandre,' he said, turning to his sleeping companion, 'wake up; an order has arrived from General

Westermann,' and he handed the despatch to his colleague.

'Who brought the order?'

'Delmar, the people's representative.'

'Very good. Where do these poor devils assemble?'

'In a wood a league and a half from this place. It is here upon the map.'

Then orders, given in a low voice, broke up the group of soldiers extended round the ashes which had once been a village. The line of soldiers descended the roadway which separates Saint-Crépin from Montfaucon, and when, some seconds after, the moon shone forth between two clouds upon the long lines of bayonets, they seemed to resemble a great black serpent with scales of steel gliding away into the darkness.

They marched thus for half an hour, Marceau at their head. The study he had made of the localities prevented him from missing the route, and after a quarter of an hour's further march they perceived before them the black mass of the forest. According to their instructions, it was there that the inhabitants of some villages and the remnants of several armies were to assemble to hear mass; altogether about eighteen hundred Royalists.

The two generals separated their little troop into several parties, with orders to surround the forest. As they advanced thus in a circle, it seemed that the glade which formed the centre of the forest was lighted up. Still approaching, they could distinguish the glare of torches, and soon, as objects became more distinct, a strange scene burst upon their sight.

Upon an altar, roughly represented by some piles of stones, stood the *curé* of the village of Sainte-Marie-de-Rhé, chanting the mass; grouped round him was a circle of old men grasping torches, and, upon their knees, women and children were praying. Between the Republicans and this group a wall of soldiers was placed. It was evident that the Royalists had been warned.

They did not wait to be attacked, but opened fire at

once upon their assailants, who advanced without firing a single shot. The priest still continued chanting the mass. When the Republicans were thirty paces from their enemies the first rank knelt down; three lines of barrels were lowered like corn before the wind; the volley burst forth. The light gleamed upon the lines of the Royalists, and some shots struck the women and children kneeling at the foot of the altar. For an instant wails of distress arose. Then the priest held up his crucifix, and all was silent again.

The Republicans still advancing, fired their second discharge, and now neither side had time to load; it was a hand-to-hand fight with bayonets, and all advantage was on the side of the well-armed Republicans. The Royalists gave way; entire ranks fell. The priest, perceiving this, made a sign. The torches were extinguished, and all was darkness. Then followed a scene of disorder and carnage, where each man struck with blind fury, and died without asking for pity.

'Mercy! mercy!' cried a heartrending voice, suddenly, at Marceau's feet, as he was about to strike. It was a young boy without weapons. 'Save me, in the name of Heaven!' he cried.

The general stooped and dragged him some paces from the affray, but as he did so the youth fainted. Such excess of terror in a soldier astonished Marceau; but, notwithstanding, he loosened his collar to give him air. His captive was a girl!

There was not an instant to lose. The Convention's orders were imperative; all Royalists taken with or without weapons, whatever their age or sex, must perish upon the scaffold. He placed the young girl at the foot of a tree, and ran towards the skirmish. Amongst the dead he perceived a young Republican officer, whose figure appeared to him about the same as that of his prisoner. He stripped him quickly of his coat and hat, and returned with them to the girl. The freshness of the night had revived her.

'My father! my father!' were her first words. 'I have abandoned him; he will be killed.'

'Mademoiselle Blanche!' suddenly whispered a voice behind the tree, 'the Marquis de Beaulieu lives; he is saved.' And he who had said these words disappeared like a shadow.

'Tinguy, Tinguy!' cried the girl, extending her arms towards the spot where he had stood.

'Silence! a word will denounce you,' said Marceau; 'and I wish to save you. Put on this coat and hat and wait here.'

He returned to his soldiers, gave orders for them to retire upon Chollet, left his companion to command, and came back to his prisoner. Finding her ready to follow him, he directed their steps to the road where his servant waited with horses. The young girl sprang into the saddle with all the grace of a practised rider. Three-quarters of an hour after they galloped into Chollet. Marceau, with his little escort, took his way to the Hôtel Sans Culotte. He engaged two rooms, and conducted the young girl to one of them, advising her, at the same time, to take some rest after the fearful night she had endured. Whilst she slept, Marceau determined on the course he would take to save her. He would take her himself to Nantes, where his mother lived. He had not seen her for three years, and it would be natural enough for him to ask permission for leave of absence. As dawn began to break he entered General Westermann's house. His demand was accorded at once, but it was necessary that his permission should be signed by Delmar. The General promised to send him with the certificate, and Marceau returned to the hotel to snatch a few moments of repose.

Marceau and Blanche were about to sit down to breakfast when Delmar appeared in the doorway. He was one of Robespierre's agents, in whose hands the guillotine was more active than intelligent.

'Ah!' he said to Marceau, 'you wish to leave us already, citizen, but you have done this night's work so well I can refuse you nothing. My only regret is that the Marquis de

Beaulieu escaped. I had promised the Convention to send them his head.'

Blanche stood erect and pale like a statue of terror. Marceau placed himself before her.

'But we will follow his track. Here is your permission,' he added; 'you can start when you choose. But I cannot quit you without drinking to the health of the Republic.' And he sat down at the table by the side of Blanche.

They were beginning to feel more at ease, when a discharge of musketry burst upon their ears. The General leapt to his feet and rushed to his arms, but Delmar stopped him.

'What noise is that?' asked Marceau.

'Oh, nothing!' replied Delmar. 'Last night's prisoners being shot.' Blanche uttered a cry of terror. Delmar turned slowly and looked at her.

'Here's a fine thing,' he said. 'If soldiers tremble like women, we shall have to dress up our women as soldiers. It is true you are very young,' he continued, catching hold of her and scanning her closely, 'you will get used to it in time.'

'Never, never!' cried Blanche, without dreaming how dangerous it was for her to manifest her feelings before such a witness. 'I could never get used to such horrors.'

'Boy,' he replied, loosing her, 'do you think a nation can be regenerated without spilling blood? Listen to my advice; keep your reflections to yourself. If ever you fall into the hands of the Royalists they will give you no more mercy than I have done to their soldiers.' And saying these words he went out.

'Blanche,' said Marceau, 'do you know, if that man had given one gesture, one sign, that he recognized you, I would have blown his brains out?'

'My God!' she said, hiding her face in her hands, 'when I think that my father might fall into the hands of this tiger, that if he had been made a prisoner, this night, before my eyes—It is atrocious. Is there no longer pity in this world? Oh! pardon, pardon,' she said, turning to

Marceau, 'who should know that better than I?'

At this instant a servant entered and announced that the horses were ready.

'Let us start, in the name of Heaven!' she cried; 'there is blood in the air we breathe here.'

'Yes, let us go,' replied Marceau, and they descended together.

Marceau found at the front door a troop of thirty men whom the General-in-Chief had ordered to escort them to Nantes.

As they galloped along the highroad, Blanche told him her history; how, her mother being dead, she had been brought up by her father; how her education, given by a man, had accustomed her to exercises which, on the insurrection breaking out, had become so useful to her in following her father.

As she finished her story, they saw twinkling before them in the mist the lights of Nantes. The little troop crossed the Loire, and some seconds after Marceau was in the arms of his mother. A few words sufficed to interest his mother and sisters in his young companion. No sooner had Blanche manifested a desire to change her dress than the two young girls led her away, each disputing which should have the pleasure of serving her as lady's-maid. When Blanche re-entered, Marceau stared in astonishment. In her first costume he had hardly noticed her extreme beauty and gracefulness, which she had now resumed with her woman's dress. It is true, she had taken the greatest pains to make herself as pretty as possible; for one instant before her glass she had forgotten war, insurrection, and carnage. The most innocent soul has its coquetry when it first begins to love.

Marceau could not utter a word, and Blanche smiled joyously, for she saw that she appeared as beautiful to him as she had desired.

In the evening the young *fiancé* of Marceau's sister came, and there was one house in Nantes—one only, perhaps—where all was happiness and love, surrounded, as it was, by tears and sorrow.

And now, from this time forth, a new life began for Marceau and Blanche. Marceau saw a happier future before him, and it was not strange that Blanche should desire the presence of the man who had saved her life. Only from time to time as she thought of her father tears would pour from her eyes, and Marceau would reassure her, and to distract her thoughts would tell her of his first campaign; how the school-boy had become a soldier at fifteen, an officer at seventeen, a colonel at nineteen, and a general at twenty-one.

Nantes at this time writhed under the yoke of Carrier. Its streets ran with blood, and Carrier, who was to Robespierre what the hyena is to the tiger, and the jackal to the lion, gorged himself with the purest of this blood. No one bore a reputation more blameless than that of the young general, Marceau, and no suspicion had as yet attacked his mother or sisters. And now the day fixed for the marriage of one of these young girls arrived.

Amongst the jewels that Marceau had sent for, he chose a necklace of precious stones, which he offered to Blanche.

She looked at it first with all the coquetry of a young girl; then she closed the box.

'Jewels are out of place in my situation,' she said. 'I cannot accept it, whilst my father, hunted from place to place, perhaps begs a morsel of bread for his food, and a granary for his shelter.'

Marceau pressed her in vain. She would accept nothing but an artificial red rose which was amongst the jewels.

The churches being closed, the ceremony took place at the village hotel. At the door of the hotel a deputation of sailors awaited the young couple. One of these men, whose face appeared familiar to Marceau, held in his hands two bouquets. One he gave to the young bride, and, advancing towards Blanche, who regarded him fixedly, he presented her with the other.

'Tinguy, where is my father?' said Blanche, growing very pale.

'At Saint-Florent,' replied the sailor. 'Take this bouquet. There is a letter inside.'

Blanche wished to stop him, to speak to him, but he had disappeared. She read the letter with anxiety. The Royalists had suffered defeat after defeat, giving way before devastation and famine. The Marquis had learnt everything through the watchfulness of Tinguy. Blanche was sad. This letter had cast her back again into all the horrors of war. During the ceremony a stranger who had, he said, affairs of the utmost importance to communicate to Marceau had been ushered into the salon. As Marceau entered the room, his head bent towards Blanche, who leant upon his arm, he did not perceive him. Suddenly he felt her tremble. He looked up. Blanche and he were face to face with Delmar. He approached them slowly, his eyes fixed on Blanche, a smile upon his lips. With his forehead beaded with cold sweat, Marceau regarded him advance as Don Juan regarded the statue of the commandant.

'You have a brother, citizeness?' he said to Blanche. She stammered. Delmar continued–

'If my memory and your face do not deceive me, we breakfasted together at Chollet. How is it I have not seen you since in the ranks of the Republican army?'

Blanche felt as if she were going to fall, for the eye of Delmar pierced her through and through. Then he turned to Marceau; it was Delmar's turn to tremble. The young general had his hand upon the hilt of his sword, which he gripped convulsively. Delmar's face resumed its habitual expression; he appeared to have totally forgotten what he was about to say, and taking Marceau by the arm he drew him into the niche of a window, and talked to him a few minutes about the situation in La Vendée, and told him he had come to consult with Carrier on certain rigorous measures about to be inflicted on the Royalists. The he quitted the room, passing Blanche, who had fallen cold and white into a chair, with a bow and a smile.

Two hours after Marceau received orders to rejoin his army, though his leave of absence did not expire for fifteen ·days. He believed this to have some connection with the scene which had just passed. He must obey, however; to hesitate were to be lost.

Marceau presented the order to Blanche. He regarded her sadly. Two tears rolled down her pale cheeks, but she was silent.

'Blanche,' he said, 'war makes us murderous and cruel; it is possible that we shall see each other no more.' He took her hand. 'Promise me, if I fall, that you will remember me sometimes, and I promise you, Blanche, that if between my life and death I have the time to pronounce one name—one alone—it shall be yours.' Blanche was speechless for tears, but in her eyes were a thousand promises more tender than that which Marceau demanded. With one hand she pressed Marceau's, and pointed with the other to his rose, which she wore in her hair.

'It shall never leave me,' she said.

An hour after he was on the road to rejoin his army. Each step he took on the road they had journeyed together recalled her to his mind, and the danger she ran appeared more menacing now that he was away from her side. Each instant he felt ready to rein in his horse and gallop back to Nantes. If Marceau had not been so intent upon his own thoughts he would have perceived at the extremity of the road and coming towards him, a horseman who, after stopping an instant to assure himself he was not mistaken, had put his horse at a gallop and joined him. He recognized General Dumas. The two friends leapt from their horses and cast themselves into each other's arms. At the same instant a man, his hair streaming with perspiration, his face bleeding, his clothing rent, sprang over the hedge and, half fainting, fell at the feet of the two friends, exclaiming—

'She is arrested!'

It was Tinguy.

'Arrested! Who? Blanche!' cried Marceau.

The peasant made an affirmative sign. He could no longer speak. He had run five leagues, crossing fields and hedges in his flight to join Marceau.

Marceau stared at him stupidly.

'Arrested! Blanche arrested!' he repeated continually, whilst his friend applied his gourd full of wine to the clenched teeth of the peasant.

'Alexandre,' cried Marceau. 'I shall return to Nantes; I must follow her; for my life, my future, my happiness, all is with her!' His teeth chattered violently, and his body trembled convulsively.

'Let him beware who has dared to put his hand on Blanche. I love her with all the strength of my soul; existence is no longer possible for me without her. Oh, fool that I was to leave her! Blanche arrested! And where has she been taken?'

Tinguy, to whom this question was addressed, commenced to recover. 'To the prison of Bouffays,' he answered.

The words were hardly out of his mouth when the two friends were galloping back to Nantes.

Marceau knew he had not an instant to lose: he directed his steps at once to Carrier's house. But neither menaces nor prayers could obtain an interview from the deputy of the 'Mountain.'

Marceau turned away quietly; he appeared in the interval to have adopted a new project, and he prayed his companion to await him at the gate of the prison with horses and a carriage.

Before Marceau's name and rank the prison gates were soon opened, and he commanded the gaoler to conduct him to the cell where Blanche was enclosed. The man hesitated; but, on Marceau repeating his desire in a more imperative tone, he obeyed, making him a sign to follow him.

'She is not alone,' said his guide, as he unlocked the low-arched door of a cell whose sombre gloom made

Marceau shudder, 'but she will not troubled long with her companion; he is to be guillotined to-day.' Saying these words he closed the door on Marceau, and determined to keep as quiet as possible concerning an interview which would be so compromising to him.

Still dazzled from his sudden passage from day to darkness, Marceau groped his way into the cell like a man in a dream. Then he heard a cry, and the young girl flung herself into his arms. She clung to him with inarticulate sobs and convulsive embraces.

'You have not abandoned me, then,' she cried. 'They arrested me, dragged me here; in the crowd which followed I recognized Tinguy. I cried out "Marceau! Marceau!" and he disappeared. Now you have come, you will take me away, you will not leave me here?'

'I wish I could tear you away this moment, if it were at the price of my life; but it is impossible. Give me two days, Blanche, but two days. Now I wish you to answer me a question on which your life and mine depend. Answer me as you would answer to God. Blanche, do you love me?'

'Is this the time and place for such a question? Do you think these walls are used to vows of love?'

'This *is* the moment, for we are between life and death. Blanche, be quick and answer me; each instant robs us of a day, each hour, of a year. Do you love me?'

'Oh! yes, yes!' These words escaped from the young girl's heart, who, forgetting that no one could see her blushes, hid her head upon his breast.

'Well! Blanche, you must accept me at once for your husband.'

The young girl trembled.

'What can be your design?'

'My motive is to tear you from death; we will see if they will send to the scaffold the wife of a Republican general.'

Then Blanche understood it all; but she trembled at the danger to which he must expose himself to save her. Her love for him increased, and with it her courage rose.

'It is impossible,' she said, firmly.

'Impossible!' interrupted Marceau, 'what can rise between us and happiness, since you have avowed you love me? Listen, then, to the reason which has made you reject your only way of escape. Listen, Blanche! I saw you and loved you; that love has become a passion. My life is yours, your fate is mine; happiness or death, I will share either with you; no human power can separate us, and if I quitted you, I have only to cry "*Vive le roi!*" and your prison gates will reopen, and we will come out no more except together. Death upon the same scaffold, that will be enough for me.'

'Oh, no, no; leave me, in the name of Heaven, leave me!'

'Leave you! Take heed what you say, for if I quit this prison without having the right to defend you, I shall seek out your father—your father whom you have forgotten, and who weeps for you—and I shall say to him: "Old man, she could have saved herself, but she has not done so; she has wished your last days to be passed in mourning, and her blood to be upon your white hair. Weep, old man, not because your daughter is dead, but because she did not love you well enough to live."'

Marceau had repulsed her, and she had fallen on her knees beside him, and he, with his teeth clenched, strode to and fro with a bitter laugh; then he heard her sob, the tears leapt to his eyes, and he fell at her feet.

'Blanche, by all that is most sacred in the world, consent to become my wife!'

'You must, young girl,' interrupted a strange voice, which made them tremble and rise together. 'It is the only way to preserve your life. Religion commands you, and I am ready to bless your union.' Marceau turned astonished, and recognised the *curé* of Saint-Marie-de-Rhé, who had made part of the gathering which he had attacked on the night when Blanche became his prisoner.

'Oh, my father,' he cried, seizing his hand, 'obtain her consent!'

'Blanche de Beaulieu,' replied the priest, with solemn accents, 'in the name of your father, whom my age and friendship give me the right of representing, I command you to obey this young man.'

Blanche seemed agitated with a thousand different emotions; at last she threw herself into Marceau's arms.

'I cannot resist any longer,' she said. 'Marceau, I love you, and I will be your wife.' Their lips joined; Marceau was at the height of joy; he seemed to have forgotten everything. The priest's voice broke in upon their ecstasy.

'We must be quick,' he said, 'for my moments are numbered.'

The two lovers trembled; this voice recalled them to earth. Blanche glanced around the cell with apprehension.

'What a moment,' she said, 'to unite our destinies! Can you think a union consecrated under vaults so sombre and lugubrious can be fortunate and happy?'

Marceau shuddered, for he himself was touched with superstitious terror. He drew Blanche to that part of the cell where the daylight struggling through the crossed bars of a narrow air-hole rendered the shadows less thick, and there, falling on their knees, they awaited the priest's blessing. As he extended his arms above them and pronounced the sacred words, the clash of arms and the tread of soldiers was heard in the corridor.

Blanche cast herself in terror into Marceau's arms.

'Can they have come to seek me already?' she cried. 'Oh, my love, how frightful death is at this moment!' The young General threw himself before the door, a pistol in each hand. The astonished soldiers drew back.

'Reassure yourselves,' said the priest; 'it is I whom they seek. It is I who must die.'

The soldiers surrounded him.

'My children,' he cried, in a loud voice, addressing himself to the young pair. 'On your knees; for with one foot in the tomb I give you my last benediction, and that of a dying person is sacred.' He drew, as he spoke, a crucifix from his breast, and extended it towards them; himself about to die, it was for them he prayed.

There was a solemn silence.

Then the soldiers surrounded him, the door closed, and all disappeared.

Blanche threw her arms about Marceau's neck.

'Oh, if you leave me, and they come to seek me, and you are not here to aid me! Oh, Marceau, think of me upon the scaffold far from you, weeping, and calling you, without response! Oh, do not go! do not go! I will cast myself at their feet; I will tell them I am not guilty, that, if they will leave me in prison with you all my life, I will bless them!'

'I am sure to save you, Blanche; I answer for your life. In less than two days I shall be here with your pardon, and then, instead of a prison and a cell, a life of happiness, a life of liberty and love!'

The door opened, the gaoler appeared. Blanche clung more closely to her lover's breast, but each instant was precious, and he gently unwound her arms from about him, and promised to return before the close of the second day.

'Love me for ever,' he said, rushing out of the cell.

'For ever,' said Blanche, half fainting, and showing him in her hair the red rose that he had given her. Then the door closed upon him like the gate of the Inferno.

Marceau found his companion waiting for him at the porter's lodge. He called for ink and paper.

'What are you about to do?' asked his friend.

'I am going to write to Carrier, to demand a respite of two days, and to tell him his own life depends on Blanche's.'

'Wretched man!' cried his friend, snatching the unfinished letter away from him. 'You threaten him, you who are in his power, you who have set his orders to rejoin your army at defiance. Before an hour passes you will be arrested, and what then can you do for yourself or her?'

Marceau let his head fall between his hands, and appeared to reflect deeply.

'You are right,' he cried, rising suddenly; and he drew his friend into the street.

A group of people were gathered round a post-chaise.

'If this evening is hazy,' whispered a voice at Marceau's ear, 'I do not know what would prevent twenty strong fellows from entering the town and freeing the prisoners. It is a pity that Nantes is so badly guarded.'

Marceau trembled, turned, and recognized Tinguy, darted a glance of intelligence at him, and sprang into the carriage.

'Paris!' he called to the postillion, and the horses darted forward with the rapidity of lightning. At eight o'clock the carriage entered Paris.

Marceau and his friend separated at the square of the Palais-Egalité, and Marceau took his way alone on foot through the Rue Saint-Honoré, descended at the side of Saint-Roch, stopped at No. 366, and asked for Robespierre. He was informed that he had gone to the Théâtre de la Nation. Marceau proceeded there, astonished to have to seek in such a place the austere member of the Committee of Public Welfare. He entered, and recognized Robespierre half hidden in the shadow of a box. As he arrived outside the door he met him coming out. Marceau presented himself, and gave him his name.

'What can I do for you?' said Robespierre.

'I desire an interview with you.'

'Here, or at my house?'

'At your house.'

'Come, then.'

And these two men, moved by feelings so opposite, walked along side by side, Robespierre indifferent and calm, Marceau passionate and excited. This was the man who held within his hands the fate of Blanche.

They arrived at Robespierre's house, entered, and ascended a narrow staircase, which led them to a chamber on the third floor. A bust of Rousseau, a table, on which lay open the *Contrat Social* and *Emile*, a chest of drawers, and some chairs, completed the furniture of the apartment.

'Here is Caesar's palace,' said Robespierre, smiling; 'what have you to demand from its president?'

'The pardon of my wife, who is condemned to death by Carrier.'

'Your wife condemned to death by Carrier! The wife of Marceau, the well-known Republican! the Spartan soldier! What is Carrier then doing at Nantes?'

Marceau gave him an account of the atrocities which Carrier was superintending at Nantes.

'See how I am always misunderstood,' cried Robespierre, with a hoarse voice, broken by emotion. 'Above all, where my eyes cannot see, nor my hand arrest. There is enough blood being spilt that we cannot avoid, and we are not at the end of it yet.'

'Then give me my wife's pardon.'

Robespierre took a leaf of white paper.

'What was her name?'

'Why do you wish to know that?'

'It is necessary in cases of identity.'

'Blanche de Beaulieu.'

Robespierre let his pen fall.

'What? The daughter of the Marquis de Beaulieu, the chief of the Royalists of La Vendée. How is it that she is *your* wife?'

Marceau told him all.

'Young fool and madman!' he said. 'Must you—' Marceau interrupted him.

'I ask from you neither insults nor abuse. I ask for her life. Will you give it me?'

'Will family ties, love's influence, never lead you to betray the Republic?'

'Never.'

'If you find yourself armed, face to face with the Marquis de Beaulieu?'

'I will fight against him as I have already done.'

'And if he falls into your hands?'

Marceau reflected an instant:

'I will bring him to you, and you shall be his judge.'

'You swear it to me?'

'Upon my honour.'

Robespierre took up his pen and finished writing.

'There is your wife's pardon,' he said. 'You can depart.'

Marceau took his hand and wrung it with force. He wished to speak, but tears choked his utterance; and it was Robespierre who said to him—

'Go! there is not an instant to lose. *Au revoir!*'

Marceau sprang down the stairs and into the street, and ran towards the Palais-Egalité, where his carriage waited.

From what a weight his heart was freed! What happiness awaited him! What joy after so much grief! His imagination plunged into the future, and he saw the moment when, appearing on the threshold of the prison-cell, he would cry—

'Blanche, you are saved! You are free! Before us lies a life of love and happiness.'

Yet from time to time a vague uneasiness tormented him; a sudden chill struck cold upon his heart. He spurred on the postillions by lavish promises of gold, and the horses flew along the road. Everything seemed to partake of the feverish agitation of his blood. In a few hours he had left Versailles, Chartres, Le Mans, La Flèche behind him. They were nearing Angers, when suddenly, with a terrible crash, the carriage heeled over on its side, and he fell. He rose hurt and bleeding, separated with his sabre the traces which bound one of the horses, and, leaping on its back, reached the next post; and, taking a fresh horse, rapidly continued his course.

And now he has crossed Angers, he perceives Nigrande, reaches Varade, passes Ancenis; his horse streams with foam and blood. He gains Saint-Donatien, then Nantes—Nantes, which encloses his life, his happiness! Some seconds after he passes the gates, he is in the town, he reins in his horse before the prison of Bouffays. He has arrived. What matters all their troubles now? He calls—

'Blanche, Blanche!'

The gaoler appears and replies—

'Two carts have just left the prison. Mademoiselle de Beaulieu was in the first.'

With a curse upon his lips, Marceau springs to the ground, and rushes with the hustling crowd towards the great square. He comes up with the last of the two carts; one of the prisoners inside recognizes him. It is Tinguy.

'Save her! save her!' he cries out, 'for I have failed.'

Marceau pushes on through the crowd; they hustle him, they press around him, but he hurls them out of his path. He arrives upon the place of execution. Before him is the scaffold. He flourishes aloft the scrap of paper, crying—

'A pardon! a pardon!'

At that instant the executioner, seizing by its long, fair hair the head of a young girl, held it up before the terrified crowd.

Suddenly from the midst of that silent crowd a cry was heard—a cry of anguish, in which there seemed to have been gathered all the forces of human agony. Marceau had recognized between the teeth of this uplifted head the red rose which he had given to his young bride.

DARK DIGNUM
and
THE VANISHING HOUSE

O

Bernard Capes

It has taken over sixty years for the rediscovery of Bernard Capes (1854–1918), in my opinion one of the finest writers of macabre fiction of the Victorian era. Yet he languished in undeserved obscurity almost from the year he died, despite writing over thirty-five books and contributing to most of the classic Victorian periodicals.

Capes was born in London and educated at Beaumont College. Originally intending to follow an army career, he was prevented by the first of a series of mishaps that dogged him throughout his life. Various unsuccessful ventures followed–brief forays into art, rabbit farming and magazine editorial work–before he found his real talent, writing. He entered a contest run by the Chicago Record in 1898, to find a new mystery novel. Capes' entry, THE LAKE OF WINE, won hands down, was published that same year and Capes became a full time writer from then on.

He was prolific and imaginative, writing weird tales, detective novels, historical romances, newspaper articles and editorials, magazine stories and verse. He wrote six books of short stories, many of them ghostly or macabre, and they are much prized by collectors now.

Capes' run of bad luck ended with him being struck down by the influenza epidemic which swept Europe after the First World War. He died in Winchester after a brief illness and heart failure.

Readers interested in seeing more of Capes' stories should consult a recent collection of his work, THE BLACK REAPER (1989). Here are two tales not included in that book, taken from his 1899 collection AT A WINTER'S FIRE. They show the neglected talents of Bernard Capes to perfection.

BERNARD CAPES

O

Dark Dignum

'I'D not go nigher, sir,' said my landlady's father.

I made out his warning through the shrill piping of the wind; and stopped and took in the plunging seascape from where I stood. The boom of the waves came up from a vast distance beneath; sky and the horizon of running water seemed hurrying upon us over the lip of the rearing cliff.

'It crumbles!' he cried. 'It crumbles near the edge like as frosted mortar. I've seen a noble sheep, sir, eighty pound of mutton, browsing here one moment, and seen it go down the next in a puff of white dust. Hark to that! Do you hear it?'

Through the tumult of the wind in that high place came a liquid vibrant sound, like the muffled stroke of iron on an anvil. I thought it the gobble of water in clanging caves deep down below.

'It might be a bell,' I said.

The old man chuckled joyously. He was my cicerone for the nonce; had come out of his chair by the ingle-nook to taste a little the salt of life. The north-easter flashed in the white cataracts of his eyes and woke a feeble activity in his scrannel limbs. When the wind blew loud, his daughter had told me, he was always restless, like an imprisoned sea-gull. He would be up and out. He would rise and flap his old draggled pinions, as if the great air fanned an expiring spark into flame.

'It *is* a bell!' he cried–'the bell of old St Dunstan's, that was swallowed by the waters in the dark times.'

'Ah,' I said. 'That is the legend hereabouts.'

'No legend, sir–no legend. Where be the tombstones of drownded mariners to prove it such? Not one to forty that they has in other sea-board parishes. For why? Dunstan bell sounds its warning, and not a craft will put out.'

'There is the storm cone,' I suggested.

He did not hear me. He was punching with his staff at one of a number of little green mounds that lay about us.

'I could tell you a story of these,' he said. 'Do you know where we stand?'

'On the site of the old churchyard?'

'Ay, sir; though it still bore the name of the *new* yard in my first memory of it.'

'Is that so? And what is the story?'

He dwelt a minute, dense with introspection. Suddenly he sat himself down upon a mossy bulge in the turf, and waved me imperiously to a place beside him.

'The old order changeth,' he said. 'The only lasting foundations of men's works shall be godliness and law-biding. Long ago they builded a new church–here, high up on the cliffs, where the waters could not reach; and, lo! the waters wrought beneath and sapped the foundations, and the church fell into the sea.'

'So I understand,' I said.

'The godless are fools,' he chattered knowingly. 'Look here at these bents–thirty of 'em, may be. Tombstones, sir; perished like man his works, and the decayed stumps of them coated with salt grass.'

He pointed to the ragged edge of the cliff a score paces away.

'They raised it out there,' he said, 'and further–a temple of bonded stone. They thought to bribe the Lord to a partnership in their corruption, and He answered by casting down the fair mansion into the waves.'

I said, 'Who—who, my friend?'

'They that builded the church,' he answered.

'Well,' I said. 'It seems a certain foolishness to set the edifice so close to the margin.'

Again he chuckled.

'It was close, close, as you say; yet none so close as you might think nowadays. Time hath gnawed here like a rat on a cheese. But the foolishness appeared in setting the brave mansion between the winds and its own graveyard. Let the dead lie seawards, one had thought, and the church inland where we stand. So had the bell rung to this day; and only the charnel bones flaked piecemeal into the sea.'

'Certainly, to have done so would show the better providence.'

'Sir, I said the foolishness *appeared*. But, I tell you, there was foresight in the disposition—in neighbouring the building to the cliff path. *For so they could the easier enter unobserved, and store their kegs of Nantes brandy in the belly of the organ.*'

'They? Who were they?'

'Why, who—but two-thirds of all Dunburgh?'

'Smugglers?'

'It was a nest of 'em—traffickers in the eternal fire o' weekdays, and on the Sabbath, who so sanctimonious? But honesty comes not from the washing, like a clean shirt, nor can the piety of one day purge the evil of six. They built their church anigh the margin, forasmuch as it was handy, and that they thought, "Surely the Lord will not undermine His own?" A rare community o' blasphemers, fro' the parson that took his regular toll of the organ-loft, to him that sounded the keys and pulled out the joyous stops as if they was so many spigots to what lay behind.'

'Of when do you speak?'

'I speak of nigh a century and a half ago. I speak of the

time o' the Seven Years' War and of Exciseman Jones,
that, twenty year after he were buried, took his revenge
on the cliff side of the man that done him to death.'

'And who was that?'

'They called him Dark Dignum, sir—a great feat smuggler, and as wicked as he was bold.'

'Is your story about him?'

'Ay, it is; and of my grandfather, that were a boy when
they laid, and was glad to lay, the exciseman deep as they
could dig; for the sight of his sooty face in his coffin was
worse than a bad dream.'

'Why was that?'

The old man edged closer to me, and spoke in a sibi-
lant voice.

'He were murdered, sir, foully and horribly, for all
they could never bring it home to the culprit.'

'Will you tell me about it?'

He was nothing loth. The wind, the place of perished
tombs, the very wild-blown locks of this "withered apple-
john", were eerie accompaniments to the tale he piped in
my ear:—

'When my grandfather were a boy,' he said, 'there
lighted in Dunburgh Exciseman Jones. P'r'aps the village
had gained an ill reputation. P'r'aps Exciseman Jones's
predecessor had failed to secure the confidence o' the
exekitive. At any rate, the new man was little to the fancy
of the village. He was a grim, sour-looking, brass-bound
galloot; and incorruptible—which was the worst. The keg
o' brandy left on his doorstep o' New Year's Eve had been
better unspiled and run into the gutter; for it led him
somehow to the identification of the innocent that done
it, and he had him by the heels in a twinkling. The squire
snorted at the man, and the parson looked askance; but
Dark Dignum, he swore he'd be even with him, if he
swung for it. They were hurt and surprised, that was the
truth, over the scrupulosity of certain people; and feelin'
ran high against Exciseman Jones.

'At that time Dark Dignum was a young man with a

reputation above his years for profaneness and audacity. Ugly things were said about him; and amongst many wicked he was feared for his wickedness. Exciseman Jones had his eye on him; and that was bad for Exciseman Jones.

'Now one murky December night Exciseman Jones staggered home with a bloody long slice down his scalp, and the red drip from it spotting the cobble-stones.

'"Summut fell on him from a winder," said Dark Dignum, a little later, as he were drinkin' hisself hoarse in the Black Boy. "Summat fell on him retributive, as you might call it. For, would you believe it, the man had at the moment been threatenin' me? He did. He said, 'I know damn well about you, Dignum; and for all your damn ingenuity, I'll bring you with a crack to the ground yet!'"'

'What had happened? Nobody knew, sir. But Exciseman Jones was in his bed for a fortnight; and when he got on his legs again, it was pretty evident there was a hate between the two men that only blood-spillin' could satisfy.

'So far as is known, they never spoke to one another again. They played their game of death in silence—the lawful, cold and unfathomable; the unlawful, swaggerin' and crool—and twenty year separated the first move and the last.

'This were the first, sir—as Dark Dignum leaked it out long after in his cups. This were the first; and it brought Exciseman Jones to his grave on the cliff here.

'It were a deep soft summer night; and the young smuggler sat by hisself in the long room of the Black Boy. Now, I tell you he were a fox-ship intriguer—grand, I should call him, in the aloneness of his villainy. He would play his dark games out of his own hand; and sure, of all his wickedness, this game must have seemed the sum.

'I say he sat by hisself; and I hear the listening ghost of him call me a liar. For there were another body present, though invisible to mortal eye; and that second party were Exciseman Jones, who was hidden up the chimney.

'How had he inveigled him there? Ah, they've met and worried that point out since. No other will ever know the truth this side the grave. But reports come to be whispered; and reports said as how Dignum had made an appointment with a bodiless master of a smack as never floated, to meet him in the Black Boy and arrange for to run a cargo as would never be shipped; and that somehow he managed to acquent Exciseman Jones o' this dissembling appointment, and to secure his presence in hidin' to witness it.

'That's conjecture; for Dignum never let on so far. But what *is* known for certain is that Exciseman Jones, who were as daring and determined as his enemy–p'r'aps more so–for some reason was in the chimney, on to a grating in which he had managed to lower hisself from the roof; and that he could, if given time, have scrambled up again with difficulty, but was debarred from going lower. And, further, this is known–that, as Dignum sat on, pretendin' to yawn and huggin' his black intent, a little soot plopped down the chimney and scattered on the coals of the laid fire beneath.

'At that–"Curse this waitin"! said he. "The room's as chill as a belfry", and he got to his feet, with a secret grin, and strolled to the hearthstone.

'"I wonder," said he, "will the landlord object if I ventur' upon a glint of fire for comfort's sake?" and he pulled out his flint and steel, struck a spark, and with no more feeling than he'd express in lighting a pipe, set the flame to the sticks.

'The trapt rat above never stirred or give tongue. My God! what a man! Sich a nature could afford to bide and bide–ay, for twenty year, if need be.

'Dignum would have enjoyed the sound of a cry; but he never got it. He listened with the grin fixed on his face; and of a sudden he heard a scrambling struggle, like as a dog with the colic jumping at a wall; and presently, as the sticks blazed and the smoke rose denser, a thick coughin', as of a consumptive man under bed-clothes. Still no cry, or any appeal for mercy; no, not from the time he lit the fire till a horrible rattle came down, which was the last twitches of somethin' that choked and died on the sooty gratin' above.

'When all was quiet, Dignum he knocks with his foot on the floor and sits hisself down before the hearth, with a face like a pillow for innocence.

'"I were chilled and lit it," says he to the landlord. "You don't mind?"

'"Mind? Who would have ventur'd to cross Dark Dignum's fancies?"

'He give a boisterous laugh, and ordered in a double noggin of humming stuff.

'"Here," he says, when it comes, "is to the health of Exciseman Jones, that swore to bring me to the ground."

'"To the ground," mutters a thick voice from the chimney.

'"My God!" says the landlord—"there's something up there!"

'Something there was; and terrible to look upon when they brought it to light. The creature's struggles had ground the soot into its face, and its nails were black below the quick.

'Were those words the last of its death-throe, or an echo from beyond? Ah! we may question; but they were heard by two men.

'Dignum went free. What could they prove agen him? Not that he knew there was aught in the chimney when he lit the fire. The other would scarcely have acquent him of his plans. And Exciseman Jones was hurried into his grave alongside the church up here.

'And therein he lay for twenty year, despite that, not a twelvemonth after his coming, the sacreligious house itself sunk roaring into the waters. For the Lord would have none of it, and, biding His time, struck through a fortnight of deluge, and hurled church and cliff into ruin. But the yard remained, and, nighest the seaward edge of it, Exciseman Jones slept in his fearful winding sheet and bided *his* time.

'It came when my grandfather were a young man of thirty, and mighty close and confidential with Dark Dignum. God forgive him! Doubtless he were led away by the older smuggler, that had a grace of villainy about him, 'tis said, and used Lord Chesterfield's printed letters for wadding to his bullets.

'By then he was a ramping, roaring devil; but, for all his bold hands were stained with crime, the memory of Exciseman Jones and of his promise dwelled with him and darkened him ever more and more, and never left him. So those that knew him said.

'Now all these years the cliff edge agen the graveyard, where it was broke off, was scabbing into the sea below. But still they used this way of ascent for their ungodly traffic; and over the ruin of the cliff they had drove a new path for to carry up their kegs.

'It was a cloudy night in March, with scud and a fitful moon, and there was a sloop in the offing, and under the shore a loaded boat that had just pulled in with muffled rowlocks. Out of this Dark Dignum was the first to sling hisself a brace of rundlets; and my grandfather followed with two more. They made softly for the cliff path—began the ascent—was half-way up.

'Whiz!—a stone of chalk went by them with a skirl, and slapped into the rubble below.

'"Some more of St Dunstan's gravel!" cried Dignum, pantin' out a reckless laugh under his load; and on they went again.

'Hwish!—a bigger lump came like a thunderbolt, and the wind of it took the bloody smuggler's hat and sent it swooping into the darkness like a bird.

'"Thunder!" said Dignum; "the cliff's breaking away!"

'The words was hardly out of his mouth, when there flew such a volley of chalk stones as made my grandfather, though none had touched him, fall upon the path where he stood, and begin to gabble out what he could call to mind of the prayers for the dying. He was in the midst of it, when he heard a scream come from his companion as froze the very marrow in his bones. He looked up, thinkin' his hour had come.

'My God! What a sight he saw! The moon had shone out of a sudden, and the light of it struck down on Dignum's face, and that was the colour of dirty parchment. And he looked higher, and give a sort of sob.

'For there, stickin' out of the cliff side, was half the body of Exciseman Jones, with its arms stretched abroad, *and it was clawin' out lumps of chalk and hurling them down at Dignum!*

'And even as he took this in through his terror, a great ball of white came hurtling, and went full on to Dignum's face with a splash—and he were spun down into the deep night below, a nameless thing.'

The old creature came to a stop, his eyes glinting with a febrile excitement.

'And so,' I said, 'Exciseman Jones was true to his word?'

The tension of memory was giving—the spring slowly uncoiling itself.

'Ay,' he said doubtfully. 'The cliff had flaked away by degrees to his very grave. They found his skelington stickin' out of the chalk.'

'His *skeleton*?' said I, with the emphasis of disappointment.

'The first, sir, the first. Ay, his was the first. There've been a many exposed since. The work of decay goes on, and the bones they fall into the sea. Sometimes, sailing off shore, you may see a shank or an arm protrudin' like a pigeon's leg from a pie. But the wind or the weather takes it and it goes. There's more to follow yet. Look at 'em! look at these bents! Every one a grave, with a skelington in it. The wear and tear from the edge will reach each one in turn, and then the last of the ungodly will have ceased from the earth.'

'And what became of your grandfather?'

'My grandfather? There were something happened made him renounce the devil. He died one of the elect.

His youth were heedless and unregenerate; but, 'tis said,
after he were turned thirty he never smiled agen. There
was a reason. Did I ever tell you the story of Dark Dignum
and Exciseman Jones?'

BERNARD CAPES

O

The Vanishing House

'MY grandfather,' said the banjo, 'drank "dog's-nose," my father drank "dog's-nose," and I drink "dog's-nose." If that ain't heredity, there's no virtue in the board schools.'

'Ah!' said the piccolo, 'you're always a-boasting of your science. And so, I suppose, your son'll drink "dog's-nose," too?'

'No,' retorted the banjo, with a rumbling laugh, like wind in the bung-hole of an empty cask; 'for I ain't got none. The family ends with me; which is a pity, for I'm a full-stop to be proud on.'

He was an enormous, tun-bellied person—a mere mound of expressionless flesh, whose size alone was an investment that paid a perpetual dividend of laughter. When, as with the rest of his company, his face was blackened, it looked like a specimen coal on a pedestal in a museum.

There was Christmas company in the Good Intent, and the sanded tap-room, with its trestle tables and sprigs of holly stuck under sooty beams, reeked with smoke and the steam of hot gin and water.

'How much could you put down of a night, Jack?' said a little grinning man by the door.

'Why,' said the banjo, 'enough to lay the dustiest ghost as ever walked.'

'*Could* you, now?' said the little man.

'Ah!' said the banjo, chuckling. 'There's nothing like settin' one sperit to lay another; and there I could give you proof number two of heredity.'

'What! Don't you go for to say you ever see'd a ghost!'

'Haven't I? What are you whisperin' about, you blushful chap there by the winder?'

'I was only remarkin', sir, 'twere snawin' like the devil!'

'*Is* it? Then the devil has been misjudged these eighteen hundred and ninety odd years.'

'But *did* you ever see a ghost?' said the little grinning man, pursuing his subject.

'No, I didn't, sir,' mimicked the banjo, 'saving in coffee grounds. But my grandfather in *his* cups see'd one; which brings us to number three in the matter of heredity.'

'Give us the story, Jack,' said the 'bones,' whose agued chins were extemporizing a rattle on their own account before the fire.

'Well, I don't mind,' said the fat man. 'It's seasonable; and I'm seasonable, like the blessed plum-pudden, I am; and the more burnt brandy you set about me, the richer and headier I'll go down.'

'You'd be a jolly old pudden to digest,' said the piccolo.

'You blow your aggravation into your pipe and sealing-wax the stops,' said his friend.

He drew critically at his 'churchwarden' a moment or so, leaned forward, emptied his glass into his capacious receptacles, and, giving his stomach a shift, as if to accommodate it to its new burden, proceeded as follows:—

'Music and malt is my nat'ral inheritance. My grandfather blew his "dog's-nose," and drank his clarinet like a artist; and my father—'

'What did you say your grandfather did?' asked the piccolo.

'He played the clarinet.'

'You said he blew his "dog's-nose."'

'Don't be an ass, Fred!' said the banjo, aggrieved. 'How the blazes could a man blow his dog's nose, unless he muzzled it with a handkercher, and then twisted its tail? He played the clarinet, I say; and my father played the musical glasses, which was a form of harmony pertiklerly genial to him. Amongst us we've piped out a good long century—ah! we have, for all I look sich a babby bursting on sops and spoon meat.'

'What!' said the little man by the door. 'You don't include them cockt hatses in your experience?'

'My grandfather wore 'em, sir. He wore a play-actin' coat, too, and buckles to his shoes, when he'd got any; and he and a friend or two made a permanency of "waits" (only they called 'em according to the season), and got their profit goin' from house to house, principally in the country, and discoursin' music at the low rate of whatever they could get for it.'

'Ain't you comin' to the ghost, Jack?' said the little man hungrily.

'All in course, sir. Well, gentlemen, it was hard times pretty often with my grandfather and his friends, as you may suppose; and never so much as when they had to trudge it across country, with the nor'-easter buzzin' in their teeth and the snow piled on their cockt hats like lemon sponge on entry dishes. The rewards, I've heard him say—for he lived to be ninety, nevertheless—was poor compensation for the drifts, and the inflienza, and the broken chilblains; but now and again they'd get a fair skinful of liquor from a jolly squire, as 'd set 'em up like boggarts mended wi' new broomsticks.'

'Ho-haw!' broke in a hurdle-maker in a corner; and then, regretting the publicity of his merriment, put his fingers bashfully to his stubble lips.

'Now,' said the banjo, 'it's of a pertikler night and a pertikler skinful that I'm a-going to tell you; and that night fell dark, and that skinful were took a hundred years ago this December, as I'm a Jack-pudden!'

He paused for a moment for effect, before he went on:—

'They were down in the sou'-west country, which they little knew; and were anighing Winchester city, or should 'a' been. But they got muzzed on the ungodly downs, and before they guessed, they was off the track. My good hat! there they was, as lost in the snow as three nut-shells a-sinkin' into a hasty pudden. Well, they wandered round; pretty confident at first, but getting madder and madder as every sense of their bearings slipped from them. And the bitter cold took their vitals, so as they saw nothing but a great winding sheet stretched abroad for to wrap their dead carcasses in.

'At last my grandfather he stopt and pulled hisself together with an awful face, and says he: "We're Christmas pie for the carrying-on crows if we don't prove ourselves human. Let's fetch out our pipes and blow our trouble into 'em." So they stood together, like as if they was before a house, and they played "Kate of Aberdare" mighty dismal and flat, for their fingers froze to the keys.

'Now, I tell you, they hadn't climbed over the first stave, when there come a skirl of wind and spindrift of snow as almost took them off of their feet; and, on the going down of it, Jem Sloke, as played the hautboy, dropped the reed from his mouth, and called out, "Sakes alive! if we fools ain't been standin' outside a gentleman's gate all the time, and not knowin' it!"

'You might 'a' knocked the three of 'em down wi' a barley straw, as they stared and stared, and then fell into a low, enjoyin' laugh. For they was standin' not six fut from a tall iron gate in a stone wall, and behind these was a great house showin' out dim, with the winders all lighted up.

'"Lord!" chuckled my grandfather, "to think o' the tricks o' this vagarious country! But, as we're here, we'll go on and give 'em a taste of our quality."

'They put new heart into the next movement, as you may guess; and they hadn't fair started on it, when the door of the house swung open, and down the shaft of light that shot out as far as the gate there come a smiling young gal, with a tray of glasses in her hands.

'Now she come to the bars; and she took and put a glass through, not sayin' nothin', but invitin' some one to drink with a silent laugh.

'Did any one take that glass? Of course he did, you'll be thinkin'; and you'll be thinkin' wrong. Not a man of the three moved. They was struck like as stone, and their lips was gone the colour of sloe berries. Not a man took the glass. For why? The moment the gal presented it, each saw the face of a thing lookin' out of the winder over the porch, and the face was hidjus beyond words, and the shadder of it, with the light behind, stretched out and reached to the gal, and made her hidjus, too.

'At last my grandfather give a groan and put out his hand; and, as he did it, the face went, and the gal was beautiful to see agen.

'"Death and the devil!" said he. "It's one or both, either way; and I prefer 'em hot to cold!"

'He drank off half the glass, smacked his lips, and stood staring a moment.

'"Dear, dear!" said the gal, in a voice like falling water, "you've drunk blood, sir!"

'My grandfather gave a yell, slapped the rest of the liquor in the faces of his friends, and threw the cup agen the bars. It broke with a noise like thunder, and at that he up'd with his hands and fell full length into the snow.'

There was a pause. The little man by the door was twisting nervously in his chair.

'He came to—of course, he came to?' said he at length.

'He come to,' said the banjo solemnly, 'in the bitter break of dawn; that is, he come to as much of hisself as he ever was after. He give a squiggle and lifted his head; and there was he and his friends a-lyin' on the snow of the high downs.'

'And the house and the gal?'

'Narry a sign of either, sir, but just the sky and the white stretch; and one other thing.'

'And what was that?'

'A stain of red sunk in where the cup had spilt.'

There was a second pause, and the banjo blew into the bowl of his pipe.

'They cleared out of that neighbourhood double quick, you'll bet,' said he. 'But my grandfather was never the same man agen. His face took purple, while his friends' only remained splashed with red, same as birth marks; and, I tell you, if he ever ventur'd upon "Kate of Aberdare", his cheeks swelled up to the reed of his clarinet, like as a blue plum on a stalk. And forty year after, he died of what they call solution of blood to the brain.'

'And you can't have better proof than that,' said the little man.

'That's what *I* say,' said the banjo. 'Next player, gentlemen, please.'

THE KING OF THE BABOONS

O

Perceval Gibbon

Africa was a fertile source of fiction for Victorian writers, in this and other genres. H. Rider Haggard was probably the supreme exponent of African adventure fiction, but there were many other writers who used Africa for their stories and never achieved Haggard's renown. The now forgotten Perceval Gibbon was one such author who perhaps deserved better.

Gibbon was born in Wales in 1879 and, like many young men of his day, travelled abroad in the merchant navy. He served on ships from Britain, America and France.

Bitten by the travelling bug, Gibbon turned to journalism and continued his journeys around the world as a war correspondent, covering the Boer War among other conflicts.

He joined the Marines in the First World War but continued his writing, being responsible for the official account of the surrender of the German Imperial fleet, published in 1919.

His book career had started in 1903 with AFRICAN ITEMS, based on his extensive journeying in south and central Africa. He was to publish another ten before his somewhat early death in 1926.

Among his most popular works was another based on his African experiences, THE VROUW GROBELAAR'S LEADING CASES *(1905). Vrouw Grobelaar is a Boer widow who sits on her verandah dispensing wisdom and creepy stories in equal quantities. 'The King of the Baboons' is a fair sample of Gibbon's skill and the Vrouw Grobelaar's way with a tall story.*

PERCEVAL GIBBON

O

The King of the Baboons

THE old yellow-fanged dog-baboon that was chained to a post in the yard had a dangerous trick of throwing stones. He would seize a piece of rock in two hands, stand erect and whirl round on his heels till momentum was obtained, and then—let go. The missile would fly like a bullet, and woe betide anyone who stood in its way. The performance precluded any kind of aim; the stone was hurled off at any chance tangent: and it was bad luck rather than any kind of malice that guided one three-pound boulder through the window, across the kitchen, and into a portrait of Judas de Beer which hung on the wall not half a dozen feet from the slumbering Vrouw Grobelaar.

She bounced from her chair and ballooned to the door with a silent swift agility most surprising to see in a lady of her generous build, and not a sound did she utter. She was of good veld-bred fighting stock, which never cried out till it was hurt, and there was even something of compassion in her face as Frikkie jumped from the stoep with a twelve-foot thong in his hand. It was, after all, the baboon that suffered most, if his yells were any index to his feelings. Frikkie could smudge a fly ten feet off with just a flick of his whip, and all the tender parts of the accomplished animal came in for ruthless attention.

'He ought to be shot,' was Frikkie's remark as he curled up the thong at the end of the discipline. 'A baboon is past teaching if he has bad habits. He is more like a man than a beast.'

The Vrouw Grobelaar seated herself in the stoep chair which by common consent was reserved for her use, and shook her head.

'Baboons are uncanny things,' she answered slowly. 'When you shoot them, you can never be quite sure how much murder there is in it. The old story is that some of them have souls and some not: and it is quite certain that they can talk when they will. You have heard them crying in the night sometimes. Well, you ask a Kafir what that means. Ask an old wise Kafir, not a young one that has forgotten the wisdom of the black people and learned the foolishness only of the white.'

'What does it mean, tante?' It was I that put the question. Katje, too, seemed curious.

The old lady eyed me gloomily.

'If you were a landed Boer, instead of a kind of schoolmaster,' she replied, witheringly, 'you would not need to ask such a question. But I will tell you. A baboon may be wicked—look at that one showing his teeth and cursing—but he is not blind nor a fool. He runs about on the hills, and steals and fights and scratches, and all the time he has all the knowledge and twice the strength of a man, if it were not for the tail behind him and the hair on his body. So it is natural that sometimes he should be grieved to be such a mean thing as a baboon when he could be a useful kind of man if the men would let him. And at nights, particularly, when their troop is in laager and the young ones are on watch among the high rocks, it comes home to the best of them, and they sob and weep like young widows, pretending that they have pains inside so that the others shall not feel offended and turn on them. Anyone may hear them in the kloofs on a windless night, and, I can tell you, the sound of their sorrow is pitiful.'

Katje threw out a suggestion to console them with buckshot, and the Vrouw Grobelaar nodded with meaning.

'To hate baboons is well enough in the wife of a Burgher,' she said sweetly. 'I am glad to see there is so much fitness and wifeliness about you, since you will naturally spend all your life on farms.'

Katje's flush was a distress signal. First blood to the Vrouw.

'Baboons,' continued the old lady, 'are among a farmer's worst enemies. They steal and destroy and menace all the year round, but for all that there are many farmers who will not shoot or trap them. And these, you will notice, are always farmers of a ripe age and sense-shaped by experience. *They* know, you may be sure. My step-sister's first husband, Shadrach van Guelder, shot at baboons once, and was so frightened afterwards that he was afraid to be alone in the dark.'

There was a story toward, and no one moved.

'There were many Kafirs on his farm, which you have not seen,' pursued the Vrouw Grobelaar, adjusting her voice to narrative pitch. 'It was on the fringe of the Drakensberg, and many spurs of hill, divided by deep kloofs like gashes, descended on to it. So plenty of water came down, and the cattle were held from straying by the rocks, on one side at any rate. The Kafirs had their kraals dotted all about the land; and as they were of the kind that works, my step-sister's husband suffered them to remain and grow their little patches of mealies, while they worked for him in between. He was, of course, a cattle Boer, as all of our family have always been, but here were so many Kafirs to be had for nothing, that he soon commenced to plough great spaces of land and sow valuable crops. There was every prospect that he would make very much money out of that farm; for corn always sells, even when cattle are going for only seven pounds a-piece, and Shadrach van Guelder was very cheerful about it.

'But when a farmer weighs an ungrown crop, you will always find that there is something or other he does not take into account. He tells off the weather and the land and the Kafirs and the water on his fingers, and forgets to bend down his thumb to represent God—or something. Shadrach van Guelder lifted up his eyes to the hills from whence came the water, but it was not until the green corn was six inches high that he saw that there came with it baboons. Armies and republics of them; more baboons than he had thought to exist—they swooped down on his sprouting lands and rioted, ate and rooted, trampled and wantoned, with that kind of bouncing devilishness that not even a Kafir can correctly imitate. In one night they undid all his work on five sown morgen of fat land, and with the first wink of the sun in the east they were back again in their kopjes, leaving devastation and foulness wherever they passed.

'It was my step-sister's husband that stood on one leg and cursed like a Jew. He was wrathful as a Hollander that has been drinking water, and what did not help to make him content was the fact that hardly anything would avail to protect his lands. Once the baboons had tasted the sweetness of the young corn, they would come again and again, camping in the kloofs overhead as long as anything remained for them, like a deaf guest. But for all that, he had no notion of leaving them to plunder at their ease. The least one can do with an unwelcome visitor is to make him uncomfortable; and he sent to certain kraals on the farm for two old Kafirs he had remarked who had the appearance of cunning old men.

'They came and squatted before him, squirming and shuffling, as Kafirs do when a white man talks to them. One was quite a common kind of Kafir, gone a little grey with age, a tuft of white wool on his chin, and little patches of it here and there on his head. But the other was a small twisted yellow man, with no hair at all, and eyes like little blots of fire on a charred stick; and his arms were so long and gnarled and lean that he had a bestial look, like a laborious animal.

'"The baboons have killed the crop on the lower lands," said Shadrach, smacking his leg with his sjambok. "If they are not checked, they will destroy all the corn on this farm. What is the way to go about it?"

'The little yellow man was biting his lips and turning a straw in his hands, and gave no answer, but the other spoke.

'"I am from Shangaanland," he said, "and there, when the baboons plague us, we have a way with them, a good way."

'He sneered sideways at his yellow companion as he spoke, and the look which the latter returned to him was a thing to shrink from.

'"What is this way?" demanded Shadrach.

'"You must trap a baboon," explained the old Kafir. "A leading baboon, for choice, who has a lot to say in the government of the troop. And then you must skin him, and let him go again. The others will travel miles and miles as soon as they see him, and never come back again."

'"It makes me sick to think of it," said Shadrach. "Surely you know some other way of scaring them?"

'The old Kafir shook his head slowly, but the yellow man ceased to smile and play with the straw and spoke.

'"I do not believe in that way, baas. A Shangaan baboon"—he grinned at his companion—"is more easily frightened than those of the Drakensberg. I am of the bushmen, and I know. If you flay one of those up yonder, the others will make war, and where one came before, ten will come every night. A baboon is not a fat lazy Kafir; one must be careful with him."

'"How would you drive them away, then?" asked Shadrach.

'The yellow man shuffled his hands in the dust, squatting on his heels. There! There! See, the baboon in the yard is doing the very same thing.

'"If I were the baas," said the yellow man, "I would

turn out the young men to walk round the fields at night, with buckets to hit with sticks, and make a noise. And I—well, I am of the bushmen—" he scratched himself and smiled emptily.

'"Yes, yes?" demanded Shadrach. He knew the wonderful ways of the bushmen with some animals.

'"I do not know if anything can be done," said the yellow man, "but if the baas is willing I can go up to the rocks and try."

'"How?"

'But he could tell nothing. None of these wizards that have charms to subdue the beasts can tell you anything about it. A Hottentot will smell the air and say what cattle are near, but if you bid him tell you how he does it, he giggles like a fool and is ashamed.

'"I do not know if anything can be done," the yellow man repeated. "I cannot promise the baas, but I can try."

'"Well, try then," ordered Shadrach, and went away to make the necessary arrangements to have the young Kafirs in the fields that night.

'They did as he bade, and the noise was loathsome-enough to frighten anything with an ear in its head. The Kafirs did not relish the watch in the dark at first, but when they found that their work was only to thump buckets and howl, they came to do it with zest, and roared and banged till you would have thought a judgement must descend on them. The baboons heard it, sure enough, and came down after a while to see what was going on. They sat on their rumps outside the circle of Kafirs, as quiet as people in a church, and watched them drumming and capering as though it were a show for their amusement. Then they went back, leaving the crops untouched, but pulling all the huts in one kraal to pieces as they passed. It was the kraal of the old white-tufted Shangaan, as Shadrach learned afterwards.

'Shadrach was pleased that the row had saved his corn, and next day he gave the twisted yellow man a lump of tobacco. The man tucked it into his cheek and smiled, wrinkling his nose and looking at the ground.

'"Did you get speech of the baboons last night among the rocks?" Shadrach asked.

'The other shook his head, grinning. "I am old," he said. "They pay no attention to me, but I will try again. Perhaps, before long, they will listen."

'"When they do that," said Shadrach, "you shall have five pounds of tobacco and five bottles of dop."

'The man was squatting on his heels all this time at Shadrach's feet, and his hard fingers, like claws, were picking at the ground. Now he put out a hand, and began fingering the laces of the farmer's shoes with a quick fluttering movement that Shadrach saw with a spasm of terror. It was so exactly the trick of a baboon, so entirely a thing animal and inhuman.

'"You are more than half a baboon yourself," he said. "Let go of my leg! Let go, I say! Curse you, get away—get away from me!"

'The creature had caught his ankle with both hands, the fingers, hard and shovel-ended, pressing into his flesh.

'"Let go!" he cried, and struck at the man with his sjambok.

'The man bounded on all-fours to evade the blow, but it took him in the flank, and he was human—or Kafir—again in a moment, and rubbed himself and whimpered quite naturally.

'"Let me see no more of your baboon tricks," stormed Shadrach, the more angry because he had been frightened. "Keep them for your friends among the rocks. And now be off to your kraal."

'That night again the Kafirs drummed all about the green corn, and sang in chorus the song which the mountain-Kafirs sing when the new moon shows like a paring from a finger-nail of gold. It is a long and very loud song, with stamping of feet every minute, and again the baboons came down to see and listen. The Kafirs saw them, many hundreds of humped black shapes, and sang the louder, while the crowd of beasts grew ever denser as fresh parties came down and joined it. It was opposite the rocks on which they sat that the singing-men collected, roaring their long verses and clattering on the buckets, doubtless not without some intention to jeer at and flout the baffled baboons, who watched them in such a silence. It was drooping now to the pit of night, and things were barely seen as shapes, when from higher up the line, where the guardians of the crops were sparser, there came a discord of shrieks.

'"The baboons are through the line," they cried, and it was on that instant that the great watching army of apes came leaping in a charge on the main force of the Kafirs. Oh, but that was a wild, a haunting thing! Great bull-headed dog-baboons, with naked fangs and clutching hands alert for murder; bounding mothers of squealing litters that led their young in a dash to the fight; terrible lean old bitches that made for the men when others went for the corn—they swooped like a flood of horror on the aghast Kafirs, biting, tearing, bounding through the air like uncouth birds, and in one second the throng of the Kafirs melted before them, and they were among the corn.

'Eight men they killed by rending, and of the others, some sixty, there was not one but had his wound—some bit to the bone, some gashed, where iron fingers had clutched and torn their way through skin and flesh. When they came to Shadrach, and woke him warily with the breathless timidity of beaten men, it was already too late to go with a gun to the corn-lands. The baboons had contented themselves with small plunder after their victory, and withdrew orderly to the hills; and even as Shadrach came to the door of the homestead, he saw the last of their marshalled line, black against the sky, moving swiftly towards the kloofs.

'He flung out his hands like a man in despair, with never a word to ease his heart, and then the old Shangaan Kafir stood up before him. He had the upper part of his right arm bitten to the bone and worried, and now he cast back the blanket from his shoulder and held out the quivering wound to his master.

'"It was the chief of the baboons that gave me this," he said, "and he is a baboon only in the night. He came through the ranks of them bounding like a boulder on a steep hillside, and it was for me that his teeth were bared. So when he hung by his teeth to my arm and tore and snarled, I drew my nails across his back, that the baas should know the truth."

'"What is this madness?" cried Shadrach.

'"No madness, but simple devilry," answered the Shangaan, and there came a murmur of support from the Kafirs about him. "The leader of the baboons is Naqua, and it was he who taught them the trick they played us to-night."

'"Naqua?" repeated Shadrach, feeling cold and weak.

'"The bushman," explained the old man. "The yellow man with the long lean arms who gave false counsel to the baas."

'"It is true," came the chorus of the Kafirs. "It is true; we saw it."

'Shadrach pulled himself together and raised a hand to the lintel of the door to steady himself.

'"Fetch me Naqua!" he ordered, and a pair of them went upon that errand. But they came back empty: Naqua was not at his hut, and none had news of him.

'Shadrach dismissed the Kafirs to patch their wounds, and at sun-up he went down to the lands where the eight dead Kafirs still lay among the corn, to see what traces remained of the night's work. He had hoped to find a clue in the tracks, but the feet of the Kafirs and the baboons were so mingled that the ground was dumb, and on the grass of the baboons' return there remained, of course, no sign. He was no fool, my step-sister's first husband, and since a wild and belly-quaking tale was the only one that offered, he was not ready to cast it aside till a better one were found. At any rate it was against Naqua that his preparations were directed.

'He had seven guns in his house for which ammunition could be found, and from among all the Kafirs on the land he chose a half-dozen Zulus, who, as you know, will always rather fight than eat. These were only too ready to face the baboons again, since they were to have guns in their hands; and a kind of ambush was devised. They were to lie among the corn so as to command the flank of the beasts, and Shadrach was to lie in the middle of them, and would give the signal when to commence firing by a shot from his own rifle. There was built, too, a pile of brushwood lying on straw soaked in oil, and this one of them was to put a light to as soon as the shooting began.

'It was dark when they took their places, and then commenced a long and anxious watch among the corn, when every bush that creaked was an alarm and every small beast of the veld that squealed set hearts to thumping. From where he lay on his stomach, with his rifle before him, Shadrach could see the line of ridge of rocks over which the baboons must come, dark against a sky only just less dark; and with his eyes fixed on this he waited. Afterwards he said that it was not the baboons he waited for, but the yellow man, Naqua, and he had in his head an idea that all the evil and pain that ever was, and all the sin to be, had a home in that bushman. So a man hates an enemy.

'They came at last. Five of them were suddenly seen on the top of the rocks, standing erect and peering round for a trap; but Shadrach and his men lay very still, and soon one of these scouts gave a call, and then was heard the pat! pat! of hard feet as the body of them came up. There was not light enough to tell one from another, except by size, and as they trooped down among the corn Shadrach lay with his finger throbbing on his trigger, peering among them. But he could see nothing except the mass of their bodies, and waiting till the main part of them was past him, so that he could have a shot at them as they came back, should it happen that they retired at once, he thrust forward his rifle, aimed into the brown, and fired.

'Almost in the same instant the rifles of the Zulus spoke, and a crackle of shots ran up and down their line. Then there was a flare of light as the bonfire was lit, and they could see the army of baboons in a fuss of panic dashing to and fro. They fired again and again into the tangle of them, and the beasts commenced to scatter and flee, and Shadrach and his men rose to their full height and shot faster, and the hairy army vanished into the darkness, defeated.

'There was a guffaw of laughter from the Zulus, but ere it was finished a shout from Shadrach brought their rifles leaping up again. The baboons were coming back, a line of them was breaking from the darkness beyond the range of the fire, racing in great leaps towards the men. As they came into the light they were a sight to terrify a host, all big tuskers, and charging without a sound. Shadrach, aiming by instinct only, dropped two as they came, and the next instant they were upon him. He heard the grunt of the Zulu next him as a huge beast leaped against his chest and bore him down, and there were screams from another. Then something heavy and swift drove at him like a bullet and he clubbed his rifle. As the beast flew, with hands and feet drawn in for the grapple, he hewed at it with the butt and smashed it to the ground. The stock struck on bone, and he felt it crush and fail, and there was the thing at his feet.

'How they broke the charge, with what a frenzy of battle they drove the baboons from them, none of the four who spoke again could ever tell. But it must have been very soon after Shadrach clubbed his rifle that the beasts wavered, were beaten, and fled screaming, and the farmer found himself leaning on his weapon and a great Zulu, shining with sweat, talking to him.

'"Never have I had such a fight," the Zulu was saying, "and never may I hope for such another. The baas is a great chief. I watched him."

'Something was picking at Shadrach's boots, and he drew back with a shudder from the form that lay at his feet.

'"Bring a stick from the fire," he ordered. "I want to see this—this baboon."

'As the man went, he ran a cartridge into the breech of his rifle, and when the burning stick was brought, he turned over the body with his foot.

'A yellow face mowed up at him, and pale yellow eyes sparkled dully.

'"Tck!" clicked the Zulu in surprise. "It is the bushman, Naqua. No, baas," as Shadrach cocked his rifle, "do not shoot him. Keep him and chain him to a post. He will like that less."

'"I shoot," answered Shadrach, and shattered the evil grin that gleamed in the face on the ground with a quick shot.

'And, as I told you, my step-sister's first husband, Shadrach van Guelder, was afraid to be alone in the dark after that night,' concluded the Vrouw Grobelaar. 'It is ill shooting baboons, Frikkie.'

'I'm not afraid,' retorted Frikkie, and the baboon in the yard rattled his chain and cursed shrilly.

THE WOMAN WITH A CANDLE

O

W. Bourne Cooke

Like Perceval Gibbon, W. Bourne Cooke passed into obscurity after his death, despite being a prolific and popular writer of children's adventure stories.

Born in 1869, Cooke became a frequent contributor to many weeklies and dailies of his time, including the Daily Chronicle, Tit Bits, Chums *and* Little Folk. *His serials were particularly popular, among them 'The Black Box' which ran in* The Captain *in 1913 and the two-year long 'Wreck Cove' in the same journal in 1915–16.*

Cooke published fifteen books as well as his periodical work. The first was THE CANON'S DAUGHTER *(1902) and the last seems to have been* RED FEATHER *(1934). He published book forms of some of his serials, like* GREY WIZARD *(1925) and the weird* THE CURSE OF AMARIS *(1924).*

He specialized in historical fiction, and occasionally tried his hand at a creepy story, as in this one. Taken from his 1908 book FOR KING AND LOVE, *a volume of stories mainly about the Civil War, this is one of a group of tales which first appeared in the author's native Nottinghamshire* Guardian. *Sub-titled 'A Charnwood Forest Mystery', it is a straightforward good old ghost story, well worth a second airing.*

W. BOURNE COOKE

O

The Woman with a Candle

In the autumn of the year 1900 I was staying at the isolated village of Knelby, which place, I need hardly inform the reader, is situated in the heart of the wild forest country known as Charnwood.

I have always had a decided weakness for antiquities, and it was, therefore, only natural that, on the day following my arrival at Knelby, I should take my way to the ancient church, which stands on a rocky eminence overlooking a precipitous and disused slate-quarry.

In the churchyard I found the sexton busily engaged in putting the final touches to a newly-dug grave. As I drew near, he came up the ladder from the depths where he had been working, and, after stretching himself, stood looking down at his handiwork with the air of one who has accomplished a hard task, and was satisfied.

He was a fine specimen of village manhood—tall, and broad in proportion; and although his white hair and beard indicated that he must be well advanced in years, his back was as straight as one of the spruce firs that fringed the churchyard in which he worked.

As he stood thus, gazing down into the grave at his feet, there was an expression of solemn thoughtfulness in his face, which betokened a mind not wholly engrossed with the doings of spade and pickaxe; while the height of his forehead and keenness of his eyes bespoke a more than ordinary intelligence.

Walking quietly over the grass, I reached the opposite side of the grave to the one on which he stood before he noticed my presence.

'Good-day, sir,' said he, touching his cap.

'Good-day,' I replied. 'You are, or rather, have been busy, I see.'

'Yes, sir,' returned he. 'I was just thinking, among other things, how many this one makes, and it's either sixty-eight or sixty-nine; but I can't be quite sure which, without referring to my figures at home.'

'You allude, I suppose, to the number of graves you have dug?'

'Yes, sir.'

'May I ask how long you have been sexton of Knelby?'

'It is forty years this very day, sir, since I was appointed.'

'Strange, that you should have had a grave to dig on the anniversary.'

'Very strange, sir; I have been thinking so, off and on, all the morning.'

'And during the forty years you have been sexton, you have probably buried every person who has died in the parish?'

'All but one, sir,' replied the sexton; and then, to my surprise, I noticed that he regarded me with an uneasy look, and evinced a desire to change the subject of our conversation.

'Perhaps you would like to look over the church, sir?' he said.

I replied that I was most anxious to do so, in fact, had come out with that intention; and so we moved off in the direction of the time-worn building, the sexton leading the way, while I followed, with the thought of the one parishoner, whose grave had not been dug by my guide, uppermost in my mind.

'You are staying at Knelby, perhaps, sir?' said the sexton, as he unlocked the ponderous door.

I replied that it was my intention to stay in the village for some weeks, in order that I might have perfect quietness and rest.

'You will certainly find our village quiet, sir,' rejoined the old man, as he threw open the door and bowed me courteously in.

As we entered, the sun was shining brightly through the ivy-clad windows, the movement of the leaves in the wind breaking the light into a hundred fantastic shapes, which quivered on the walls.

The chancel was a large one in proportion to the church, and in it there reposed in stony watchfulness, two knights in armour, with their ladies beside them; for the Androvil family, who still lived at the Hall, had been lords of the manor far back in the Middle Ages.

After looking for some time on the cold, expectant faces of these effigies, trying, as I did so, to make them live again in my imagination, I raised my eyes and noticed a small brass plate on the north wall of the chancel. Following a habit I have, I read aloud the following inscription:–

Sacred to the Memory
of
DOROTHY LESLIE HOWARD,

Who disappeared mysteriously on the 18th of December, 1858. Her remains were found by a strange coincidence on the 5th day of March, 1865, and now rest in the churchyard.
'Until the day dawns, and the shadows flee away.'

As I finished reading the inscription I turned round, and looking at the sexton, noticed the same half-fearful expression which had so impressed me at the side of the newly-made grave. I think as our eyes met, he saw the questioning look in mine, for, with a hasty remark about its being a long time ago, and best forgotten, he turned and led the way to another part of the church. But in spite of the interest I felt in a most perfect specimen of a cross-legged knight, I found my thoughts and eyes continually wandering to the brass tablet in the chancel, and I was not sorry when, after seeing everything worthy of notice, I found myself once more in the churchyard and the sunshine.

When we came to the grave I left the sexton to gather up his tools, and, walking across to the south side of the churchyard, seated myself on the low stone wall. It was then that I noticed for the first time a mournful-looking house, standing in somewhat extensive grounds, and surrounded by trees—most of which were ancient yews of gigantic growth.

Surely, thought I, this must be the rectory, and yet I marvelled to see that it was in a state of utter neglect and decay, as though it had been unoccupied for many years. The windows were close-shuttered, except in the case of one in the upper storey, where a shutter had in some way become loose and hung by a single hinge, creaking in the wind. One end of the house was covered with ivy, which, unchecked by the pruner's knife, had overgrown itself, and now waved its long tendrils above the chimney stack like the arms of some mighty octopus feeling for its prey. Truly this ancient and deserted house was the most eerie one I had ever seen.

I am of a decidedly imaginative temperament, and at once began to indulge in all sorts of wild fancies to account for the gloomy scene before me.

My reverie was broken by the sound of a footstep at my side, and, looking up, I found the sexton standing beside me, his spade and pickaxe over his shoulder, and his gaze fixed on the lifeless old house which had so fascinated me.

'Is that the rectory?' I asked.

'Yes, sir,' replied the sexton, 'or rather it still goes by

that name, although no rector has lived there these thirty years.'

'Indeed,' replied I, 'that is singular, for although the house has evidently fallen into great decay through neglect, it still bears evidence of having once been a pleasant and commodious residence; besides which, the grounds are extensive and beautiful, and the close situation of the rectory to the church must have been extremely convenient.'

'Yes, sir,' rejoined the sexton, 'I daresay you're right in your way of looking at it, but I happen to know that there were good reasons for the rector refusing to live there.'

'Reasons!' I exclaimed, my curiosity now thoroughly awakened by the mysterious tone of my informant's voice. 'It must, indeed, have been a very strong reason that could drive a man from a spot like this to new surroundings and a new house.'

The sexton seated himself on the wall beside me, and lowering his voice to a solemn whisper, said:—

'The reason, sir, was one that would have driven a man from any house, even though the surroundings were like Paradise. Sir, the house you are looking at is haunted.'

'Haunted!' I exclaimed, in an incredulous and bantering tone. 'By what?'

The sexton drew closer to me, and looking round with an air of one who was half-fearful of being overheard, whispered in my ear:—'By a woman, sir—an old and ghastly woman—who walks the house at dead of night with a lighted candle in her hand.'

'But, surely,' said I, 'you do not believe in such a foolish tale as that. It must be one of those village superstitions, which one finds handed down from generation to generation in all remote country districts; and most probably the rector's reasons for removing to a new house was that he might have the benefit of more modern conveniences; for certainly yonder house is very ancient.'

But the sexton passed over unheeded the latter part of my speech, and replied in even more set and solemn tones than before:—

'Sir, it is no foolish tale, for I, who now speak to you, have met the woman face to face.'

Even had I felt so inclined, I could not, looking into the old man's face as he uttered these words, have made light of them.

'Pray tell me all about it,' I said eagerly, placing my hand upon his arm.

'Sir,' he replied, 'I have told no one for many years, and even now when I think of it, all the horror of that night comes back upon me, making me tremble like an aspen leaf; but as you have shown such interest in the matter, I will do my best to tell you the story, asking you to excuse me if I am unable to finish it.'

Having said this, the sexton sat for some moments gazing in absorbed silence on the eerie scene before us; then, with a shrug of his broad shoulders, as though bracing himself for a great effort, he thus began:—

'First of all, sir, I must tell you that my name is William Harness, and that I have lived in Knelby all my life, succeeding my father as sexton forty years ago. I was then a young man of about thirty-two, and had, up to the time of entering upon my new duties, been in the service of the rector for over ten years as coachman and gardener; but it was always an understood thing that I should follow my father in the sextonship, that office having been in our family for many generations; and though it may seem hard and strange to you, sir, I began my new duties by digging my father's grave; this, too, being an understood thing in our family, my father having done the same in the case of my grandfather, and so on right back for nearly one hundred and fifty years.

'In the year 1858, two years before I became sexton, a mysterious event happened which cast a gloom and horror over the whole district.

'There lived with the then rector, who was childless, his niece, a Miss Howard, the tablet to whose memory you saw in the church this morning. She was as good as she was beautiful, and was beloved by everyone in the parish,

from the highest to the lowest. Her time was spent in
doing good, and her sunny face and cheery voice brought
happiness and gladness wherever she went. Needless to
say that she was worshipped by the old rector and his
wife, of whose home she was the life and light. Judge,
then, of our dismay when the news spread one dark
December morning that Miss Howard had disappeared.
As she did not make her appearance at breakfast, a
servant was sent to her room, when it was found that the
door was open, and that she had evidently left her bed
during the night.

'The old rector and his wife were nearly frantic, and I
can truly say that I was hardly less affected, for Miss
Howard had been my dearest friend, and many a long
talk we had had together.

'During the whole day the rector and myself led search
parties, beating every part of the country for miles
around; but all to no purpose—we found not a trace of the
missing one; and although the search was continued day
after day for more than a week, all our efforts ended in
failure and despair; so that we had, at last, to face the
awful fact that our dear young friend had gone from us
for ever. It was the rector's death-blow, and ere a year had
passed away we laid him to rest in the churchyard,
whither, within a few weeks, he was followed by his
sorrowing wife.

'And here I must tell you that for some years a tale had
been rife in the village—of the rectory being haunted by
an old woman, who walked the house at night with a
lighted candle in her hand. Several of the servants vowed
that they had seen her, and had refused to stay in consequence; and, moreover, the rector, shortly before he died,
had confided in me that he had also met her, when one
night, being unable to sleep, he had gone down to his
study to read.

'I shall never forget how the old man's face went ashy
pale as he told me how the woman came upon him
suddenly as he sat reading; how hideous was her face, and

how she beckoned to him to follow her. But at that sight he swooned away, and knew no more until he found himself in bed, with his wife bending anxiously over him.

'He, however, desired that I would not speak of this to anyone, for fear of strengthening a story that he had always ridiculed as foolish and superstitious. And, indeed, when I considered the shattered state of his health since the disappearance of his niece, and being moreover myself a decided disbeliever in ghosts of any kind—I say, when I considered these things, I readily came to the conclusion that the old man's senses had deceived him, and that he had seen nothing.

'I was, however, soon to find how greatly in error I had been in coming to this hasty conclusion.

'In the spring of the year 1860 our new rector settled among us, taking up his residence at the old rectory; and I continued to occupy the same position I had done in the time of his predecessor; for I knew well the ways of both house and garden, and could be relied upon to do my best for my new master.

'So the spring and summer ran on to autumn, when my father died, and, as I have already told you, the duties of sexton and grave-digger fell to my lot. But my new employment, though it occupied a great part of my time, did not take me wholly out of the rector's private service, and I continued to work a day or two each week on his garden. It was one morning in the early spring of 1865 that the rector came to me, as I was engaged in pruning some rose trees, and after greeting me as was his wont, said:—

'"William, you will be sorry to hear that Mrs Rennard is so poorly that the doctor has ordered me to take her away at once for a complete change of scene. I have, therefore, decided to start tomorrow, and to close the rectory, taking the two children and servants with us."

'I told him how sorry I was to hear it, but hoped the change and rest would soon pull Mrs Rennard round again. Then, not knowing what more to say, I continued my work, thinking that the rector would pass on; but as he did not do so I looked round, and was surprised to find that he was eyeing me in an anxious way, and tapping the ground uneasily with his stick, as though there was something more which he wished to say, and yet did not know how to begin.

'At length, after an awkward pause, which I did my best to cover by the loud click of my pruning shears, he came close to where I stood, and said:–

'"William, you are not a superstitious man, are you?"

'"I don't think so, sir," I answered, laughing.

'"I thought not,' went on the rector, still playing uneasily with his stick among the pebbles on the path. "No doubt you have heard a tale about the rectory being haunted."

'"Yes sir," I replied, "I have heard it."

'"But you don't believe it, of course, William?"

'"Not a bit of it, sir," said I, laughing again.

'"Well," went on the rector, looking down at the ground, "the reason I mention it is that Mrs Rennard declares that she last night saw this old woman, who is said to walk the house with a lighted candle in her hand; and I will tell you in strict confidence that it is this that has helped to make her so much worse."

'"Indeed, sir," I replied, "I am very sorry to hear what you say, but no doubt Mrs Rennard's health accounts for the delusion."

'"Exactly, William; exactly what I think and believe; but the doctor insists on the necessity of taking her away at once, and so, as I have said, we start tomorrow. Now there is another thing I wish to ask you, and that is, if you will mind sleeping at the rectory during our absence, just as a kind of guard against burglary or anything of that sort. You will be about the grounds pretty often during the day, and if you do not mind sleeping in the house at night, we shall leave home more comfortably, for I know everything will be safe in your care. What do you say, William; do you mind?"

'"Not in the least, sir," I replied, "if it will make you and Mrs Rennard more satisfied."

'"Thank you," said the rector. "That is a great relief to me. You will, of course, have the free run of the place and come and go as you please. Good morning, William, I must be off." And with that he left me and went towards the door which leads from the rectory garden to the churchyard. On reaching the door he turned, with his hand upon the latch, and said, laughing:

'"Remember, William, no tales of ghosts when we return."

'"Aye, aye, sir," I replied, and then fell to my work again; but I could not help thinking that the rector's laugh was of a forced kind, and my mind went back to what he had just told me concerning Mrs Rennard.

'Also I thought of what the late rector had told me with regard to the same woman with the candle. But I persuaded myself that in both cases weakened nerves, the result of continued bad health, were responsible for the hallucination.

'On the following day I saw them drive off to the station which, as you know, is some five miles distant. The rector and children were in good spirits, but Mrs Rennard looked old and broken, and I fancied that, as the carriage moved off, she shuddered on looking back quickly at the house. When they were out of sight I walked slowly back to my work in the garden.

'I was a young man in those days, sir, and not over troubled with nerves; still, when night came on and I found myself sitting alone in the rectory kitchen, I couldn't help my mind running on the mystery of poor Miss Howard's sudden disappearance and also on the creature who was said to haunt the house. However, I did my best to put these thoughts away from me, and even started a song (for I was a bit of a singer in those days); but my voice sounded so unnatural and hollow in the silence, that I was quiet again ere I had sung one verse; and after trying in vain to give my attention to reading, I rose as the church clock struck nine, and went upstairs to bed.

'The room I occupied was one of the upper row overlooking the churchyard, and was that which, as you may perhaps have noticed, has a shutter hanging loosely by a single hinge. I was a heavy sleeper, and little troubled by dreams, so that I soon fell into a heavy slumber, from which I awoke to find the sun streaming brightly into the room. Then I laughed at the idea of ghosts and springing out of bed, threw open the lattice, and took deep draughts of the pure morning air.

'Villagers who knew where I had passed the night, questioned me, with solemn faces, as to whether I had seen anything; but I returned one answer to them all, namely—that ghosts only show themselves to those who believe in them. And so the second night came on.

'Having had a heavy day, I retired to rest earlier than on the previous night, and hardly had my head touched the pillow before I fell into a deep sleep.

'How long I slept I cannot tell, but suddenly I awoke to find myself in utter darkness. I have heard it said that the sound of a footstep at dead of night, will, in some mysterious way, penetrate to the brain of the deepest sleeper, and cause sudden wakefulness, where a louder but more usual noise, such as the howling of the wind, will but lull him into heavier slumber. Whether it was so in my case, or whether what I had been told had so impressed itself on my brain as to make me dream of a footstep, I cannot say; but certain it is that I now found myself lying wide awake, listening with an intensity that was almost overpowering, to the sound of a stealthy tread in the passage outside my room. It was a halting step, as of one who was lame, and by the flap on the stone floor, I knew the feet were bare.

'The sound came nearer and nearer, and then I remembered, with sudden fright, that the door was not fastened. I could not move, but lay stark still, and listened.

'Presently the halting tread ceased, and the latch of my door clicked. A moment later the door was opened, and then such a sight met my horrified gaze as to think of, even after all these years, makes my blood run cold.'

Here the sexton passed his hand over his brow, on which a cold sweat was plainly to be seen. After a short time he thus continued:

'As I was saying, the door slowly opened, and there appeared a bare and shrivelled arm, and in the hand a lighted candle. I could not move; a cold sweat broke out upon me, and although I tried to shout, all utterance was frozen on my lips. But if the candle-bearing hand and arm were terrible, a thousand times more so was the figure belonging to them, which now came slowly into the room. It was that of a woman, well advanced in years, whose haggard face and wild, staring eyes were now turned full upon me. Grizzled hair hung about a face of such diabolical ugliness as is impossible to describe in words.

'Her lips were parted in a horrid grin, exposing to view flaccid gums, studded with broken stumps of teeth; a loose, flowing garment of some ancient make was thrown about her shoulders, and reached to the ground; and at every step she went down on one side, as one afflicted with a shortened limb or stiffened knee-joint. Thus she came slowly towards me, her mouth twitching horribly the while. When within a few feet of my bed, she raised her left hand and beckoned to me as if to follow. But I could neither move nor speak, and my eyes felt as though they must roll from their sockets, so intense and fixed was my horrified gaze.

'Closer and closer she came, step by step, until with one frantic effort, born of the fear that she would touch me, my voice rushed from my lips, and I gave one loud, piercing scream.

'She stopped, and, regarding me with a look that I could pray might be blotted out from my memory for ever, again beckoned with her left hand, turning her body partly round as she did so, but still keeping her ghastly face towards me.

'Unable to resist the power of those wild, drawing eyes, I rose straightaway from my bed and followed her as one bereft of his senses. Perceiving this, she turned round and led the way from the room, ever and anon casting a hideous glance at me over her shoulder.

'Along the silent passages we passed; down the broad creaking stairs, and so out into the dark still night.

'I was as powerless as a child, and if, at any moment, a thought of turning back shot through my brain, one sight of that twitching face cast back upon its shoulder was sufficient to make me follow as though I were drawn along by some great mesmeric force.

'Across the rectory lawn she led the way—under the great yew trees, which looked like weird funeral plumes in their inky blackness. Not a breath of wind stirred the trees, and not a star relieved the frowning, clouded sky.

'So on and on we went, until we came to the little wood which stands upon the verge of one of the oldest slate pits. Skirting this wood, the old hag led the way to the further end of the pit, where the deep water may be approached, even to its very brink. There she stopped, and beckoned to me with her bony hand to come to her—for I was some yards behind.

'I had no power but to obey, and so, when I was within a yard of her, she moved on again, leading the way along a narrow and dangerous shelf of rock, which was in some parts under water. Suddenly I saw her stop, and bend down towards a chasm or small cave in the side of the pit, which, from the splash of a stone which fell from near her feet, I knew must contain water. Holding the candle to the opening, she motioned me to look in. At first I would not, but the fury of her face and gestures compelled me at last to do so, and stooping down I beheld, by the glittering light of the candle, a sight that froze me to the spot with horror; for there, lying in the water, which was three feet deep, lay a skeleton, with the face of the skull turned towards me, while round the neck there hung, by a chain, a metal cross, which told me at once whose remains they were I looked upon.

'I was as one turned to stone—without thought or feeling, or any sense of life; and for some time—I know not how long—I stood there, forgetful of everything, even of the scene before me. Then again, for a second time, I realized that in those bleaching bones beneath the water, I saw all that was left of my first rector's niece, and of our dear friend of years ago—Miss Howard.

'The flaring of the candle in its socket broke the spell, and looking quickly round I found the old hag's horrible face so close to mine that her grizzled locks nearly touched my cheek. That was the final straw to my already cracking nerves, and with a shriek that echoed round and round the pit, I sank down into a deep swoon.

'When I came to myself the dawn was breaking and I was alone. For some moments I lay dazed, but gradually the horrors of the night came back to me, and turning my head I looked into the cave, hoping, I believe, to find that it was all a dream; but to my horror I saw the skeleton, with the chain about its neck, lying beneath the water. The next moment I rushed wildly from the spot, never stopping until I reached the Hall, where the servants, who were just astir, doubtless took me for a madman.

'I insisted on seeing Lord Androvil, and presently he came to me in the study, in his dressing gown. To him I told my tale, he listening, I remember, with a pitying look; then, as I rose to go, I fell senseless at his feet.

'I remember no more until I awoke to consciousness, after a dangerous illness, some weeks later.

'When I was strong enough to bear it, I learned from Lord Androvil himself how, after bringing me home, he had organized and led a search party to the spot I had indicated; how they there found the skeleton, which was at once identified as Miss Howard's (for the metal cross bore the significant initials "D.L.H."), and how the remains had been buried in the churchyard, the sexton of a neighbouring village digging the grave.

'And that, sir,' concluded the sexton, 'ends my story of the woman with the candle, and of the one grave I did not dig: and if you are disposed to question it or put it down to a delusion of the senses, I can only point to the fact of the finding of the skeleton and ask you to account for that.'

'I do not question it for one moment,' I replied, 'though it is the strangest tale I have ever listened to. But I would like to ask you one thing. How do you think Miss Howard met her death?'

The old man bent upon me a most serious look as he replied in a deep and solemn voice:–

'My only answer to that question, sir, is that I firmly believe Miss Howard was led from her room by the same hideous creature who led me; that she was taken along the same way; and that, coming to the cave, and being beckoned to look in, she saw there something–I cannot tell what–something that caused her to swoon and lose her life by falling into the water.'

'One more question,' said I. 'Are you a believer in ghosts?'

'Yes, sir,' replied the sexton, more solemnly than ever; 'I am.'

THE PIG-SKIN BELT

O

Edward Lucas White

The life of Edward Lucas White (1866–1934) was blighted by illness and ended in tragedy. Born in New Jersey, he started writing early on and specialized in historical fiction, often based in ancient Greece or Rome.

His first book to be published here was NARRATIVE LYRICS (1908) but he had spent many years working on massive novels, such as his 700-page epic EL SUPREMO (1916), the life of a Paraguayan dictator, or ANDIVIUS HEDULO (1925), a Roman historical novel. He gained some reputation as well for his novel on the Trojan Wars, HELEN (1925).

White was one of the small, tragic band of authors in this genre who killed themselves. All his life, he suffered from migraine—this is not borne easily, even now with improved treatment—and in the end, unable to bear the pain any longer, he gassed himself.

His macabre stories are collected in one prized volume, LUKUNDOO (1927). The title story is the most famous of the lot, and has been reprinted often since it first appeared.

White's tales of terror were all based on dreams of the author: he says in his book the tales are 'paragon night-

mares ... it will be easy to realise that anyone dreaming such narratives as "The Pig-Skin Belt" just had to write them into stories to get them out of his system.'

Certainly, this tale of unusual lycanthropy, written in 1907, has the quality of nightmare, particularly in its nocturnal scenes.

EDWARD LUCAS WHITE

O

The Pig-Skin Belt

I

BE it noted that I, John Radford, always of sound mind and matter-of-fact disposition, being entirely in my senses, here set down what I saw, heard and knew. As to my inferences from what occurred I say nothing, my theory might be regarded as more improbable than the facts themselves. From the facts anyone can draw conclusions as well as I.

The first letter read:

'San Antonio, Texas,
January 1st, 1892.

'MY DEAR RADFORD:

'You have forgotten me, likely enough, but I have not forgotten you nor anyone (nor anything) in Brexington. I saw your advertisement in the New York *Herald* and am glad to learn from it that you are alive and to infer that you are well and prosperous.

'I need a lawyer's help. I want to buy real estate and I mean to return home, so you are exactly the man I am

looking for. I am writing this to ask that you take charge
of any and all of my affairs falling within your province,
and to learn whether you are willing to do so.

'I am a rich man now, and without any near ties of kin
or kind. I want to come home to Brexington, to live there
if I can, to die there if I must. Along with other matters
which I will explain if you accept I want to buy a house in
the town and a farm near-by, if not the Shelby house and
estate then some others like them.

'If willing to act for me please reply at once care of the
Hotel Menger. Remember me to any cousins of mine you
may see.

                    'Faithfully yours,
                                   'CASSIUS M. CASE.'

The name I knew well enough, of course, but my efforts
to recall the individual resulted only in a somewhat hazy
recollection of a tall, thin, red-cheeked lad of seventeen
or so. It was almost exactly twenty-eight years since
Colonel Shelby Case had left Brexington taking with him
his son. Colonel Shelby had died some six years later. I
remembered hearing of his death, in Egypt, I thought.
Since his departure from Brexington I had never heard of
or from Cassius.

My reply I wrote at once, professing my readiness to do
anything in my power to serve him.

As soon as the mails made it possible, I had a second
letter from him.

'MY DEAR RADFORD:

'Your kind letter has taken a load off my mind. I am
particular about any sort of arrangements I make,
exacting as to the accurate carrying out of small details
and I feared I might have difficulty in finding a painstaking man in a community so easy-going as Brexington.
I remember your precise ways as a boy and am basking in
a sense of total relief and complete reliance on you.

'I should buy the Shelby house and estate on your representations, but I must see for myself first. If they are the best I can get I shall take them anyhow. But please be ready to show me over every estate of five hundred acres or more, lying within ten miles of the Court House. I wish to examine every one which is now for sale or which you can induce the owners to consider selling. I want the best which is to be had. Also I want a small place of fifty acres or so, two miles or more from the larger place I buy. Money is no object to me and the condition of the buildings on the places will not weigh with me at all.

'So with the town house: I may tear it down entirely and rebuild from the cellar up. What I want in the town is a place of half an acre to two acres carrying fine, tall trees, with well-developed trunks. I want shade and plenty of it, but no limbs or branches growing or hanging within eight feet of the ground. I do not desire shrubbery, but if there is any I can have it removed, while I cannot create stout trees. Those I must have on the place when I buy it, for I will have the shade and I will have a clear sweep for air and an unobstructed view all round.

'I am not at the Menger as you naturally suppose. I merely have my mail sent there. I am living in a tent half a mile or more from the town. At Los Angeles I had the luck to fall in with a Brexington negro, Jeff Twibill. He knew of another, Cato Johnson, who was in Frisco. I have the two of them with me now, Jeff takes care of the horses and Cato of me and I am very comfortable.

'That brings me to the arrangements I want you to make for me. Buy or lease or rent or borrow a piece of a field, say four acres, free of trees or bushes and sloping enough to shed the rain. Be sure there is good water handy. Have four tents; one for me, one for the two servants (and make it big enough for three or four); one to cook in and one for my four horses, they are luxurious beasts and live as well as I do. Have the tents pitched in the middle of the field so I shall have a clear view all around. The field must be clear of bushes or trees, must

be at least four acres and may be any size larger than
that: forty would be none too big for me. I want no houses
too close to me.

'You see I am at present averse to houses, hotels and
public conveyances. I mean to ride across the continent
camping as I go. And in Brexington I mean to tent it until
I have my own house ready to live in. I am resolute to be
no man's guest nor any man's lodger, nor any company's
passenger.

'I am coming home, Radford, coming home to be a
Colonel with the rest of them. And I shall be no mere
colonel-by-courtesy: I have won my right to the title, I
won it twice over, years ago in Egypt and later in Asia.

'Thank you for all the news of the many cousins, I did
not realize they were so very numerous. I am sorry that
Mary Mattingly is dead, of all the many dear people in
Brexington I loved her best.

'I shall keep you advised of my progress across the
continent. And as questions come up about the details of
the tent-equipment you can confer with me by letter.

'Gratefully yours,

'CASSIUS M. CASE.'

I showed the letters to one and another of my elder
acquaintances, who remembered Cassius.

Dr Boone said:

'I presume it is a case of advanced tuberculosis. He
should have remained in that climate. Of course, he may
live a long time here, tenting in the open or living with
the completest fresh air treatment. His punctiliousness in
respect to self isolation does him credit, though he carries
it further than is necessary. We must do all we can for
him.'

Beverly said:

'Poor devil. "Live if he can, die if he must." He'll die all
right. They'd call him a "lunger" out there and he had
better stay there.'

The minister said:

'The lode-star of old sweet memories draws him homeward. "Mary Mattingly," yes we all remember how wildly he loved Mary Mattingly. While full of youth he could find forgetfulness fighting in strange lands. Now he must be near her although she lies in her grave. The proximity even of her tomb will be a solace to his last days.'

We were prepared to do all that sympathy could suggest. Mr Hall and Dr Boone gravely discussed together the prolongation of Case's life and the affording of spiritual support. Beverly I found helpful on my line of finances and creature comforts. As Case's leisurely progress brought him nearer and nearer our interest deepened. When the day came on which he was to arrive Beverly and I rode out to meet him.

II

Language has no words to picture our dumbfounded amazement. And we were astonished in more ways than one. Chiefly, instead of the lank invalid we expected to see, we beheld a burly giant every characteristic of whom, save one, bespoke rugged health. He was all of six foot three, big boned, overlaid with a surplus of brawn, a Samsonian musculature that showed plain through his negligent, loose clothing; and withal he was plump and would have been sleek but for the roughness of his weather-beaten skin.

He wore grey; a broad-brimmed felt hat, almost a sombrero; a flannel shirt, a sort of jacket, and corduroy trousers tucked into his boots. It was before the days of khaki.

His head was rather large and round, but not at all a bullet head, rather handsome and well set. His face was round too, and good-natured, but not a particle as is the usual round face, vacuous and like a full-moon. His was agreeable, but lit with character and determination. His

neck was fat but showed great cords through its
rotundity. He had a big barrel of a chest and his voice
rumbled out of it. He dominated the landscape the
moment he entered it.

Even in our astonishment three things about him
struck me, and, as I afterwards found out, the same three
similarly struck Beverly.

One was his complexion. He had that build which
leads one to expect floridity of face, a rubicund countenance or, at least, ruddy cheeks. But he was dead pale, with
a peculiar tint I never had seen before. His face showed
an abundance of solid muscle and over it a skin rough-
ened by exposure, toughened, even hardened, by wind
and sun. Yet its colour was not in agreement with its
texture. It had the hue which belongs to waxy skin over
suety, tallowy flesh, an opaque whiteness, a pallidity
almost corpse-like.

The second was his glance: keen, glittering, hard, blue-
grey eyes he had, gallant and far younger than himself.
But it was not the handsome eyes so much as their way of
looking that whetted our attention. They pierced us
through and through, they darted incessantly here and
there, they peered to right and left, they kept us generally
in view, indeed, and never let us feel that his attention
wandered from us, yet they incessantly swept the world
about him. You should say they saw all they looked at,
looked at everything seeable.

The third was his belt, a mellowed old belt of pig-skin,
with two capacious holsters, from each of which
protruded the butt of a large-calibre revolver.

He greeted us in the spirit of old comradeship
renewed. Behind him Jeff and Cato grinned from their
tired mounts. He sat his big horse with no sign of fatigue
and surveyed the landscape from the crossroad's knoll
where we had met him.

'I seem to recall the landmarks here,' he said, 'the left
hand road by which you came, would take me through to
Brexington.'

Beverly confirmed his recollection.

'The one straight ahead,' he went on, 'goes past the big new distillery you wrote me about.'

'Right again,' I said.

'The road to the right,' he continued, 'will take us by the old mill, and I can swing round to my camp without nearing town.'

'You could,' Beverly told. 'But it is a long way round.'

'Not too far for me,' he announced positively. 'No towns or distilleries for me. I go round. Will you ride with me, gentlemen?'

We rode with him.

On the way I told him I expected him to supper that evening.

'With all my writing, Radford,' he said. 'You don't seem to get the idea. I flock by myself for the present and eat alone. If you insist I'll explain tomorrow.'

Beverly and I left him to his camp supper.

Dr Boone and Mr Hall were a good deal taken aback upon learning that their imagined invalid had no existence and that the real Colonel Case needed neither medical assistance nor spiritual solace. We four sat for some time expressing our bewilderment.

Next morning I drove out to Case's camp. I found him sitting in his tent, the flaps of which were looped up all around. He was as pale as the day before. As I approached I saw him scrutinize me with a searching gaze, a gaze I found it difficult to analyze.

He wore his belt with the holsters and the revolver-butts showed from those same holsters. I was astonished at this. When I saw it on him the day before I had thought the belt a piece of bad taste. It might have been advisable in portions of his long ride, might have been imperatively necessary in some districts; but it seemed a pose or a stupidity to wear it so far east. Pistols were by no means unknown in our part of the world, but they were carried in the seclusion of the hip-pocket or inside the breast of one's coat, not flaunted in the face of the populace in low-hung pig-skin holsters.

Case greeted me cheerily.

'I got up too early,' he stated. 'I've had my breakfast and done my target practice twice over. Apparently you expect me to go with you in that buggy?'

I told him that I did.

'Come in and sit down a moment,' he said in a some-what embarrassed way. 'This suggestion of our driving together is in line with your kind invitation for last night. I see I must explain somehow.'

He offered me a cigar and though I seldom smoke in the morning, I took it, for, I thought smoking would fill up the silences I expected.

He puffed a while, in fact.

'Have you ever been among feudists in the mountains?' he queried.

'More than a little,' I told him.

'Likely enough then,' he went on, 'you know more about their ways than I do. But I saw something of them myself, before I left America. Did you ever notice how a man at either focus of a feud, the king-pin of his end of it so to speak, manifests the greatest care to avoid permitting others to expose themselves to any degree of the danger always menacing him; how such men, in the black shadow of doom, as it were, are solicitous to prevent outsiders from straying into the penumbra of the eclipse which threatens themselves?'

'I have observed that,' I replied.

'Have you noticed on the other hand,' he continued, 'that they never show any concern for acquaintances who comprehend the situation, but pay them the compliment of assuming that they have sense enough to know what they are doing and to take care of themselves?'

'I have observed that same too,' I affirmed.

He puffed again for a while.

'My father,' he returned presently, 'used to say that there are two ends to a quarrel, the right end and the wrong end, but that either end of a feud is the wrong end. I am one end of a feud. Wherever I am is one focus of that feud. The other focus is local, and I have removed myself as far as may be from it. But I am not safe here, should not be safe anywhere on earth; doubt if I should be safe on the moon, or Mars, on a planet of some other sun, or the least conspicuous satellite of the farthest star. I am obnoxious to the hate of a power as far-reaching' ... he took off his broad felt hat and looked up at the canvas of the tent-roof ... 'as far-reaching as the displeasure of God.'

'And as implacable,' he almost whispered. 'As the malice of Satan.'

He looked sane, healthy and self-possessed.

'I am nowhere safe,' he recommenced in his natural voice, 'while my chief adversary is alive. My enemies are many and malignant enough, but their power is negligible, and their malignancy vicarious. Without fomenting their hostility would evaporate. Could I but know that my chief enemy were no more I should be free from all alarm. But while that arch-foe survives I am liable to attack at any moment, to attacks so subtle that I am at a loss to make you comprehend their possible nature, so crude that I could not make you realize the danger you are in at this instant.'

I looked at him, unmoved.

'I shall say no more to you,' he said. 'You must do as you please. If you regard my warnings as vapours, I have at least warned you. If you are willing to share my danger, in such degree as my very neighbourhood is always full of danger, you do so at your own risk. If you consider it advisable to have no more to do with me, say so now.'

'I see no reason,' I told him without even a preliminary puff, 'why your utterances should make any difference in my treatment of you.'

'I thought you would say that,' he said. 'But my conscience is clear.'

'Shall we proceed to business?' I asked.

'There is one point more,' he replied. 'Have you ever been in mining camps or amid other frontier conditions?'

'Several times,' I answered, 'and for some time at that.'

'Have you ever noticed that when two men have been mutually threatening to shoot each other at sight, pending the final settlement, neither will expose women or children to danger by being in their neighbourhood or permitting them in his, if he can prevent their nearing them?'

'Such scrupulosity can be observed,' I told him drily, 'nearer home than mining camps or frontier towns.'

'So I have heard,' he replied stiffly. 'When I left America the personal encounter had not yet taken the place of the formal duel in these regions.'

He puffed a bit.

'However,' he continued, 'it makes no difference from what part of the world you draw the illustration; it is equally in point. The danger of being near me is a hundred times, a thousand times greater than that of running the risk of stopping a wild or random bullet. I cannot bring myself to expose innocent beings to such danger.'

'How about Jeff and Cato?' I asked.

'A good servant,' declared Colonel Case (and he looked all the colonel as he spoke it) 'is like a dog or a horse, he shares his master's dangers as a matter of course. I speak of women and children and unsuspecting men. I am resolute to sit at no man's table, to enter no man's house, uninvited or invited. All who come to me knowingly I shall welcome. When you bring any one with you I shall assume that he has been forewarned. But I shall intrude upon no one.'

'How then are you to inspect,' I queried, 'the properties I expected to show you?'

'Business,' said Colonel Case, 'is different. When people propose to do business they assume any and all risks. Are you afraid to assume the risk of driving me about in that buggy of yours?'

'Not a particle,' I disclaimed. 'Are you willing to expose the people of Brexington to these dangers on which you descant so eloquently and which I fail to comprehend?'

Colonel Case fixed me with a cold stare. He looked every inch a warrior, accustomed to dominate his environment, to command and be obeyed, impatient of any opposition, ready to flare up if disbelieved in the smallest trifle.

'Radford,' he said, slowly and sternly, 'I am willing to take any pains to avoid wronging any one, I am unwilling to make myself ridiculous by attempting impossibilities.'

'I see,' I concluded. 'Let us go.'

III

As we drove through the town he said:

'This is like coming back to earth from another world. It is like a dream too. Some streets are just as they were, only the faces are unfamiliar. I almost expect to see the ghosts of thirty years ago.'

I made some vague comment and as we jogged along talked of the unchanged or new owners of the houses. Then I felt him make a sudden movement beside me, and I looked round at him. He could not turn any paler than he was, yet there had been a change in his face.

'I do see ghosts,' he said slowly and softly.

I followed his glance as he gazed past me. We were approaching the Kenton homestead and nearly opposite it. It had an old-fashioned classic portico with four big white columns. At the top of the steps, between the two middle columns, stood Mary Kenton, all in pink with a rose in her jetty hair. She was looking intently at us, but not at me. Case stared at her fixedly.

'Mary Kenton is the picture of her mother,' I told him.

'Her very image,' he breathed, his eyes steadily on her.

She continued gazing at us. Of course she knew whom I was driving. My horses were trotting slowly and when we were opposite her, she waved her hand.

'Welcome home, Cousin Cassius,' she called cheerily.

Colonel Case waved his hat to her and bowed, but said nothing.

The Shelby mansion did not suit Colonel Case. What he wanted, he said, was a house at the edge of the town. When he had made his selection he bought it promptly. He had the outbuildings razed, the shrubbery torn up and the trees trimmed so that no limb hung within ten feet of the ground; above they were left untouched, tall and spreading as they were and almost interlacing with each other. The house he practically rebuilt. Its all-round veranda he had torn down and replaced by one even broader, but at the front only, facing the entrance, the only entrance he left. For he entirely closed the backway to the kitchen and side-gate to the stable, cutting instead a loop-drive around the house from the one front entrance.

Except for this stone-posted carriage-gate with the little foot-path gate beside it, he had the whole place surrounded with a fence the like of which Brexington had never seen. The posts were T-beams, of rolled steel, eight feet tall above ground, reaching six feet below it and bedded down in rammed concrete. To these was bolted a four-foot continuous, square-mesh wire fencing, the meshes not over six inches at its top and as small as two inches at the bottom, which was sunk a hand's breadth below the surface and there held by close-set clamps upon sections of gas-pipe, extending from post to post and bolted to them. Inside this mesh-fencing, as high as it reached, and above it to the top of the posts, were strung twenty strands of heavy barbed wire, the upper wires six inches apart, the lower strands closer. Inside the fence he had set a close hedge. As the plants composing it were large and vigorous when they arrived from the nurseryman, this was soon thick and strong. It was kept clipped to about three feet high. The flower-beds he abolished and from house to drive and drive to hedge soon had the whole place in well-kept turf.

Behind the house he had two outbuildings erected; at one corner a small carriage-house and stable, capable of holding two vehicles and three horses; at the other a structure of about the same size as the stable, half wood-shed and half hen-house.

Watching the carpenters at work on this and regarding the nine-days-wonder of a fence, several negroes stood in talk one day as I passed. They were laughing and I overheard one say:

'Mahs'r Case shuah ain' gwine tuh lose no hains awf the roos'. Mus be gwine tuh be powerful fine hains he gwine raise. He sutt'nly mus' sot stoah by them hains. He sutt'nly dun spen' cunnsdd'ble money awn the fAince.'

The interior of the house was finished plainly and furnished sparingly. The very day it was ready for occupancy he moved into it and ceased his camp life. Besides Cato, an old negro named Samson acted as cook, and another named Pompey as butler. These three made up all his household. Jeff was quartered in a room over the carriage-house.

Before his residence was prepared and while he was still camping he bought Shelby Manor.

'Nothing like obliging one's cousins,' he said. He also bought two adjoining farms, forming a property of over a thousand acres. This he proceeded to equip as a stud farm, engaging a competent manager; refitting the house for him and the two smaller houses for his assistants, the overseer and farmer; abolishing the old outbuildings; putting up barns and stables in the most lavish fashion. He bought many blooded mares and created an establishment on a large scale.

About two miles out of town on the road past his house, nearly halfway to Shelby Manor, he bought a worthless little farm of some forty acres. This he had fenced and put in grass, except a small garden-patch by the house, which he had made snug and where he had installed an elderly negro couple as caretakers. The old man had formerly belonged to the Colonel's father, and was named Erastus Everett. All the other buildings he had removed, except a fair-sized hay barrack standing on a knoll near the middle of the largest field. This he had new roofed and repaired and given two coats of shingle stain, moss green on the roof and weather grey on the sides. In it he had ranked up some forty cords of fat pine wood. Near the house was built a small stable, which harboured the two mules Case allowed Uncle Rastus.

Besides this he had built a number of low sheds, opening on spaces enclosed with wire netting. Soon the enclosures swarmed with dogs, not blooded dogs, but mere mongrel curs. Not a small dog among them, all were big or fairly large. Uncle Rastus drove about the country in his big close-covered wagon, behind his two mules. Wherever he found an utterly worthless dog of some size he bought it, if it could be had cheap, and turned it in with the rest. Before a year had passed uncle Rastus had more than a hundred no-account brutes to feed and care for.

Colonel Case was not a man to whom anyone, least of all a stranger, would put a direct unsolicited question. Uncle Rastus was more approachable. But the curious gained little information from him.

'Mahs'r Case ain' tole me wuff'r he keepin' awl dees yeah houns. He ain' spoke nuffin. He done tole me to buy 'um, he done tole me to feed 'um. Ahze buyed 'um en' ah feeds 'um.'

Once he had established himself Case lived an extremely regular life. He rose early, breakfasted simply, and whatever the weather, drove out to Shelby Manor. He never rode in the forenoon. At his estate he had a pistol-range and a rifle-range. He spent nearly an hour each morning in pistol and rifle practice. He never used a shot-gun, but shot at targets, running marks, and trap-sprung clay-pigeons with both repeating rifle and revolver. He always carried his two repeating rifles with him, and brought them back with him. Several times, when I happened to accompany him, I watched him shoot.

The first time I was rather surprised. He emptied the chambers of one revolver, made some fifty shots with it, cleaned it, replaced the six cartridges which had been in it, and put it in its holster. Then he did the like with the other. Then he similarly emptied the magazines of one of his rifles, made some fifty shots with that, cleaned it and reloaded it with the original cartridges. So with the second rifle.

I asked him why he did so.

'The cartridges I go about with,' he said, 'are loaded with silver bullets. I can't afford to fire away two or three pounds of silver every day. Lead keeps my hand in just as well as silver, and the silver bullets are always ready for an emergency.'

Against such an imaginary emergency, I conceived he wore his belt and kept his two rifles always at hand.

After his target practice he talked with his manager, looked over the place, discussed his stock or watched his jockeys exercising their mounts, for an hour or two. Once a week or so on his way back to town he stopped to inspect Uncle Rastus' charges, and investigate his doings. His early lunch was almost as simple as his breakfast. After his lunch he slept an hour or more. Later he took a long ride, seldom towards Shelby Manor. Always, both in going and in returning, he rode past Judge Kenton's mansion. At first his hour of starting on his ride varied. Before many days he so timed his setting forth as to pass the Kenton house when Mary was likely to be at her window, and his riding homeward when she was likely to be on the portico. After a time she was sure to be at her window when he passed and on the portico when he repassed, and his departure and return occurred with clockwork regularity. When she was at her window, they never gave any sign of mutual recognition, but when she was on the portico she waved her hand to him and he his hat to her.

Towards dusk in summer, after lamp-light in winter, he ate a deliberate dinner. It never seemed to make a particle of difference to him how early he went to bed or how late, or whether he went to bed at all. He was quite capable of sitting all night at cards if the game was especially interesting. Yet he never made a habit of late hours. He was an inveterate card-player, but play at his house generally ceased before midnight and often much earlier. He could drink all night long, four fingers deep and often, and never seem the worse for it. Yet it was very seldom he did so. Habitually he drank freely after dinner, but no effects of liquor were ever visible on him. His liquors were the best and always set out in abundance. His cigars were as good as his liquors and spread out in similar profusion. His wines at dinner were unsurpassable and numerous. The dinners themselves could not have been beaten. Uncle Samson was an adept at marketing and a superlative cook. Pompey was an ideal butler. They seemed always ready to serve dinner for their master alone without waste or for a dozen more also without any sign of effort or dismay. As Case made welcome to his dinner table as to his card table anyone who happened to drop in, he had no lack of guests. All the bachelors of Brexington flocked to him as a matter of course. The heads of families were puzzled. One after another they invited him to their houses. His refusals were courteous but firm: for explanations he referred them to me. Most of them accepted my dilution of his utterances and acquiesced in his lop-sided hospitality. One or two demurred and laid special siege to him. Particularly Judge Kenton would not be denied. When he was finally convinced that Colonel Case would not respond to any invitation, he declared his resolution not to cross Case's threshold until his several visits there were properly acknowledged by a return call at his house. Intercourse between him and Case thereupon ceased. Judge Kenton, however, was alone in his punctilious attitude. Everybody else frequented Case's house and table.

His house indeed became a sort of informal club for all the most agreeable men of the town and neighbourhood. It was not mere creature comforts or material attractions which drew them there, but the very real charm of the host. Even while he was tenting, before the house was ready for occupancy, he had made friends, according to their degree, with every man in and about Brexington, white or black. Everybody knew him, everybody liked him, everybody wondered at him.

IV

Case was in fact the most discussed man in our region of the world. Some called him a lunatic, dwelling especially on his dog-ranch, as he called it, and his everlasting pigskin belt with the holstered revolvers, without which he was never seen at any hour of the day, by any one. It was difficult for his most enthusiastic partisans to assign any colourable reason why he should maintain a farm for the support of some two hundred totally worthless dogs. Their worthlessness was the main point which Uncle Rastus made in buying them. Often he rejected a dog proffered for little or almost nothing.

'No suh,' he would say. 'Dat dawg ain' no 'count enuff. Mah'sr Case he dun awdah me dat 'ah ain' buy no dawg wot ain' pintedly no 'count. Dey gotter be no 'count. Ah ain' buyin' um lessen dey's wuffless en' onery.'

Scarcely less easy was it to defend his wearing his twin revolvers even with dinner-dress, for he put on evening-dress for dinner, with the punctiliousness of an Englishman in the wilderness, put it on as often as he dined and yet wore it so naturally and unobtrusively, that no more than the incongruous belt did it embarrass the guests he made at home in any kind of clothes they happened to be wearing. His admirers pointed to this as a kind of exploit, as something of which only a perfectly sane and exceptionally fine man could be capable. They

adduced his clear-headed business sense, his excellent
judgement on matters pertaining to real estate, his knowledge of horseflesh, his horsemanship, his coolness, skill
and exceptional good temper at cards, as cumulative
proofs of his perfect sanity. They admitted he was peculiar on one or two points but minimized these as negligible eccentricities. They were ready to descant to any
extent on his personal charm, and this indeed all were
agreed upon. To attract visitors by good dinners, good
liquors, good cigars and endless card playing was easy. To
keep his visitors at their ease and entertained for hours
with mere conversations while seated on his veranda, was
no small feat in itself and a hundred times a feat when
their host obtruded upon them the ever visible butts of
his big revolvers and kept a repeating rifle standing
against each jamb of his front door. This tension of
perpetual preparedness for an imminent attack might
well have scared away everybody and left Case a hermit. It
did nothing of the kind. It was acquiesced in at first, later
tacitly accepted and finally ignored altogether. With it
was ignored his strange complexion. I had myself puzzled
over this: after long groping about in my mind I had realized what it reminded me of, and I found others who
agreed with me in respect to it. It was like the paleness
one sees for the half of a breath on the face of a strong,
healthy man when in sudden alarm, astonishment or
horror his blood flows momently back to his heart. Under
such stress of unforeseen agitation a normal countenance
might exhibit that hue for a fraction of a second; on
Case's visage it was abiding, like the war paint on an
armour-clad, drab-grey and dreary. Yet it produced no
effect of gloom in his associates. He not only did not put a
damper upon high spirits but diffused an atmosphere of
gaiety and good fellowship.

And he did so not only in spite of his ever-visible
weapons and of his uncanny, sombre complexion, but
also in spite of the strange and daunting habit of his eyes.
I had seen something like it once and again in a frontiers-

man who knew that his one chance of surviving his enemy was to shoot first and who expected the crucial instant at any moment. I had watched in more than one town the eyes of such an individual scan each man who approached with one swift glance of inquiry, of keen uncertainty dying instantly into temporary relief. Such was the look with which Case invariably met me. It had in it hesitation, doubt, and, as it were, an element of half-conscious approach to alarm. It was as if he said to himself:

'Is that Radford? It looks like him. If it is Radford, all right. But is it really Radford after all?'

I grew used in time to this lightning scrutiny of me every time he caught sight of me. His other friends grew used to it. But it was the subject of endless talk among us. His eyes had an inexplicable effect on every one. And not the least factor in their mystery was that he bestowed this glance not only upon all men, but upon women, children, animals, birds, even insects. He regarded a robin or a butterfly with the same flash of transient interest which he bestowed upon a horse or a man. And his eyes seemed to keep him cognizant of every moving thing before, behind and above him. Nothing living which entered his horizon seemed to escape his notice.

Beverly remarked:

'Case is afraid of something, is always looking for something. But what the devil is it he is looking for? He acts as if he did not know what to expect and suspected everything.'

Dr Boone said:

'Case behaves somewhat as if he were suffering from a delusion of persecution. But most of the symptoms are conspicuously absent. I am puzzled like the rest of you.'

The effect upon strangers of this eerie quality of Case's vision was by no means pleasant. Yet his merest acquaint-ances soon became used to it and his intimates ceased to notice it at all. His personal charm made it seem a trifle. Night after night his card room was the scene of jollity.

His table gathered the most desirable comrades the countryside afforded. Evening after evening his cronies sat in the comfortable wicker chairs on his broad veranda, little Turkish tables bearing decanters and cigars set among them, Colonel Case the centre and life of the group.

He talked easily and he talked well. To start him talking of the countries he had seen was not easy, but, once he began, his stories of Egypt and Abyssinia, of Persia and Burmah, of Siam and China were always entertaining. Very seldom, almost never, did he tell of his own experiences. Generally he told of having heard from others the tales he repeated, even when he spoke so that we suspected him of telling events in which he had taken part.

It was impossible to pin him down to a date, almost as hard to elicit the definite name of a locality. He gave minute particulars of incidents and customs, but dealt in generalities as to place and time. Especially he was strong in local superstitions and beliefs.

He told countless tales, all good, of crocodiles and ichneumons in Egypt, gazelles and ghouls in Persia, elephants and tigers in Burmah, deer and monkeys in Siam, badgers and foxes in China and sorcerers and enchanters anywhere. He spoke of the last two in as matter-of-fact a tone as of any of the others.

He told legends of the contests of various Chinese sages and saints, with magicians and wizards; of the malice and wiles of these wicked practitioners of sombre arts; of the sort of super-sense developed by the adepts, their foes, enabling them to tell of the approach or presence of a sorcerer whatever disguise he assumed, even if he had the power of making himself invisible.

Several legendary anecdotes turned on this point of the invisibility of the wicked enemy and the prescience of his intended victim.

One was of a holy man said to have lived in Singan Fu about the time of the crusades. Knowing that he was threatened with the vengeance of a wizard, he provided himself with a sword entirely of silver, since the flesh of a wizard was considered proof against all baser metals. He likewise had at hand a quantity of the ashes of a sacred tree.

While seated in his study he felt an inimical presence. He snatched up his silver blade, stood upon the defensive and shouted a signal previously agreed upon. Hearing it his servants locked the doors of the house and rushed in with boxes of the sacred ashes. Scattering it on the floor, they could see on the fresh ashes the footsteps of the wizard. One of the servants, according to his master's instructions, had brought a live fowl. Slicing off its head he waved the spouting neck towards the air over the footprints. According to Chinese belief fowls' blood has the magical property of disclosing anyone invisible through incantation. In fact where the blood drops fell upon the wizard, they remained visible, there appeared a gory eye and cheek. Slashing at his revealed enemy the sage slew him with the silver sword, after which his body was with all speed burned to ashes. This was the invariable ending of all his similar tales.

Stories like this Case delighted in, but beyond this penchant for the weird and occult, for even childish tales of distant lands, his conversation in general showed no sign of peculiarity or eccentricity. Only once or twice did he startle us. Some visitors to town were among the gathering on his veranda and fell into a discussion of the contrasting qualities of Northerners and Southerners. Inevitably the discussion degenerated into a rather acrimonious and petty citation of all the weak points of each section and a rehash of all the stale sneers at either. The wordy Alabamian who led one side of the altercation descanted on the necessary and inherited vileness of the descendants of the men who burnt the Salem witches. Case had been listening silently. Then he cut in with an emphatic, trenchant directness unusual to him.

'Witches,' he announced, 'ought to be burnt always and everywhere.'

We sat a moment startled and mute.

The Alabamian spoke first.

'Do you believe in witches, sir?' he asked.

'I do,' Case affirmed.

'Ever been bewitched?' the Alabamian queried. He was rather young and dogmatically assertive.

'Do you believe in Asiatic cholera?' Case queried in his turn.

'Certainly, sir,' the Alabamian asserted.

'Ever had it?' Case inquired meaningly.

'No,' the Alabamian admitted. 'No, sir, never.'

'Ever had the yellow fever?' Case questioned him.

'Never, sir, thank God,' the Alabamian replied fervently.

'Yet I'll bet,' Case hammered at him, 'that you would be among the first to join a shot-gun quarantine if an epidemic broke out within a hundred miles of you. You have never had it, but you believe in it with every fibre of your being.

'That's just the way with me. I've never been bewitched, but I believe in witchcraft. Belief in witchcraft is like faith in any one of a dozen fashionable religions, not a subject for argument or proof, but a habit of mind. That's my habit of mind. I won't discuss it, but I've no hesitation about asserting it.

'Witchcraft is like leprosy; both spread among nations indifferent to them, both disappear before unflinching severity. The horror of both among our ancestors abolished both in Europe and kept them from gaining a foothold in this country. Both exist and flourish in other corners of the world, along with other things undreamed of in some complacent philosophies. Leprosy can be repressed only by isolation, the only thing that will abolish witchcraft is fire, fire sir.'

That finished that discussion. No one said another word on the subject. But it started a round of debates on Case's mental condition, which ran on for days, everywhere except at Case's house, and which brought up all that could be said about personal aloofness, pensioned dogs, exposed revolvers and pig-skin belts.

V

The mellow fall merged into Indian summer. The days were short and the afternoons chill. The weather did not permit the evening gatherings on Case's veranda. No more did it allow Mary Kenton to sit in her rocker between the two left-hand columns of the big white portico. Yet it was both noticeable and noticed that she never failed to step out upon that portico, no matter what the weather, each afternoon; that in the twilight or in the late dusk the wave of her hand and the sweep of the horseman's big, broad-brimmed felt hat answered each other unfailingly.

The coterie of Case's chums, friends and hangers-on gathered in his ample drawing-room, when they were not in the card-room, the billiard-room or at table. I made one of that coterie frequently and enjoyed my hours there with undiminished zest. When I dined there I habitually occupied the foot of the long table, facing Case at the head. The hall door of the dining-room was just at my right hand.

One evening in early December I was so seated at the foot of the table. The weather had been barely coolish for some days, the skies had been clear and everything was dry. That night was particularly mild. We had sat down rather early and it was not yet seven o'clock when Pompey began to pass the cigars. No one had yet lit up. Some one had asked Case a question and the table was still listening for his answer. I, like the rest, was looking at him. Then it all happened in a tenth, in a hundredth of the time necessary to tell it; so quickly that, except Case, no one had time to move a muscle.

Case's eyes were on his questioner. I did not see the door open, but I saw his gaze shift to the door, saw his habitual glance of startled uncertainty. But instead of the

lightning query of his eyes softening into relief and indifference, it hardened instantaneously into decision. I saw
his hand go to his holster, saw the revolver leap out, saw
the aim, saw his face change, heard his explosive exclamation:

'Good God, it is!' We saw the muzzle kick up as the
report crushed our ear drums and through the smoke saw
him push back his chair and spring up.

The rest of us were all too dazed to try to stand. Like
me they all looked towards the door.

There stood Mary Kenton, all in pink, a pink silk
opera cloak half off her white shoulders, a single strand
of pale coral round her slender throat, a pink pompom in
her glossy hair. She was standing as calmly as if nothing
had happened, her arms hidden in the cloak, her right
hand holding it together in front. Her rings sparkled on
her low corsage.

'Cousin Cassius,' she said, 'you have a theatrical way of
receiving unexpected visitors.'

'Good God, Mary,' he said. 'It is really you. I saw it was
really you just in time.'

'Of course it is really I,' she retorted. 'Whom or what
did you think it really was?'

'Not you,' he answered thickly. 'Not you.'

His voice died away.

'Now you know it is really I,' she said crisply, 'you
might at least offer me a chair.'

At that the spell of our amazement left us and we all
sprang to our feet.

She seated herself placidly to the right of the fireplace.

'I hear your port is excellent,' she said laughingly.

Before Case could hand her the glass she wavered a
little in the chair, but a mere swallow revived her.

'I had not anticipated,' she said, 'so startling a reception.'

We stood about in awkward silence.

'Pray ask your guests to be seated, Cousin Cassius,' she
begged. 'I did not mean to disturb your gaiety.'

We took our chairs, but those on her side of the table

were turned outwards toward the fireplace, where Case stood facing her.

'I owe you an explanation,' she said easily. 'Milly Wilberforce is staying with me and she bet me a box of Maillard's that I would not pay you a call. As I never take a dare, as the weather is fine, and as we have all your guests for chaperones, I thought a brief call between cousins could do no harm.'

'It has not,' said Case fervently; 'but it very nearly did. And now will you let me escort you home? The Judge will be anxious about you.'

'Papá doesn't know I am here, of course,' she said. 'When he finds out, I'll quiet him. If you won't come to see me, at least I have once come to see you.'

Case held the door wide for her, shut it behind him, and left us staring at the bullet hole in the door frame.

One morning of the following spring Case was driving me townward from Shelby Manor, when, not a hundred feet in front of us, Mary Kenton's buggy entered the pike from a cross-road. As it turned, mare, vehicle and all went over sideways with a terrific crash. Mary must have fallen clear for the next instant she was at the mare's head.

Case did succeed in holding his fiery colts and in pulling them to a stand-still alongside the wreck, but it was all even he could do. I jumped out, meaning to take the colts' bits and let Case help Mary. But she greeted me imperiously.

'Cousin Jack, please come sit on Bonnie's head.'

I took charge of Bonnie in my own fashion and she stood up entirely unhurt.

'How on earth did you come to do it, Mary?' Colonel Case wondered, for she was a perfect horsewoman.

'Accidents will happen,' she answered lightly, 'and I'm glad of this one. You have really spoken to me, and that is worth a hundred smashes.'

'But I wrote to you,' he protested, 'I wrote to you and explained.'

'One letter,' she sniffed contemptuously. 'You should have kept on, you silly man, I might have answered the fifth or sixth or even the second.'

He stared at her and no wonder for she was fascinatingly coquettish.

'I don't mind Jack a bit, you know,' she went on. 'Jack is my loyal knight and unfailing partisan. He keeps my secrets and does everything I ask of him. For instance, he will not demur an atom now when I ask him to throw Bonnie's harness into the buggy and ride her to town for me.

'You see,' she smiled at him dazzlingly, 'another advantage of my upset is that the buggy is so smashed that you cannot decently refuse to drive me home.'

'But Mary,' he protested, 'I explained fully to you.'

'You didn't really expect me to believe all that fol-de-rol?' she cried. 'Suppose I did, I don't see any dwergs around, and if all Malebolge were in plain sight I'd make you take me anyhow.'

Inevitably he did, but that afternoon their daily ceremony of hand-wave from the portico and hat-wave from horseback was resumed and was continued as their sole intercourse.

VI

It was full midsummer when a circus came to Brexington. Case and I started for a ride together on the afternoon of its arrival, passed the tents already raised and met the procession on its way through town from the freight yard of the railroad. We pulled our horses to one side of the street and sat watching the show.

There were Cossacks and cowboys, Mexican vaqueros and Indians on mustangs. There were two elephants, a giraffe, and then some camels which set our mounts snorting and swerving about. Then came the cages, one of monkeys, another of parrots, cockatoos and macaws, others with wolves, bears, hyenas, a lion, a lioness, a tiger, and a beautiful leopard.

Case made a movement and I heard a click. I looked round and beheld him with his revolver cocked and pointed at the leopard's cage. He did not fire but kept the pistol aimed at the cage until it was out of range. Then he thrust it back into its holster and watched the fag-end of the procession go by. All he said was:

'You will have to excuse me, Radford, I have urgent business at home.'

Towards dusk Cato came to me in great agitation.

'Mahs'r Case done gone off'n his haid,' he declared. 'He shuah done loss his sainsus.' I told him to return home and I would stroll up there casually.

I found Case in the woodshed, Uncle Rastus with him. Hung by the hind legs like new-slaughtered hogs were a dozen of the biggest dogs of which Rastus had charge. Their throats were cut and each dripped into a tin pail. Rastus, his ebony face paled to a sort of mud-grey, held a large tin pail and a new white-washer's brush.

Case greeted me as usual, as if my presence there were a matter of course and he were engaged upon nothing out of the common.

'Uncle,' he said, 'I judge those are about dripped out. Pour it all into the big pail.'

He took the brush from Rastus, who followed him to the gate.

There Case dipped the brush into the blood and painted a broad band across the gravel of the drive and the flagstones of the footpath. He proceeded as if he were using lime white-wash to mark off a lawn-tennis court in the early days of the game, when wet markers were not yet invented and dry markers were still undreamed of. He continued the stripe of blood all round his place, just inside the hedge. He made it about three inches wide and took great pains to make it plain and heavy.

When he had come round to the entrance again he

went over the stripe on the path and drive a second time.
Then he straightened up and handed the brush to Rastus.

'Just enough,' he remarked. 'I calculated nicely.'

I had so far held my tongue. But his air of self-
approval, as if in some feat of logic led me to blurt out:

'What is it for?'

'The Chinese,' said Case, 'esteem dogs' blood a defence
against sorcery. I doubt its efficacy, but I know of no
better fortification.'

No reply seemed expected and I made none.

That evening I was at Case's, with some six or seven
others. We sat indoors, for the cloudy day had led up to a
rainy evening. Nothing unusual occurred.

Next day the town was plastered with posters of the circus
company offering five hundred dollars reward for the
capture of an escaped leopard.

Cato came to my office just as I was going out to lunch.

'Mahs'r Case done gone cunjuhin' agin,' he announced.

I found that a second batch of dogs had been brought
in by Uncle Rastus in his covered wagon behind his
unfailing mules, had been butchered like the former
convoy and the band of blood gone over a second time.
Case had not gone outside that line since he first made it,
no drive to Shelby Manor that morning.

The day was perfect after the rain of the day before, and
the bright sunlight dried everything. The evening was
clear and windless with a nearly full moon intensely
bright and very high. Practically the whole population
went to the circus.

Beverly and I dined at Case's. He had no other guests,
but such was his skill as a host that our dinner was
delightfully genial. After dinner the three of us sat on the
veranda.

The brilliance of the moonlight on and through the
unstirred trees made a glorious spectacle and the mild,
cool atmosphere put us in just the humour to enjoy it and

each other. Case talked quietly, mostly of art galleries in
Europe, and his talk was quite as charming and entertaining as usual. He seemed a man entirely sane and altogether at his ease.

We had been on the veranda about half an hour and in
that time neither team nor pedestrian had passed. Then
we saw the figure of a woman approaching down the
middle of the roadway from the direction of the country.
Beverly and I caught sight of her at about the same
instant and I saw him watching her as I did, for she had
the carriage and bearing of a lady and it seemed strange
that she should be walking, stranger that she should be
alone, and strangest that she should choose the road
instead of the footpath which was broad and good for half
a mile.

Case, who had been describing a carved set of ivory
chessmen he had seen in Egypt, stopped speaking and
stared as we did. I began to feel as if I ought to recognize
the advancing figure, it seemed unfamiliar and yet familiar
too in outline and carriage, when Beverly exclaimed:

'By Jove, that is Mary Kenton.'

'No,' said Colonel Case in a combative, resonant tone
like the slow boom of a big bell. 'No, it is not Mary
Kenton.'

I was astonished at the animus of his contradiction and
we intensified our scrutiny. The nearing girl really
suggested Mary Kenton and yet, I felt sure, was not she.
Her bearing made me certain that she was young, and she
had that indefinable something about her which leads a
man to expect that a woman will turn out to be good
looking. She walked with a sort of insolent, high-stepping
swing.

When she was nearly opposite us Case exclaimed in a
sort of chopped-off, guttural bark:

'Nay, not even in that shape, foul fiend, not even in
that.'

The tall, shapely young woman turned just in front of
the gateway and walked towards us.

'I think,' said Beverly, 'the lady is coming in.'

'No,' said Colonel Case, again with that deep, baying reverberation behind his voice. 'No, not coming in.'

The young woman laid her hand on the pathway gate and pushed it open. She stepped inside and then stopped, stopped suddenly, abruptly, with an awkward half-stride, as if she had run into an obstacle in the path, a low obstruction like a wheelbarrow. She stood an instant, looked irresolutely right and left, and then stepped back and shut the gate. She turned and started across the street, fairly striding in a sort of incensed, wrathful haste.

My eyes, like Beverly's were on the figure in the road. It was only with a sort of sidelong vision that I felt rather than saw Case whip a rifle from the door jamb to his shoulder and fire. Almost before the explosion rent my ear drums I saw the figure in the roadway crumple and collapse vertically. Petrified with amazement I was frozen with my stare upon the huddle on the macadam. Beverly had not moved and was as dazed as I. My gaze still fixed as Case threw up a second cartridge from the magazine and fired again. I saw the wretched heap on the piking leap under the impact of the bullet with the yielding quiver of totally dead flesh and bone. A third time he fired and we saw the like. Then the spell of our horror broke and we leapt up, roaring at the murderer.

With a single incredibly rapid movement the madman disembarrassed himself of his rifle and held us off, a revolver at each of our heads.

'Do you know what you have done?' we yelled together.

'I am quite sure of what I have done,' Case replied in a big calm voice, the barrels of his pistols steady as the pillars of the veranda. 'But I am not quite so clear whether I have earned five hundred dollars reward. Will you gentlemen be kind enough to step out into the street and examine that carcass?'

Woodenly, at the muzzles of those unwavering revolvers, we went down the flagged walk side by side, moving in a nightmare dream.

I had never seen a woman killed before and this woman was presumably a lady, young and handsome. I felt the piking of the roadway under my feet, and looked everywhere, except downward in front of me.

I heard Beverly give a coughing exclamation:

'The leopard!'

Then I looked, and I too shouted:

'The leopard!'

She lay tangible, unquestionable, in plain sight under the silver moonrays with the clear black shadows of the maple leaves sharp on her sleek hide.

Gabbling our excited astonishment we pulled at her and turned her over. She had six wounds, three where the bullets entered and three where they came out, one through spine and breast-bone and two through the ribs.

We dropped the carcass and stood up.

'But I thought ...' I exclaimed.

'But I saw ...' Beverly cried.

'You gentlemen,' thundered Colonel Case, 'had best not say what you saw or what you thought you saw.'

We stood mute, looking at him, at each other, and up and down the street. No one was in sight. Apparently the circus had so completely drained the neighbourhood that no one had heard the shots.

Case addressed me in his natural voice:

'If you will be so good Radford, would you oblige me by stepping into my house and telling Jeff to fetch the wheelbarrow. I must keep watch over this carrion.'

There I left him, the two cocked revolvers pointed at the dead animal.

Jeff, and Cato with him, brought the wheelbarrow. Upon it the two negroes loaded the warm, inert mass of spotted hide and what it contained. Then Jeff lifted the handles and taking turns they wheeled their burden all the way to Uncle Rastus', Case walking on one side of the barrow with his cocked revolvers, we on the other, quite as a matter of course.

Jeff trundled the barrow out to the hay barrack on the

knoll. He and Cato and Uncle Rastus carried out cord-wood until they had an enormous pile well out in the field. Then they dug up a barrel of kerosene from near one corner of the barrack. When the leopard had been placed on the top of the firewood they broached the barrel and poured its contents over the carcass and its pyre. When it was set on fire Case gave an order to Jeff, who went off. We stood and watched the pyre burn down to red coals. By that time Jeff had returned from Shelby Manor with a double team.

Case let down the hammers of his revolvers, holstered them, unbuckled his belt and threw it into the dayton.

Never had we suspected he could sing a note. Now he started 'Dixie' in a fine, deep baritone and we sang that and other rousing songs all the way home. When we got out of the dayton he walked loungingly up the veranda steps, his belt hanging over his arm. He took the rifles from the door jamb.

'I have no further use for these trusty friends,' he said. 'If you like, you may each have one as a souvenir of the occasion. My defunct pistols and otiose belt I'll even keep myself.'

Next morning as I was about to pass Judge Kenton's house I heard heavy footsteps rapidly overtaking me. Turning I saw Case, not in his habitual grey clothes and broad-brimmed semi-sombrero, but wearing a soft brown felt hat, a blue serge suit, set off by a red necktie and tan shoes. He was conspicuously beltless.

'You might as well come with me, Radford,' he said. 'You will probably be best man later anyhow.'

We found Judge Kenton on his porch, and Mary, all in pink, with a pink rose in her hair, seated between her father and her pretty step-mother.

'I sent Jeff with a note,' Case explained as we approached the steps, 'to make sure of finding them.'

After the greetings were over Case said:

'Judge, I am a man of few words. I love your daughter

and I ask your permission to win her if I can.'

'You have my permission, Suh,' the Judge answered.

Case rose.

'Mary,' he said, 'would you walk with me in the garden, say to the grape arbor?'

When they returned Mary wore a big ruby ring set round with diamonds. Her colour was no bad match for the ruby. And, beyond a doubt, Case's cheeks showed a trace of colour, too.

'Father,' Mary said as she seated herself, 'I am going to marry Cousin Cassius.'

'You have my blessing, my dear,' the Judge responded. 'I am glad of it.'

'Everybody will be glad, I believe,' said Mary. 'Cassius is glad, of course, and he is glad of two other things. One is that he feels free to dine with us tonight, he has just told me so.

'The other' (a roguish light sparkled in her eyes) 'he has not confessed. But I just know that, next to marrying me, the one thing in all this world that makes him gladdest is that now at last he feels at liberty to see a horse race and go to the races every chance he gets.'

In fact, when they returned from their six-months' wedding tour, they were conspicuous at every race meeting. Case's eyes had lost their restlessness and his cheeks showed as healthy a colouring as I ever saw on any human being.

It might be suggested that there should be an explanation to this tale. But I myself decline to expound my own theory. Mary never told what she knew, and her husband, in whose after life there has been nothing remarkable as far as I know, has never uttered a syllable.

THE BLACK KNIGHT

O

Raymund Allen

Raymund Allen was one of the many, now obscure, contributors to the Strand Magazine, that storehouse of so much Victorian macabre fiction. Allen does not appear in any works of reference for this time, literary or otherwise. In fact, the only Raymund Allen I can trace with that spelling is the co-author with Albert Parsons of the third and fourth editions of THE WORKMEN'S COMPENSATION ACTS (1906-1907). I leave it to you to judge from this story whether they are one and the same!

Raymund Allen wrote several stories for the Strand Magazine, contributing one to every Christmas issue from 1913 to 1916. 'The Black Knight' comes from a much earlier edition, that of April 1892, and as far as I can trace, has never before appeared in book form. It is a typically Victorian tale of Indian fun and games and stands up well after its 100-year neglect.

RAYMUND ALLEN

O

The Black Knight

A storm of wind and rain had come on suddenly, and, as there were no cabs to be got near at hand, there was nothing for it but to set out on foot. I was going to dine with old Colonel Bradshaw, whose acquaintance I had lately made at the local chess club, and I was due at half-past seven, so I pulled my coat collar up to my ears and started off through the muddy streets. Several times in the course of my exceedingly unpleasant walk the foulness of the weather had given rise to a wish on my part that I had invented some excuse for staying by my own comfortable fireside. Once arrived, however, the cheery welcome of the old soldier quickly dispersed all regrets for my own hearth, and restored me to the good humour necessary for the proper appreciation of a good dinner.

Colonel Bradshaw had served in India during the time of the Mutiny, had received a severe wound in the left leg, which still caused him to limp, and had led to his comparatively early retirement from the service. He had returned to England on his retirement, and had lately leased a snug little house in our town, which he apparently intended to occupy for the rest of his days in the quiet enjoyment of peaceful obscurity. I had made his acquaintance, as I have said, at the chess club, where, I believe, he used to spend most of his evenings, and where he had earned the reputation of a decidedly strong player. I had not as yet encountered him over the board.

In his note of invitation, the Colonel had asked me to bring my men with me, as he had left his own at the club-rooms, on the occasion of a match for which they had been called into requisition, and it was accordingly my set of chessmen which we now arranged in the customary order of battle. To my annoyance, however, I found that one of my black knights was missing, and I cast my eyes round the room in search of some article on which we might for the occasion confer the spurs of knighthood. On the Colonel's writing-table, acting as a paperweight, I saw the very object we were in want of—a black knight. Not of the orthodox Staunton pattern, it is true, nor indeed were its grotesquely protruding eyes and maliciously grinning mouth characteristic of any pattern with which I was familiar; but still it was undeniably a black chess knight, and would serve our turn admirably. My host hesitated, and even seemed the least trifle annoyed when I suggested the expediency of pressing it into the service. The beast certainly looked incongruous among my Stauntons, but something in his human eyes and life-like expression of malicious humour caught my fancy, and I asked to be allowed to play with the black men. The Colonel acquiesced, but declined the privilege of first move, which usually goes with the white. We accordingly drew for the move, and I won it.

Led partly by my fancy for the black knight, and partly 'to take my opponent out of the books,' I began the game by making the paperweight first take the field. As I did so, I fancied my host gave a little start, and, as he certainly appeared to be annoyed at my irregular opening, I was sorry that I had begun by a move which I supposed he objected to on the ground that it generally leads to a close game. He said nothing, however, and the game was con-tinued for some time by very ordinary moves on both

sides, and presently I began to be absorbed in the study
of the position and in the endeavour to gauge the
strength of my opponent. For a time he seemed to play a
decidedly good game, and, in spite of continuous concen-
tration on my part, to maintain some superiority of position. Presently, however, he embarked on a series of
moves which appeared to give me a decisive advantage
and to have no more rational object than the capture of
my swarthy champion at a ruinous sacrifice of his own
pieces. This eccentric proceeding puzzled me, and, added
to his previous hesitation about using the substitute,
excited my curiosity. So, relinquishing the object of
winning the game in the ordinary way, I devoted all my
skill to the defence of my king's knight, as though it were
a *pièce coiffée* with which I was pledged to give
checkmate. Rooks were sacrificed for bishops, and
bishops exchanged for inoffensive pawns, while the kings
stood disregarded on their knights' squares, and the fight
raged hotly round the black knight, who seemed to bear a
charmed life and sprang nimbly about the board, always
evading my opponent's headlong attempts at his capture.
At last, in desperation, he offered the bribe of the white
queen, but I obstinately refused to part at any price with
my dusky cavalier, and a few moves later brought the
game to a successful end with a smothered mate, the very
bone of contention inflicting the deathblow.

The Colonel leaned back in his armchair and for some
minutes continued silently to blow out thick clouds of
smoke. After a pause, during which his brow was
compressed into a frown, as though by the contemplation
of some bewildering enigma to which he could not find
the clue, he broke silence with the remark, that 'there
were more things in heaven and earth–' and then again
relapsed into silence in apparent forgetfulness of my
presence. As he made no further remark for some time, I
rose from my seat, and, muttering something about its
being late, prepared to take my leave. 'Wait a moment;
look here,' said the Colonel, rising to stop me with the air

of a man who has formed a sudden determination, and pointing to the board, 'I daresay you wonder what on earth I was driving at in that game?'

'Well, you appeared to me to be driving mainly at that outlandish black knight instead of at my king,' I replied.

'Exactly, and perhaps I ought to apologise for having spoilt the game by giving way to an absurd fancy; but if you will sit down again and refill your pipe, I will tell you a curious experience which I had many years ago in India, and which you will perhaps admit as an excuse for my eccentric play to-night.'

'Nothing I should like better,' I replied; 'for I confess you have considerably roused my curiosity.'

'Well then, I think I can partly satisfy it'; and my host threw a fresh log on to the fire, stretched himself in the chair, and began.

'I don't know whether you take any interest in such subjects as hypnotism, thought-reading, and so on; but, if you do, you may perhaps be able to form some scientific theory to explain my story. Personally I used to be very unbelieving in such matters, but my scepticism was considerably modified by the adventure I am going to tell you of. Very well, then. On one occasion in India, many years ago, I had got leave from my regiment for a few weeks in order to join a shooting expedition which had been got up by one of my greatest friends, a man many years older than I was then, and of much higher rank in the service. When, however, I arrived at our appointed meeting-place, I found my friend, the General, preparing for a more warlike excursion against a marauding tribe who had lately been extending their cattle raids across our frontier. The shooting expedition having fallen through, I readily accepted the General's suggestion that I should accompany his force as a volunteer, and see some sport of a more exciting kind. A common risk, even when comparatively insignificant, inclines men to readier cordiality towards the companions they may shortly be going to lose, and I was soon on excellent terms with the other officers, who were as pleasant a set of fellows as I have ever met. Nothing of any interest happened till we were across the enemy's frontier and the force was encamped one night under a brilliant moon on a hill overlooking a thickly wooded valley.

'I was strolling round camp with a cigar, when I was joined by one of the younger officers, who, not being on duty, was refreshing himself after the day's march in the same way, and we continued our walk together. We stopped to admire the view at a point where we could look down on the valley, and presently we fell into an argument as to whether a bright surface which caught the moonlight in a glade of the wood below was water or a smooth slab of rock. It happened that my companion particularly prided himself on the keenness of his sight, and a few days before had won a small bet from me on the subject. I, too, thought that I had good eyes, and, feeling sure that he was wrong in his contention that he could detect a gentle ripple on the surface in dispute, I offered him a second bet that it was rock, and proposed to settle the question by myself going down to the spot. He accepted my bet, and, as he was not at liberty to leave the camp, I gaily started down the hill alone, telling him with a laugh to have the stakes ready by the time I returned, and never for a moment supposing that I was running any risk in the affair.

'I rapidly made my way down over the short grass of the hillside, and, marking the direction of the spot in question, soon plunged into the darkness of that wood, the cavernous depth of whose shadows was enhanced by an occasional glint of moonshine. I am not naturally superstitious. I have no particular aversion to midnight graveyards or haunted rooms, but I must confess I felt an uncommonly disagreeable feeling of something like dread when I got inside the wood. Everything was absolutely dead and still. Not the faintest rustle of a leaf, not the crick of an insect, nor murmur of water, but dense and awful blackness! It excited my nerves. I almost imagined I saw black shapes moving under the trees, though it was quite impossible that anything not luminous should show against such an inky background. I felt my way cautiously, stopping constantly to hear if anything was moving near me. What cracks the twigs under my feet gave! What a resounding crash reverberated in the gloomy shades when my foot set a loose stone rolling! My nerve was gone, and I felt horribly uncomfortable. I would gladly have paid my bet to be back again in camp, but I was bound to go through with my search now that I had once begun, and I should make myself a butt for the wit of the regiment if I turned back halfway to confess myself scared by the dark. After a longer time and with more difficulty than I had anticipated, I reached the slab of rock, for such it proved to be. Here I was clear of the trees, and I stood for a few moments in the bright moonlight, so that my friend above, who I knew would be watching for me to emerge from the shadow, might see that it was not water on which I stood. Then I turned, and struck out energetically for the camp.

'I had not, however, pushed my way far through the undergrowth when I was tripped up suddenly by what I at first took to be some stout creeper or protruding root. I fell forward on my hands, and had not time to get on my feet again before I learnt that it was no accident which had overthrown me. Before I had time to offer the least resistance, or even to utter a shout for help, I felt myself seized round the neck by a grip like a vice; a few seconds more, and I was gagged, bound, and carried off through the forest, quickly, but in silence. As soon as subsiding astonishment left room for any other sensation, I felt a paroxysm of rage, as well against my own folly in running into such a trap as against my sudden assailants, whom I cursed none the less heartily for my inability to utter a sound. The futility of passion under the circumstances gradually subdued me, if not to philosophic fortitude, at least to sufficient calmness to speculate on my probable fate and on the chances of escape. For some time I seemed to be borne down hill and over irregular ground; then we must have emerged from the jungle on to more even ground, for the pace became quicker and smoother. This may have gone on for some twenty minutes or half an hour, and then my captors came to a halt. I was set on my feet, and my eyes and mouth released from their bandages. This change of condition did not, however, conduce to my comfort or reassurance; for, while an armed native on each side held me firmly by my pinioned arms, a third presented a huge horse-pistol at my head at a yard's distance. For a few instants I endured an agony of suspense. I involuntarily shut my eyes, and waited for the bullet to crash through my brain.

'I have met many men who have at some time or other looked death pretty closely in the face, and you must often have heard it said that a man's mind at such moments reviews in a flash long periods of past time with an almost supernatural vividness of perception, but I didn't feel anything of this. I only felt that I might be dead in another second, and then, with a determination to "die game," which was rather an animal sensation than an articulate thought, I set my teeth and opened my eyes to meet those of my enemy. The pistol was still directed at my head, and the grim Indian still kept his finger on the trigger. I faced him defiantly, and, as though unwilling to change a dramatic situation which interested him, he still kept the same menacing posture, while I longed for the flash and the end before my nerve should fail.

'At last he spoke. He spoke a dialect which I only imperfectly followed, but I understood him to say that if I tried to escape I should be shot on the spot. I felt no confidence that I was not being reserved for a more horrible death, but the instinct of self-preservation kept me passive. When at last the pistol was lowered, and I no longer stood in momentary expectation of death, I looked round me and perceived that I was in the middle of a group of some half dozen Indians, and as many horses. On to one of these latter I was lifted, and secured in the saddle by leathern thongs, my captors not choosing to give me the chance of escape by leaving me the management of my horse.

'After about an hour's hard riding, during which the rapid motion and the blowing of the cool night air on my face and hands acted as a sedative on my racked nerves, we reached the encampment of the hostile tribe against which the expedition had been sent out. And now came the strangest part of my adventures; the part which bears on my eccentric play to-night.'

Here Colonel Bradshaw paused to stir the smouldering log in the grate to a bright blaze and then, staring into the fire and keeping the poker in his hands as he leaned forward in his chair, went on with his story, more slowly at first, but with growing animation of voice, which gradually rose to the eloquence of excitement as he seemed to forget his immediate surroundings, and to live once again through the distant scene he was describing.

'The human brain,' he resumed, 'is incapable, I imagine, of continuing to experience any intense sensation for very long. It reaches the maximum tension, and then one set of perceptive faculties becomes deadened. The previous incidents of the night had exhausted my capacity for fear, and, as I was led before the chief of the tribe to hear his decree concerning me, I awaited the decision with indifference. I was keenly alive to every detail of my surroundings, and noted the expression of every face, and yet I seemed somehow to have lost my own individuality; to be watching myself as an actor in a scene with which I had no personal concern, but only looked at from some outside point of view. The moon was now hidden behind a hill, but some twenty torches lit up the spot with their lurid flames. The party that had caught me had obviously been sent out to reconnoitre the movements of the English force, and the chief had been beguiling the time of their absence with nothing less than a game of chess.

'I was the less surprised at the nature of his pastime, as

I knew that the game was widely spread in India, and had played it with natives myself, and knew in what points their game differed from our European rules. The chief's antagonist was a man whom I imagined, though I can't say exactly what suggested the idea, to be the priest of the tribe. He was shorter than the others, but his face suggested an extraordinarily active mind, and this, combined with his regularity of feature, would have made him a strikingly handsome type if it had not been for the fearful malignity of his expression. I wish I could give you some faint idea of that man's face, for it was the most terribly sinister face I have ever seen. His back had been turned towards me at first, but from the moment when I met the scrutiny of his black deepset eyes, which glared on me with a look of mocking, triumphant devilry that must have been borrowed from the fiend below, I was fascinated, and could see nothing but that one diabolical face. If there is any truth in the Eastern belief in possession by evil spirits, a demon looked through that man's eyes. A shiver ran through my frame as I met his gaze, and I felt that he was exercising some subtle influence over me, against which every fibre of my body, every atom of my being, stiffened in revolt. I felt that unless I exerted the whole of my will-force in resistance to the dread spell he was casting over me, I should lose myself in his identity, and become the creature of his wicked will. It was not physical fear that I felt. I had passed through that stage, and I believe I should have met death with firmness, but I felt that my whole personality was at the death-grapple with that fearful being—a mysterious deadly struggle, fought in neither act nor word, with the powers of darkness impersonated.

'While all this was going on in me, the chief must have been listening to an account of my capture, though I was unconscious of any words being spoken near me, till the priest turned from me to him, and, pointing to the chess-board which stood on a sort of low table, made a suggestion which at first I did not fully grasp. Its meaning was soon made clear to me, however. I had some knowledge of their dialect, and most expressive pantomime conveyed the rest. I was to play a game of chess with the chief; the stakes, my life against a safe conduct to the English lines. Never before had I encountered so terrible an opponent, and never in the history of the royal game had so fateful an issue been fought out on the battlefield of the sixty-four squares. I took my seat opposite the chief, and the torchbearers formed a wide ring round the table, looking, as the dancing torch-flames shone on their dark faces and limbs, like so many stalwart statues of bronze. Within the circle, and a little behind the king, stood the evil priest, motionless, with folded arms, including me and the board in his keen, hateful gaze. I knew exactly where he stood before I looked at him, and again I felt the same dread fascination working on me that I had felt when I first set eyes on him. The chief moved the pieces indeed, but I was conscious in some subtle way that it was against his attendant's mind that I was pitted—that the former was scarcely more than an automaton under the thraldom of the priest's marvellous will, and the game itself only a sort of emblem or shadow of our inward contest of mind and personality.

'I played appropriately enough, with the white pieces, and the game itself might have afforded an expressive symbol of the antagonism of the light and dark races, of the clear, bright West with the mystic, sombre East, but the thought did not occur to me then. To me it was rather a struggle between the intangible powers of good and evil—a realization in my own self of the eternal struggle of the universe. We played very slowly, and in absolute silence. No word was spoken nor sign made when either king was checked. Hour after hour the priest kept the same motionless posture behind his chief, who played with the same monotonously mechanical movement of the hand, the same vacant mesmerised expression on his face. Hour passed after hour, unmeasured by any clock, unmarked by any change except in the position of the pieces on the board. The chief, or rather the priest, played well; and, though time after time I seemed on the point of gaining a decisive advantage, some unforeseen move always deferred my victory.

'One piece in particular repeatedly thwarted my combinations. Again and again it constituted the weak point in a series of moves which should have brought me victory. Again and again, when, after straining every faculty of my brain, I made my move and raised my eyes to watch in the priest's face the effect of a stroke to which I saw no reply, a faint mocking smile would curl for a moment his cruel lips, and the black knight would be moved once more, threatening dangers which I had overlooked, and dashing my premature hopes to the ground. It was as though some secret link existed between that particular bit of bone and the grim, ghoulish spectator of our game. Piece after piece was taken from the board and dropped on the sand at our feet; the ranks of pawns grew thinner and thinner, but still that one black knight, now the only piece left to my antagonist, sprang over the board, evading my deep-laid plans for his capture. The opening was long passed, the wavering fortune of the middle-game had waned with the long hours to an end-game. The inexorable moment which must decide my fate was close upon me.

'I turned for a moment from the board to ease the throbbing fever of my brain. A black veil of formless mist hid the stars and gave back the earth's heat, till I gasped for breath, and drops of nervous sweat ran down my forehead. There was a stifling oppression in the still air, as in the minutes before the first lightning flash darts from the charged thunder-cloud. The chief moved and I spurred my flagging energies once more to the study of the game. Suddenly I seemed to be gifted with extraordinary powers of calculation. I shut my eyes, and saw mentally the position change through every possible variation like the moving pattern of a kaleidoscope. I could have announced a mate. I knew, to the exclusion of any doubt, that I must win. I made my move, and then, concentrating every particle of the hatred and loathing with which the diabolical priest had inspired me into one flashing look of defiance, I tried to hurl from me the cursed influence of his malignant spirit and to crush it into subjection to mine. His face changed with a hideous contortion of defeated evil purpose, and then the whole devil in him rose to one supreme effort in answer to mine. He passed his hand lightly across his eyes, and leaning over his chief scored his forehead with a malevolent frown, the glare of his glittering eyes seeming to pierce to the brain of the head they nearly touched. The new spell began to work on the chief. An uneasy, puzzled look came into his face, and this time it was with an uncertain, vacillating movement that he raised his hand to play. Again I looked at the priest. His expression was more bitterly mocking and more exultingly fiendish than ever as he directed my glance by a movement of his own to the hand which hovered over the board. His treacherous design was transmitted in a flash to my mind by some unexplained interaction of our brains. An illegal move with the black knight, in defiance of the rules of the game, was to snatch the nearly won victory from my grasp. I saw the fatal square on which the piece would be placed, and I felt that if it reached it I was lost. There were no spectators to whom I could appeal against the glaring illegality, unconscious, no doubt, on the part of the hypnotised chief, and I should never be able to convince him afterwards of having won unfairly. I must prevent the move.

'The struggle entered on the final phase. I had shaken off the priest's mesmeric influence over my own will; now I must wrest the chief's will from the same thraldom by the exertion of a counter influence. It was the critical moment, the culminating point of conflict which must at last be decisive. The chief's hand raised the black knight slowly from the board, and as it began more slowly still to descend, I exerted all my power of will on one burst of straining endeavour to compel another move than the false one the priest intended. Every nerve in my body seemed strung to cracking. The wonderful sensation of my individuality, of the intangible essence which constitutes self, wrestling grimly for life with the demon-possessed priest, became intensified till my brain reeled. The chief's hand came slowly, slowly down; wavered as though uncertain on which square to place the piece. One final effort of will exhausted my faculties of brain and volition.

'The ordeal was over; light had triumphed over darkness as day had risen on night. I knew the priest's influence had been overcome, his spell cast off, without the evidence of the chess-board; I saw him fall backwards on the ground, every muscle of his body twisted in horrible contortion, as though some invisible power of the air were wreaking its vengeance on his ghastly, spasm-shaken form. The gruesome sight ended quickly, the violence of the seizure was resistless; the muscles relaxed, the limbs stretched out, and he lay a corpse.

'How I parted from my strange entertainers I can't tell you. I only know that the chief honourably fulfilled his pledge, and that, as I galloped away with a guide for the English camp, over the fair, green earth, the woods and fields dancing to the breeze in the sunlight, the bright clouds carrying my thoughts to the depths of the blue expanse they sailed in, I experienced a new sensation of keen, ecstatic enjoyment of life for its own sake. All nature seemed to have a fuller, better meaning to me than ever before, to be the physical expression of boundless power and happiness moving with all-inclusive purpose towards some eternal end, and I myself was filled with a thrilling vitality in the consciousness of being a part of the joyous whole.'

The Colonel made a long pause, and then, with a reluctant sigh, as he dismissed the wide expanse of glorious landscape which lay stretched out before his mind's eye, to return to the commonplace of his immediate surroundings, he picked up the paperweight from the board, and replacing it on the writing-table, concluded:

'Later in the day, and after my return to the English camp, I found this little fellow in a pocket of my coat. Whether I had put it there myself or how it got there I don't know, and to what extent the incidents of the night were coloured by my own excited imagination is a chess problem, I must leave to your own solution.'

THE TERROR BY NIGHT

O

Lewis Lister

Lewis Lister, like Raymund Allen, is one of the annoying mystery men who turn up increasingly as you delve further into the forgotten regions of this genre.

I can find out even less about Lister than Allen. He is not listed anywhere (excuse the pun) nor did he appear to have published any books of his own. What we have is this story.

It first appeared in the Novel Magazine in July 1915 and was later reprinted in UNCANNY STORIES (1916), an anthology of tales gathered from that magazine and issued by Pearson. The anthology and a sequel two years later were reissued by Pearson in the 1920s as one volume, GHOST STORIES AND OTHER QUEER TALES.

The anonymous editor of that book remarked that 'the study of ghosts will always fascinate even if it fails to convince. Few of us, in spite of an avowed scepticism, would willingly spend the night in a haunted room or a moonlit graveyard. While we doubt we dare not experiment'.

Lister's hero doesn't even doubt; he has not the faintest idea of what he's doing when he disposes of his fish and we can enjoy the consequences.

LEWIS LISTER

O

The Terror by Night

MAYNARD disencumbered himself from his fishing-creel, stabbed the butt of his rod into the turf, and settled down in the heather to fill a pipe. All round him stretched the undulating moor, purple in the late summer sunlight. To the southward, low down, a faint haze told where the sea lay. The stream at his feet sang its queer, crooning moor-song as it rambled onward, chuckling to meet a bed of pebbles somewhere out of sight, whispering mysteriously to the rushes that fringed its banks of peat, dèepening to a sudden contralto as it poured over granite boulders into a scum-flecked pool below.

For a long time the man sat smoking. Occasionally he turned his head to watch with keen eyes the fretful movements of a fly hovering above the water. Then a sudden dimple in the smooth surface of the stream arrested his attention. A few concentric ripples widened, travelled towards him, and were absorbed in the current. His lips curved into a little smile and he reached for his rod. In the clear water he could see the origin of the ripples; a small trout, unconscious of his presence, was waiting in its hover for the next titbit to float downstream. Presently it rose again.

'The odds are ten to one in your favour,' said the man. 'Let's see!'

He dropped on one knee and the cast leapt out in feathery coils. Once, twice it swished ; the third time it alighted like thistledown on the surface. There was a tiny splash, a laugh, and the little greenheart rod flicked a trout high over his head. It was the merest baby—half an ounce, perhaps—and it fell from the hook into the herbage some yards from the stream.

'Little ass!' said Maynard. 'That was meant for your big brother.'

He recovered his cast and began to look for his victim. Without avail he searched the heather, and as the fateful seconds sped, at last laid down his rod and dropped on hands and knees to probe among the grass-stems.

For a while he hunted in vain, then the sunlight showed a golden sheen among some stones. Maynard gave a grunt of relief, but as his hand closed round it a tiny flutter passed through the fingerling ; it gave a final gasp and was still. Knitting his brows in almost comical vexation, he hastened to restore it to the stream, holding it by the tail and striving to impart a life-like wriggle to its limpness.

'Buck up, old thing!' he murmured encouragingly. 'Oh, buck up! You're all right, really you are!'

But the 'old thing' was all wrong. In fact, it was dead.

Standing in the wet shingle, Maynard regarded the speckled atom as it lay in the palm of his hand.

'A matter of seconds, my son. One instant in all eternity would have made just the difference between life and death to you. And the high gods denied it you!'

On the opposite side of the stream, set back about thirty paces from the brink, stood a granite boulder. It was as high as a man's chest, roughly cubical in shape; but the weather and clinging moss had rounded its edges, and in places segments had crumbled away, giving foothold to clumps of fern and starry moor-flowers. On three sides the surrounding ground rose steeply, forming an irregular horseshoe mound that opened to the west. Perhaps it was the queer amphitheatrical effect of this setting that connected up some whimsical train of thought in Maynard's brain.

'It would seem as if the gods had claimed you,' he mused, still holding the corpse. 'You shall be a sacrifice—a burnt sacrifice to the God of Waste Places.'

He laughed at the conceit, half ashamed of his own childishness, and crossing the stream by some boulders, he brushed away the earth and weed from the top of the great stone. Then he retraced his steps and gathered a handful of bleached twigs that the winter floods had left stranded along the margin of the stream. These he arranged methodically on the cleared space; on the top of the tiny pyre he placed the troutlet.

'There!' he said, and smiling gravely struck a match. A faint column of smoke curled up into the still air, and as he spoke the lower rim of the setting sun met the edge of the moor. The evening seemed suddenly to become incredibly still, even the voice of the stream ceasing to be a sound distinct. A wagtail bobbing in the shallows fled into the waste. Overhead the smoke trembled upwards, a faint stain against a cloudless sky. The stillness seemed almost acute. It was as if the moor were waiting, and holding its breath while it waited. Then the twigs upon his altar crackled, and the pale flames blazed up. The man stepped back with artistic appreciation of the effect.

'To be really impressive, there ought to be more smoke,' he continued.

Round the base of the stone were clumps of small flowers. They were crimson in colour and had thick, fleshy leaves. Hastily, he snatched a handful and piled it on the fire. The smoke darkened and rose in a thick column; there was a curious pungency in the air.

Far off the church-bell in some unseen hamlet struck the hour. The distant sound, coming from the world of men and everyday affairs, seemed to break the spell. An ousel fluttered across the stream and dabbled in a puddle among some stones. Rabbits began to show themselves and frisk with lengthened shadows in the clear spaces. Maynard looked at his watch, half mindful of a train to be caught somewhere miles away, and then, held by the peace of running water, stretched himself against the sloping ground.

The glowing world seemed peopled by tiny folk, living out their timid, inscrutable lives around him. A water-rat, passing bright-eyed upon his lawful occasion, paused on the border of the stream to consider the stranger, and was lost to view. A stagnant pool among some reeds caught the reflection of the sunset and changed on the instant into raw gold.

Maynard plucked a grass-stem and chewed it reflectively, staring out across the purple moor and lazily watching the western sky turn from glory to glory. Over his head the smoke of the sacrifice still curled and eddied upwards. Then a sudden sound sent him on to one elbow—the thud of an approaching horse's hoofs.

'Moor ponies!' he muttered, and, rising, stood expectant beside his smoking altar.

Then he heard the sudden jingle of a bit, and presently a horse and rider climbed into view against the pure sky. A young girl, breeched, booted and spurred like a boy, drew rein, and sat looking down into the hollow.

For a moment neither spoke; then Maynard acknowledged her presence by raising his tweed hat. She gave a little nod.

'I thought it was somebody swaling—burning the heather.' She considered the embers on the stone, and then her grey eyes travelled back to the spare, tweed-clad figure beside it.

He smiled in his slow way—a rather attractive smile.

'No. I've just concluded some pagan rites in connection with a small trout!' He nodded gravely at the stone. 'That was a burnt sacrifice.' With whimsical seriousness he told her of the trout's demise and high destiny.

For a moment she looked doubtful; but the inflection

of breeding in his voice, the wholesome, lean face and humorous eyes, reassured her. A smile hovered about the corners of her mouth.

'Oh, is that it? I wondered ... '

She gathered the reins and turned her horse's head.

'Forgive me if I dragged you out of your way,' said Maynard, never swift to conventionality, but touched by the tired shadows in her eyes. The faint droop of her mouth, too, betrayed intense fatigue. 'You look fagged. I don't want to be a nuisance or bore you, but I wish you'd let me offer you a sandwich. I've some milk here, too.'

The girl looked round the ragged moor, brooding in the twilight, and half hesitated. Then she forced a wan little smile.

'I am tired, and hungry, too. Have you enough for us both?'

'Lots!' said Maynard. To himself he added, 'And what's more, my child, you'll have a little fainting affair in a few minutes, if you don't have a feed.'

'Come and rest for a minute,' he continued aloud.

He spoke with pleasant, impersonal kindliness, and as he turned to his satchel she slipped out of the saddle and came towards him, leading her horse.

'Drink that,' he said, holding out the cup of his flask. She drank with a wry little face, and coughed. 'I put a little whisky in it,' he explained. 'You needed it.'

She thanked him and sat down with the bridle linked over her arm. The colour crept back into her cheeks. Maynard produced a packet of sandwiches and a pasty.

'I've been mooning about the moor all the afternoon and lost myself twice,' she explained between frank mouthfuls. 'I'm hopelessly late for dinner, and I've still got miles to go.'

'Do you know the way now?' he asked.

'Oh, yes! It won't take me long. My family are sensible, too, and don't fuss.' She looked at him, her long-lashed eyes a little serious. 'But you—how are you going to get home? It's getting late to be out on the moor afoot.'

Maynard laughed.

'Oh, I'm all right, thanks!' He sniffed the warm September night. 'I think I shall sleep here, as a matter of fact. I'm a gipsy by instinct—

> "Give to me the life I love,
> Let the lave go by me,
> Give the jolly Heaven above—"'

He broke off, arrested by her unsmiling eyes. She was silent a moment.

'People don't as a rule sleep out—about here.' The words came jerkily, as if she were forcing a natural tone into her voice.

'No?' He was accustomed to being questioned on his unconventional mode of life, and was prepared for the usual expostulations. She looked abruptly towards him.

'Are you superstitious?'

He laughed and shook his head.

'I don't think so. But what has that got to do with it?'

She hesitated, flushing a little.

'There is a legend—people about here say that the moor here is haunted. There is a Thing that hunts people to death!'

He laughed outright, wondering how old she was. Seventeen or eighteen, perhaps. She had said her people 'didn't fuss.' That meant she was left to herself to pick up all these old wives' tales.

'Really! Has anyone been caught?'

She nodded, unsmiling.

'Yes; old George Toms. He was one of Dad's tenants, a big purple-faced man, who drank a lot and never took much exercise. They found him in a ditch with his clothes all torn and covered with mud. He had been run to death; there was no wound on his body, but his heart was broken.' Her thoughts recurred to the stone against which they leant, and his quaint conceit. 'You were rather rash to go offering burnt sacrifices about here, don't you think?' Dad says that stone is the remains of an old Phœnician altar, too.'

She was smiling now, but the seriousness lingered in her eyes.

'And I have probably invoked some terrible heathen deity–Ashtoreth, or Pugm, or Baal! How awful!' he added, with mock gravity.

The girl rose to her feet.

'You are laughing at me. The people about here are superstitious, and I am a Celt, too. I belong here.'

He jumped up with a quick protest.

'No, I'm not laughing at you. Please don't think that! But it's a little hard to believe in active evil when all around is so beautiful.' He helped her to mount and walked to the top of the mound at her stirrup. 'Tell me, is there any charm or incantation, in case–?' His eyes were twinkling, but she shook her fair head soberly.

'They say iron–cold iron–is the only thing it cannot cross. But I must go!' She held out her hand with half-shy friendliness. 'Thank you for your niceness to me.' Her eyes grew suddenly wistful. 'Really, though, I don't think I should stay there if I were you. Please!'

He only laughed, however, and she moved off, shaking her impatient horse into a canter. Maynard stood looking after her till she was swallowed by the dusk and surrounding moor. Then, thoughtfully, he retraced his steps to the hollow.

A cloud lay across the face of the moon when Fear awoke Maynard. He rolled on to one elbow and stared round the hollow, filled with inexplicable dread. He was ordinarily a courageous man, and had no nerves to speak of; yet, as his eyes followed the line of the ridge against the sky, he experienced terror, the elementary, nauseating terror of childhood, when the skin tingles, and the heart beats at a suffocating gallop. It was very dark, but momentarily his eyes grew accustomed to it. He was conscious of a queer, pungent smell, horribly animal and corrupt.

Suddenly the utter silence broke. He heard a rattle of stones, the splash of water about him, realized that it was the brook beneath his feet, and that he, Maynard, was running for his life.

Neither then nor later did Reason assert herself. He ran without question or amazement. His brain—the part where human reasoning holds normal sway—was dominated by the purely primitive instinct of flight. And in that sudden rout of courage and self-respect one conscious thought alone remained. Whatever it was that was even then at his heels, he must not see it. At all costs it must be behind him, and, resisting the sudden terrified impulse to look over his shoulder, he unbuttoned his tweed jacket and disengaged himself from it as he ran. The faint haze that had gathered round the full moon dispersed, and he saw the moor stretching before him, grey and still, glistening with dew.

He was of frugal and temperate habits, a wiry man at the height of his physical powers, with lean flanks and a deep chest.

At Oxford they had said he was built to run for his life. He was running for it now, and he knew it.

The ground sloped upwards after awhile, and he tore up the incline, breathing deep and hard; down into a shallow valley, leaping gorse bushes, crashing through whortle and meadowsweet, stumbling over peat-cuttings and the workings of forgotten tin-mines. An idiotic popular tune raced through his brain. He found himself trying to frame the words, but they broke into incoherent prayers, still to the same grotesque tune.

Then, as he breasted the flank of a boulder-strewn tor, he seemed to hear snuffling breathing behind him, and, redoubling his efforts, stepped into a rabbit hole. He was up and running again in the twinkling of an eye, limping from a twisted ankle as he ran.

He sprinted over the crest of the hill and thought he heard the sound almost abreast of him, away to the right. In the dry bed of a watercourse some stones were

dislodged and fell with a rattle in the stillness of the
night; he bore away to the left. A moment later there was
Something nearly at his left elbow, and he smelt again the
nameless, fœtid reek. He doubled, and the ghastly truth
flashed upon him. The Thing was playing with him! He
was being hunted for sport—the sport of a horror
unthinkable. The sweat ran down into his eyes.

He lost all count of time; his wrist-watch was smashed
on his wrist. He ran through a reeling eternity, sobbing
for breath, stumbling, tripping, fighting a leaden weari-
ness; and ever the same unreasoning terror urged him on.
The moon and ragged skyline swam about him; the blood
drummed deafeningly in his ears, and his eyeballs felt as
if they would burst from their sockets. He had nearly
bitten his swollen tongue in two falling over an unseen
peat-cutting, and blood-flecked foam gathered on his lips.

God, how he ran! But he was no longer among bog and
heather. He was running—shambling now—along a road.
The loping pursuit of the nameless, shapeless Something
sounded like an echo in his head.

He was nearing a village, but saw nothing save a red
mist that swam before him like a fog. The road underfoot
seemed to rise and fall in wavelike undulations. Still he
ran, with sobbing gasps and limbs that swerved under his
weight; at his elbow hung death unnamable, and the fear
of it urged him on while every instinct of his exhausted
body called out to him to fling up his hands and end it.

Out of the mist ahead rose the rough outline of a
building by the roadside; it was the village smithy, half
workshop, half dwelling. The road here skirted a patch of
grass, and the moonlight, glistening on the dew, showed
the dark circular scars of the turf where, for a generation,
the smith's peat fires had heated the great iron hoops that
tyred the wheels of the wains. One of these was even then
lying on the ground with the turves placed in readiness
for firing in the morning, and in the throbbing darkness
of Maynard's consciousness a voice seemed to speak
faintly—the voice of a girl:

'*There's a Thing that hunts people to death. But iron—cold iron—it cannot cross.*'

The sweat of death was already on his brow as he reeled sideways, plunging blindly across the uneven tufts of grass. His feet caught in some obstruction and he pitched forward into the sanctuary of the huge iron tyre—a spasm of cramp twisting his limbs up under him.

As he fell a great blackness rose around him, and with it the bewildered clamour of awakened dogs.

Dr Stanmore came down the flagged path from the smith's cottage, pulling on his gloves. A big car was passing slowly up the village street, and as it came abreast the smithy the doctor raised his hat.

The car stopped, and the driver, a fair-haired girl, leant sideways from her seat.

'Good morning, Dr Stanmore! What's the matter here? Nothing wrong with any of Matthew's children, is there?'

The doctor shook his head gravely.

'No, Lady Dorothy; they're all at school. This is no one belonging to the family—a stranger who was taken mysteriously ill last night just outside the forge, and they brought him in. It's a most queer case, and very difficult to diagnose—that is to say, to give a diagnosis in keeping with one's professional—er—conscience.'

The girl switched off the engine, and took her hand from the brake-lever. Something in the doctor's manner arrested her interest.

'What is the matter with him?' she queried. 'What diagnosis have you made, professional or otherwise?'

'Shock, Lady Dorothy; severe exhaustion and shock, heart strained, superficial lesions, bruises, scratches, and so forth. Mentally he is in a great state of excitement and terror, lapsing into delirium at times—that is really the most serious feature. In fact, unless I can calm him I am afraid we may have some brain trouble on top of the other thing. It's most mysterious!'

The girl nodded gravely, holding her underlip between her white teeth.

'What does he look like—in appearance, I mean? Is he young?'

The shadow of a smile crossed the doctor's eyes.

'Yes, Lady Dorothy—quite young, and very good-looking. He is a man of remarkable athletic build. He is calmer now, and I have left Matthew's wife with him while I slip out to see a couple of other patients.'

Lady Dorothy rose from her seat and stepped down out of the car.

'I think I know your patient,' she said. 'In fact, I had taken the car to look for him, to ask him to lunch with us. Do you think I might see him for a minute? If it is the person I think it is I may be able to help you diagnose his illness.'

Together they walked up the path and entered the cottage. The doctor led the way upstairs and opened a door. A woman sitting by the bed rose and dropped a curtsey.

Lady Dorothy smiled a greeting to her and crossed over to the bed. There, his face grey and drawn with exhaustion, with shadows round his closed eyes, lay Maynard; one hand lying on the counterpane opened and closed convulsively, his lips moved. The physician eyed the girl interrogatively.

'Do you know him?' he asked.

She nodded, and put her firm, cool hand over the twitching fingers.

'Yes,' she said. 'And I warned him. Tell me, is he very ill?'

'He requires rest, careful nursing, absolute quiet—'

'All that he can have at the Manor,' said the girl softly. She met the doctor's eyes and looked away, a faint colour tinging her cheeks. 'Will you go and telephone to father? I will take him back in the car now if he is well enough to be moved.'

'Yes, he is well enough to be moved,' said the doctor. 'It

is very kind of you, Lady Dorothy, and I will go and telephone at once. Will you stay with him for a little while?'

He left the room, and they heard his feet go down the narrow stairs. The cottage door opened and closed.

The two women, the old and the young, peasant and peer's daughter, looked at each other, and there was in their glance that complete understanding which can only exist between women.

'Do 'ee mind old Jarge Toms, my lady?'

Lady Dorothy nodded.

'I know, I know! And I warned him! They won't believe, these men! They think because they are so big and strong that there is nothing that can hurt them.'

''Twas th' iron that saved un, my lady. 'Twas inside one of John's new tyres as was lyin' on the ground that us found un. Dogs barkin' wakened us up. But it'd ha' had un else—' A sound downstairs sent her flying to the door. ''Tis the kettle, my lady. John's dinner spilin', an' I forgettin'.'

She hurried out of the room and closed the door.

The sound of their voices seemed to have roused the occupant of the bed. His eyelids fluttered and opened; his eyes rested full on the girl's face. For a moment there was no consciousness in their gaze; then a whimsical ghost of a smile crept about his mouth.

'Go on,' he said in a weak voice. 'Say it!'

'Say what?' asked Lady Dorothy. She was suddenly aware that her hand was still on his, but the twitching fingers had closed about hers in a calm, firm grasp.

'Say "I told you so!"'

She shook her head with a little smile.

'I told you that cold iron—'

'Cold iron saved me.' He told her of the iron hoop on the ground outside the forge. 'You saved me last night.'

She disengaged her hand gently.

'I saved you last night—since you say so. But in future—'

Someone was coming up the stairs. Maynard met her eyes with a long look.

'I have no fear,' he said. 'I have found something better than cold iron.'

The door opened and the doctor came in. He glanced at Maynard's face and touched his pulse.

'The case is yours, Lady Dorothy!' he said with a little bow.

THE DARK SHADOW

O

Wirt Gerrare

For reasons now obscure, the historian William Wellington Greener (1834–1921) adopted the odd pen-name Wirt Gerrare for the bulk of his book output. As well as being an expert on small arms and shooting, Greener wrote a text book on the Russian empire through the ages and a history of Moscow. He also wrote a couple of adventure stories, one set in the future, THE WARSTOCK (1898).

He is now almost forgotten, apart from one book, the ghost story volume PHANTASMS (1895). This was a very odd volume indeed, published by the Roxburghe Press, a small London firm, and given an advertising campaign that included announcing that the book would not be available after 31 March 1895. It is not recorded if this got the customers rushing in the right direction or not, alas.

PHANTASMS was the collected cases of a psychic detective named Vesey, who, in keeping with the book's odd background, did not appear in many of the stories, restricting himself to comments before and after. In some cases, like this one, he didn't even manage that. Vesey was of the opinion there were two types of phantom: the natural phantom—'those of persons whose earthly life is cut short before naturally developed'; and the unnatural phantom—'those of persons who, during earth life, have been able to attract to themselves some of the world-force, or energy, without intelligence'.

Vesey left it to the reader to figure out which kind is the phantom in 'The Dark Shadow'. It was certainly not a friendly one. And note what a marvellously doom-laden atmosphere Mr Gerrare creates, right from the very first page.

It would be interesting to find out if Greener ever read Edith Nesbit's famous ghost story 'The Shadow', first published not long before this. Readers may notice an intriguing similarity.

WIRT GERRARE

O

The Dark Shadow

IN November, 1888, I was ordered to relieve Nurse Rose at
Bracknal House, Ebery, where she had been her full term
of six weeks. It was a hopeless case, and I had of late had
so many that I felt disheartened, and was so dismayed at
the cheerless aspect of the deserted, straggling village,
and more particularly of the lonely house on its outskirts,
that I was inclined to sacrifice my career and return
forthwith to Kyrwick with Nurse Rose: many times since I
have wished that I had done so. Nurse Rose was not long
in getting away; as a farmer drove her to the station. I
watched the spring-cart as long as it was in sight, then
shut the heavy iron gate in the old high wall, and burst
out crying. I walked slowly up the weedy path through
the neglected and desolate garden, with its dark gloomy
evergreens and leafless old trees. It was already becoming
dark, and I saw, or thought I saw, something like a human
figure, dimly discernible, crouching behind some overgrown and gnarled espaliers at the far end of the garden. I
hastened to the front door, which I had left ajar; but it
closed with a bang before I reached it, and no sooner had
the echo it produced died out than I heard an ominous
chuckle; it seemed close at my side. There was nothing

for it but to make my way round by the espaliers to the other door, and this I did with face averted and as fast as my legs could take me. The little village girl, our sole establishment, was astonished to see me out of breath and sobbing in her kitchen; my manner frightened her, and she never got over her aversion, which was unfortunate, for she and her mother who came once or twice to char, were the only people to speak to.

My unfortunate patient, however, required constant care. Poor woman, I hardly knew how to take her at first; she was so importunate, so querulous, so insistent upon constant and immediate attention, that I thought she would weary me to death; but I found that it was because she was afraid to be alone, and not that she had determined to have the full value of her money in service, as it is the manner of some coarse natures to exact. For fifty years she had lived alone and uncared for in that dreary village, unloving and unloved; there appeared to be no relative to solace her age, or comfort her dying moments with sympathy. To the doctor also she was almost a stranger, and although she suffered from a wondrous number of diseases, not one had the merit of being uncommon or interesting. Chronic bronchitis, with dropsy, a sphacelitic limb and senile atrophy, are merely troublesome and hopeless.

It was indeed a dreadful time. The close, stuffy sick-room with bronchitis-kettle always steaming, and the air reeking of iodoform, nauseous compounds, and the ever-prevailing odour of death; the huge four-post bedstead and its heavy curtains; the heavy, well-polished press; the equally substantial and inelegant chest-upon-chest; the dirty and foxed engravings in their worm-eaten frames; the badly-polished bare floor and rush-bottomed, cruelly angular, and impossible chairs; these and other reminders of that age when people regarded hardship, torture, and agony as daily necessaries, all added to the prevailing gloom—a gloom which was not enlivened by such glimpses of day as one obtained through the small

latticed window, o'ershadowed by the huge arms of an
elm from which the vigour of youth had long since
departed.

Then the doctor, a grumpy, dried up, ill-at-ease old
bachelor, whom nothing could please, barely noticed
me—I suppose I have Nurse Rose to thank for *that*—and
had nothing to say to his patient. Then the mild-faced,
soulless curate, who was a sort of hereditary incumbent,
nephew to a vicar who invariably wintered in the South
and passed the summer in Scotland. The charwoman,
Kate's mother, a grasping, cruel, bargain-driving peasant
woman, and a young, very boorish, taciturn farmer, who
drove me back to the station at Soltun-in-the-Marsh, were
the only other persons to whom I spoke except the village
lawyer, Mr Shum. He came but once, ostensibly to see Mrs
Bailey, and assure me that the nursing-fee would be paid;
really I think to see *me*; for he asked me to visit him at
Frog Hall—what a name for a house!—on Sunday afternoon and try his Madeira. A would-be waggish and not at
all nice man, Mr Shum. I was glad when his visit ended.

Then out of doors dull November; dead leaves strewn
thickly over dank grass, and muddy roads, rotten sticks
which cracked, and bursting acorns which crunched
beneath one's feet; a sleepy village, with dirty cottages,
dilapidated church, and a barn for a school; pools of
water in fields and roads, and ponds hidden by dead
rushes; drizzle, fog, the churchyard smell of Nature *in
extremis*; no paint, no life, no colour, no solidity
anywhere visible; rather decrepit walls, worn-out thatch,
cracking boughs, huge, waving black poplars—their
sooty trunks at every angle but a right one—moist leaves
and skeletons of leaves; old withered hags; children of
stunted growth; dejected curs too ill to yelp; heavy-
limbed, leaden-eyed, listless men; lazy pigs rooting for
offal. Such are my recollections of Ebery.

All through, the house was cheerless. In the damp,
unused hall an old mildewed hunting-whip hung against
the wall over the head of a mangy fox, which, cut off close

behind the ears, and with only one glass eye, grinned like
a death's head at a moth-eaten jay perched in a broken
case over the door. The rooms were even more gloomy:
threadbare carpets, the furniture rickety and angular and
scant; the curtains thin, colourless, and patched; the
linen blinds of Isabella hue and full of holes, and the
ceiling cracked and dirty, and ornamented with long-
deserted cobwebs; and peering into the gloom of the
corners one noticed tiny heaps of wood dust and the shri-
velled-up corpses of insects long since dead. There was no
sign of life, neither cat, nor dog, neither mouse nor fly; a
stray reptile which had wandered from the congenial
dampness of the moss-covered yard had yielded its low
life, and lay mummified on the flagged floor at the edge
of a mat too rotten to raise.

On the second day Kate, our tiny, juvenile maid-of-all-
work, told me that on the third floor, in the room farthest
from that in which my patient lay, a man lived. 'The
woman's son,' she said, 'a poor creature, but evil disposed;
at enmity with his dying mother, and barely able to keep
life in his own body.' Kate attended to him, but he mostly
foraged for himself when she was absent from the
kitchen, for he possessed the cunning common to those
whose intellect has only in part developed.

For more than a fortnight my life there was simply
dull. There was no change in the condition of the patient;
she was not only resigned to death, but anxious for a
termination to her suffering. The little girl attended to us
as she was able, but was an unconscionable time on her
errands. The doctor came in and hummed and hahed; the
curate called thrice, the postman called once—with a note
for me from the matron—and time dragged on, my odd
hours being spent in reading aloud Paley's *Evidences*, or
Jeremy Taylor's *Holy Dying*, to my listless patient.

The monotony was becoming dreadful; it wanted but a
month to Christmas, and it seemed possible that I should
have to while it away amidst the infestivity of Ebery.

In the middle drawer of the chest-upon-chest was a

little store of money upon which we drew for our daily supplies. As I saw it dwindle to very small proportions, I fear I longed for it to become exhausted; only in order to see where the next supply, if any, would come from; everything was so insulse. My patient, I thought, took very little interest in it, until one day she accidentally lisped something which made me more careful of her trifling hoard; she was not a lovable object, barely likable, but really I felt more for her than for many who were far more interesting.

On the last Friday in November I noticed a change; there could be no doubt she was sinking fast. This the doctor corroborated; she had repeatedly asked him when the end would come. He was now able to tell her. 'At four o'clock to-day,' he said shortly. He bade her a more kindly farewell than I thought him capable of, gave me a few final instructions, bade me goodbye, and went.

My patient seemed much relieved; she would not allow me to send for the curate. 'Not again, nurse, not again—you will stay with me—tell no one,' she whispered. Of course I reassured her, and I told no one.

'When's her goin' to die?' asked Kate bluntly, the next time I entered the kitchen.

I answered as kindly as I could.

''Cos I ain't a goin' to stay here while her's dyin'. Mother says I needn't.'

'What has your mother to do with it?'

'D'yer think I'd be here now if't warn't fur mother? Her'd thrape me if I went whum, but her sed I needn't stay while her's dyin'.'

'Are you afraid?'

'Afeared! A course I'm afeared, so you'll be by-and-bye. I suppose you dursen't leave?'

'I should not think of leaving, nor must you,' I replied, and I escaped quickly from the kitchen, for there was something in the girl's manner which alarmed me.

Slowly the hours went by, the silence broken only by the often reiterated 'How long?' or 'What time is it now?'

of my patient, in whose condition there was no change. As
it grew dusk I put the clock on half an hour and lit my
small lamp. Four o'clock came; five o'clock; my patient
grew restless. Six; seven; she accused me of deceiving her.
And so on until midnight, when she fell into a troubled
sleep. In the morning she seemed stronger, but depressed
in spirits, and I could not rouse her. On Saturdays Kate's
mother went to char at Frog Hall. No one came to
Bracknal House. Hour after hour crawled slowly by. My
patient besought me to end her suffering; if only I would
give her a treble dose of medicine, or snatch from under
her the pillows on which she was propped; anything
which would snap the slender thread which held her to
this world. These requests were so earnest, so often
repeated, the state of the patient so piteous, that I fear I
became somewhat unnerved. Once only I looked out of
the window; and saw an old man with his spade over his
shoulder limping towards the churchyard. I turned
quickly away, and my patient recommenced. She
upbraided me with want of heart; reproached me for my
attentions to her, and cried at my refusal to do her wish.
'If I only had more money to give, you would do it, you
know you would,' she gasped exasperatingly, and all I
could do was to sit at the dressing table, with my back
towards her, my head upon my hand, and bear with it. All
through that long Saturday, all through the long, long
dreary night, I had to hear it; often with hands clenched
and grinding teeth, and my heart listening to what I
could not shut my ears to.

At last day broke. My patient was worn, and I half mad;
our solitude was unbearable. I told Kate she would have
to sit with my patient, and I went to church and made my
way through the thick fog which hung over the village,
but cleared to show me a newly dug grave yawning
beneath the dripping yew. Everyone knew that Mrs Bailey
was dead; the doctor had told them so. They appeared,
too, surprised to see me, but after service no one spoke to
me except the doctor. 'Why has not Shum sent up his man

to take you to the station?' he asked. I told him it was probably because his patient was not yet dead. 'She died at four o'clock on Friday afternoon,' he said. 'Confound it, won't you understand?'

'I am afraid I do not.'

The doctor fumed. 'The thing is *done*,' he said. 'I made out the certificate yesterday, Fluck has it now, he'll be round for the body to-morrow. You understand, don't you?'

'I think it will be best for you to come with me now,' I answered.

'I? Oh, no, not again. I can do nothing. Good morning.'

I went back alone, Kate seemed stupefied with terror at having been left so long; in an hour or so things resumed their usual course.

As soon as possible I shut out the heavy day, but I could not make the room cheery; even my lamp refused to burn, and had to be replaced with snuffy candles. As I turned over the words of the doctor, and looked at the patient, I thought it strange that the woman was not dead. 'Why could she not die?'

Perhaps I spoke the question; at any rate the patient understood; she groaned. 'I will tell you, nurse, I will tell you. I shall not die to-day unless *you*—ah, you won't! but listen to me.'

I drew a chair near, and bent over to hear her story, told in short gasps: painfully, disconnectedly, but understandable.

More than fifty years ago, she said, she had loved the man who owned the house in which we were. During his absence she was faithless, or rather was coerced into marrying Mr Bailey, a man of fierce temper and violent disposition, and who was both cruel and resentful. When her lover returned he committed suicide, 'here in this room,' she gasped—'with a saddle-pistol—at dead of night, on the last day of November, fifty years ago.'

'And your husband?'

'He swore that I had been false, and left me, but vowed

that–in fifty years–dead or alive–he would return and be avenged on me. "When your dead lover will no longer be able to protect you," as he said.'

'But your husband is dead?'

'Yes, yes, dead.'

'And your son?'

'That *thing*! He hates me–hates me–more than his father did.'

'But you have not injured him?'

'No, but–I could not love–him–and he has–cursed me.'

'What can you fear? None can hurt you.'

'What can you know, child? For fifty years I have never been outside but ill befell me, it is only here–in the house where *he* died–that there is peace–for I am forgiven by *him*; I must join *him* before the other returns.'

'No, no,' I replied quickly, 'you will soon be at peace; where nought can trouble you more.'

'No. It is not true.'

The death-bed is no place for argument. My patient was terribly agitated, so anxious did she appear to hear my answer, that her look frightened me. I took her hard, wrinkled hand in mine, and kneeling prayed for her earnestly, and as I prayed I heard short mocking laughs, and at each she clutched at my hand convulsively as if in terror. I dared not look up, my tongue was stilled, I shook with fright. Then all was silent except the heavy short breathing of the patient, her broken sobs and bronchial hiss. In time I gained sufficient courage to look up. Her terror-stricken gaze filled me with despair; I would have prayed but could not.

My patient was the first to speak.

'You are afraid.'

'No, no,' I answered.

'Then pray.'

I could not. I passed my hand over my face, tried to persuade myself that I was only weak, nervous from long watching, that really I was not afraid; but I got up from

the bedside, and said that I would call Kate to serve tea—
that I felt faint. The look of anguish on my patient's face
as I made these poor excuses was heart-rending, and
filled me with shame. Nevertheless, and notwithstanding
her piteous appeal to remain with her, I went along the
corridor to the head of the stairs, and called Kate. There
was no answer. I went down to the kitchen; it was empty,
and the fire had burned out. I called again and again, but
obtained no reply. Loneliness brought back the feeling of
fright, and I turned upstairs eager for companionship—
even that of my dying patient.

I paused at the top of the stairs, determining to regain
courage. Everything was explicable. Kate had run away
home. There was nothing to fear; no harm could come to
me. I ought to be ashamed of my cowardice. I was too
familiar with death for that to frighten me, and these and
kindred thoughts resolved me to be brave; but my newly
recovered courage quickly left me, when, as I neared the
bedroom door, I heard sounds which my patient,
bedridden as she was, could not possibly have made.
Footsteps were audible, the drawing out of drawers, angry
exclamations, splutterings, mingled with the groans of my
patient. I remember peering into the room and seeing the
strange form of a man, at the head of the bed, bending
over it. I drew hastily back. Then came a faint cry. 'Nurse!
Nurse!' I fear that I staggered rather than walked into the
room. Something told me that it was only the son; and
with any living creature I felt able to deal.

This strange creature was gesticulating violently a few
inches from his mother's face, muttering incoherently,
occasionally spluttering words which were half intelli-
gible, 'Papersh—crrsse.'

'What is it you want?' I asked firmly. He turned his
face towards me, a small, pinched-up hairless face, with
eyes deep sunken, and lips drawn tightly across broken
teeth. He was wretchedly clothed, and his ill-shapen form
thin to attenuation; his limbs were long, but his body
bowed—a tabid, fleshless, cretinous creature who might

have been seventeen or seventy for all one could tell, but evidently weak and unable to control his movements.

He hissed a reply, the import of which I did not understand.

'You must go, if you please,' I said. 'I have to attend to my patient.'

He understood, for he expostulated energetically.

'At once, please,' I said, holding the door.

I never saw a face so full of evil, perfectly demoniacal in its malignance. 'Crsse womssh,' he hissed; but he did not go.

Unfortunately I could not hear my patient, nor could I approach closer whilst he was there. I therefore grasped him firmly by the arm, thinking to remove him; but as my fingers closed I felt that he was as strong and unyielding as one in a cataleptic fit, and instinctively my fingers relaxed until there was but the slightest pressure. 'You must go now, please,' I said. 'Come again if you wish—in an hour.'

Somewhat to my surprise he yielded, reluctantly it is true, and with jerky movements made his way to the door, hissing and muttering and gesticulating wildly with his hands. No sooner had he passed the threshold than I sprang to the door, shut it upon him, and locked it.

He turned in a terrific fury, hammered at the door, and made the house echo with weird, horrible noises. I appreciated the mistake I had made, and opened the door, but blocked the entrance by confronting him.

'Have you forgotten anything?' I asked as calmly as I could.

A grimace was his only reply.

'Come when you will after eight o'clock,' I continued, 'but come quietly; you must go now.' I tendered him a candle, pretending it was that he had forgotten. He motioned that he did not need it, and turned away. 'The door will be unlocked after eight, but do not trouble us without cause,' I called after him.

The poor patient was decidedly worse. I comforted her

as well as circumstances permitted. I must confess that I was elated at the success of my encounter with the intruder. After I had made and taken tea, and thought the matter over, I concluded that my senses had been deceived, and that I had frightened myself needlessly; in short, I recovered my nerve, and awaited composedly to carry out whatever wishes my patient might express. She requested that I should read to her, and this I did. It seemed to distract her attention from herself, but not for long; then she made me promise that I would not leave her again that night for anything; to this I agreed. I sat close to the bed and kept her hand in mine, only loosing it when I needed both to minister to her wants. I remember well looking into her face, and trying to trace in the coarse features the beauty which half a century before had attracted two men, and years before that had doubtless been the happy, smiling face of a child. I was not very successful, for surely never were human lineaments so brutalised by selfishness and fear; but I felt an intimacy as of years. What little there was in her life I *knew*, and I remember that I felt puzzled then, as I am puzzled now, as to what useful purpose such an existence as hers had been could serve.

She regarded me as her sole hope, gazed at me with a look of longing that was akin to love, and listened to every trifling thing I said, as though her salvation depended upon understanding it. No one, I am sure, had extended sympathy to her, and it was *that* she lacked. My talk was of such trifling matters as are distinctly human, and she became so far interested as to forget her immediate state. I was pleased that I had calmed her terrors, and she appeared to be so grateful for the relation of the few trifling private occurrences which concerned only myself, that I ventured to tell her of a weightier matter, one which I approached with some diffidence, and blushing like a schoolgirl; a matter I would have confided to a loving mother, perhaps to one other; but its relation to this poor dying woman was as pleasing to her as it was

surprising to me. How I came to say so much I do not
know; perhaps because I knew she was dying, and would
keep my poor little secret. Of course I was crying when
my story finished, and the tears were rolling down her fat,
furrowed cheeks too. It was unutterably silly, but I kissed
her; then dried my eyes, and stood at the foot of the bed
looking at her confusedly.

'God bless you, dear,' she whispered, and turned her
face away. Perhaps I had touched a chord which the
orthodox and usual conversation would have missed.

Then I sat down at the table and wrote for a short time
in my journal; read again to my patient, but she seemed
to wish to chat. She complimented me upon the prettiness
of our uniform, expressed herself as satisfied with the
white cuffs and long streamers to the cap. I wished to
humour her, and crossed over and snuffed the candle,
that she could see better, and she told me that I was really
handsome and carried my years like a girl of seventeen. I
just bowed my head and replaced the snuffers, and when
I looked up I saw a man's face staring at me *out* of the
highly polished wood of the wardrobe. I remember that
I drew a very quick breath, and the face, which had
anything but a pleasing expression upon it, slowly died
away from view as I looked.

I did not cry out; I do not think that I betrayed my fear
by any tremor. I could not trust myself to speak, nor
should I have spoken of what I had seen; but the very
silence seemed to convey a knowledge of all to the dying
woman.

'What time?' she murmured.

'A quarter past twelve,' I replied.

'No. You are fast.'

I remembered then that I had put on my clock fully
thirty minutes the day upon which she was to have died.

'Perhaps,' I replied.

'Yes, yes. Do not leave me—you do not know.' Then
came some terrible gasps, and she was shaken with
convulsive tremors.

I made a supreme effort to be calm; I felt that I must see something beyond that terrible room. I went to the window, and pulling aside the blind looked out into the night. I was surprised to see that the fog had lifted, the moon shone brightly, the whole garden from the house to the gate was clearly visible. There was of course no one stirring; the silence was only broken by the dripping of the fog-damp from the boughs. As I gazed at the gate I distinctly heard it clang as though pushed to in haste, but it had not stirred. There was something coming along the path, for I heard the footsteps as of a person stealing, as on tip-toe, towards the house; it was clearer than day, but I could see no one—no thing.

'Nurse—nurse—it comes!'

I went to the bed, and took the woman's hand in mine; she clung to it with all the strength of her feeble grasp.

'I will not leave you,' I stammered.

Again that face appeared in the wardrobe—*was* there when I looked, and faded away before my gaze.

The head of the bedstead was towards the door. I stood with my back to the door, facing the fireplace; on my left, the window; on the right, the bed; and beyond it, at the foot, the table, with the candle burning brightly upon it. I am thus particular because the occurrences of that night can be set down only as I remember then, not perhaps in the order of their exact sequence.

First (of that I am sure) the son came into the room, staggering, staring blindly, and ever blinking his strange deeply-sunk eyes. He groped his way to the wardrobe, opened it, and passed his hands along the upper shelves; brought from there a small bundle of yellow papers, waved them above his head in an unmeaning fashion, and with them tottered from the room. His young-old wizened face, his terribly emaciated frame, and his expression of wicked cunning, I can see now as plainly as though he stood before me as he did then, and as I write I hear the peculiar chuckle, the only sound he made then.

His footsteps died away in the corridor. All around, in

the house and out of it, everything was still—still as the dreadful calm before the hurricane. The silence was broken by two sharp blows, as though struck with a withy switch on the windowpane. There was a firmer grip of my hand, a muttered cry of 'Help!' and I reeled as I saw glide into the room a shapeless, shadowy pillar of sooty blackness, larger than human size, but with a form no better defined than that of a huge cactus: without marks, or lines, or excrescences.

It passed round to the foot of the bed, my gaze firmly riveted upon it. For a moment it passed between me and the candle, and obscured the light, and I remember noticing that the bronchitis-kettle on the fire ceased to emit its tiny puff of steam; then it again moved to the foot of the bed, and the room instantly and perceptibly darkened, just like the darkening of the stage at a second-rate theatre, when they alter the scene from noonday to dusk. Then this thing extended; as it were a shapeless shadowy arm or limb *was* stretching from one side and closing the door of the wardrobe; then instantly another, like the trunk of an elephant, reached out to the candle, enveloped, and extinguished it; all in very much less time than I can recall the memory. Then, in the glow of the fire and the dim light of the moon shining through the dirty, stained blinds, this sooty shadow extended upwards, bent under the canopy of the bedstead, reached in a straight line from the head to the foot of the bed immediately above the dying woman, then spread out in breadth and descended. There was a bright flash of light, a loud shriek from the corridor, a convulsive tug at my hand; voices, the hurrying of many feet, low groans, ear-piercing yells, sobs, stifled cries—but I had swooned.

When I recovered, the room was still dark, and I was alone. The candle had burned out in the socket; there was a dull, red glow from the lower bars of the grate, and all was still, the silence broken only by the almost inaudible slow ticking of my clock.

I knew that my patient was dead.

There is very little more to tell. The affairs of the dead are no concern of mine, and the little I said to the doctor next day elicited only the fact that Mrs Bailey had occupied the house at a peppercorn rent for fifty years. The lease ended, strange to say, the day of her death; and as she appeared to be very poor it is possible that this may have made her anxious to quit the world when she did.

My stay at the house of the dark shadow almost terminated my career as a nurse. My nerve was shattered, and for a long time I was too ill to undertake any duty. However, twelve months amid the brighter surroundings of a convalescent home have assisted my recovery, although, I am sure, the events will never fade from my memory, nor, I fancy, will their freshness be impaired by new adventures.

THE MYSTERY OF THE FELWYN TUNNEL

O

Mrs L.T. Meade and Robert Eustace

Now for two mystery writers who left behind a real-life mystery all their own. It seems there are two candidates for the role of the pen-name Robert Eustace—it is by no means certain which is the right one.

Elizabeth Thomasina Meade (1844–1914)—who was incorrectly called Mrs Meade, when she should have been named Mrs Toulmin Smith—was born in Ireland, the daughter of a Cork rector.

She became a prolific and well respected writer, both of children's books (over 150!) and detective stories, which she wrote in collaboration with two writers, Clifford Halifax (six books) and Robert Eustace (five books).

Space prevents me setting out the full story here, but I recommend interested readers to consult Trevor Hall's valuable book DOROTHY L. SAYERS: NINE LITERARY STUDIES (1980), where he sets out his argument in a chapter on Eustace and Sayers. He finds two likely candidates for the role of Robert Eustace: Dr Eustace Robert Barton or Eustace Rawlins, both of whom have good credentials. Both wrote under other names than their own.

Hall favours Dr Barton, but whichever one it was, they made a good job of their collaboration with Mrs Meade.

One book which resulted from the Meade/Eustace partnership was A MASTER OF MYSTERIES *(1898), the adventures of a detective called Mr John Bell, clearly modelled—as many were in those days—on Sherlock Holmes.*

Bell investigated haunted houses as his speciality, and called himself a 'professional exposer of ghosts'. Note the word 'exposer'—that was indeed the fate of many of Bell's cases. As he put it, his cases were 'enveloped at first in mystery, and apparently dark with portent, but, nevertheless, when grappled with in the true spirit of science, capable of explanation.'

'The Mystery of the Felwyn Tunnel' was one of John Bell's better cases, here returned to print after an absence of over ninety years. It bears an interesting resemblance to Charles Dickens' famous story 'The Signalman', and I do not think it over-fanciful to see in the line on page 287 starting 'What the ... ' an affectionate nod at the famous author.

MRS L.T. MEADE AND ROBERT EUSTACE

O

The Mystery of the Felwyn Tunnel

I WAS making experiments of some interest in South Kensington, and hoped that I had perfected a small but not unimportant discovery, when, on returning home one evening in late October in the year 1893, I found a visiting card on my table. On it were inscribed the words, 'Mr Geoffrey Bainbridge.' This name was quite unknown to me, so I rang the bell and inquired of my servant who the visitor had been. He described him as a gentleman who wished to see me on most urgent business, and said further that Mr Bainbridge intended to call again later in the evening. It was with both curiosity and vexation that I awaited the return of the stranger. Urgent business with me generally meant a hurried rush to one part of the country or the other. I did not want to leave London just then; and when at half-past nine Mr Geoffrey Bainbridge was ushered into my room, I received him with a certain coldness which he could not fail to perceive. He was a tall, well-dressed, elderly man. He immediately plunged into the object of his visit.

'I hope you do not consider my unexpected presence an intrusion, Mr Bell,' he said. 'But I have heard of you from our mutual friends, the Greys of Uplands. You may remember once doing that family a great service.'

'I remember perfectly well,' I answered more cordially. 'Pray tell me what you want; I shall listen with attention.'

'I believe you are the one man in London who can help me,' he continued. 'I refer to a matter especially relating to your own particular study. I need hardly say that whatever you do will not be unrewarded.'

'That is neither here nor there,' I said; 'but before you go any further, allow me to ask one question. Do you want me to leave London at present?'

He raised his eyebrows in dismay.

'I certainly do,' he answered.

'Very well; pray proceed with your story.'

He looked at me with anxiety.

'In the first place,' he began, 'I must tell you that I am chairman of the Lytton Vale Railway Company in Wales, and that it is on an important matter connected with our line that I have come to consult you. When I explain to you the nature of the mystery, you will not wonder, I think, at my soliciting your aid.'

'I will give you my closest attention,' I answered; and then I added, impelled to say the latter words by a certain expression on his face, 'if I can see my way to assisting you I shall be ready to do so.'

'Pray accept my cordial thanks,' he replied. 'I have come up from my place at Felwyn today on purpose to consult you. It is in that neighbourhood that the affair has occurred. As it is essential that you should be in possession of the facts of the whole matter, I will go over things just as they happened.'

I bent forward and listened attentively.

'This day fortnight,' continued Mr Bainbridge, 'our quiet little village was horrified by the news that the signalman on duty at the mouth of the Felwyn Tunnel had been found dead under the most mysterious circumstances. The tunnel is at the end of a long cutting between Llanlys and Felwyn stations. It is about a mile long, and the signal-box is on the Felwyn side. The place is extremely lonely, being six miles from the village across the mountains. The name of the poor fellow who met his death in this mysterious fashion was David Pritchard. I have known him from a boy, and he was quite one of the steadiest and most trustworthy men on the line. On Tuesday evening he went on duty at six o'clock; on Wednesday morning the day-man who had come to relieve him was surprised not to find him in the box. It was just getting daylight, and the 6.30 local was coming down, so he pulled the signals and let her through. Then he went out, and looking up the line towards the tunnel, saw Pritchard lying beside the line close to the mouth of the tunnel. Roberts, the day-man, ran up to him and found, to his horror, that he was quite dead. At first Roberts naturally supposed that he had been cut down by a train, as there was a wound at the back of his head; but he was not lying on the metals. Roberts ran back to the box and telegraphed through to Felwyn Station. The message was sent on to the village, and at half-past seven o'clock the police inspector came up to my house with the news. He and I, with the local doctor, went off at once to the tunnel. We found the dead man laying beside the metals a few yards away from the mouth of the tunnel, and the doctor immediately gave him a careful examination. There was a depressed fracture at the back of the skull, which must have caused his death; but how he came by it was not so clear. On examining the whole place most carefully, we saw, further, that there were marks on the rocks at the steep side of the embankment as if someone had tried to scramble up them. Why the poor fellow had attempted such a climb, God only knows. In doing so he must have slipped and fallen back on to the line, thus causing the fracture of the skull. In no case could he have gone up more than eight or ten feet, as the banks of the cutting run sheer up, almost perpendicularly, beyond that point for more than a hundred and fifty feet. There are some sharp boulders beside the line, and it was possible that he might have fallen on one of these and so sustained the injury. The affair must have occurred some time between 11.45 p.m. and 6 a.m., as the engine-driver of the express at 11.45 p.m. states that the line was signalled clear, and he also caught sight of Pritchard in his box as he passed.'

'This is deeply interesting,' I said; 'pray proceed.'

Bainbridge looked at me earnestly; he then continued:–

'The whole thing is shrouded in mystery. Why should Pritchard have left his box and gone down to the tunnel? Why, having done so, should he have made a wild attempt to scale the side of the cutting, an impossible feat at any time? Had danger threatened, the ordinary course of things would have been to run up the line towards the signal-box. These points are quite unexplained. Another curious fact is that death appears to have taken place just before the day-man came on duty, as the light at the mouth of the tunnel had been put out, and it was one of the night signalman's duties to do this as soon as daylight appeared; it is possible, therefore, that Pritchard went down to the tunnel for that purpose. Against this theory, however, and an objection that seems to nullify it, is the evidence of Dr Williams, who states that when he examined the body his opinion was that death had taken place some hours before. An inquest was held on the following day, but before it took place there was a new and most important development. I now come to what I consider the crucial point in the whole story.

'For a long time there had been a feud between Pritchard and another man of the name of Wynne, a platelayer on the line. The object of their quarrel was the blacksmith's daughter in the neighbouring village–a remarkably pretty girl and an arrant flirt. Both men were madly in love with her, and she played them off one against the other. The night but one before his death Pritchard and Wynne had met at the village inn, had quarrelled in the bar–Lucy, of course, being the subject of their difference. Wynne was heard to say (he was a man of powerful build and subject to fits of ungovernable rage) that he would have Pritchard's life. Pritchard swore a great oath that he would get Lucy on the following day to promise to marry him. This oath, it appears, he kept, and on his way to the signal-box on Tuesday evening met Wynne, and triumphantly told him that Lucy had promised to be his wife. The men had a hand-to-hand fight on the spot, several people from the village being witnesses of it. They were separated with difficulty, each vowing vengeance on the other. Pritchard went off to his duty at the signal-box and Wynne returned to the village to drown his sorrows at the public-house.

'Very late that same night Wynne was seen by a villager going in the direction of the tunnel. The man stopped him and questioned him. He explained that he had left some of his tools on the line, and was on his way to fetch them. The villager noticed that he looked queer and excited, but not wishing to pick a quarrel thought it best not to question him further. It has been proved that Wynne never returned home that night, but came back at an early hour on the following morning, looking dazed and stupid. He was arrested on suspicion, and at the inquest the verdict was against him.'

'Has he given any explanation of his own movements?' I asked.

'Yes; but nothing that can clear him. As a matter of fact, his tools were nowhere to be seen on the line, nor did he bring them home with him. His own story is that being considerably the worse for drink, he had fallen down in one of the fields and slept there till morning.'

'Things look black against him,' I said.

'They do; but listen, I have something more to add. Here comes a very queer feature in the affair. Lucy Ray, the girl who had caused the feud between Pritchard and Wynne, after hearing the news of Pritchard's death, completely lost her head, and ran frantically about the village declaring that Wynne was the man she really loved, and that she had only accepted Pritchard in a fit of rage with Wynne for not himself bringing matters to the point. The case looks very bad against Wynne, and yesterday the magistrate committed him for trial at the coming assizes. The unhappy Lucy Ray and the young man's parents are in a state bordering on distraction.'

'What is your own opinion with regard to Wynne's guilt?' I asked.

'Before God, Mr Bell, I believe the poor fellow is innocent, but the evidence against him is very strong. One of the favourite theories is that he went down to the tunnel and extinguished the light, knowing that this would bring Pritchard out of his box to see what was the matter, and that he then attacked him, striking the blow which fractured the skull.'

'Has any weapon been found about, with which he could have given such a blow?'

'No; nor has anything of the kind been discovered on Wynne's person; that fact is decidedly in his favour.'

'But what about the marks on the rocks?' I asked.

'It is possible that Wynne may have made them in order to divert suspicion by making people think that Pritchard must have fallen, and so killed himself. The holders of this theory base their belief on the absolute want of cause for Pritchard's trying to scale the rock. The whole thing is the most absolute enigma. Some of the country folk have declared that the tunnel is haunted (and there certainly has been such a rumour current among them for years). That Pritchard saw some apparition, and in wild terror sought to escape from it by climbing the rocks, is another theory, but only the most imaginative hold it.'

'Well, it is a most extraordinary case,' I replied.

'Yes, Mr Bell, and I should like to get your opinion of it. Do you see your way to elucidate the mystery?'

'Not at present; but I shall be happy to investigate the matter to my utmost ability.'

'But you do not wish to leave London at present?'

'That is so; but a matter of such importance cannot be set aside. It appears, from what you say, that Wynne's life hangs more or less on my being able to clear away the mystery?'

'That is indeed the case. There ought not to be a single stone left unturned to get at the truth, for the sake of Wynne. Well, Mr Bell, what do you propose to do?'

'To see the place without delay,' I answered.

'That is right; when can you come?'

'Whenever you please.'

'Will you come down to Felwyn with me tomorrow? I shall leave Paddington by the 7.10, and if you will be my guest I shall be only too pleased to put you up.'

'That arrangement will suit me admirably,' I replied. 'I will meet you by the train you mention, and the affair shall have my best attention.'

'Thank you,' he said, rising. He shook hands with me and took his leave.

The next day I met Bainbridge at Paddington Station, and we were soon flying westward in the luxurious private compartment that had been reserved for him. I could see by his abstracted manner and his long lapses of silence that the mysterious affair at Felwyn Tunnel was occupying all his thoughts.

It was two o'clock in the afternoon when the train slowed down at the little station of Felwyn. The station-master was at the door in an instant to receive us.

'I have some terribly bad news for you, sir,' he said, turning to Bainbridge as we alighted; 'and yet in one sense it is a relief, for it seems to clear Wynne.'

'What do you mean?' cried Bainbridge. 'Bad news? Speak out at once!'

'Well, sir, it is this: there has been another death at Felwyn signal-box. John Davidson, who was on duty last night, was found dead at an early hour this morning in the very same place where we found poor Pritchard.'

'Good God!' cried Bainbridge, starting back, 'what an awful thing! What, in the name of Heaven, does it mean.

Mr Bell? This is too fearful. Thank goodness you have come down with us.'

'It is as black a business as I ever heard of, sir,' echoed the station-master; 'and what we are to do I don't know. Poor Davidson was found dead this morning, and there was neither mark nor sign of what killed him—that is the extraordinary part of it. There's a perfect panic abroad, and not a signalman on the line will take duty to-night. I was quite in despair, and was afraid at one time that the line would have to be closed, but at last it occurred to me to wire to Lytton Vale, and they are sending down an inspector. I expect him by a special every moment. I believe this is he coming now,' added the station-master, looking up the line.

There was the sound of a whistle down the valley, and in a few moments a single engine shot into the station, and an official in uniform stepped on to the platform.

'Good-evening, sir,' he said, touching his cap to Bainbridge; 'I have just been sent down to inquire into this affair at the Felwyn Tunnel, and though it seems more of a matter for a Scotland Yard detective than one of ourselves, there was nothing for it but to come. All the same, Mr Bainbridge, I cannot say that I look forward to spending tonight alone at the place.'

'You wish for the services of a detective, but you shall have some one better,' said Bainbridge, turning towards me. 'This gentleman, Mr John Bell, is the man of all others for our business. I have just brought him down from London for the purpose.'

An expression of relief flitted across the inspector's face.

'I am very glad to see you, sir,' he said to me, 'and I hope you will be able to spend the night with me in the signal-box. I must say I don't much relish the idea of tackling the thing single-handed; but with your help, sir, I think we ought to get to the bottom of it somehow. I am afraid there is not a man on the line who will take duty until we do. So it is most important that the thing should be cleared, and without delay.'

I readily assented to the inspector's proposition, and Bainbridge and I arranged that we should call for him at four o'clock at the village inn and drive him to the tunnel.

We then stepped into the wagonette which was waiting for us, and drove to Bainbridge's house.

Mrs Bainbridge came out to meet us, and was full of the tragedy. Two pretty girls also ran to greet their father, and to glance inquisitively at me. I could see that the entire family was in a state of much excitement.

'Lucy Ray has just left, father,' said the elder of the girls. 'We had much trouble to soothe her; she is in a frantic state.'

'You have heard, Mr Bell, all about this dreadful mystery?' said Mrs Bainbridge as she led me towards the dining-room.

'Yes,' I answered; 'your husband has been good enough to give me every particular.'

'And you have really come here to help us?'

'I hope I may be able to discover the cause,' I answered.

'It certainly seems most extraordinary,' continued Mrs Bainbridge. 'My dear,' she continued, turning to her husband, 'you can easily imagine the state we were all in this morning when the news of the second death was brought to us.'

'For my part,' said Ella Bainbridge, 'I am sure that Felwyn Tunnel is haunted. The villagers have thought so for a long time, and this second death seems to prove it, does it not?' Here she looked anxiously at me.

'I can offer no opinion,' I replied, 'until I have sifted the matter thoroughly.'

'Come, Ella, don't worry Mr Bell,' said her father; 'if he is as hungry as I am, he must want his lunch.'

We then seated ourselves at the table and commenced the meal. Bainbridge, although he professed to be hungry, was in such a state of excitement that he could scarcely eat. Immediately after lunch he left me to the care of his family and went into the village.

'It is just like him,' said Mrs Bainbridge; 'he takes these sort of things to heart dreadfully. He is terribly upset about Lucy Ray, and also about the poor fellow Wynne. It is certainly a fearful tragedy from first to last.'

'Well, at any rate,' I said, 'this fresh death will upset the evidence against Wynne.'

'I hope so, and there is some satisfaction in the fact. Well, Mr Bell, I see you have finished lunch; will you come into the drawing-room?'

I followed her into a pleasant room overlooking the valley of the Lytton.

By and by Bainbridge returned, and soon afterwards the dog-cart came to the door. My host and I mounted, Bainbridge took the reins, and we started off at a brisk pace.

'Matters get worse and worse,' he said the moment we were alone. 'If you don't clear things up to-night, Bell, I say frankly that I cannot imagine what will happen.'

We entered the village, and as we rattled down the ill-paved streets I was greeted with curious glances on all sides. The people were standing about in groups, evidently talking about the tragedy and nothing else. Suddenly as our trap bumped noisily over the paving-stones, a girl darted out of one of the houses and made frantic motions to Bainbridge to stop the horse. He pulled the mare nearly up on her haunches, and the girl came up to the side of the dog-cart.

'You have heard it?' she said, speaking eagerly and in a gasping voice. 'The death which occurred this morning will clear Stephen Wynne, won't it, Mr Bainbridge? It will, you are sure, are you not?'

'It looks like it, Lucy, my poor girl,' he answered. 'But there, the whole thing is so terrible that I scarcely know what to think.'

She was a pretty girl with dark eyes, and under ordinary circumstances must have had the vivacious expression of face and the brilliant complexion which so many of her countrywomen possess. But now her eyes were swollen with weeping and her complexion more or less disfigured by the agony she had gone through. She looked piteously at Bainbridge, her lips trembling. The next moment she burst into tears.

'Come away, Lucy,' said a woman who had followed her out of the cottage; 'Fie—for shame! don't trouble the gentlemen; come back and stay quiet.'

'I can't, mother, I can't' said the unfortunate girl. 'If they hang him, I'll go clean off my head. Oh, Mr Bainbridge, do say that the second death has cleared him!'

'I have every hope that it will do so, Lucy,' said Bainbridge, 'but now don't keep us, there's a good girl; go back into the house. This gentleman has come down from London on purpose to look into the whole matter. I may have good news for you in the morning.'

The girl raised her eyes to my face with a look of intense pleading. 'Oh, I have been cruel and a fool, and I deserve everything,' she gasped; 'but, sir, for the love of Heaven, try to clear him.'

I promised to do my best.

Bainbridge touched up the mare, she bounded forward, and Lucy disappeared into the cottage with her mother.

The next moment we drew up at the inn where the Inspector was waiting, and soon afterwards were bowling along between the high banks of the country lanes to the tunnel. It was a cold, still afternoon; the air was wonderfully keen, for a sharp frost had held the countryside in its grip for the last two days. The sun was just tipping the hills to westward when the trap pulled up at the top of the cutting. We hastily alighted, and the Inspector and I bade Bainbridge goodbye. He said that he only wished that he could stay with us for the night, assured us that little sleep would visit him, and that he would be back at the cutting at an early hour on the following morning; then the noise of his horse's feet was heard fainter and fainter as he drove back over the frost-bound roads. The Inspector and I ran along the little path to the wicket-

gate in the fence, stamping our feet on the hard ground to
restore circulation after our cold drive. The next moment
we were looking down upon the scene of the mysterious
deaths, and a weird and lonely place it looked. The
tunnel was at one end of the rock cutting, the sides of
which ran sheer down to the line for over a hundred and
fifty feet. Above the tunnel's mouth the hills rose one
upon the other. A more dreary place it would have been
difficult to imagine. From a little clump of pines a
delicate film of blue smoke rose straight up on the still
air. This came from the chimney of the signal-box.

As we started to descend the precipitous path the
Inspector sang out a cheery 'Hullo!' The man on duty in
the box immediately answered. His voice echoed and
reverberated down the cutting, and the next moment he
appeared at the door of the box. He told us that he would
be with us immediately; but we called back to him to stay
where he was, and the next instant the Inspector and I
entered the box.

'The first thing to do,' said Henderson the Inspector, 'is
to send a message down the line to announce our arrival.'

This he did, and in a few moments a crawling goods
train came panting up the cutting. After signalling her
through we descended the wooden flight of steps which
led from the box down to the line and walked along the
metals towards the tunnel till we stood on the spot where
poor Davidson had been found dead that morning. I
examined the ground and all around it most carefully.
Everything tallied exactly with the description I had
received. There could be no possible way of approaching
the spot except by going along the line, as the rocky sides
of the cutting were inaccessible.

'It is a most extraordinary thing, sir,' said the
signalman whom we had come to relieve. 'Davidson had
neither mark nor sign on him—there he lay stone dead
and cold, and not a bruise nowhere; but Pritchard had an
awful wound at the back of the head. They said he got it
by climbing the rocks—here, you can see the marks for

yourself, sir. But now, is it likely that Pritchard would try to climb rocks like these, so steep as they are?'

'Certainly not,' I replied.

'Then how do you account for the wound, sir?' asked the man with an anxious face.

'I cannot tell you at present,' I answered.

'And you and Inspector Henderson are going to spend the night in the signal-box?'

'Yes.'

A horrified expression crept over the signalman's face.

'God preserve you both,' he said; 'I wouldn't do it—not for fifty pounds. It's not the first time I have heard tell that Felwyn Tunnel is haunted. But, there, I won't say any more about that. It's a black business, and has given trouble enough. There's poor Wynne, the same thing as convicted of the murder of Pritchard; but now they say that Davidson's death will clear him. Davidson was as good a fellow as you would come across this side of the country; but for the matter of that, so was Pritchard. The whole thing is terrible—it upsets one, that it do, sir.'

'I don't wonder at your feelings,' I answered; 'but now, see here, I want to make a most careful examination of everything. One of the theories is that Wynne crept down this rocky side and fractured Pritchard's skull. I believe such a feat to be impossible. On examining these rocks I see that a man might climb up the side of the tunnel as far as from eight to ten feet, utilizing the sharp projections of rock for the purpose; but it would be out of the question for any man to come down the cutting. No; the only way Wynne could have approached Pritchard was by the line itself. But, after all, the real thing to discover is this,' I continued, 'what killed Davidson? Whatever caused his death is, beyond doubt, equally responsible for Pritchard's. I am now going into the tunnel.'

Inspector Henderson went in with me. The place struck damp and chill. The walls were covered with green, evil-smelling fungi, and through the brickwork the moisture was oozing and had trickled down in long lines to the ground. Before us was nothing but dense darkness.

When we re-appeared the signalman was lighting the red lamp on the post, which stood about five feet from the ground just above the entrance to the tunnel.

'Is there plenty of oil?' asked the Inspector.

'Yes, sir, plenty,' replied the man. 'Is there anything more I can do for either of you gentlemen?' he asked, pausing, and evidently dying to be off.

'Nothing,' answered Henderson; 'I will wish you good-evening.'

'Good-evening to you both,' said the man. He made his way quickly up the path and was soon lost to sight.

Henderson and I then returned to the signal-box.

By this time it was nearly dark.

'How many trains pass in the night?' I asked of the Inspector.

'There's the 10.20 down express.' he said, 'it will pass here at about 10.40; then there's the 11.45 up, and then not another train till the 6.30 local tomorrow morning. We shan't have a very lively time,' he added.

I approached the fire and bent over it, holding out my hands to try and get some warmth into them.

'It will take a good deal to persuade me to go down to the tunnel, whatever I may see there,' said the man. 'I don't think, Mr Bell, I am a coward in any sense of the word, but there's something very uncanny about this place, right away from the rest of the world. I don't wonder one often hears of signalmen going mad in some of these lonely boxes. Have you any theory to account for these deaths, sir?'

'None at present,' I replied.

'This second death puts the idea of Pritchard being murdered quite out of court,' he continued.

'I am sure of it,' I answered.

'And so am I, and that's one comfort,' continued Henderson. 'That poor girl, Lucy Ray, although she was to be blamed for her conduct, is much to be pitied now; and as to poor Wynne himself, he protests his innocence through thick and thin. He was a wild fellow, but not the sort to take the life of a fellow-creature. I saw the doctor this afternoon while I was waiting for you at the inn, Mr Bell, and also the police sergeant. They both say they do not know what Davidson died of. There was not the least sign of violence on the body.'

'Well, I am as puzzled as the rest of you,' I said. 'I have one or two theories in my mind, but none of them will quite fit the situation.'

The night was piercingly cold, and, although there was not a breath of wind, the keen and frosty air penetrated into the lonely signal-box. We spoke little, and both of us were doubtless absorbed by our own thoughts and speculations. As to Henderson, he looked distinctly uncomfortable, and I cannot say that my own feelings were too pleasant. Never had I been given a tougher problem to solve, and never had I been so utterly at my wits' end for a solution.

Now and then the Inspector got up and went to the telegraph instrument, which intermittently clicked away in its box. As he did so he made some casual remark and then sat down again. After the 10.40 had gone through, there followed a period of silence which seemed almost oppressive. All at once the stillness was broken by the whirr of the electric bell, which sounded so sharply in our ears that we both started. Henderson rose.

'That's the 11.45 coming,' he said, and, going over to the three long levers, he pulled two of them down with a loud clang. The next moment, with a rush and a scream, the express tore down the cutting, the carriage lights streamed past in a rapid flash, the ground trembled, a few sparks from the engine whirled up into the darkness, and the train plunged into the tunnel.

'And now,' said Henderson, as he pushed back the levers, 'not another train till daylight. My word, it is cold!'

It was intensely so. I piled some more wood on the fire and, turning up the collar of my heavy ulster, sat down at one end of the bench and leant my back against the wall.

Henderson did likewise; we were neither of us inclined to speak. As a rule, whenever I have any night work to do, I am never troubled with sleepiness, but on this occasion I felt unaccountably drowsy. I soon perceived that Henderson was in the same condition.

'Are you sleepy?' I asked of him.

'Dead with it, sir,' was his answer; 'but there's no fear, I won't drop off.'

I got up and went to the window of the box. I felt certain that if I sat still any longer I should be in a sound sleep. This would never do. Already it was becoming a matter of torture to keep my eyes open. I began to pace up and down; I opened the door of the box and went out on the little platform.

'What's the matter, sir?' inquired Henderson, jumping up with a start.

'I cannot keep awake,' I said.

'Nor can I,' he answered, 'and yet I have spent nights and nights of my life in signal-boxes and never was the least bit drowsy; perhaps it's the cold.'

'Perhaps it is,' I said; 'but I have been out on as freezing nights before, and....'

The man did not reply; he had sat down again; his head was nodding.

I was just about to go up to him and shake him, when it suddenly occurred to me that I might as well let him have his sleep out. I soon heard him snoring, and he presently fell forward in a heap on the floor. By dint of walking up and down, I managed to keep from dropping off myself, and in torture which I shall never be able to describe, the night wore itself away. At last, towards morning, I awoke Henderson.

'You have had a good nap,' I said; 'but never mind, I have been on guard and nothing has occurred.'

'Good God! have I been asleep?' cried the man.

'Sound,' I answered.

'Well, I never felt anything like it,' he replied. 'Don't you find the air very close, sir?'

'No,' I said; 'it is as fresh as possible; it must be the cold.'

'I'll just go and have a look at the light at the tunnel,' said the man; 'it will rouse me.'

He went on to the little platform, whilst I bent over the fire and began to build it up. Presently he returned with a scared look on his face. I could see by the light of the oil lamp which hung on the wall that he was trembling.

'Mr Bell,' he said, 'I believe there is somebody or something down at the mouth of the tunnel now.' As he spoke he clutched me by the arm. 'Go and look,' he said; 'whoever it is, it has put out the light.'

'Put out the light?' I cried. 'Why, what's the time?'

Henderson pulled out his watch.

'Thank goodness, most of the night is gone,' he said; 'I didn't know it was so late, it is half past five.'

'Then the local is not due for an hour yet?' I said.

'No; but who should put out the light?' cried Henderson.

I went to the door, flung it open, and looked out. The dim outline of the tunnel was just visible looming through the darkness, but the red light was out.

'What the dickens does it mean, sir?' gasped the Inspector. 'I know the lamp had plenty of oil in it. Can there be anyone standing in front of it, do you think?'

We waited and watched for a few moments, but nothing stirred.

'Come along,' I said, 'let us go down together and see what it is.'

'I don't believe I can do it, sir; I really don't!'

'Nonsense' I cried. 'I shall go down alone if you won't accompany me. Just hand me my stick, will you?'

'For God's sake, be careful, Mr Bell. Don't go down, whatever you do. I expect this is what happened before, and the poor fellows went down to see what it was and died there. There's some devilry at work, that's my belief.'

'That is as it may be,' I answered shortly; 'but we certainly shall not find out by stopping here. My business

is to get to the bottom of this, and I am going to do it.
That there is danger of some sort, I have very little doubt;
but danger or not, I am going down.'

'If you'll be warned by me, sir, you'll just stay quietly
here.'

'I must go down and see the matter out,' was my
answer. 'Now listen to me, Henderson. I see that you are
alarmed, and I don't wonder. Just stay quietly where you
are and watch, but if I call come at once. Don't delay a
single instant. Remember I am putting my life into your
hands. If I call "Come," just come to me as quick as you
can, for I may want help. Give me that lantern.'

He unhitched it from the wall, and taking it from him.
I walked cautiously down the steps on to the line. I still
felt curiously, unaccountably drowsy and heavy. I
wondered at this, for the moment was such a critical one
as to make almost any man wide awake. Holding the lamp
high above my head, I walked rapidly along the line. I
hardly knew what I expected to find. Cautiously along the
metals I made my way, peering right and left until I was
close to the fatal spot where the bodies had been found.
An uncontrollable shudder passed over me. The next
moment, to my horror, without the slightest warning, the
light I was carrying went out, leaving me in total darkness. I started back, and stumbling against one of the
loose boulders reeled against the wall and nearly fell.
What was the matter with me? I could hardly stand. I felt
giddy and faint, and a horrible sensation of great tight-
ness seized me across the chest. A loud ringing noise
sounded in my ears. Struggling madly for breath, and
with the fear of impending death upon me, I turned and
tried to run from a danger I could neither understand nor
grapple with. But before I had taken two steps my legs
gave way from under me, and uttering a loud cry I fell
insensible to the ground.

Out of an oblivion which, for all I knew, might have
lasted for moments or centuries, a dawning consciousness

came to me. I knew that I was lying on hard ground; that I was absolutely incapable of realizing, nor had I the slightest inclination to discover, where I was. All I wanted was to lie quite still and undisturbed. Presently I opened my eyes.

Some one was bending over me and looking into my face.

'Thank God, he is not dead,' I heard in whispered tones. Then, with a flash, memory returned to me.

'What has happened?' I asked.

'You may well ask that, sir,' said the Inspector gravely. 'It has been touch and go with you for the last quarter of an hour, and a near thing for me too.'

I sat up and looked around me. Daylight was just beginning to break, and I saw that we were at the bottom of the steps that led up to the signal-box. My teeth were chattering with the cold and I was shivering like a man with ague.

'I am better now,' I said; 'just give me your hand.'

I took his arm, and holding the rail with the other hand staggered up into the box and sat down on the bench.

'Yes, it has been a near shave,' I said; 'and a big price to pay for solving a mystery.'

'Do you mean to say you know what it is?' asked Henderson eagerly.

'Yes,' I answered, 'I think I know now; but first tell me how long was I unconscious?'

'A good bit over half an hour, sir, I should think. As soon as I heard you call out I ran down as you told me, but before I got to you I nearly fainted. I never had such a horrible sensation in my life. I felt as weak as a baby, but I just managed to seize you by the arms and drag you along the line to the steps, and that was about all I could do.'

'Well, I owe you my life,' I said; 'just hand me that brandy flask, I shall be the better for some of its contents.'

I took a long pull. Just as I was laying the flask down Henderson started from my side.

'There;' he cried, 'the 6.30 is coming.' The electric bell at the instrument suddenly began to ring. 'Ought I to let her go through, sir?' he inquired.

'Certainly,' I answered. 'That is exactly what we want. Oh, she will be all right.'

'No danger to her, sir?'

'None, none; let her go through.'

He pulled the lever and the next moment the train tore through the cutting.

'Now I think it will be safe to go down again,' I said. 'I believe I shall be able to get to the bottom of this business.'

Henderson stared at me aghast.

'Do you mean that you are going down again to the tunnel?' he gasped.

'Yes,' I said; 'give me those matches. You had better come too. I don't think there will be much danger now; and there is daylight, so we can see what we are about.'

The man was very loth to obey me, but at last I managed to persuade him. We went down the line, walking slowly, and at this moment we both felt our courage revived by a broad and cheerful ray of sunshine.

'We must advance cautiously,' I said, 'and be ready to run back at a moment's notice.'

'God knows, sir, I think we are running a great risk,' panted poor Henderson; 'and if that devil or whatever else it is should happen to be about—why, daylight or no daylight—'

'Nonsense, man!' I interrupted; 'if we are careful, no harm will happen to us now. Ah! and here we are!' We had reached the spot where I had fallen. 'Just give me a match, Henderson.'

He did so, and I immediately lit the lamp. Opening the glass of the lamp, I held it close to the ground and passed it to and fro. Suddenly the flame went out.

'Don't you understand now?' I said, looking up at the Inspector.

'No, I don't, sir,' he replied with a bewildered expression.

Suddenly, before I could make an explanation, we both heard shouts from the top of the cutting, and looking up I saw Bainbridge hurrying down the path. He had come in the dog-cart to fetch us.

'Here's the mystery,' I cried as he rushed up to us, 'and a deadlier scheme of Dame Nature's to frighten and murder poor humanity I have never seen.'

As I spoke I lit the lamp again and held it just above a tiny fissure in the rock. It was at once extinguished.

'What is it?' said Bainbridge, panting with excitement.

'Something that nearly finished *me*,' I replied. 'Why, this is a natural escape of choke damp. Carbonic acid gas—the deadliest gas imaginable, because it gives no warning of its presence, and it has no smell. It must have collected here during the hours of the night when no train was passing, and gradually rising put out the signal light. The constant rushing of the trains through the cutting all day would temporarily disperse it.'

As I made this explanation Bainbridge stood like one electrified, while a curious expression of mingled relief and horror swept over Henderson's face.

'An escape of carbonic acid gas is not an uncommon phenomenon in volcanic districts,' I continued, 'as I take this to be; but it is odd what should have started it. It has sometimes been known to follow earthquake shocks, when there is a profound disturbance of the deep strata.'

'It is strange that you should·have said that,' said Bainbridge, when he could find his voice.

'What do you mean?'

'Why, that about the earthquake. Don't you remember, Henderson,' he added, turning to the Inspector, 'we had felt a slight shock all over South Wales about three weeks back?'

'Then that, I think, explains it,' I said. 'It is evident that Pritchard really did climb the rocks in a frantic attempt to escape from the gas and fell back on to these boulders. The other man was cut down at once, before he had time to fly.'

'But what is to happen now?' asked Bainbridge. 'Will it go on for ever? How are we to stop it?'

'The fissure ought to be drenched with lime water, and then filled up; but all really depends on what is the size of the supply and also the depth. It is an extremely heavy gas, and would lie at the bottom of a cutting like water. I think there is more here just now than is good for us.' I added.

'But how,' continued Bainbridge, as we moved a few steps from the fatal spot, 'do you account for the interval between the first death and the second?'

'The escape must have been intermittent. If wind blew down the cutting, as probably was the case before this frost set in, it would keep the gas so diluted that its effects would not be noticed. There was enough down here this morning, before that train came through, to poison an army. Indeed, if it had not been for Henderson's promptitude, there would have been another inquest–on myself.'

I then related my own experience.

'Well, this clears Wynne, without doubt.' said Bainbridge; 'but alas! for the two poor fellows who were victims. Bell, the Lytton Vale Railway Company owe you unlimited thanks; you have doubtless saved many lives, and also the Company, for the line must have been closed if you had not made your valuable discovery. But now come home with me to breakfast. We can discuss all those matters later on.'

OLD GERVAIS

O

Mrs Molesworth

Like Mrs Meade, Mary Louisa Molesworth (1839–1921) wrote books for children (over 100!) and occasionally tried her hand at ghost stories. Alas, unlike Mrs Meade, she has failed to keep much of a name in the macabre genre, which is sad, for she brought to it a touch of elegance and charm that is rare to find.

Born Mary Stewart in Holland, she does not seem to have left much behind in the way of biographical details. We know she married a Bevil Molesworth (who collaborated with her on some books), and that she produced over a hundred volumes in the period 1870–1911. Of interest to macabre fiction enthusiasts, of course, are her two books of ghost stories FOUR GHOST STORIES (1888) which was reprinted in America in 1976, and UNCANNY TALES (1896). They are both scarce books indeed.

However, scattered among her various other collections of stories was the odd ghostly tale, one of which is to be found in her 1893 book STUDIES AND STORIES. 'Old Gervais' is well worth reviving. Like her famous story 'The Shadow in the Moonlight', Mrs Molesworth uses children for her protagonists. This tale has been out of print for the best part of a century and I think readers will find it much to their taste now.

MRS MOLESWORTH

O

Old Gervais

... AND now, as to your questions about that long-ago story. What put it into your head, I wonder? You have been talking 'ghosts' like everybody else nowadays, no doubt, and you want to have something to tell that you had at 'first hand.' Ah well, I will try to recall my small experience of the kind as accurately as my old brain is capable of doing at so long a distance. Though, after all, that is scarcely a correct way of putting it. For, like all elderly people, I find it true, strikingly true, that the longer ago the better, as far as memory is concerned. I can recollect events, places—nay, words and looks and tones, material impressions of the most trivial, such as scents and tastes, of forty or fifty years ago, far more vividly, more minutely, than things of a year or even a month past. It is strange, but I like it. There is something consolatory and suggestive about it. It seems to show that we are still all there, or all here, rather; that there is a something—an innermost 'I'—which goes on, faithful and permanent, however rusty and dull the machinery may grow with the wear and tear of time and age.

But you won't thank me for reflections of this kind. You want my little personal experience of the 'more things,' and you shall have it.

You know, of course, that by birth—by descent, that is to say—I am a little, a quarter or half a quarter, French. And by affection I have always felt myself much more than that. It is often so; there is a sort of loyalty in us to the weaker side of things. Just because there is really so much less French than English in me, because I have spent nearly all my threescore and —! years in Great Britain, I feel bound to stand up for the Gallic part of me, and to feel quite huffed and offended if France or 'Frenchness' is decried. It is silly, I dare say; but somehow I cannot help it. We don't know, we can't say in what proportions our ancestors are developed in us. It is possible that I am really, paradoxical as it may sound, more French than English, after all.

You know all about me, but if you want to tell my bit of a ghost-story to others, you will understand that I am not actuated by egotism in explaining things. It was through my being a little French that I came to pay long visits to old friends of my mother's in Normandy. *They* were not relations, but connections by marriage, and bound by the closest ties of association and long affection to our cousins. And the wife of the head of the family, dear Madame de Viremont, was my own godmother. She had visited us in England and Scotland—she loved both, and she was cosmopolitan enough to think it only natural that even as a young girl I should be allowed to cross the Channel to stay with her for weeks, nay, months at a time, in her old château of Viremont-les-bocages. Not that I travelled over there *alone*—ah no, indeed! Girls, even of the unmistakably upper classes, *do* travel alone now, I am assured, still I can't say that it has ever come within my own knowledge that a young lady should journey by herself to Normandy, though I believe such things are done. But it was very different in my young days. My father himself took me to Paris—I am speaking just now of the first time I went, with which indeed only, I am at present concerned—and after a few days of sightseeing there, Madame de Viremont's own maid came to escort me to my destination—the château.

We travelled by diligence, of course—the journey that five or six hours would now see accomplished took us the best part of two days. At Caen, my godmother met us, and I spent a night in her 'hotel' there—the town residence of the family—dear old house that it was! Many a happy day have I spent there since. And then, at Caen, I was introduced for the first time to my godmother's grand-daughters, her son's children, Albertine and Virginie. Albertine was older than I, Virginie two years younger. We were dreadfully shy of each other, though Albertine was too well bred to show it, and talked formalities in a way that I am sure made her grandmother smile. Virginie, dear soul, did not speak at all, which you must remember is *not* bad manners in a French girl before she is out, and I, as far as I recollect, spoke nonsense in very bad French, and blushed at the thought of it afterwards. It was stupid of me, for I really could speak the language very decently.

But that all came right. I think we took to each other in spite of our shyness and awkwardness, at once. It must have been so, for we have remained friends ever since, staunch friends, though Albertine's life has been spent among the great ones of the earth (she is a great-grand-mother now) and I only see my Virginie once a year, or once in two or three years, for a few hours, at the convent of which she has long, long been the head; and *I* am an old-fashioned, narrow-minded perhaps, Scotch maiden lady of a very certain age, who finds it not always easy to manage the journey to France even to see her dear old friends.

How delightful, how unspeakably exciting and inter-esting and fascinating that first real glimpse into the home life of another nation was! The queernesses, the extraordinary differences, the indescribable mingling of primitiveness with ultra refinement, of stateliness and dignity of bearing and customs with odd unsophisticated-ness such as I had imagined mediæval at least—all added to the charm.

How well I remember my first morning's waking in my bedroom at the château! There was no carpet on the floor; no looking-glass, except a very black and unflattering one which might have belonged to Noah's wife, over the chimney-piece; no attempt at a dressing-table; a ewer and basin in the tiny cabinet-de-toilette which would have delighted my little sister for her dolls. Yet the cup in which old Désirée brought me my morning chocolate was of almost priceless china, and the chocolate itself such as I do not *think* I ever have tasted elsewhere, so rich and fragrant and steaming hot—the roll which accompanied it, though sour, lying on a little fringed doyley marked with the Viremont crest in embroidery which must have cost somebody's eyes something.

It seemed to me like awaking in a fairy-tale in a white cat's château. And the charm lasted till I had come to feel so entirely at home with my dear, courteous, kindly hosts, that I forgot to ask myself if I were enjoying myself or no. Nay, longer than till then, did it last—indeed, I have never lost the *feeling* of it—at any moment I can hear the tapping of my godmother's stoutly shod feet as she trotted about early in the morning, superintending her men and maidens, and giving orders for the day; I can scent the perfume of Monsieur's pet roses; I hear the sudden wind, for we were not far from the sea, howling and crying through the trees as I lay in my alcove bed at night.

It was not a great house, though called a château. It was one of the still numerous moderate-sized old country houses which escaped the destruction of that terrible time now nearly a century past. The De Viremonts were of excellent descent, but they had never been extremely wealthy, nor very prominent. They were pious, home-loving, cultivated folk—better read than most of their class in the provinces, partly perhaps thanks to their English connections which had widened their ideas, partly because they came of a scholarly and thoughtful race. The house was little changed from what it must have

been for a century or more. The grounds, so Madame de
Viremont told me, were less well tended than in her
husband's childhood, for it was increasingly difficult to
get good gardeners, and she herself had no special gift in
that line, such as her mother-in-law had been famed for.
And though Monsieur loved his roses, his interest in
horticulture began and ended with them. I don't think he
minded how untidy and wilderness-like the grounds
were, provided the little bit near the house was pretty
decent. For there, round the 'lawn' which he and Madame
fondly imagined was worthy of the name, bloomed his
beloved flowers.

If it had been my own home, the wildness of the
unkempt grounds would have worried me sadly. I have
always been old-maidish about neatness and tidiness, I
think. But as it was not my home, and I therefore felt no
uncomfortable responsibility, I think I rather liked it. It
was wonderfully picturesque—here and there almost
mysterious. One terrace I know, up and down which
Virginie and I were specially fond of pacing, always
reminded me of the garden in George Sand's *Château de
Pictordu*, if only there had been a broken statue at one
end!

The time passed quickly, even during the first two or
three weeks, when my only companions were 'Marraine,'
as Madame made me call her, and her husband. I was not
at all dull or bored, though my kind friends would
scarcely believe it, and constantly tried to cheer my
supposed loneliness by telling me how pleasant it would
be when *les petites*—Albertine and Virginie—joined us, as
they were to do before long. I didn't feel very eager about
their coming. I could not forget my shyness; though, of
course, I did not like to say so. I only repeated to my
godmother that I *could* not feel dull when she and
Monsieur de Viremont were doing so much to amuse me.
And for another reason I was glad to be alone with my old
friends at first. I was very anxious to improve my French,
and I worked hard at it under Monsieur's directions. He

used to read aloud to us in the evenings; he read splen-
didly, and besides the exercises and dictations he gave
me, he used to make me read aloud too. I hated it at first,
but gradually I improved very much, and then I liked it.

So passed three or four weeks; then at last one
morning came a letter announcing the grand-daughters'
arrival on the following day. I could not but try to be
pleased, for it was pretty to see how delighted every one at
the château was, to hear the news.

'They must be nice girls,' I thought, 'otherwise all the
servants and people about would not like them so much,'
and I made myself take an interest in going round with
my godmother superintending the little preparations she
was making for the girls.

They were to have separate rooms. Albertine's was
beside mine, Virginie's on the floor above. There was a
good deal of excitement about Virginie's room, for a
special reason. Her grandmother was arranging a surprise
for her, in the shape of a little oratory. It was a tiny
closet—a dark closet it had been, used originally for
hanging up dresses, in one corner of her room, and here
on her last visit, the girl had placed her *prie-Dieu*,
and hung up her crucifix. Madame de Viremont had noticed
this, and just lately she had had the door taken away, and
the little recess freshly painted, and a small window
knocked out, and all made as pretty as possible for the
sacred purpose.

I felt quite interested in it. It was a queer little recess—
almost like a turret—and Madame showed me that it ran
up the whole height of the house from the cellars where it
began, as an out-jut, with an arched window to give light
to one end of the large 'cave' at that side, which would
otherwise have been quite dark.

'The great cellar used to be a perfect rat-warren,' she
told me, 'till light and air were thus thrown into it. What
that odd out-jut was originally, no one knows. There goes
a story that a secret winding-staircase, very, very narrow,
of course, once ran up it to the roof. There were some

doubts, I know, as to the solidity of the masonry—it has
sunk a little at one side, you can see it in the cellar. But I
expect it has all "settled," as they call it, long ago. Old
Gervais, whom we employed to knock out the new
window in Virginie's little oratory, had no doubt about it,
and he is a clever mason.'

'Old Gervais,' I repeated; 'who is he, Marraine? I don't
think I have seen him, have I?'

For she had spoken of him as if I must have known
whom she meant.

'Have you not?' she said. 'He is a dear old man—one of
our great resources. He is so honest and intelligent. But
no—I dare say you have not seen him. He does not live
in our village, but at Plaudry, a mere hamlet about three
miles off. And he goes about a good deal; the neighbouring families know his value, and he is always in
request for some repairs or other work. He is devout, too,'
my godmother added; 'a simple, sincere, and yet intelligent Christian. And that is very rare nowadays: the
moment one finds a thoughtful or intelligent mind
among our poor, it seems to become the prey of all the
sad and hopeless teaching so much in the air.'

And Madame de Viremont sighed. But in a moment or
two she spoke again in her usual cheerful tone.

'It was quite a pleasure to see Gervais' interest in this
little place,' she said—we were standing in the oratory at
the time. 'He has the greatest admiration for our Virginie,
too,' she added, 'as indeed every one has who knows the
child.'

'She does look *very* sweet,' I said, and truly. But as I
had scarcely heard Virginie open her lips, I could not
personally express admiration of anything *but* her looks!
In those days too, the reputation of unusual 'goodness'—as
applied to Virginie de Viremont, I see now that the word
'sanctity' would scarcely be too strong to use—in one so
young, younger than myself, rather alarmed than
attracted me.

But her grandmother seemed quite pleased.

'You will find the looks a true index,' she said.

I was examining the oratory—and wondering if there was any little thing I could do to help to complete it. Suddenly I exclaimed to my godmother—

'Marraine, the floor does sink decidedly at one side—just move across slowly, and you will feel it.'

'I know,' she replied composedly, 'that is the side of the settling I told you of. It is the same in the two intermediate storeys—one of them is my own cabinet-de-toilette. If Virginie does not observe it at once, we shall have Albertine discovering it some day, and teasing the poor child by saying she has weighed down the flooring by kneeling too much—it is just where she will kneel.'

'Is Albertine a tease?' I asked; and in my heart I was not sorry to hear it.

'Ah, yes indeed,' said Madame. 'She is full of spirits. But Virginie, too, has plenty of fun in her.'

My misgivings soon dispersed.

The two girls had not been forty-eight hours at Vire-mont before we were the best of friends, Virginie and I especially. For though Albertine was charming, and truly high-principled and reliable, there was not about her the quite indescribable fascination which her sister has always possessed for me. I have never known anyone like Virginie, and I am quite sure I never shall. Her character was the most childlike one in certain ways that you could imagine—absolutely single-minded, unselfish, and sunny—and yet joined to this a strength of principle like a rock, a resolution, determination, and courage, once she was convinced that a thing was *right*, such as would have made a martyr of her without a moment's flinching. I have often tried to describe her to you; and the anecdote of her childhood, which at last I am approaching—she was barely out of childhood—shows what she was even then.

Those were very happy days. Everything united to make them so. The weather was lovely, we were all well, even Monsieur's gout and Madame's occasional rheumatism having for the time taken to themselves wings and fled, while we girls were as brilliantly healthful and full of life as only young things can be. What fun we had! Games of hide-and-seek in the so-called garden—much of it better described as a wilderness, as I have said—races on the terrace; explorations now and then, on the one or two partially rainy days, of Madame's stores—from her own treasures of ancient brocades and scraps of precious lace and tapestry, to the 'rubbish,' much of it really rubbish, though some of it quaint and interesting, hoarded for a century or two in the great 'grenier' which extended over a large part of the house under the rafters. I have by me now, in this very room where I write, some precious odds and ends which we extracted from the collection, and which my godmother told me I might take home with me to Scotland, if I thought it worth the trouble.

One day we had been running about the grounds till, breathless and tired, we were glad to sit down on the seat at the far end of the terrace. And, while there, we heard some one calling us.

'Albertine, Virginie, Jeannette,' said the voice.

'It is grandpapa,' said Virginie, starting up, and running in the direction indicated, Albertine and I following her more leisurely.

'Where have you been, my children?' said the old gentleman, as we got up to him. 'I have been seeking you—what are your plans for the afternoon? Your grandmother is going to pay some calls, and proposes that one of you should go with her, while I invite the other two to join me in a good walk—a long walk, I warn you— to Plaudry. What do you say to that?'

The two girls looked at me. As the stranger, they seemed to think it right that I should speak first.

'I should like the walk best,' I said with a smile. 'I have not been to Plaudry, and they say it is so pretty. And— perhaps Marraine would prefer one of you two to pay calls—I have already visited most of your neighbours with her before you came, and every one was asking when you were coming.'

'Albertine, then,' said her grandfather. 'Yes, that will be best. And you two little ones shall come with me.'

The arrangement seemed to please all concerned, especially when Monsieur went on to say that the object of his expedition was to see Gervais the mason.

'Oh,' said Virginie, 'I am so glad. I want to thank him for all the interest he took in my dear little oratory. Grandmamma told me about it.'

Her eyes sparkled. I think I have omitted to say that Madame de Viremont had been well rewarded for her trouble by Virginie's delight in the little surprise prepared for her.

'I want him to see the arch of the window in the "cave,"' said Monsieur. 'Some stones are loosened, one or two actually dropped out. Perhaps his knocking out of your little window, Virginie, has had to do with it. In any case, it must be looked to, without delay. Come round that way, and you shall see what I mean.'

He led us to the far side of the house. The window in question had been made in the out-jut I have described; but as it was below the level of the ground, a space had been cleared out in front of it, making a sort of tiny yard, and two or three steps led down to this little spot. It seems to have been used as a receptacle for odds and ends— flower-pots, a watering-can, etc., were lying about. Monsieur went down the steps to show us the crumbling masonry. He must have had good eyes to see it, I thought, for only by pushing aside with his stick the thickly growing ivy, could he show us the loosened and falling stones. But then in a moment he explained.

'I saw it from the inside. I was showing the men where to place some wine I have just had sent in, in the wood. And the proper cellar is over-full—yes, it must certainly be seen to. Inside it looks very shaky.'

So we three walked to Plaudry that afternoon. It was a lovely walk, for Monsieur knew the shortest way, partly through the woods, by which we avoided the long, hot stretch of high-road. And when we reached our destin-

ation—a hamlet of only half a dozen cottages at most—by
good luck Gervais was at home, though looking half
ashamed to be caught idle, in spite of his evident pleasure
at the visit.

He had not been very well lately, his good wife
explained, and she had insisted on his taking a little rest.
And though I had never seen him before, it seemed to me
I could have discerned a worn look—the look of pain
patiently borne—in the old man's quiet, gentle face and
eyes.

'Gervais not well!' said Monsieur. 'Why, that is something new. What's been the matter, my friend?'

Oh, it was nothing—nothing at all. The old wife frightened herself for nothing, he said. A little rheumatism, no
doubt—a pain near the heart. But it was better, it would
pass. What was it Monsieur wanted? He would be quite
ready to see to it by to-morrow.

Then Monsieur explained, and I could see that at once
the old mason's interest was specially aroused. 'Ah yes,
certainly,' he interjected. It must be seen to—he had had
some misgivings, but had wished to avoid further
expense. But all should be put right. And he was so glad
that Mademoiselle was pleased with the little oratory, his
whole face lighting up as he said it. Tomorrow by
sunrise, or at least as soon as possible after, he would be
at the château.

Then we turned to go home again, though not till
Madame Gervais had fetched us a cup of milk, to refresh
us after our walk; for they were well-to-do, in their way,
and had a cow of their own, though the bare, dark
kitchen, which in England would scarcely seem better
than a stable, gave little evidence of any such prosperity. I
said some words to that effect to my companions, and
then I was sorry I had done so.

'Why, did you not see the armoire?' said Virginie. 'It is
quite a beauty.'

'And the bed and bedding would put many such com-
modities in an English cottage to shame, I fancy,' added

Monsieur, which I could not but allow was probably true.

Gervais kept his word. He was at his post in the 'cave' long before any of us were awake, and Virginie's morning devotions must have been disturbed by the knocking and hammering far below.

He was at it all day. Monsieur went down to speak to him once or twice, but Gervais had his peculiarities. He would not give an opinion as to the amount of repair necessary till he was sure. And that afternoon we all went for a long drive—to dine with friends, and return in the evening. When we came home, there was a message left for Monsieur by the old mason to the effect that he would come again 'tomorrow,' and would then be able to explain all. Monsieur must not mind if he did not come early, as he would have to get something made at the forge—something iron, said the young footman who gave the message.

'Ah, just so,' said Monsieur. 'He has found it more serious than he expected, I fancy; but it will be all right, now it is in his hands.'

So the next morning there was no early knocking or tapping to be heard in the old cellar. Nor did Gervais return later, as he had promised.

'He must have been detained at the forge,' said Monsieur. 'No doubt he will come tomorrow.'

Tomorrow came, but with it no Gervais. And Monsieur de Viremont, who was old and sometimes a little irascible, began to feel annoyed. He went down to the cellar, to inspect the work.

'It is right enough,' he said, when he came upstairs to the room where we four ladies were sitting—there had been a change in the weather, and it was a stormily rainy day—'I see he has got out the loose stones, and made it all solid enough, but it looks unsightly and unfinished. It wants pointing, and—'

'What was it Alphonse said about an iron band or something?' said Madame. 'Perhaps Gervais is getting one made, and it has taken longer than he expected.'

'It is not necessary,' said the old gentleman. 'Gervais is

over-cautious. No—a girder would be nonsense; but I do not like to see work left so untidy; and it is not his usual way.'

So little indeed was it the old mason's way, that when another day passed, and there was no news of Gervais, Monsieur determined to send in the morning to hunt him up.

'I would have walked over this afternoon myself,' he said, 'if the weather had been less terrible.'

For it really was terrible—one of those sudden storms to which, near the sea, we are always liable, even in summer—raging wind, fierce beating, dashing rain, that take away for the time all sensation of June or July.

But whatever the weather was, orders were given that night that one of the outdoor men was to go over to Plaudry first thing the next morning.

Monsieur had a bad night, a touch of gout, and he could not get to sleep till very late, or rather early. So Madame told us when we met at table for the eleven o'clock *big* breakfast.

'He only awoke an hour ago, and I wanted him to stay in bed all day,' she said. 'But he would not consent to do so. Ah! there he comes,' as our host at that moment entered the room with apologies for his tardiness.

The wind had gone down, though in the night it had been fiercer than ever; but it was still raining pitilessly.

'I do hope the storm is over,' said Virginie. 'Last night, when I was saying my prayers, it almost frightened me. I really thought I felt the walls rocking.'

'Nonsense, child!' said her grandfather, sharply. Incipient gout is not a sweetener of the temper. But Virginie's remark had reminded him of something.

'Has Jean Pierre come back from Plaudry?' he asked the servant behind his chair; 'and what message did he bring?'

Alphonse started. He had been entrusted with a message, though not the one expected, but had forgotten to give it.

'He did not go, Monsieur,' he said; hastily adding, before there was time for his master to begin to storm. 'There was no need. Old Gervais was here this morning—very early, before it was light almost; so Nicolas'—Nicolas was the bailiff—'said no one need go.'

'Oh—ah, well,' said Monsieur, mollified. 'Then tell Gervais I want to speak to him before he leaves.'

Then Alphonse looked slightly uneasy.

'He is gone already, unfortunately—before Monsieur's bell rang. He must have had but little to do—by eight o'clock, or before, he was gone.'

Monsieur de Viremont looked annoyed.

'Very strange,' he said, 'when he left word he would explain all to me. Did you see him? Did he say nothing?'

No, Alphonse had not seen him—he had only heard him knocking. But he would inquire more particularly if there was no message.

He came back in a few moments, looking perplexed. *No one*, it appeared, had really seen the mason; no one, at least, except a little lad, Denis by name—who worked in the garden—'the little fellow who sings in the choir,' said Alphonse. He—Denis—had seen Gervais' face from the garden, at the window. And he had called out, 'Good morning,' but Gervais did not answer.

'And the work is completed? Has he perhaps left his tools? If so, he may be coming back again,' asked Monsieur.

Alphonse could not say. Impatient, the old gentleman rose from the table, and went off to make direct inquiry.

'Very odd, very odd indeed,' he said when he returned and sat down again. 'To all appearance, the work is exactly as it was when he left it three days ago. Not tidied up or finished. And yet the cook and all heard him knocking for two hours certainly, and the child, Denis, saw him.'

'I dare say he will be returning,' said Madame, soothingly. 'Let us wait till this evening.'

So they did; but no Gervais came back, and the rain

went on falling, chill, drearily monotonous.

Just before dinner Monsieur summoned the bailiff.

'Someone must go first thing tomorrow,' he began at once, when Nicolas appeared, 'and tell Gervais sharply that I won't be played the fool with. What has come over the old fellow?'

'No, Monsieur, certainly not. Monsieur's orders must be treated with respect,' replied Nicolas, ignoring for the moment his master's last few words. 'But–' and then we noticed that he was looking pale. 'Someone has just called in from Plaudry–a neighbour–he thought we should like to know. Gervais is *dead*–he died last night. He has been ill these three days–badly ill; the heart, they say. And the weather has stopped people coming along the roads as much as usual, else we should have heard. Poor old Gervais–peace to his soul.' And Nicolas crossed himself.

'*Dead!*' Monsieur repeated.

'*Dead!*' we all echoed.

It seemed incredible. Monsieur, I know, wished he had not spoken so sharply.

'Virginie, Jeanette,' whispered Albertine. 'It must have been his ghost!'

But she would not have dared to say so to her grandfather.

'It is sad, very sad,' said Monsieur and Madame. Then a few directions were given to the bailiff, to offer any help she might be in want of, to the poor widow, and Nicolas was dismissed.

'It just shows what imagination will do,' said Monsieur; 'all these silly servants believing they heard him, when it was *impossible*.'

'Yes,' whispered Albertine again, 'and Denis Blanc, who saw him. And Denis, who is so truthful; a little saint indeed! You know, Virginie, the boy with the lovely voice.'

Virginie bent her head in assent, but said nothing. And the subject was not referred to again that evening.

But–

The storm was over, next day was cloudless, seeming as if such things as wind and rain and weather fury had never visited this innocent-looking world before. Again we went off to a neighbouring château, returning late and tired, and we all slept soundly. Again an exquisite day. Monsieur was reading aloud to us in the salon that evening; it was nearly bedtime, when a sort of skirmish and rush—hushed, yet excited voices, weeping even – were heard outside.

Monsieur stopped. 'What is it?' he said. Then rising, he went to the door.

A small crowd of servants was gathered there, arguing, vociferating, yet with a curious hush over it all.

'What is it?' repeated the master sternly.

Then it broke out. They could stand it no longer; something must be done; though Monsieur had forbidden them to talk nonsense—it was not nonsense, only too true.

'*What?*' thundered the old gentleman.

About Gervais. He was there again—at the present moment. He had been there the night before, but no one had dared to tell. He had returned, no notice having been taken of his first warning. And he *would* return. There now, if every one would be perfectly still, even here, his knockings could be heard.

The speaker was the cook. And truly, as an uncanny silence momentarily replaced the muffled hubbub, far-off yet distinct taps, coming from below, were to be heard.

'Some trick,' said Monsieur. 'Let us go down, all of us together, and get to the bottom of this affair.'

He led the way; we women, and after us the crowd of terrified servants, following. Monsieur paused at the kitchen door.

'It is dark in the "cave",' he said.

'No, no' cried the cook. 'There is a beautiful moon. Not a light, pray Monsieur; he might not like it.'

All was silent.

We reached the cellar, and entered it a little way. Quite a distance off, so it seemed, was the arched window, the

moonlight gleaming through it eerily, the straggling ivy
outside taking strange black shapes; but no one to be
seen, nothing to be heard.

Ah, what was that? The knocking again, unmistakable,
distinct, *real*. And why did one side of the window grow
dark, as if suddenly thrown into shadow? Was there
something intercepting the moonlight? It seemed misty,
or was it partly that we scarcely dared look?

Then, to our surprise, the grandfather's voice sounded
out clearly.

'Virginie, my child,' he said, 'you are the youngest, the
most guileless, perhaps the one who has least cause for
fear. Would you dread to step forward and—*speak?* If so
be it is a message from the poor fellow, let him tell it.
Show every one that those who believe in the good God
need not be afraid.'

Like a white angel, Virginie, in her light summer dress,
glided forward, silent. She walked straight on; then,
rather to our surprise, she crossed the floor, and stood
almost out of sight in the dark corner, at the further side
of the window. Then she spoke—

'Gervais, my poor Gervais,' she said. 'Is it you? I think I
see you, but I cannot be sure. What is troubling you, my
friend? What is keeping you from your rest?'

Then all was silent again. I should have said that as
Virginie went forward, the knocking ceased—*so* silent that
we could almost hear our hearts beat. And then—Virginie
was speaking again, and *not repeating her questions!*
When we realized this, it did seem awful. She was
carrying on a conversation. *She had been answered.*

What she said I cannot recall. Her voice was lower now;
it sounded almost dreamy. And in a moment or two she
came back to us, straight to her grandfather.

'I will tell you all,' she said. 'Come upstairs—all will be
quiet now,' she added, in a tone almost of command, to
the awestruck servants. And upstairs she told.

'I do not know if he spoke,' she said, in answer to
Albertine's eager inquiries. 'I cannot tell. I know what he

wanted, that is enough. No; I did not *exactly* see him; but—he was there.'

And this was the message, simple enough. The wall was *not* safe, though he had done what could be done to the stonework. Iron girders must be fixed and that without delay. He had felt too ill to go to the forge that night as he had intended, and the unfinished work, the possible danger, was sorely on his mind.

'He thanked me,' said Virginie, simply. 'He feared that grandfather would think all the solid work was done, and that the wall only needed finishing for appearance.'

As, indeed, Monsieur de Viremont *had* thought.

Afterwards the old woman told us a little more. Gervais had been alternately delirious and unconscious these two or three days. He had talked about the work at Viremont, but she thought it raving, till just at the last he tried to whisper something, and she saw he was clear-headed again, about letting Monsieur know. She had meant to do so when her own first pressure of grief and trouble was over. She never knew that the warning had been fore-stalled.

That is all. And it was long ago, and there are thrillingly sensational ghost-stories to be had by the score nowadays. It seems nothing. But I have always thought it touching and impressive, knowing it to be true.

If I have wearied you by my old woman's garrulity, forgive it. It has been a pleasure to me to recall those days.

Your ever affectionate,

JANET MARIE BETHUNE.

IN THE LIGHT OF THE RED
LAMP
and
THE TEST

O

Maurice Level

The term 'horror story' has become much debased over the years, coming to cover a wide range of tales, not all strictly containing horror but in themselves horrible. That is an Irish view of the situation, some may no doubt argue, but I have always thought the term 'horror story' should best be reserved for the tales where the supernatural doesn't enter into the proceedings, but instead tell of the horrible things people do to each other.

The French have a term for it, 'conte cruel', which sums it up nicely. As a form of story, it has attracted many writers but very few have ever been able to do the job well. The longest-running series of horror story anthologies in the UK, for instance, settled down after some years into printing only this kind of story and using examples by inept writers who cheapened and coarsened the whole sub-genre.

The French, however, not only had a term for it, they also produced one of the finest exponents of this sort of story in Maurice Level (1875–1926).

Level was born into a military family, and spent much

of his early life in Algeria. His father came from Alsace and instilled in Maurice a violent hatred of all things German.

The young Level studied medicine and started writing stories to while away the hours of his night shift as a Paris house-surgeon. He showed his first story to the editor of the Paris magazine Le Journal who bought it on the spot. Level took up writing full-time, producing short stories of powerful and cruel content.

Not surprisingly, the famous Grand Guignol theatre in Paris—which specialized in stage work of tales of horror—took up Level's stories with relish.

Level had a skating accident in 1910 which cut down his activities considerably. Nevertheless, he got out of his sickbed at a Swiss sanatorium to enlist in the Moroccan Tirailleurs at the outbreak of the first world war, such was his hatred of Germany. His military service didn't last long—his health gave way yet again—and he settled for army medical work thereafter. His early death followed more illness, but not before he was decorated by the French government with the order of Chevalier of the Legion of Honour.

Level is almost forgotten now. CRISES (1920), his book of short, grim stories translated by Alys Eyre Macklin, has become one of the most sought-after titles by collectors of macabre fiction. These two short stories are taken from CRISES and show Level at his best. In both, what is left in the reader's mind is even worse than what is described. This is the conte cruel at its finest.

MAURICE LEVEL

O

In the Light of the Red Lamp

SEATED in a large armchair near the fire, his elbows on his knees, his hands held out to the warmth, he was talking slowly, interrupting himself abruptly now and again with a murmured: 'Yes ... yes ...' as if he were trying to gather up, to make sure of his memories; then he would continue his sentence.

The table beside him was littered with papers, books, odds and ends of various kinds. The lamp was turned low; I could see nothing of him except his pallid face and his hands, long and thin in the firelight.

The purring of a cat that lay on the hearthrug and the crackling of the logs that sent up strangely shaped flames were the only sounds that broke the silence. He was speaking in a far-away voice as a man might in his sleep:

'Yes ... yes ... It was the great, the greatest misfortune of my life. I could have borne the loss of every penny I possess, of my health ... anything ... everything ... but not that! To have lived for ten years with the woman you adore, and then to watch her die and be left to face life alone ... quite alone ... it was almost more than I could bear ... It is six months since I lost her ... How long ago it seems! And how short the days used to be … If only she had been ill for some time, if only there had been some warning! … It seems a horrible thing to say, but when you know beforehand, the mind gets prepared, doesn't it? … little by little, the heart readjusts its outlook … you grow used to the idea … but as it was …'

'But I thought she had been ill for some time?' I said.

He shook his head:

'Not at all, not at all … It was quite sudden … The doctors were never even able to find out what was the matter with her … It all happened and was over in two days. Since then I don't know how or why I have gone on living. All day long I wander round the house looking for some reminder of her that I never find, imagining that she will appear to me from behind the hangings, that a breath of her scent will come to me in the empty rooms …'

He stretched out his hand towards the table:

'Look, yesterday I found that … this veil, in one of my pockets. She gave it to me to carry one evening when we were at the theatre, and I try to believe it still smells of her perfume, is still warm from its contact with her face … But no! Nothing remains … except sorrow … though there is something, only it … it …

'In the first shock of grief, you sometimes have extraordinary ideas … Can you believe that I photographed her lying on her death-bed? I took my camera into the white, silent room, and lit the magnesium wire: yes, overwhelmed as I was with grief, I did with the most scrupulous precaution and care things from which I should shrink today, revolting things…. Yet it is a great consolation to know she is there, that I shall be able to see her again as she looked that last day.'

'Where is this photograph?' I asked.

Leaning forward, he replied in a low voice:

'I haven't got it, or rather, I have it…. I have the plate, but I have never developed it … It is still in the camera … I have never had the courage to touch it … Yet how I have longed to see it!'

He laid his hand on my arm:

'Listen ... tonight ... your visit ... the way I have been able to talk about her ... it makes me feel better, almost strong again ... Would you, will you come with me to the dark-room? Will you help me to develop the plate?'

He looked into my face with the anxious, questioning expression of a child who fears he may be refused something he longs to have.

'Of course I will,' I answered.

He rose quickly:

'Yes ... with you it will be different. With you I shall keep calm.... and it will do me good ... I shall be much happier ... you'll see ...'

We went to the dark-room, a closet with bottles ranged round on shelves. A trestle-table, littered with dishes, glasses and books, ran along one side of the wall.

By the light of a candle that threw flickering shadows round him, he silently examined the labels on the bottles and rubbed some dishes.

Presently he lit a lamp with red glass, blew out the candle, and said to me:

'Shut the door.'

There was something dramatic about the darkness relieved only by the blood-red light. Unexpected reflections touched the sides of the bottles, played on his wrinkled cheeks, on his hollow temples. He said:

'Is the door closely shut? Then I will begin.'

He opened a dark slide and took out the plate. Holding it carefully at the corners between his thumbs and first fingers, he looked at it intently for a long time as if trying to see the invisible picture which was so soon to appear.

'She is there,' he murmured. 'How wonderful!'

With great care he let it glide into the bath and began to rock the dish.

I cannot say why, but it seemed to me that the tapping of the porcelain on the boards at regular intervals made a curiously mournful sound; the monotonous lapping of the liquid suggested a vague sobbing, and I could not lift

my eyes from the milk-coloured piece of glass which was
slowly taking on a darker line round its edges.

I looked at my friend. His lips were trembling as he
murmured words and sentences which I failed to catch.

He drew out the plate, held it up to the level of his
eyes, and as I leant over his shoulder, said:

'It's coming up ... slowly ... My developer is rather
weak ... But that's nothing ... Look, the high lights are
coming ... Wait ... you'll see ... '

He put the plate back, and it sank into the developer
with a soft, sucking sound.

The grey colour had spread uniformly over the whole
plate. His head bent over it, he explained:

'That dark rectangle is the bed ... up above, that
square ...' he pointed it out with a motion of his chin ...
'is the pillow; and in the middle, that lighter part with the
pale streak outlined on the background ... that is ...
Look, there is the crucifix I put between her fingers. My
poor little one ... my darling! ...'

His voice was hoarse with emotion; the tears were
running down his cheeks as his chest rose and fell.

'The details are coming up,' he said presently, trying to
control himself. 'I can see the lighted candles and the
flowers ... her hair, which was so beautiful ... the hands
of which she was so proud ... and the little white rosary
that I found in her Book of Hours ... My God, how it
hurts to see it all again, yet somehow it makes me happy
... very happy ... I am looking at her again, my poor
darling ...'

Feeling that emotion was again overcoming him and
wishing to soothe, I said:

'Don't you think the plate is ready now?'

He held it up near the lamp, examined it closely, and
put it back in the bath. After a short interval he drew it
out afresh, re-examined it, and again put it back,
murmuring:

'No ... no ... '

Something in the tone of his voice and the abruptness

of his gesture struck me, but I had no time to think, for he at once began to speak again.

'There are still some details to come up ... It's rather long, but as I told you, my developer is weak ... So they only come up one by one.'

He counted; 'One ... two ... three ... four ... five ... This time it will do. If I force it, I shall spoil it ... '

He took out the plate, waved it vertically up and down, dipped it in clean water, and held it towards me:

'Look!'

But as I was stretching out my hand, he started and bent forward, holding the plate up to the lamp, and his face, lit up by the light, had suddenly become so ghastly that I cried:

'What is it? What's the matter?'

His eyes were fixed in a wide terrified stare, his lips were drawn back and showed teeth that were chattering: I could hear his heart beating in a way that made his whole body rock backwards and forwards.

I put my hand on his shoulder, and unable to imagine what could possibly cause such terrible anguish, I cried for the second time:

'But what is it? Tell me. What's the matter?'

He turned his face to me, so drawn it no longer seemed human, and as his blood-shot eyes looked into mine, he seized me by the wrist with a grip that sent his nails into my flesh.

Thrice he opened his mouth, trying to speak, then, brandishing the plate above his head, he shrieked into the crimson-lit darkness:

'The matter! ... the matter! ... My God! ... I have murdered her! ... She wasn't dead! ... the eyes have moved! ...'

MAURICE LEVEL

o

The Test

Not a muscle quivered as the man stood with his gaze fixed on the dead woman.

Through half-closed eyes he looked at the white form on the marble slab with a red gash between the breasts where the cruel knife had entered. In spite of its rigidity, the body had kept its rounded beauty and seemed alive. Only the hands, with their too-transparent skin and violet finger-nails, and the face with its glazed, wide-open eyes and blackened mouth, a mouth that was set in a horrible grin, told of the eternal sleep.

An oppressive silence weighed on the dreary stone-paved hall. Lying on the ground beside the dead woman was the sheet that had covered her: there were blood-stains on it. The magistrates were closely watching the accused man as he stood unmoved between the two warders, his head well up, a supercilious expression on his face, his hands crossed behind his back.

The examining magistrate opened the proceedings:

'Well, Bourdin, do you recognize your victim?'

The man moved his head, looking first at the magistrate, then with reflective attention at the dead woman as if he were searching in the depths of his memory.

'I do not know this woman,' he said at length in a slow voice. 'I have never seen her before.'

'Yet there are witnesses who will state on oath that you were her lover ...'

'The witnesses are mistaken. I never knew this woman.'

'Think well before you answer,' said the magistrate, after a moment's silence. 'What is the use of trying to mislead us? This confrontation is the merest formality, not at all necessary in your case. You are intelligent, and if you wish for any clemency from the jury, I advise you in your own interests to confess.'

'Being innocent, I have nothing to confess.'

'Once again, remember that these denials have no weight at all. I myself am prepared to believe that you gave way to a fit of passion, one of these sudden madnesses when a man sees red ... Look again at your victim ... Can you see her lying there like that and feel no emotion, no repentance? ...'

'Repentance, you say? How can I repent of what I have not done? ... As for emotion, if mine was not entirely deadened, it was at least considerably lessened by the simple fact that I knew what I was going to see when I came here. I feel no more emotion than you do yourself. Why should I? I might just as well accuse you of the crime because you stand there unmoved.'

He spoke in an even voice, without gestures, as a man would who had complete control of himself. The overwhelming charge left him apparently undisturbed, and he confined his defence to calm, obstinate denials.

One of the minor officials said in an undertone:

'They will get nothing out of him ... He will deny it even on the scaffold.'

Without a trace of anger, Bourdin replied:

'That is so, even on the scaffold.'

The sultry atmosphere of an impending thunderstorm added to the feeling of exasperation caused by this struggle between accusers and accused, by this obstinate 'no' to every question in the face of all evidence.

Through the dirty window-pane the setting sun threw a vivid golden glare on the corpse.

'So be it,' said the magistrate: 'You do not know the victim. But what about this?'

He held out an ivory-handled knife, a large knife with clotted blood on its strong blade.

The man took the weapon in his hands, looked at it for a few seconds, then handed it to one of the warders and wiped his fingers.

'That? ... I have never seen it before.'

'Systematic denial ... that is your plan, is it?' sneered the magistrate. 'This knife is yours. It used to hang in your study. Twenty people have seen it there.'

The prisoner bowed.

'That proves nothing but that twenty people have made a mistake.'

'Enough of this,' said the magistrate. 'Though there is not a shadow of doubt about your guilt, we will make one last decisive test. There are marks of strangulation on the neck of the victim. You can clearly see the traces of five fingers, particularly long fingers, the medical expert tells us. Show these gentlemen your hands. You see?'

The magistrate raised the chin of the dead woman.

There were violet marks on the white skin of the neck: at the end of every bruise the flesh was deeply pitted, as if the nails had been dug in. It looked like the skeleton of a giant leaf.

'There is your handiwork. Whilst with your left hand you were trying to strangle this poor woman, with your free right hand you drove this knife into her heart. Come here and repeat the action of the night of the murder. Place your fingers on the bruises of the neck ... Come along ...'

Bourdin hesitated for a second, then shrugged his shoulders and said in a sullen voice:

'You wish to see if my fingers correspond? ... and suppose they do? ... What will that prove? ...'

He moved towards the slab: he was noticeably paler,

his teeth were clenched, his eyes dilated. For a moment he stood very still, his gaze fixed on the rigid body, then with an automaton-like gesture, he stretched out his hand and laid it on the flesh.

The involuntary shudder that ran through him at the cold, clammy contact caused a sudden, sharp movement of his fingers, which contracted as if to strangle.

Under this pressure, the set muscles of the dead woman seemed to come to life. You could see them stretch obliquely from the collar-bone to the angle of the jaw: the mouth lost its horrible grin and opened as if in an atrocious yawn, the dry lips drew back to disclose teeth encrusted with thick, brown slime.

Everyone started with horror.

There was something enigmatic and terrifying about this gaping mouth in this impassive face, this mouth open as if for a death-rattle from beyond the portals of the grave, the sound only held back by the swollen tongue that was doubled back in the throat.

Then, all at once, there came from that black hole a low, undefined noise, a sort of humming that suggested a hive, and an enormous blue-bottle with shining wings, one of these charnel-house flies that live on death, an unspeakably filthy beast, flew out, hissing as it circled round the cavern as if to guard the approach. Suddenly it paused ... then made a straight course for the blue lips of Bourdin.

With a motion of horror, he tried to drive it away: but the monstrous thing came back, clinging to his lip with all the strength of its poisonous claws.

With one bound the man leapt backwards, his eyes wild, his hair on end, his hands stretched out, his whole body quivering as he shrieked like a madman:

'I confess! ... I did it! ... Take me away! ... Take me away! ...'

MRS RIVERS'S JOURNAL

○

Perceval Landon

Perceval Landon (1869–1927) is one of those authors (lucky or unlucky, depending on your point of view) who is now only remembered for just one story. In his case, the story is a classic, 'Thurnley Abbey', from his 1908 collection RAW EDGES, one of the most reprinted tales in the genre.

But there was more to Landon than ghost stories. He was a barrister and journalist who gained his reputation as a war correspondent covering the Boer War. He knew Africa well, and travelled extensively in the Far East and India.

Landon's knowledge of Asia came to fruition when he joined the Younghusband expedition to Lhasa in 1903, at first as a special correspondent for The Times *but eventually becoming the expedition's official recorder. His massive two volume (870 pages!) book LHASA: AN ACCOUNT OF THE COUNTRY AND PEOPLE OF CENTRAL TIBET was published in 1905.*

Landon's first book was as editor of HELIOTROPES (1903), a revised edition of a seventeenth century work by John Parmenter. He put his knowledge of the East to good use again in a later book, UNDER THE SUN (1906), a volume on Indian cities.

Though his book output was limited, Landon wrote for over twenty years as the Daily Telegraph's eastern correspondent, and covered the First World War for all its four years.

RAW EDGES and 'Thurnley Abbey' is now all he is remembered for in the literary field. I thought it might be worth while having another look at RAW EDGES to see if there were any further stories that merit revival.

'Mrs Rivers's Journal', from that book, seems to have been overlooked for 80 years. For most of its length, an intriguing Victorian morality drama, right at the end it brings in the supernatural in a scene worthy of M.R. James. It is most definitely worth reprinting.

PERCEVAL LANDON

O

MRS RIVERS'S JOURNAL

I

'*May 19th.* Two or three people to dinner and a play.
Dennis, Mr and Mrs Richmond, Lady Alresford, and
Colonel Wyke. D. saw me home after. I think something
must be the matter. D. was very much upset last night,
I'm sure. It all happened very suddenly, as he had been as
delightful as ever all the evening. I can't think what it is.
It was about midnight when he said something to himself,
as he was looking out of the window, and changed
completely.'

Later in the day Mrs Rivers added, almost in another
hand, these notes:

'D. called here this afternoon. At first he was very
silent, and I asked him what the matter was. He said that
it was not my fault in any way, and that he would explain
some day. Meanwhile he asked me not to worry. But I'm
sure something is very wrong, and if it is not my fault I'm
half afraid that it may be on my behalf that Dennis is so
upset. But he won't say anything, and I can't think that
there is anything really to be feared. He only stayed half
an hour, and went away saying that he would like to see

me tomorrow morning. I thought it was a pity that he
should come too often to the house, and said that I would
meet him in the National Gallery at twelve o'clock. I
wonder what it all means.'

Mrs Rivers, whose locked journal is here quoted, was
in herself a very ordinary kind of pretty woman. So far as
the world knew, she was a widow, and a rich widow. Her
husband had died about four years before this date, and
it is unlikely that he was very seriously mourned. Colonel
Rivers—his title was really a Volunteer distinction, but the
man deserved no little credit for the way in which he
worked up his battalion—was an inordinately jealous
man, and though no one believed he had the least reason
for suspecting his wife's acquaintance with Captain
Dennis Cardyne, there is no doubt that, shortly before he
died, it became almost a monomania with him, it may
even have been a symptom of the trouble from which he
must even then have been suffering acutely. Cardyne, a
remarkably straight and loyal friend, with no brains, but a
good sense of humour and principles which were at least
as correct as those of his fellow-officers, was surprised one
day by being peremptorily forbidden the house by
Colonel Rivers. Human nature being what it is, it is
possible that Cardyne then felt that the least impediment
which friendship or loyalty could impose was removed,
and there is no doubt that a general feeling of sympathy
and affection for Mrs Rivers took on quite another
colouring by this idiotic proceeding on the part of Mrs
Rivers's husband. Cardyne's eyes were opened for the first
time to the life that Mrs Rivers must have led since her
marriage four years before, though indeed she had previously taken some pains that he should quite understand
her unhappiness at home. But Cardyne, who knew and
liked the Colonel—in the patronizing way that the most
junior of regular officers will regard a volunteer—unconsciously discounted a good deal, knowing that most
women like to think that their husbands misunderstand
them. Hitherto he had neither disbelieved nor believed

what Mrs Rivers was insinuating. Now, however, his pity was aroused, though nothing in his conduct showed it at the moment.

I do not suggest for a moment that Mrs Rivers was either a very interesting or a very virtuous person. But she had the little fluffy pleading ways by which many men are strangely attracted, and even if Cardyne had made any advances, her respect for conventionality, which was far more sacred to her than she quite realized, fully supplied the place of morality during the few months that elapsed between Colonel Rivers's explosion of jealousy and his sudden death.

There were not many people, except the very nearest of kin, who were aware of a curious clause which Colonel Rivers had inserted in his will about the time that he forbade Dennis Cardyne to come to the house. Personal references of an unpleasant kind are not copied into the volumes in Somerset House, which contain the wills to which probate has been granted. A proviso in the will that Mrs Rivers, in the event of her marrying again, was to forfeit one-half of the somewhat large fortune bequeathed to her by her husband was public property, but only to those who were chiefly concerned it was allowed to be known that in the event of her marrying Captain Dennis Cardyne—whose name was preceded by an epithet—she was to forfeit every penny.

When Mrs Rivers heard the terms of her husband's will, she lost the last tinge of respect she had ever had for her departed helpmeet. The prohibition certainly achieved its end, but it was not long before Cardyne and Mrs Rivers settled down to a hole-and-corner flirtation, which probably brought far more terror than pleasure into the latter's life. Cardyne assured me that there was never anything more, and I am accustomed to believe that Dennis Cardyne speaks the truth. But the world thought otherwise and found many excuses for them. Mrs Rivers could always justify to herself what she was doing by a remembrance of her husband's insane and ungenerous jealousy; but the fact remained that, however much this suffced to quiet her own conscience, Mrs Rivers was, to the very marrow of her, a common little thing, utterly afraid of the world's opinion, and quite unable to carry through the unconventionality of her affection for Cardyne without a burden of misery. And they did the silliest of things. After all, if a man will see a woman home from the play night after night and stay till two in the morning, he must be ready for a howl or two from the brute world. We have all done it, and done it most platonically, but at least we knew that it wasn't over wise.

I used to meet her at one time. She was always to be found in houses of a certain type. Her friends were women who took their views of life from one another, or from Society weekly papers. In the wake of Royalty they did no doubt achieve a certain amount of serviceable work for others, and at least it could be said of them that none of them seemed likely to scandalize the susceptibilities of their comfortable, if somewhat narrow, circle. Never twice would you meet a clever man, or a brilliant woman, at these feasts.

If you will take the names of those who were present at Mrs Rivers's small dinner-party on 18 March, you will see exactly what I mean. Colonel Wyke was an old friend of her husband's. He had a little place in the country in which he grew begonias very well, and was, I believed, writing the history of the parish, from such printed material as he could find in the library of the county town. Lady Alresford lent her name to every charity organization without discrimination or inquiry. She was a president of a rescue home in London, which probably did much harm to conventional morality. Mr and Mrs Richmond were a quiet, and somewhat colourless, little couple of considerable wealth, but without any real interest or purpose in life except that, if the truth must be told, of gossiping about their neighbours. I have never known Richmond at a loss for an inaccurate version of any scandal in London.

I have set out the circumstances in which Mrs Rivers lived at greater length than may be thought necessary. But I am inclined to think that it was very largely the facts of her surroundings, and the influence unconsciously exerted by her friends, that eventually led Mrs Rivers into the most awful trouble. As I have said, I am a somewhat silent person, and I meditate more perhaps than talkative folk upon the reversals and eccentricities of fate. I think I could safely affirm that though I did not then know the real relations that existed between Mrs Rivers and Cardyne—who, by the way, for all his density, was head and shoulders above this crowd—I still could never have dreamed that fate would have whetted her heaviest shaft to bring down such poor and uninteresting game as this. But, as a matter of fact, I did not know that Mrs Rivers was nothing more than a close friend of Cardyne's. On the face of it I thought that Cardyne could never be very long attracted by any one possessed of so little interest as Mrs Rivers; but, against that, I admitted that Cardyne's constancy was quite in keeping with his general simple loyalty; and, on the other hand, I was not sure that Mrs Rivers might not be more interesting in that relation than she might have seemed likely to be to a mere outsider like myself. She might have been possessed, like many other women, of the two entirely distinct and mutually exclusive natures that Browning thanks God for.

I came to know Cardyne pretty well in those months, and if any feeling of anger should be caused by the story I am going to tell with the help of Mrs Rivers's journal, it is only fair to say that Cardyne did all he could. It is a grim tale.

Cardyne, as he had promised, went to the National Gallery at twelve o'clock on 20 May. It was a Friday, and in consequence there were very few present except the young ladies in brown holland over-alls, who were painting copies of deceased masters in the intervals of conversation. But in the central room there was one industrious figure labouring away at a really important copy of the Bronzino at the other end of the room. Mrs Rivers was sitting in a chair opposite the Michael Angelo—a picture, by the way, which she would certainly have relegated to a housemaid's bedroom had she possessed it herself.

Cardyne was punctual. But it was clear from the moment he entered the gallery that the interview was going to be unpleasant. He walked listlessly, and with a white face, up to where Mrs Rivers was sitting.

She was really alarmed at the sight of him, and, putting out a hand, said to him:

'Good gracious, Dennis, don't frighten me like this!'

Cardyne sat down and said:

'You've got to listen, Mary. It is a matter that concerns you.'

Mrs Rivers grew rather white, and said:

'Nobody knows, surely? Nobody would believe. We are perfectly safe if we deny it absolutely?'

Cardyne shook his head.

'Listen,' he said wearily, 'did you see the posters of the *Star* as you came along?'

Mrs Rivers thought that he was going mad.

'Yes,' she said; 'there was a speech by Roosevelt and a West End murder, but what has that got to do with us?'

Dennis put his hand in front of his eyes for a moment, and then said:

'Everything—at least the murder has.'

Mrs Rivers grew rather cross.

'For Heaven's sake tell me what you mean!' she said; 'I don't understand anything. What can this murder have to do with you and me?'

Cardyne said, in a dull and rather monotonous voice:

'A man called Harkness was murdered on the night of 18 May. He lived at No. 43 Addistone Place.'

Mrs Rivers began a remark, but Cardyne impatiently stopped her.

'That house, as you know, is exactly opposite yours. The old man was found murdered yesterday, the police were making inquiries all day, the newspapers have just got hold of it, and an arrest has been made. They have taken into custody a maidservant called Craik, who had apparently one of the best of reasons for hating Harkness.'

Cardyne broke off. Mrs Rivers breathed again.

'But what in the name of Heaven has all this to do with me or you?

Cardyne paused for thirty seconds before he answered:

'The maidservant is innocent.' His sentences fell slowly and heavily. 'The murder was committed by the man-servant.'

Mrs Rivers was not a person of very quick imagination, but she vaguely felt that there was something horrible impending over her, and, after an indrawn breath, she said quickly:

'Where did you see it from?'

Dennis turned round and looked at her straight in the eyes and did not say a word. Mrs Rivers felt the whole gallery swinging and swirling round her. She seemed to be dropping through space, and the only certain things were Dennis Cardyne's two straight grey eyes fixed in mingled despair and misery upon her own. A moment later the girl at the other end of the room looked up with a start, and went quickly across the gallery to ask if she could be of any use. Mrs Rivers, in a high falsetto that was almost a scream, had said, 'What are you going to do?' and fallen forward out of her chair. She pulled herself together as the girl came up, and muttered a conventional excuse, but she hardly knows how it was that she got home and found herself lying on her own bed, vaguely conscious that Cardyne had just left the room after giving her the strictest instructions as to what she was to do to keep well, and assuring her that there might not be the slightest risk or trouble of any kind. And he added that he would return about six o'clock in the evening, and tell her all there was to be known.

II

I heard this story some time afterwards, but I remember,
as if it were yesterday, the remark which some one made
to me about Mrs Rivers during the season of 1904.

'The woman's going mad. She goes to every lighted
candle she can scrape up an invitation to, and last week,
to my certain knowledge, she—she, poor dear!—went to
two Primrose League dances.'

Right enough this feverish activity was regarded as a
sign and portent, for Mrs Rivers was one of those people
who thought that her social position was best secured by
kicking down her ladders below her. I confess that a night
or two later I was amazed indeed at finding her at my
poor old friend Miss Frankie's evening party. Miss
Frankie was the kindest and dullest soul in London. She
was also the only real conscientious Christian I have ever
known. She refrained from malicious criticism of those
around her. This perhaps made her duller than ever, and
I will admit that there was a curious species of mental
exercise associated with visits to her house. As a rule, one
found the earnest district visitor sitting next one at
dinner, or it might be some well-intentioned faddist with
elastic-sided boots, bent on the reformation of the butter-
flies of society, or the House of Lords. But among those
who really understood things, there were many who used
to put up with the eccentricities of a night out at Miss
Frankie's if only because of the genuine pleasure that it
obviously gave to the little lady to entertain her old
friends. I twice met San Iguelo the painter there, and for
the first time began to like the man, if only for going.
Now this was particularly, I fancy, the social level from
which Mrs Rivers had herself risen; but precisely therefore was it the social level which she took particular pains
now to ignore. A year ago Mrs Rivers would have regarded
an evening with Miss Frankie as an evening worse than
wasted.

That night, I was sitting in a corner of the room. I was

talking to a young artist who had not yet risen in the world, and probably never will; still, she had a sense of humour, and knew Mrs Rivers by sight. She watched her entrance and, without a touch of malice, she turned to me and said:

'What on earth has made Mrs Rivers honour us with her presence to-night?'

I did not know, and said so, but I watched Mrs Rivers for some minutes. Of course it was Mrs Rivers, but I doubt if any one who knew her in a merely casual way would have been quite sure. I am prefectly certain that the woman was painted. Now Mrs Rivers never painted in old days. Moreover, she never stopped talking, which was also unlike her. (The woman had her good points, you see.) However, there she was. Once, our eyes met, and probably neither of us liked to define the uneasiness that I am sure we both felt.

She had a way of leaving her mouth open and allowing the tip of a very pink tongue to fill one corner of it. I knew it well in the old days. Somebody must have told her that it was arch. It was a touch of vulgarity of just that sort of which no one could very well break her after she had once started climbing the society ladder, and in time it grew to be a trick. At one moment, when Miss Frankie was occupied with a newcomer, Mrs Rivers's face fell into a mask that convinced me that the woman was ill. As soon as her forced vivacity left her, the whole face fell away on to the bones, the eyes became unnaturally bright, and there was a quick, hunted look about them. She was evidently quite oblivious for the moment, and I saw her tongue go up into the corner of her mouth. It was a small matter, but the contrast between the expression of her face, and this silly little affectation no one could fail to notice.

She stayed for half an hour and went on somewhere, I suppose to a dance. She was alone, and as I happened to be at the foot of the stairs as she came down, I thought it was only civil, as I was myself hatted and coated for going

away, to ask if she had her servant there to call the
carriage. It was all rather awkward. I moved across the
floor to her with the conventional offer so obviously on
my lips and even in my gait, that I could not well be
stopped going on with my part, even though at the last
moment, almost after she might have recognized me, she
shut her eyes and said in a tone of broken helplessness:
'O my God, have mercy upon me!' She opened her eyes
again a moment afterwards, saw me with a start,
recovered herself, and pressed me almost hysterically to
be dropped somewhere by her, she did not seem to care
where. But I refused. I did not much want to be dropped
by Mrs Rivers, and I am quite sure that my humble
diggings did not lie anywhere on the route to her next
engagement that evening.

A few days after that I met Cardyne, and with the usual
fatuity of any one who tries with all his might to keep off
a subject, I said to him that I had seen Mrs Rivers, and
that she seemed to me to be strangely upset and unlike
herself. He looked at me rather hard for a moment and
said:

'Oh, I know all about that: she is worried about her
people.'

Now that is absurd, for nobody ever is worried to that
extent about her people, or at least she doesn't say, 'O my
God, have mercy upon me!' if she is. However, it was no
business of mine, and I went on in my humble way of life,
though from time to time I heard some notice taken of
Mrs Rivers's hysterical behaviour during that season.

Cardyne told me afterwards that at the moment when I
had noticed Mrs Rivers's behaviour, she was almost determined to make the sacrifice by which alone, as it was now
too clear, could the unfortunate maidservant at No. 43 be
cleared from the charge against her. The excitement
caused by the murder had died down somewhat since the
middle of May when it had taken place, but every one was
looking forward with gladiatorial interest to the trial. It

was appointed to begin on 30 June at the Old Bailey, and though, as I have said, from a legal point of view the case looked very black against Martha Craik, the servant, it was still felt that something more was needed before the jury would accept as proved a crime which for some reasons a woman seemed hardly likely to carry out. Cardyne told me that, of course, his first duty was to reassure Mrs Rivers. This he did at first with such effect that the woman regarded the likelihood of any serious issue to the trial as most improbable, and eagerly hugged to herself the relief which her lover thus held out to her.

'On Thursday afternoon,' said Cardyne to me, 'after our meeting in the National Gallery, the unhappy woman had so convinced herself that there was nothing really to fear, that she went down on her knees in her own drawing-room beside the tea-table and made me kneel with her.' Cardyne's face, as he said this, almost made me smile, though it was hardly an occasion for mirth. 'She rose, gave me tea, and all the time asked me to see in it the kindness and tenderness of God, and hoped it would be a warning to me.' Of what, I really hardly think either Cardyne or myself knew. 'But at any rate,' said Cardyne, 'I had cheered her up for the time being. But I lied like a trooper.'

As a matter of fact, the case against Craik grew blacker and blacker every day. She was the only servant who slept alone in the house, and all the others were ready to swear, with unanimity, that neither they nor their stable-companions had left their rooms all night. To this I ought to have attached little importance, as servants, when frightened, are always ready to swear that they did not sleep a wink all night. But it made a very great impression on the public.

The knife with which the murder was done was found in rather a curious way. The police inspector was asking some questions of the manservant in the passage outside Mr Harkness's bedroom door. Another servant came by, and both men took a step inwards to allow room for him to pass. The manservant, whose name was Steele, in taking a sharp pace up to the wall, actually cut his boot upon the knife, which was stuck upright in the floor, blade outwards, between the jamb of the door and the wainscoting, where it had escaped notice. It was an ordinary kitchen table-knife, worn and very sharp, and the fact that Steele cut his boot upon it was taken as proof beyond all hesitation or question that Steele at least was totally ignorant of everything connected with the crime. But Steele was the man whom Cardyne had seen in Harkness's room.

To return to Mrs Rivers. Cardyne found that it was impossible to conceal from her much longer the fact that things were going badly indeed against Craik. One afternoon, about a fortnight before the trial opened, he found it his terrible duty to make Mrs Rivers see that unless his evidence was forthcoming, an innocent woman might be condemned to death. For a long time Mrs Rivers had understood that all was not well. Perhaps if all had been well she would have had just the same nervous breakdown. The woman was at her tether's end, and there is no doubt that in spite of her hysterical attempts to distract her thoughts, she was coming to realize what the position was.

Here are some extracts from her diary at different times:–

'*June 20th.* All going as well as possible. D. tells me that he still thinks there may be no real reason for alarm. He hears at the club that the verdict at the inquest is thought unreasonable by people in town.'

(Let every woman remember that there is no more worthless authority for any statement than that a man has heard it at his club. As a rule, it is worth no more than her maid's opinion as she does her hair that evening.)

'*July 1st.* Lady Garrison came across this afternoon and upset me a good deal. D. never told me about the door of 43 having been chained all night. Will see him about this tomorrow.

'*June 10th.* [This was about the time when I saw Mrs Rivers.] Worse and worse. Of course everything must go right, but I would give five years of my life to be over the next two months. All must be right. D. tells me so. The suspense is awful.

'*July 14th.* Sampson gave me warning this morning. I was horribly frightened when he actually told me, and I'm rather afraid that he noticed it. He says he is going to his brother in Canada, and of course he has always told me that he would go as soon as he could. He said nothing to make me uneasy, spoke very respectfully, and offered to suit his convenience to mine at any time. I don't know what to do. I must ask D. Perhaps it would be better if he left at once.'

I am sure it passed through that wretched woman's brain that if her butler could, so to speak, be made to look as if he had bolted from the country a week before the trial took place, some suspicion would be aroused which might, perhaps, cause a postponement of the sentence, if the worst came to the worst. More than that, she was, of course, anxious to get rid thus easily of some one who, for all her precautions, might have known about Cardyne's visit, and finally, in the event of her having to go through a great nervous strain at the time of the trial, she hardly knew whether it would be better to have a new butler who might simply look upon her with unpleasant inquisitiveness as an hysterical subject, or the old one who, for all his discretion and sympathy, could hardly fail to see that something very new, very odd, and very wrong was going on in her life.

It was clear, in fact, that Mrs Rivers was slowly realizing that there was actually a probability of the trial resulting in the conviction of Craik, and when, a fortnight later, Cardyne took his courage in his hands and went to Addistone Terrace to break the news to her of Craik's conviction and sentence to death, I fancy she knew all before he opened his lips. Cardyne never intentionally told me much about that interview. Indirectly he let me know a good deal, and I am perfectly sure that any feeling of repugnance or horror that he ever felt against Mrs Rivers was that afternoon changed into the deepest and most heartfelt pity. It was one of those interviews from which both parties emerge old and broken. Mrs Rivers apparently saw what was going to be urged by Cardyne, rattled off his arguments one after the other, with horrible fluency, and then, while he sat in white silence on the sofa, flung at him:

'And you've come to tell me that as things have gone wrong, I'm to sacrifice my honour and my reputation for that wretched woman's life!'

All Cardyne could say was simply, 'I have.'

At this Mrs Rivers leant against the mantelpiece and spoke clearly and monotonously for half a minute, as if she had been long conning the lesson, and drew out before Cardyne's dazed understanding a dramatic but unconvincing picture of what a woman's reputation means to her. She declaimed with pathos that, like any other woman, she would rather die than be disgraced in the eyes of the world. Poor Cardyne's one interruption was not a happy one, yet it is one which, from a man's standpoint, had a touch of nobility. He said:

'But it isn't a question of *your* dying.'

When Mrs Rivers said that she would rather die than suffer dishonour, his involuntary ejaculation told her plainly enough that, up to that moment, he had not conceived it possible that any woman could be so vile as to sacrifice the life of an innocent woman for her own social ambitions.

There was a silence of a quarter of a minute. Mrs Rivers fidgeted with the fire-screen. Then she said:

'So you intend to betray me?'

At this poor Cardyne was more hopelessly bewildered than ever.

'Good God, no!' he said: 'of course I can only do what you decide. The matter is entirely in your hands; but surely-'

Mrs Rivers stopped him with a gesture.

'I absolutely forbid you to say a word. I will decide the matter, and I will let you know; but, understand me, except with my express permission, I rely upon your honour to keep the secret for ever, if I wish it.'

This at least Cardyne could understand, and he gave the promise with unquestionable earnestness. But he was to realize that a man placed in such a position, with honour tearing him in two opposite ways, is condemned to the worst anguish which the devil knows how to inflict.

However, he had given his word—a quite unnecessary proceeding, if only Mrs Rivers had known it—and it only remained for him to try and make her see the matter from the point of view from which he himself regarded it. He could not bring himself to believe that she would refuse. This continual appeal resulted in almost daily scenes. Cardyne, with the best of intentions, was not a tactful person, and in season and out of season he presented the case to Mrs Rivers from a standpoint she never understood, and never could have understood. She in turn, driven to bay like an animal, wholly failed to see that in this matter Cardyne's secrecy might be trusted to his death, and shook with terror as the date for the execution drew on. These two wretched souls, during the last fortnight in July, fought out this dreary fight between themselves, until poor Cardyne came to wonder how it was that he had ever in the wildest moment of infatuation cared for such a woman as Mrs Rivers daily proved herself to be.

All this while Mrs Rivers was steadily going out to dinners and dances, and in the afternoons she attended more regularly than anyone the committee meetings presided over by Royalty with which her name had been so long and honourably connected.

III

It is strange in the light of after events to remember
Cardyne's life among us during the days which followed
the trial of Martha Craik. I have never supposed, nor do I
now suppose, that Cardyne had in him many of the necessary constituents of an actor, but I am perfectly sure that
there were few among us, his friends, who noticed at that
time anything in him except perhaps a certain absent-
mindedness and irritability. Perhaps the man's simple
nature was its own salvation. To his mind there could be
no two views as to his own personal duty. He was clearly
bound to adopt Mrs Rivers's decision in this matter, just
as on a doubtful field of battle he would not have
dreamed of disobeying his colonel's most desperate order.
What must have made it doubly hard for him, however,
was the feeling that though he was thus bound he was
obliged to use every fair argument in his power to make
Mrs Rivers see that she had adopted a course which, to
him, and I believe to any man, was almost unthinkable.
Here his plain, blunt tactlessness served him poorly
indeed. One afternoon, after an hour's conversation–if
any discussion between a man and a woman of such a
topic can rightly be called conversation–it happened that
he blurted out what, in his simple soul, he had imagined
Mrs Rivers had understood from the beginning. To her
incessant argument that death was better than dishonour
he opposed, as if it were the most natural thing in the
world, the remark: 'But there is not the least reason why
we should survive. Provided this woman's life is saved you
will have done everything that is necessary, and I think
you would be right. I will gladly die with you.'

Upon Mrs Rivers's fevered brain and throbbing conscience this last suggestion had at least the effect of making
the woman and the man understand each other at last.
Disregarding, forgetting all that she had said, the
haggard, red-eyed woman, dressed as it chanced in the
most becoming of biscuit-coloured cloth gowns, turned

upon Cardyne with a scream.

'Die!' she echoed. 'Do you mean that I ought to get that woman off and then kill myself? Good God, what a brute you are!'

And then Cardyne understood what manner of woman wretched Mrs Rivers was. Perhaps a clever man might have availed himself of her reaction, which set in the next day and which was necessarily great, but poor Cardyne had had neither the capacity nor the inclination to conceal from Mrs Rivers, as he had left the house the previous day, that he detested and despised her. He never went back till the afternoon before the day set for Craik's execution.

Now and then, during the course of the next day, Mrs Rivers saw things with Cardyne's eyes. So far, however, from this leading to any permanent change of her intentions, it merely made her suspect in abject cowardly terror that those considerations might, as the fatal day approached, prove too much for Cardyne, and that on his own initiative he would blurt out the story. The days went on. Mrs Rivers still clung to the hope that though Craik had been sentenced to death, something would be done, something must happen to prevent the execution. What was God in His heaven for if not for this? She had a blind hope that somehow or other a wholly innocent person could not be allowed by God to suffer capital punishment in these days of modern civilization.

There had been a time in these miserable weeks when she attempted to persuade Cardyne that what he had seen would not, after all, make much difference to the fate of Martha Craik. But upon his point he was as clear as the ablest of barristers. He had seen the manservant in the house opposite, stripped to the skin, with a knife in his hand, moving about in Mr Harkness's room at midnight. Cardyne was the only man in England who knew why it was that so barbarous a murder could have taken place without the murderer receiving even a splash or smear upon his or her clothes. Mere proof of the presence of a naked man moving about in the house that night would beyond all question have saved the unhappy maidservant.

Martha Craik had been sentenced to be hanged at eight o'clock on Monday morning, 30 July.

Cardyne spent Sunday afternoon with Mrs Rivers.

Sunday evening he spent in his own rooms. He did not leave them for three months. I suppose if ever a man had an excuse for intentional and continuous self-intoxication, Cardyne was that man. He had done his best. He had used every argument, entreaty, and exhortation he knew of. He had failed completely, and his sense of honour bound him with a band of iron. Few men will dare to criticise him. He would have killed himself if he had been sober, I think.

Mrs Rivers was in a state that night which clearly bordered on insanity. Twice over she wrote out a confession. Once she actually rang the bell and gave the letter, which was addressed to Cardyne, into her servant's hands, but she was at the door calling for it again before he had reached the bottom of the stairs. About one o'clock she got into a dressing-gown, and with dry, hot eyes and scorching brain she watched the small hours of the morning go by. She was up in her room alone. The servants had long gone to bed.

Daylight came small thin, and blue, between the crack of the curtains. Six o'clock. Mrs Rivers was kneeling by the side of her bed with her face buried in the quilt. One hand dropped beside her, the other was stretched out and clutched a prettily designed Italian crucifix.

She had prayed at intervals all night long, and had even denounced the injustice of God that no mercy or comfort was extended to her in what she even then called her hour of trial. You will have grossly misunderstood the nature of Mrs Rivers if you think that this was mere blasphemy. It was the solemn conviction in that poor little mind that God was treating her very hardly in not deadening the last appeals of her conscience against her own wickedness.

Dry-eyed and with aching brain she watched, with her chin on the quilt like a dog, the daylight grow. Seven o'clock. There was a clock on a church near which gave the chimes with astonishing clearness in the morning air. The milk-carts had ceased to rattle through the street. Vans took up their daily work, and the foot-passengers hurried by, sometimes with a low murmur of conversation, under the bright, ashy sky of a London July morning. She still knelt there unmoved. She could not have moved, I think, if she had wished; anyway she told herself that physically she could not do anything now, much as she wanted to. It was now too late.

In the curious half-light of her curtained room she could distinguish things pretty well, and one of the three slants of light fell upon herself. There was a glass between the windows, and as the light increased she could see herself in it. Even then she had time to pity the drawn and haggard misery which was stamped upon the face that met her own.

The first chime of eight o'clock struck from the church clock. With a shudder Mrs Rivers drew her face down again and buried it in the side of the bed, convulsively clutching the crucifix. The four quarters tinkled out, and then the hour struck.

There was a light knock at the door.

Mrs Rivers did not answer. With her face buried in the side of the bed, she was still trying to pray, but she heard it and she listened.

There was a step across the room, and someone was clearly standing at her side. She moved her eyes enough to look downwards, and she saw, three feet away from her, the end of a common skirt and two coarse boots. They did not belong either to her maid or to anyone else in the house. With a sudden icy hand at her heart, she turned back with shut eyes to the position she had occupied for so long. At last she let her eyes open. She fixed them horribly upon the reflection in the glass. And she has known little or nothing since.

Sometimes in sheer defence of Cardyne himself, I think that he *must* have lied to me about their relations. Sometimes I feel sure he did lie.

THE WOMAN OF THE SÆTER

O

Jerome K. Jerome

Not a name instantly associated with ghost stories, Jerome K. Jerome (1859–1927) is remembered as a humorist, in particular for his novel THREE MEN IN A BOAT (1889). But Jerome was quite fond of an occasional tale of terror and even wrote one of the very few satires on ghost stories, his hilarious TOLD AFTER SUPPER (1891).

Jerome was born in Walsall, the son of a coal mine owner. Brought up in London when the family moved there in the 1860s, Jerome tried his hand at several jobs, among them solicitor's clerk, teacher and actor, before turning to writing. He scored an immediate success with his first book, ON THE STAGE AND OFF (1888) and wrote full time thereafter.

He enjoyed magazine work and even founded a couple of his own, The Idler, which he started with fellow writer Robert Barr, and the later Today, a weekly paper that very nearly bankrupted Jerome after a ruinously expensive libel case.

His writing covered many fields, not just humour, and he was a successful dramatist for many years. Tucked away among his copious output are some now-forgotten tales of terror and ghost stories.

In NOVEL NOTES *(1893) he wrote one of the most reprinted items in this genre, the sardonic tale 'The Dancing Partner' and two overlooked little tales, 'The Skeleton' and 'The Snake'.*

This particular story comes from his 1894 collection JOHN INGERFIELD *and first saw magazine publication shortly before. It is a very odd tale indeed, set in a Norwegian location (most unusual in those days but see John Shannon's story earlier) where man and the unknown live in close and terrifying proximity.*

If the only Jerome you've read up to now has been THREE MEN IN A BOAT, *you're in for a very pleasant surprise.*

JEROME K. JEROME

O

THE WOMAN OF THE SÆTER

WILD-REINDEER stalking is hardly so exciting a sport as the evening's verandah talk in Norroway hotels would lead the trustful traveller to suppose. Under the charge of your guide, a very young man with the dreamy, wistful eyes of those who live in valleys, you leave the farmstead early in the forenoon, arriving towards twilight at the desolate hut which, for so long as you remain upon the uplands, will be your somewhat cheerless headquarters.

Next morning, in the chill, mist-laden dawn, you rise; and after a breakfast of coffee and dried fish, shoulder your Remington, and step forth silently into the raw, damp air; the guide locking the door behind you, the key grating harshly in the rusty lock.

For hour after hour you toil over the steep, stony ground, or wind through the pines, speaking in whispers, lest your voice reach the quick ears of your prey, that keeps its head ever pressed against the wind. Here and there, in the hollows of the hills lie wide fields of snow, over which you pick your steps thoughtfully, listening to the smothered thunder of the torrent, tunnelling its way beneath your feet and wondering whether the frozen arch above it be at all points as firm as is desirable. Now and again, as in single file you walk cautiously along some jagged ridge, you catch glimpses of the green world, three thousand feet below you; though you gaze not long upon the view, for your attention is chiefly directed to watching the footprints of the guide, lest by deviating to the right or left you find yourself at one stride back in the valley— or, to be more correct, are found there.

These things you do, and as exercise they are healthful and invigorating. But a reindeer you never see, and unless, overcoming the prejudices of your British-bred conscience, you care to take an occasional pop at a fox, you had better have left your rifle at the hut, and, instead, have brought a stick which would have been helpful. Notwithstanding which the guide continues sanguine, and in broken English, helped out by stirring gesture, telling of the terrible slaughter generally done by sportsmen under his superintendence, and of the vast herds that generally infest these fjelds; and when you grow sceptical upon the subject of Reins he whispers alluringly of Bears.

Once in a way you will come across a track, and will follow it breathlessly for hours, and it will lead to a sheer precipice. Whether the explanation is suicide, or a reprehensible tendency on the part of the animal towards practical joking, you are left to decide for yourself. Then, with many rough miles between you and your rest, you abandon the chase.

But I speak from personal experience merely.

All day long we had tramped through the pitiless rain, stopping only for an hour at noon to eat some dried venison and smoke a pipe beneath the shelter of an overhanging cliff. Soon afterwards Michael knocked over a ryper (a bird that will hardly take the trouble to hop out of your way) with his gun-barrel, which incident cheered us a little; and, later on, our flagging spirits were still further revived by the discovery of apparently very recent deer-tracks. These we followed, forgetful, in our eagerness, of the lengthening distance back to the hut, of the fading daylight, of the gathering mist. The track led us higher and higher, farther and farther into the mountains, until on the shores of a desolate rock-bound vand it abruptly ended, and we stood staring at one another, and the snow began to fall.

Unless in the next half-hour we could chance upon a sæter, this meant passing the night upon the mountain. Michael and I looked at the guide; but though, with characteristic Norwegian sturdiness, he put a bold face upon it, we could see that in that deepening darkness he knew no more than we did. Wasting no time on words, we made straight for the nearest point of descent, knowing that any human habitation must be far below us.

Down we scrambled, heedless of torn clothes and bleeding hands, the darkness pressing closer round us. Then suddenly it became black—black as pitch—and we could only hear each other. Another step might mean death. We stretched out our hands, and felt each other. Why we spoke in whispers, I do not know, but we seemed afraid of our own voices. We agreed there was nothing for it but to stop where we were till morning, clinging to the short grass; so we lay there side by side for what may have been five minutes or may have been an hour. Then, attempting to turn, I lost my grip and rolled. I made convulsive efforts to clutch the ground, but the incline was too steep. How far I fell I could not say, but at last something stopped me. I felt it cautiously with my foot: it did not yield, so I twisted my self round and touched it with my hand. It seemed planted firmly in the earth. I passed my arm along to the right, then to the left. I shouted with joy. It was a fence.

Rising and groping about me, I found an opening, and passed through, and crept forward with palms outstretched until I touched the logs of a hut; then, feeling my way round, discovered the door, and knocked. There came no response, so I knocked louder; then pushed, and the heavy woodwork yielded, groaning. But the darkness within was even darker than the darkness without. The others had contrived to crawl down and join me. Michael struck a wax vesta and held it up, and slowly the room came out of the darkness and stood round us.

Then something rather startling happened. Giving one swift glance about him, our guide uttered a cry, and rushed out into the night. We followed to the door, and called after him, but only a voice came to us out of the blackness, and the only words that we could catch, shrieked back in terror, were: '*Sætervronen! Sætervronen!*' ('The woman of the sæter').

'Some foolish superstition about the place, I suppose,' said Michael. 'In these mountain solitudes men breed ghosts for company. Let us make a fire. Perhaps, when he sees the light, his desire for food and shelter may get the better of his fears.'

We felt about in the small enclosure round the house, and gathered juniper and birch-twigs, and kindled a fire upon the open stove built in the corner of the room. Fortunately, we had some dried reindeer and bread in our bag, and on that and the ryper and the contents of our flasks we supped. Afterwards, to while away the time, we made an inspection of the strange eyrie we had lighted on.

It was an old log-built sæter. Some of these mountain farmsteads are as old as the stone ruins of other countries. Carvings of strange beasts and demons were upon its blackened rafters, and on the lintel, in runic letters, ran this legend: 'Hund builded me in the days of Haarfager.' The house consisted of two large apartments. Originally, no doubt, these had been separate dwellings standing beside one another, but they were now connected by a long, low gallery. Most of the scanty furniture was almost as ancient as the walls themselves, but many articles of a comparatively recent date had been added. All was now, however, rotting and falling into decay.

The place appeared to have been deserted suddenly by its last occupants. Household utensils lay as they were left, rust and dirt encrusted on them. An open book, limp and mildewed, lay face downwards on the table, while many others were scattered about both rooms, together with much paper, scored with faded ink. The curtains hung in shreds about the windows; a woman's cloak, of an antiquated fashion, drooped from a nail behind the door. In an oak chest we found a tumbled heap of yellow letters. They were of various dates, extending over a period of four months; and with them, apparently intended to receive them, lay a large envelope, inscribed with an address in London that has since disappeared.

Strong curiosity overcoming faint scruples, we read them by the dull glow of the burning juniper twigs, and, as we lay aside the last of them, there rose from the depths below us a wailing cry, and all night long it rose and died away, and rose again, and died away again; whether born of our brain or of some human thing, God knows.

And these, a little altered and shortened, are the letters:—

Extract from first letter:
'I cannot tell you, my dear Joyce, what a haven of peace this place is to me after the racket and fret of town. I am almost quite recovered already, and am growing stronger every day; and joy of joys, my brain has come back to me, fresher and more vigorous, I think, for its holiday. In this silence and solitude my thoughts flow freely, and the difficulties of my task are disappearing as if by magic. We are perched upon a tiny plateau halfway up the mountain. On one side the rock rises almost perpendicularly, piercing the sky; while on the other, two thousand feet below us, the torrent hurls itself into the black waters of the fiord. The house consists of two rooms—or, rather, it is two cabins connected by a passage. The larger one we use as a living room, and the other is our sleeping apartment. We have no servant, but do everything for ourselves. I fear sometimes Muriel must find it lonely. The nearest human

habitation is eight miles away, across the mountain, and
not a soul comes near us. I spend as much time as I can
with her, however, during the day, and make up for it by
working at night after she has gone to sleep; and when I
question her, she only laughs, and answers that she loves
to have me all to herself. (Here you will smile cynically, I
know, and say, "Humph, I wonder will she say the same
when they have been married six years instead of six
months.") At the rate I am working now I shall have
finished my first volume by the spring, and then, my dear
fellow, you must try and come over, and we will walk and
talk together "amid these storm-reared temples of the
gods." I have felt a new man since I arrived here. Instead
of having to "cudgel my brains," as we say, thoughts
crowd upon me. This work will make my name.'

*Part of the third letter, the second being mere talk
about the book (a history apparently) that the man was
writing:*

'MY DEAR JOYCE, I have written you two letters—this will
make the third—but have been unable to post them. Every
day I have been expecting a visit from some farmer or
villager, for the Norwegians are kindly people towards
strangers—to say nothing of the inducements of trade. A
fortnight having passed, however, and the commissariat
question having become serious, I yesterday set out
before dawn, and made my way down to the valley; and
this gives me something to tell you. Nearing the village, I
met a peasant woman. To my intense surprise, instead of
returning my salutation, she stared at me, as if I were
some wild animal, and shrank away from me as far as the
width of the road would permit. In the village the same
experience awaited me. The children ran from me, the
people avoided me. At last a grey-haired old man
appeared to take pity on me, and from him I learnt the
explanation of the mystery. It seems there is a strange
superstition attaching to this house in which we are
living. My things were brought up here by the two men

who accompanied me from Drontheim, but the natives are afraid to go near the place, and prefer to keep as far as possible from any one connected with it.

'The story is that the house was built by one Hund, "a maker of runes" (one of the old saga writers, no doubt), who lived here with his young wife. All went peacefully until, unfortunately for him, a certain maiden stationed at a neighbouring sæter grew to love him.

'Forgive me if I am telling you what you know, but a "sæter" is the name given to the upland pastures to which, during the summer, are sent the cattle, generally under the charge of one or more of the maids. Here for three months these girls will live in their lonely huts, entirely shut off from the world. Customs change little in this land. Two or three such stations are within climbing distance of this house, at this day, looked after by the farmers' daughters, as in the days of Hund, "maker of runes."

'Every night, by devious mountain paths, the woman would come and tap lightly at Hund's door. Hund had built himself two cabins, one behind the other (these are now, as I think I have explained to you, connected by a passage): the smaller one was the homestead, in the other he carved and wrote, so that while the young wife slept the "maker of runes" and the sæter woman sat whispering.

'One night, however, the wife learnt all things, but said no word. Then, as now, the ravine in front of the enclosure was crossed by a slight bridge of planks, and over this bridge the woman of the sæter passed and repassed each night. On a day when Hund had gone down to fish in the fiord, the wife took an axe, and hacked and hewed at the bridge, yet it still looked firm and solid; and that night, as Hund sat waiting in his workshop, there struck upon his ears a piercing cry, and a crashing of logs and rolling rock, and then again the dull roaring of the torrent far below.

'But the woman did not die unavenged; for that winter a man, skating far down the fiord, noticed a curious object embedded in the ice; and when, stooping, he looked closer, he saw two corpses, one gripping the other by the throat, and the bodies were the bodies of Hund and his young wife.

'Since then, they say, the woman of the sæter haunts Hund's house, and if she sees a light within she taps upon the door, and no man may keep her out. Many, at different times, have tried to occupy the house, but strange tales are told of them. "Men do not live at Hund's sæter," said my old grey-haired friend, concluding his tale, "they die there."

'I have persuaded some of the braver of the villagers to bring what provisions and other necessaries we require up to a plateau about a mile from the house and leave them there. That is the most I have been able to do. It comes somewhat as a shock to one to find men and women—fairly educated and intelligent as many of them are—slaves to fears that one would expect a child to laugh at. But there is no reasoning with superstition.'

Extract from the same letter, but from a part seemingly written a day or two later:

'At home I should have forgotten such a tale an hour after I had heard it, but these mountain fastnesses seem strangely fit to be the last stronghold of the supernatural. The woman haunts me already. At night, instead of working, I find myself listening for her tapping at the door; and yesterday an incident occurred that makes me fear for my own common sense. I had gone out for a long walk alone, and the twilight was thickening into darkness as I neared home. Suddenly looking up from my reverie, I saw, standing on a knoll the other side of the ravine, the figure of a woman. She held a cloak about her head, and I could not see her face. I took off my cap, and called out a good-night to her, but she never moved or spoke. Then—God knows why, for my brain was full of other thoughts at the time—a clammy chill crept over me, and my tongue grew dry and parched. I stood rooted to the spot, staring

at her across the yawning gorge that divided us; and
slowly she moved away, and passed into the gloom, and I
continued my way. I have said nothing to Muriel, and
shall not. The effect the story has had upon myself warns
me not to do so.'

From a letter dated eleven days later:

'She has come. I have known she would, since that
evening I saw her on the mountain; and last night she
came, and we have sat and looked into each other's eyes.
You will say, of course, that I am mad—that I have not
recovered from my fever—that I have been working too
hard—that I have heard a foolish tale, and that it has filled
my overstrung brain with foolish fancies: I have told
myself all that. But the thing came, nevertheless—a creature of flesh and blood? a creature of air? a creature of my
own imagination?—what matter? it was real to me.

'It came last night, as I sat working, alone. Each night I
have waited for it, listened for it—longed for it, I know
now. I heard the passing of its feet upon the bridge, the
tapping of its hand upon the door, three times—tap, tap,
tap. I felt my loins grow cold, and a pricking pain about
my head; and I gripped my chair with both hands, and
waited, and again there came the tapping—tap, tap, tap. I
rose and slipped the bolt of the door leading to the other
room, and again I waited, and again there came the
tapping—tap, tap, tap. Then I opened the heavy outer
door, and the wind rushed past me, scattering my papers,
and the woman entered in, and I closed the door behind
her. She threw her hood back from her head, and
unwound a kerchief from about her neck, and laid it on
the table. Then she crossed and sat before the fire, and I
noticed her bare feet were damp with the night dew.

'I stood over against her and gazed at her, and she
smiled at me—a strange, wicked smile, but I could have
laid my soul at her feet. She never spoke or moved, and
neither did I feel the need of spoken words, for I understood the meaning of those upon the Mount when they said,

"Let us make here tabernacles: it is good for us to be here."

'How long a time passed thus I do not know, but suddenly the woman held her hand up, listening, and there came a faint sound from the other room. Then swiftly she drew her hood about her face and passed out, closing the door softly behind her; and I drew back the bolt of the inner door and waited, and hearing nothing more, sat down, and must have fallen asleep in my chair.

'I awoke, and instantly there flashed through my mind the thought of the kerchief the woman had left behind her, and I started from my chair to hide it. But the table was already laid for breakfast, and my wife sat with her elbows on the table and her head between her hands, watching me with a look in her eyes that was new to me.

'She kissed me, though her lips were cold; and I argued to myself that the whole thing must have been a dream. But later in the day, passing the open door when her back was towards me, I saw her take the kerchief from a locked chest and look at it.

'I have told myself it must have been a kerchief of her own, and that all the rest has been my imagination; that, if not, then my strange visitant was no spirit, but a woman; and that, if human thing knows human thing, it was no creature of flesh and blood that sat beside me last night. Besides, what woman would she be? The nearest sæter is a three-hours' climb to a strong man, and the paths are dangerous even in daylight: what woman would have found them in the night? What woman would have chilled the air around her, and have made the blood flow cold through all my veins? Yet if she come again I will speak to her. I will stretch out my hand and see whether she be mortal thing or only air.'

The fifth letter:

'MY DEAR JOYCE, Whether your eyes will ever see these letters is doubtful. From this place I shall never send them. They would read to you as the ravings of a madman. If ever I return to England I may one day show them to you, but when I do it will be when I, with you, can laugh over them. At present I write them merely to hide away—putting the words down on paper saves my screaming them aloud.

'She comes each night now, taking the same seat beside the embers, and fixing upon me those eyes, with the hell-light in them, that burn into my brain; and at rare times she smiles, and all my being passes out of me, and is hers. I make no attempt to work. I sit listening for her footsteps on the creaking bridge, for the rustling of her feet upon the grass, for the tapping of her hand upon the door. No word is uttered between us. Each day I say: "When she comes tonight I will speak to her. I will stretch out my hand and touch her." Yet when she enters, all thought and will goes out from me.

'Last night, as I stood gazing at her, my soul filled with her wondrous beauty as a lake with moonlight, her lips parted, and she started from her chair; and, turning, I thought I saw a white face pressed against the window, but as I looked it vanished. Then she drew her cloak about her, and passed out. I slid back the bolt I always draw now, and stole into the other room, and, taking down the lantern, held it above the bed. But Muriel's eyes were closed as if in sleep.'

Extract from the sixth letter:
'It is not the night I fear, but the day. I hate the sight of this woman with whom I live, whom I call "wife." I shrink from the blow of her cold lips, the curse of her stony eyes. She has seen, she has learnt; I feel it, I know it. Yet she winds her arms around my neck, and calls me sweetheart, and smooths my hair with her soft, false hands. We speak mocking words of love to one another, but I know her cruel eyes are ever following me. She is plotting her revenge, and I hate her, I hate her, I hate her!'

Part of the seventh letter:
'This morning I went down to the fiord. I told her I should not be back until the evening. She stood by the

door watching me until we were mere specks to one another, and a promontory of the mountain shut me from view. Then, turning aside from the track, I made my way, running and stumbling over the jagged ground, round to the other side of the mountain, and began to climb again. It was slow, weary work. Often I had to go miles out of my road to avoid a ravine, and twice I reached a high point only to have to descend again. But at length I crossed the ridge, and crept down to a spot from where, concealed, I could spy upon my own house. She—my wife—stood by the flimsy bridge. A short hatchet, such as butchers use, was in her hand. She leant against a pine trunk, with her arm behind her, as one stands whose back aches with long stooping in some cramped position; and even at that distance I could see the cruel smile about her lips.

'Then I recrossed the ridge, and crawled down again, and, waiting until evening, walked slowly up the path. As I came in view of the house she saw me, and waved her handkerchief to me, and in answer I waved my hat, and shouted curses at her that the wind whirled away into the torrent. She met me with a kiss, and I breathed no hint to her that I had seen. Let her devil's work remain undisturbed. Let it prove to me what manner of thing this is that haunts me. If it be a spirit, then the bridge will bear it safely; if it be woman——

'But I dismiss the thought. If it be human thing, why does it sit gazing at me, never speaking? why does my tongue refuse to question it? why does all power forsake me in its presence, so that I stand as in a dream? Yet if it be spirit, why do I hear the passing of her feet? and why does the night-rain glisten on her hair?

'I force myself back into my chair. It is far into the night, and I am alone, waiting, listening. If it be spirit, she will come to me; and if it be woman, I shall hear her cry above the storm—unless it be a demon mocking me.

'I have heard the cry. It rose, piercing and shrill, above the storm, above the riving and rending of the bridge, above the downward crashing of the logs and loosened stones. I hear it as I listen now. It is cleaving its way upward from the depths below. It is wailing through the room as I sit writing.

'I have crawled upon my belly to the utmost edge of the still standing pier, until I could feel with my hand the jagged splinters left by the fallen planks, and have looked down. But the chasm was full to the brim with darkness. I shouted, but the wind shook my voice into mocking laughter. I sit here, feebly striking at the madness that is creeping nearer and nearer to me. I tell myself the whole thing is but the fever in my brain. The bridge was rotten. The storm was strong. The cry is but a single one among the many voices of the mountain. Yet still I listen; and it rises, clear and shrill, above the moaning of the pines, above the sobbing of the waters. It beats like blows upon my skull, and I know that she will never come again.'

Extract from the last letter:

'I shall address an envelope to you, and leave it among these letters. Then, should I never come back, some chance wanderer may one day find and post them to you, and you will know.

'My books and writings remain untouched. We sit together of a night—this woman I call "wife" and I—she holding in her hands some knitting thing that never grows longer by a single stitch, and I with a volume before me that is ever open at the same page. And day and night we watch each other stealthily, moving to and fro about the silent house; and at times, looking round swiftly, I catch the smile upon her lips before she has time to smooth it away.

'We speak like strangers about this and that, making talk to hide our thoughts. We make a pretence of busying ourselves about whatever will help us to keep apart from one another.

'At night, sitting here between the shadows and the dull glow of the smouldering twigs, I sometimes think I hear the tapping I have learnt to listen for, and I start from my seat, and softly open the door and look out. But only the Night stands there. Then I close-to the latch, and she—the living woman—asks me in her purring voice what sound I heard, hiding a smile as she stoops low over her work; and I answer lightly, and, moving towards her, put my arm about her, feeling her softness and her suppleness, and wondering, supposing I held her close to me with one arm while pressing her from me with the other, how long before I should hear the cracking of her bones.

'For here, amid these savage solitudes, I also am grown savage. The old primeval passions of love and hate stir within me, and they are fierce and cruel and strong, beyond what you men of the later ages could understand. The culture of the centuries has fallen from me as a flimsy garment whirled away by the mountain wind; the old savage instincts of the race lie bare. One day I shall twine my fingers about her full white throat, and her eyes will slowly come towards me, and her lips will part, and the red tongue creep out; and backwards, step by step, I shall push her before me, gazing the while upon her bloodless face, and it will be my turn to smile. Backwards through the open door, backwards along the garden path between the juniper bushes, backwards till her heels are overhanging the ravine, and she grips life with nothing but her little toes, I shall force her, step by step, before me. Then I shall lean forward, closer, closer, till I kiss her purpling lips, and down, down, down, past the startled sea-birds, past the white spray of the foss, past the downward peeping pines, down, down, down, we will go together, till we find the thing that lies sleeping beneath the waters of the fiord.'

With these words ended the last letter, unsigned. At the first streak of dawn we left the house, and, after much wandering, found our way back to the valley. But of our guide we heard no news. Whether he remained still upon the mountain, or whether by some false step he had perished upon that night, we never learnt.

THE DEVIL'S MANUSCRIPT

O

S. Levett-Yeats

*Here's a final story to gladden the heart of any publisher:
the definitive method of finding a sure-fire best seller.
Whether all publishers would welcome the cost is another
matter.*

*It comes from a book of short stories by a now-
forgotten writer of the turn of the century, Sidney Kilner
Levett-Yeats. Levett-Yeats served in the cavalry in India
for some years, and then went into government service.
He was mentioned in the Birthday Honours in 1912 as
Accountant-General, Posts and Telegraphs in the Indian
civil service but seems to have sunk into obscurity thereafter.*

*He published nine books between 1893 and 1904,
starting with an interesting book of short stories, THE
ROMANCE OF GUARD MULLIGAN (1893). His last
listed work is the novel ORRAIN (1904).*

*'The Devil's Manuscript' comes from his second book
of short stories, THE HEART OF DENISE (1899). Why it
has escaped reprinting for ninety years is a mystery.*

S. LEVETT-YEATS

O

The Devil's Manuscript

CHAPTER I
THE BLACK PACKET

'M DE BAC? De Bac? I do not know the name.'

'Gentleman says he knows you, sir, and has called on urgent business.'

There was no answer, and John Brown, the ruined publisher, looked about him in a dazed manner. He knew he was ruined; tomorrow the world would know it also, and then—beggary stared him in the face, and infamy too. For this the world would not care. Brown was not a great man in 'the trade,' and his name in the *Gazette* would not attract notice; but his name, as he stood in the felon's dock, and the ugly history a cross-examination might disclose would probably arouse a fleeting interest, and then the world would go on with a pitiless shrug of its shoulders. What does it matter to the moving wave of humanity if one little drop of spray from its crest is blown into nothing by the wind? Not a jot. But it was a terrible business for the drop of spray, otherwise John Brown, publisher. He was at his best not a good-looking man, rather mean-looking than otherwise, with a thin, angular face, eyes as shifty as a jackal's and shoulders shaped like a champagne-bottle. As the shadow of coming ruin darkened over him, he seemed to shrink and look meaner than ever. He had almost forgotten the presence of his clerk. He could think of nothing but the morrow, when Simmonds' voice again broke the stillness.

'Shall I say you will see him, sir?'

The question cut sharply into the silence, and brought Brown to himself. He had half a mind to say 'No.' In the face of the coming tomorrow, business, urgent or otherwise, was nothing to him. Yet, after all, there could be no harm done in receiving the man. It would, at any rate, be a distraction, and, lifting his head, Brown answered:

'Yes, I will see him, Simmonds.'

Simmonds went out, closing the green baize door behind him. There was a delay of a moment, and M De Bac entered—a tall, thin figure, bearing an oblong parcel, packed in shiny, black paper, and sealed with flame-coloured wax.

'Good-day, Mr Brown;' and M De Bac, who, for all his foreign name, spoke perfect English, extended his hand.

Brown rose, put his own cold fingers into the warm grasp of his visitor, and offered him a seat.

'With your permission, Mr Brown, I will take this other chair. It is nearer the fire. I am accustomed to warm climates, as you doubtless perceive;' and De Bac, suiting his action to his words, placed his packet on the table, and began to slowly rub his long, lean fingers together. The publisher glanced at him with some curiosity. M De Bac was as dark as an Italian, with clear, resolute features, and a moustache, curled at the ends, thick enough to hide the sarcastic curve of his thin lips. He was strongly if sparely built, and his fiery black eyes met Brown's gaze with a look that ran through him like a needle.

'You do not appear to recognize me, Mr Brown?'—De Bac's voice was very quiet and deep-toned.

'I have not the honour—' began the publisher; but his visitor interrupted him.

'You mistake. We are quite old friends; and in time will always be very near each other. I have a minute or two to spare'—he glanced at a repeater—'and will prove to you that I know you. You are John Brown, that very religious young man of Battersea, who, twelve years ago, behaved like a blackguard to a girl at Homerton, and sent her to—but no matter. You attracted my attention then; but, unfortunately, I had no time to devote to you. Subsequently, you effected a pretty little swindle—don't be angry, Mr Brown—it *was* very clever. Then you started in business on your own account, and married. Things went well with you; you know the art of getting at a low price, and selling at a high one. You are a born "sweater." Pardon the word. You know how to keep men down like beasts, and go up yourself. In doing this, you did me yeoman's service, although you are even now not aware of this. You had one fault, you have it still, and had you not been a gambler you might have been a rich man. Speculation is a bad thing, Brown—I mean gambling speculation.'

Brown was an Englishman, and it goes without saying that he had courage. But there was something in De Bac's manner, some strange power in the steady stare of those black eyes, that held him to his seat as if pinned there.

As De Bac stopped, however, Brown's anger gave him strength. Every word that was said was true, and stung like the lash of a whip. He rose white with anger.

'Sir!' he began with quivering lips, and made a step forward. Then he stopped. It was as if the sombre fire in De Bac's gaze withered his strength. An invisible hand seemed to drag him back into his seat and hold him there.

'You are hasty, Mr Brown;' and De Bac's even voice continued: 'you are really very rash. I was about to tell you a little more of your history, to tell you you are ruined, and tomorrow every one in London—it is the world for you, Brown—will know you are a beggar, and many will know you are a cheat.'

The publisher swore bitterly under his breath.

'You see, Mr Brown,' continued his strange visitor, 'I know all about you, and you will be surprised, perhaps, to hear that you deserve help from me. You are too useful to let drift. I have therefore come to save you.'

'Save me?'

'Yes. By means of this manuscript here,' he pointed to the packet, 'which you are going to publish.'

Brown now realized that he was dealing with a lunatic. He tried to stretch out his arm to touch the bell on the table; but found that he had no power to do so. He made an attempt to shout to Simmonds; but his tongue moved inaudibly in his mouth. He seemed only to have the faculty of following De Bac's words, and of answering them. He gasped out:

'It is impossible!'

'My friend'—and De Bac smiled mirthlessly—'you will publish that manuscript. I will pay. The profits will be yours. It will make your name, and you will be rich. You will even be able to build a church,'

'Rich!' Brown's voice was very bitter. 'M De Bac, you said rightly. I am a ruined man. Even if you were to pay for the publication of that manuscript I could not do it now. It is too late. There are other houses. Go to them.'

'But not other John Browns. You are peculiarly adapted for my purpose. Enough of this! I know what business is, and I have many things to attend to. You are a small man, Mr Brown, and it will take little to remove your difficulties. See! Here are a thousand pounds. They will free you from your present troubles,' and De Bac tossed a pocket-book on the table before Brown. 'I do not want a receipt,' he went on. 'I will call tomorrow for your final answer, and to settle details. If you need it I will give you more money. This hour—twelve—will suit me. *Adieu!*' He was gone like a flash, and Brown looked around in blank amazement. He was as if suddenly aroused from a dream. He could hardly believe the evidence of his senses, although he could see the black packet, and the neat leather pocket-book with the initials 'L. De B.' let in in silver on the outside. He rang his bell violently, and Simmonds appeared.

'Has M De Bac gone?'

'I don't know, sir. He didn't pass out through the door.'

'There is no other way. You must have been asleep.'

'Indeed I was not, sir.'

Brown felt a chill as of cold fingers running down his backbone, but pulled himself together with an effort. 'It does not matter, Simmonds. You may go.'

Simmonds went out scratching his head. 'How the demon did he get out?' he asked himself. 'Must have been sleeping after all. The guv'nor seems a bit dotty to-day. It's the smash coming—sure.'

He wrote a letter or two, and then taking his hat, sallied forth to an aërated bread-shop for his cheap and wholesome lunch, for Simmonds was a saving young man, engaged to a young lady living out Camden Town way. Simmonds perfectly understood the state of affairs, and was not a little anxious about matters, for the mother of his fiancée, a widow who let lodgings, had only agreed to his engagement after much persuasion; and if he had to announce the fact that, instead of 'thirty bob a week,' as he put it, his income was nothing at all, there would be an end of everything.

'M'ria's all right,' he said to his friend Wilkes, in trustful confidence as they sat over their lunch; 'but that old torpedo'—by which name he designated his mother-in-law-elect—'she'll raise Cain if there's a smash-up.'

In the meantime, John Brown tore open the pocket-book with shaking hands, and, with a crisp rustling, a number of new bank-notes fell out, and lay in a heap before him. He counted them one by one. They totalled to a thousand pounds exactly. He was a small man. M De Bac had said so truly, if a little rudely, and the money was more than enough to stave off ruin. De Bac had said, too, if needed he would give him more, and then Brown fell to trembling all over. He was like a man snatched from the

very jaws of death. At Battersea he wore a blue ribbon;
but now he went to a cabinet, filled a glass with raw
brandy, and drained it at a gulp. In a minute or so the
generous cordial warmed his chilled blood, and picking
up the notes, he counted them again, and thrust them
into his breast-pocket. After this he paced the room up
and down in a feverish manner, longing for the morrow
when he could settle up the most urgent demands against
him. Then, on a sudden, a thought struck him. It was
almost as if it had been whispered in his ear. Why trouble
at all about matters? He had a clear thousand with him,
and in an hour he could be out of the country! He hesitated, but prudence prevailed. Extradition laws stretched
everywhere; and there was another thing—that extraordinary madman, De Bac, had promised more money on the
morrow. After all, it was better to stay.

As he made this resolve his eyes fell on the black
packet on the table. The peculiar colour of the seals
attracted his attention. He bent over them, and saw that
the wax bore an impress of a V-shaped shield, within
which was set a trident. He noticed also that the packet
was tied with a silver thread. His curiosity was excited. He
sat down, snipped the threads with a penknife, tore off
the black paper covering, flung it into the fire, and saw
before him a bulky manuscript exquisitely written on
very fine paper. A closer examination showed that they
were a number of short stories. Now Brown was in no
mood to read; but the title of the first tale caught his eye,
and the writing was so legible that he had glanced over
half a dozen lines before he was aware of the fact. Those
first half-dozen lines were sufficient to make him read
the page, and when he had read the page the publisher
felt he was before the work of a genius.

He was unable to stop now; and, with his head resting
between his hands, he read on tirelessly. Simmonds came
in once or twice and left papers on the table, but his
master took no notice of him. Brown forgot all about his
lunch, and turning over page after page read as if spell-

bound. He was a businessman, and was certain the book would sell in thousands. He read as one inspired to look into the author's thoughts and see his design. Short as the stories were, they were Titanic fragments, and everyone of them taught a hideous lesson of corruption. Some of them cloaked in a religious garb, breathed a spirit of pitiless ferocity; others were rich with the sensuous odours of an Eastern garden; others, again, were as the tender green of moss hiding the treacherous deeps of a quicksand; and all of them bore the hall-mark of genius. They moved the man sitting there to tears, they shook him with laughter, they seemed to rock his very soul asleep; but through it all he saw, as the mariner views the beacon fire on a rocky coast, the deadly plan of the writer. There was money in them—thousands—and all was to be his. Brown's sluggish blood was running to flame, a strange strength glowed in his face, and an uncontrollable admiration for De Bac's evil power filled him. The book, when published, might corrupt generations yet unborn; but that was nothing to Brown. It meant thousands for him, and an eternal fame to De Bac. He did not grudge the writer the fame as long as he kept the thousands.

'By Heaven!' and he brought his fist down on the table with a crash, 'the man may be a lunatic; but he is the greatest genius the world ever saw—or he is the devil incarnate.'

And somebody laughed softly in the room.

The publisher looked up with a start, and saw Simmonds standing before him.

'Did you laugh, Simmonds?'

'No sir!' replied the clerk with a surprised look.

'Who laughed then?'

'There is no one here but ourselves, sir—and I didn't laugh.'

'Did you hear nothing?'

'Nothing, sir.'

'Strange!' and Brown began to feel chill again.

'What time is it?' he asked with an effort.

'It is half-past six, sir.'

'So late as that? You may go, Simmonds. Leave me the keys. I will be here for some time. Good evening.'

'Mad as a coot,' muttered Simmonds to himself; 'must break the news to M'ria to-night. Oh, Lor'!' and his eyes were very wet as he went out into the Strand, and got into a blue omnibus.

When he was gone, Brown turned to the fire, poker in hand. To his surprise he saw that the black paper was still there, burning red hot, and the wax of the seals was still intact—the seals themselves shining like orange glow-lights. He beat at the paper with the poker; but instead of crumbling to ashes it yielded passively to the stroke, and came back to its original shape. Then a fury came on Brown. He raked at the fire, threw more coals over the paper, and blew at the flames with his bellows until they roared up the chimney; but still the coppery glare of the packet-cover never turned to the grey of ashes. Finally, he could endure it no longer, and, putting the manuscript into the safe, turned off the electric light, and stole out of his office like a thief.

CHAPTER II
THE BED TRIDENT

When Beggarman, Bowles & Co., of Providence Passage, Lombard Street, called at eleven o'clock on the morning following De Bac's visit, their representative was not a little surprised to find the firm's bills met in hard cash, and Simmonds paid him with a radiant face. When the affair was settled, the clerk leaned back in his chair, saying half-aloud to himself, 'By George! I am glad after all M'ria did not keep our appointment in the Camden Road last night.' Then his face began to darken, 'Wonder where she could have been, though?' his thoughts ran on; 'half sorry I introduced her to Wilkes last Sunday at Victoria Park. Wilkes ain't half the man I am though,' and he tried to look at himself in the window-pane, 'but he has two pound ten a week—Lord! There's the guv'nor ringing.' He hurried into Brown's room, received a brief order, and was about to go back when the publisher spoke again.

'Simmonds!'

'Sir.'

'If M De Bac calls, show him in at once.'

'Sir,' and the clerk went out.

Left to himself, Brown tried to go on with the manuscript; but was not able to do so. He was impatient for the coming of De Bac, and kept watching the hands of the clock as they slowly travelled towards twelve. When he came to the office in the morning Brown had looked with a nervous fear in the fireplace, half expecting to find the black paper still there; and it was a considerable relief to his mind to find it was not. He could do nothing, not even open the envelopes of the letters that lay on his table. He made an effort to find occupation in the morning's paper. It was full of some absurd correspondence on a trivial subject, and he wondered at the thousands of fools who could waste time in writing and in reading yards of print on the theme of 'Whether women should wear neckties.' The ticking of the clock irritated him. He flung the paper aside, just as the door opened and Simmonds came in. For a moment Brown thought he had come to announce De Bac's arrival; but no—Simmonds simply placed a square envelope on the table before Brown.

'Pass-book from Bransom's, sir, just come in;' and he went out.

Brown took it up mechanically, and opened the envelope. A type-written letter fell out with the pass-book. He ran his eyes over it with astonishment. It was briefly to inform him that M De Bac had paid into Brown's account yesterday afternoon the sum of five thousand pounds, and that, adjusting overdrafts, the balance at his credit was four thousand seven hundred and twenty pounds thirteen shillings and three pence. Brown rubbed his eyes. Then he hurriedly glanced at the pass-book. The figures tallied—there was no error, no mistake. He pricked himself with his penknife to see if he was awake, and finally shouted to Simmonds:

'Read this letter aloud to me, Simmonds,' he said.

Simmonds' eyes opened, but he did as he was bidden, and there was no mistake about the account.

'Anything else, sir?' asked Simmonds when he had finished.

'No—nothing,' and Brown was once more alone. He sat staring at the figures before him in silence, almost mesmerizing himself with the intentness of his gaze.

'My God!' he burst out at last, in absolute wonder.

'Who is your God, Brown?' answered a deep voice.

'I—I—M De Bac! How did you come?'

'I did not drop down the chimney,' said De Bac with a grin; 'your clerk announced me in the ordinary way, but you were so absorbed you did not hear. So I took the liberty of sitting in this chair, and awaiting your return to earthly matters. You were dreaming, Brown—by the way, who *is* your God?' he repeated with a low laugh.

'I—I do not understand, sir.'

'Possibly not, possibly not. I wouldn't bother about the matter. Ah! I see Bransom's have sent you your pass-book! Sit down, Brown. I hate to see a man fidgeting about—I paid in that amount yesterday on a second thought. It is enough—eh?'

Brown's jackal eyes contracted. Perhaps he could get more out of De Bac? But a look at the strong impassive face before him frightened him.

'More than enough, sir,' he stammered; and then, with a rush, 'I am grateful—anything I can do for you?'

'Oh! I know, I know, Brown—by the way, you do not object to smoke?'

'Certainly not. I do not smoke myself.'

'In Battersea, eh?' And De Bac, pulling out a silver cheroot case, held it out to Brown. But the publisher declined.

'Money wouldn't buy a smoke like that in England,' remarked De Bac, 'but as you will. I wouldn't smoke if I were you. Such abstinence looks respectable and means nothing.' He put a cigar between his lips, and pointed his forefinger at the end. To Brown's amazement an orange-flame licked out from under the fingernail, and vanished like a flash of lightning; but the cigar was alight, and its fragrant odour filled the room. It reached even Simmonds, who sniffed at it like a buck scenting the morning air. 'By George!' he exclaimed in wonder, 'what baccy!'

M De Bac settled himself comfortably in his chair, and spoke with the cigar between his teeth. 'Now you have recovered a little from your surprise, Brown, I may as well tell you that I never carry matches. This little scientific discovery I have made is very convenient, is it not?'

'I have never seen anything like it.'

'There are a good many things you have not seen, Brown—but to work. Take a pencil and paper and note down what I say. You can tell me when I have done if you agree or not.'

Brown did as he was told, and De Bac spoke slowly and carefully.

'The money I have given you is absolutely your own on the following terms. You will publish the manuscript I left you, enlarge your business, and work as you have hitherto worked—as a "sweater." You may speculate as much as you like. You will not lose. You need not avoid the publication of religious books, but you must never give in charity secretly. I do not object to a big cheque for a public object, and your name in all the papers. It will be well for you to hound down the vicious. Never give them a chance to recover themselves. You will be a legislator. Strongly uphold all those measures which, under a moral cloak, will do harm to mankind. I do not mention them. I do not seek to hamper you with detailed instructions. Work on these general lines, and you will do what I want. A word more. It will be advisable whenever you have a chance to call public attention to a great evil which is also a vice. Thousands who have never heard of it before will hear of it then—and human nature is very frail. You have noted all this down?'

'I have. You are a strange man, M De Bac.'

M De Bac frowned, and Brown began to tremble.

'I do not permit you to make observations about me, Mr Brown.'

'I beg your pardon, sir.'

'Do not do so again. Will you agree to all this? I promise you unexampled prosperity for ten years. At the end of that time I shall want you elsewhere. And you must agree to take a journey with me'

'A long one, sir?' Brown's voice was just a shade satirical.

M De Bac smiled oddly. 'No—in your case I promise a quick passage. These are all the conditions I attach to my gift of six thousand pounds to you.'

Brown's amazement did not blind him to the fact of the advantage he had, as he thought, over his visitor. The six thousand pounds were already his, and he had given no promise. With a sudden boldness he spoke out.

'And if I decline?'

'You will return me my money, and my book, and I will go elsewhere.'

'The manuscript, yes—but if I refuse to give back the money?'

'Ha! ha! ha!' M De Bac's mirthless laugh chilled Brown to the bone. 'Very good, Brown—but you won't refuse. Sign that like a good fellow,' and he flung a piece of paper towards Brown, who saw that it was a promissory note, drawn up in his name, agreeing to pay M De Bac the sum of six thousand pounds on demand.

'I shall do no such thing,' said Brown stoutly.

M De Bac made no answer, but calmly touched the bell. In a half-minute Simmonds appeared.

'Be good enough to witness Mr Brown's signature to that document,' said De Bac to him, and then fixed his gaze on Brown. There was a moment of hesitation and then—the publisher signed his name, and Simmonds did likewise as a witness. When the latter had gone, De Bac carefully put the paper by in a letter-case he drew from his vest pocket.

'Your scientific people would call this an exhibition of odic force, Brown—eh?'

Brown made no answer. He was shaking in every limb, and great pearls of sweat rolled down his forehead.

'You see, Brown,' continued De Bac, 'after all you are a free agent. Either agree to my terms and keep the money, or say you will not, pay me back, receive your note-of-hand, and I go elsewhere with my book. Come—time is precious.'

And from Brown's lips there hissed a low 'I agree.'

'Then that is settled,' and De Bac rose from his chair. 'There is a little thing more—stretch out your arm like a good fellow—the right arm.'

Brown did so; and De Bac placed his forefinger on his wrist, just between what palmists call 'the lines of life.' The touch was as that of a red-hot iron, and with a quick cry Brown drew back his hand and looked at it. On his wrist was a small red trident, as cleanly marked as if it had been tattooed into the skin. The pain was but momentary; and, as he looked at the mark, he heard De Bac say, 'Adieu once more, Brown. I will find my way out—don't trouble to rise.' Brown heard him wish Simmonds an affable 'Good-day,' and he was gone.

CHAPTER III
'THE MARK OF THE BEAST'

It was early in the spring that Brown published *The Yellow Dragon*—as the collection of tales left with him by De Bac was called—and the success of the book surpassed his wildest expectations. It became the rage. There were the strangest rumours afloat as to its authorship, for no one knew De Bac, and the name of the writer was supposed to be an assumed one. It was written by a clergyman: it was penned by a schoolgirl; it had employed the leisure of a distinguished statesman during his retirement; it was the work of an ex-crowned head. These, and such-like statements, were poured forth one day to be contradicted the next. Wherever the book was noticed it was either with the most extravagant praise or the bitterest rancour. But friend and foe were alike united on one thing—that of ascribing to its unknown author a princely genius. The greatest of the reviews, after pouring on *The Yellow Dragon* the vials of its wrath, concluded with these words of unwilling praise: 'There is not a sentence of this book which should ever have been written, still less published; but we do not hesitate to say that, having been written and given to the world, there is hardly a line of this terrible work which will not become immortal—to the misery of mankind.'

Be this as it may, the book sold in tens of thousands, and Brown's fortune was assured. In ten years a man may do many things; but during the ten years that followed the publication of *The Yellow Dragon*, Brown did so many things that he astonished 'the City,' and it takes not a little to do that. It was not alone the marvellous growth of his business—although that advanced by leaps and bounds until it overshadowed all others—it was his wonderful luck on the Stock Exchange. Whatever he touched turned to gold. He was looked upon as the Napoleon of finance. His connection with *The Yellow Dragon* was forgotten when his connection with the yellow sovereign was remembered. He had a palace in Berkshire; another huge pile owned by him overlooked Hyde Park. He was a county member and a cabinet-minister. He had refused a peerage and built a church. Could ambition want more? He had clean forgotten De Bac. From him he had heard no word, received no sign, and he looked upon him as dead. At first, when his eyes fell on the red trident on his wrist, he was wont to shudder all over; but as years went on he became accustomed to the mark, and thought no more of it than if it had been a mole. In personal appearance he was but little changed, except that his hair was thin and grey, and there was a bald patch on the top of his head. His wife had died four years ago, and he was now contemplating another marriage—a marriage that would ally him with a family dating from the Confessor.

Such was John Brown, when we meet him again ten years after De Bac's visit, seated at a large writing-table in his luxurious office. A clerk standing beside him was cutting open the envelopes of the morning's post, and placing the letters one by one before his master. It is our friend Simmonds—still a young man, but bent and old beyond his years, and still on 'thirty bob' a week. And the history of Simmonds will show how Brown carried out De Bac's instructions.

When *The Yellow Dragon* came out and business began to expand, Simmonds, having increased work, was ambitious enough to expect a rise in his salary, and addressed his chief on the subject. He was put off with a promise, and on the strength of that promise Simmonds, being no wiser than many of his fellows, married M'ria; and husband and wife managed to exist somehow with the help of the mother-in-law. Then the mother-in-law died, and there was only the bare thirty shillings a week on which to live, to dress, to pay Simmonds' way daily to the City and back, and to feed more than two mouths—for Simmonds was amongst the blessed who have their quivers full. Still the expected increase of pay did not come. Other men came into the business and passed over Simmonds. Brown said they had special qualifications. They had; and John Brown knew Simmonds better than he knew himself. The other men were paid for doing things Simmonds could not have done to save his life; but he was more than useful in his way. A hundred times it was in the mind of the wretched clerk to resign his post and seek to better himself elsewhere. But he had given hostages to fortune. There was M'ria and her children, and M'ria set her face resolutely against risk. They had no reserve upon which to fall back, and it was an option between partial and total starvation. So 'Sim,' as M'ria called him, held on and battled with the wolf at the door, the wolf gaining inch by inch. Then illness came, and debt, and then—temptation. 'Sim' fell, as many a better man than he has fallen.

Brown found it out, and saw his opportunity to behave generously, and make his generosity pay. He got a written confession of his guilt from Simmonds, and retained him in his service forever on thirty shillings a week. And Simmonds' life became such as made him envy the lot of a Russian serf, of a Siberian exile, of a negro in the old days of the sugar plantations. He became a slave, a living machine who ground out his daily hours of work; he became mean and sordid in soul, as one does become when hope is extinct. Such was Simmonds as he cut open the envelopes of Brown's letters, and the great man, reading them quickly, endorsed them with terse remarks in blue pencil, for subsequent disposal by his secretary. A sudden exclamation from the clerk, and Brown looked up.

'What is it?' he asked sharply.

'Only this, sir,' and Simmonds held before Brown's eyes a jet black envelope; and as he gazed at it, his mind travelled back ten years, to that day when he stood on the brink of public infamy and ruin, and De Bac saved him. For a moment everything faded before Brown's eyes, and he saw himself in a dingy room, with the gaunt figure of the author of 'The Yellow Dragon,' and the maker of his fortune, before him.

'Shall I open it, sir?' Simmonds' voice reached him as from a far distance, and Brown roused himself with an effort.

'No,' he said, 'give it to me, and go for the present.'

When the bent figure of the clerk had passed out of the room, Brown looked at the envelope carefully. It bore a penny stamp and the impress of the postmark was not legible. The superscription was in white ink and it was addressed to Mr John Brown. The 'Mr' on the letter irritated Brown, for he was now The Right Hon'ble John Brown, and was punctilious on that score. He was so annoyed that at first he thought of casting the letter unopened into the waste-paper basket beside him, but changed his mind, and tore open the cover. A note-card discovered itself. The contents were brief and to the point:

'*Get ready to start. I will call for you at the close of the day.* L. De B.'

For a moment Brown was puzzled, then the remembrance of his old compact with De Bac came to him. He fairly laughed. To think that he, The Right Hon'ble John Brown, the richest man in England, and one of the most powerful, should be written to like that! Ordered to go somewhere he did not even know! Addressed like a servant! The cool insolence of the note amused Brown first, and then he became enraged. He tore the note into fragments and cast it from him. 'Curse the madman,' he said aloud, 'I'll give him in charge if he annoys me.' A sudden twinge in his right wrist made him hurriedly look at the spot. There was a broad pink circle, as large as a florin, around the mark of the trident, and it smarted and burned as the sting of a wasp. He ran to a basin of water and dipped his arm in to the elbow; but the pain became intolerable, and, finally, ordering his carriage, he drove home. That evening there was a great civic banquet in the city, and amongst the guests was The Right Hon'ble John Brown.

All through the afternoon he had been in agony with his wrist, but towards evening the pain ceased as suddenly as it had come on, and Brown attended the banquet, a little pale and shaken, but still himself. On Brown's right hand sat the Bishop of Browboro', on his left a most distinguished scientist, and amongst the crowd of waiters was Simmonds, who had hired himself out for the evening to earn an extra shilling or so to eke out his miserable subsistence. The man of science had just returned from Mount Atlas, whither he had gone to observe the transit of Mercury, and had come back full of stories of witchcraft. He led the conversation in that direction, and very soon the Bishop, Brown, and himself were engaged in the discussion of *diablerie*. The Bishop was a learned and a saintly man, and was a 'believer'; the scientist was puzzled by what he had seen, and Brown openly scoffed.

'Look here!' and pulling back his cuff, he showed the red mark on his wrist to his companions, 'if I were to tell you how that came here, you would say the devil himself marked me.'

'I confess I am curious,' said the scientist; and the Bishop fixed an inquiring gaze upon Brown. Simmonds was standing behind, and unconsciously drew near. Then the man, omitting many things, told the history of the mark on his wrist. He left out much, but he told enough to make the scientist edge his chair a little further from him, and a look of grave compassion, not untinged with scorn, to come into the eyes of the Bishop. As Brown came to the end of his story he became unnaturally excited, he raised his voice, and, with a sudden gesture, held his wrist close to the Bishop's face, 'There!' he said, 'I suppose you would say the devil did that?'

And as the Bishop looked, a voice seemed to breathe in his ear: '*And he caused all ... to receive a mark in their right hand, or in their foreheads.*' It was as if his soul was speaking to him and urging him to say the words aloud. He did not; but with a pale face gently put aside Brown's hand. 'I do not know, Mr Brown—but I think you are called upon for a speech.'

It was so; and, after a moment's hesitation, Brown rose. He was a fluent speaker, and the occasion was one with which he was peculiarly qualified to deal. He began well; but as he went on those who looked upon him saw that he was ghastly pale, and that the veins stood out on his high forehead in blue cords. As he spoke he made some allusion to those men who have risen to eminence from an obscure position. He spoke of himself as one of these, and then began to tell the story of 'The Devil's Manuscript,' as he called it, with a mocking look at the Bishop. As he went on he completely lost command over himself, and the story of the manuscript became the story of his life. He concealed nothing, he passed over nothing. He laid all his sordid past before his hearers with a vivid force. His listeners were astonished into silence; perhaps curiosity kept them still. But, as the long tale of infamy went on, some, in pity for the man, and believing him struck mad, tried to stop him, but in vain. He came at last to the incident of the letter, and told how De Bac was to call for him tonight. 'The Bishop of Browboro',' he said with a jarring laugh, 'thought De Bac was the fiend himself,' but he (Brown) knew better; he–he stopped, and, with a half-inarticulate cry, began to back slowly from the table, his eyes fixed on the entrance to the room. And now a strange thing happened. There was not a man in the room who had the power to move or to speak; they were as if frozen to their seats; as if struck into stone. Some were able to follow Brown's glance, but could see nothing. All were able to see that in Brown's face was an awful fear, and that he was trying to escape from a horrible presence which was moving slowly towards him, and which was visible to himself alone. Inch by inch Brown gave way, until he at last reached the wall, and stood with his back to it, with his arms spread out, in the position of one crucified. His face was marble white, and a dreadful terror and a pitiful appeal shone in his eyes. His blue lips were parted as of one in the dolors of death.

The silence was profound.

There were strong men there; men who had faced and overcome dangers, who had held their lives in their hands, who had struggled against desperate odds and won; but there was not a man who did not now feel weak, powerless, helpless as a child before that invisible, advancing terror that Brown alone could see. They could move no hand to aid, lift no voice to pray. All they could do was to wait in that dreadful silence and to watch. Time itself seemed to stop. It was as if the stillness had lasted for hours.

Suddenly Brown's face, so white before, flushed a crimson purple, and with a terrible cry he fell forwards on the polished woodwork of the floor.

As he fell it seemed as if the weight which held all still was on the moment removed, and they were free. With scared faces they gathered around the fallen man and raised him. He was quite dead; but on his forehead, where there was no mark before, was the impress of a red trident.

A man, evidently one of the waiters, who had forced his way into the group, laid his finger on the mark and looked up at the Bishop. There was an unholy exultation in his face as he met the priest's eyes, and said:

'He's marked twice—*curse him!*'

TRUE CRIME DIARY

James Bland

One hundred and eighty real-life modern murder stories, quirky, gory, ingenious, bungled, or just plain horrifying, arranged in diary form for the delectation of all true crime addicts.

4 January 1964: the Boston Strangler's last victim found naked, trussed, raped and strangled with a New Year greetings card against her right foot.

15 May 1948: June Anne Devaney, aged three years and eleven months, found raped and murdered a hundred yards from the Blackburn hospital where she had been recovering from pneumonia.

23 July 1943: invalid Archibald Brown, of Essex, blown to pieces by an anti-tank mine attached to the seat of his wheelchair.

23 November 1910: Dr Crippen hanged at Pentonville Prison for the murder of his second wife. He had poisoned her, and concealed her dismembered remains beneath the cellar floor of their home.

29 December 1969: Muriel McKay abducted from her London home. The body was never found, but two Trinidadian brothers, Arthur and Nizamodeen Hosein, were convicted of her murder – it is popularly believed that she was fed to the pigs on Arthur Hosein's farm.

FUTURA PUBLICATIONS
NON-FICTION/CRIME
0 7088 3264 4

TRUE CRIME DIARY
VOLUME 2

James Bland

A gruesome new gallery of murders – ingenious, tragic, sadistic and downright horrifying – which will send a shiver down the spine of the most hardened of true crime addicts.

1 February 1935: the body of Gertrina Opperman was found by a railway line near Pretoria. Her murderer was one of the detectives investigating the crime.

8 February 1983: the celebrated Nilsen case opened with the discovery of human flesh in a north London manhole.

26 July 1984: death of Ed Gein, murderer, body-snatcher and necrophile. His ghoulish activities provided the inspiration for Hitchcock's *Psycho*.

2 November 1979: Jacques Mesrine, infamous murderer and robber, was killed in a police ambush in Paris. Overjoyed at his death, the police danced in the street.

30 December 1916: Grigori Rasputin was murdered by conspirators in Russia. He survived poison, shooting and battering, only to drown in the icy River Neva.

FUTURA PUBLICATIONS
NON-FICTION/CRIME
0 7088 4213 5

VOICES IN MY EAR
THE AUTOBIOGRAPHY OF A MEDIUM

Doris Stokes
with Linda Dearsley

She's helped to solve murder cases.

She filled the Sydney Opera House three nights in a row.

Once, she even had to convince a man he was dead.

Now she's written her own astonishing life story.

Her name is Doris Stokes.

As a child she often saw things others couldn't. During the War she was officially informed her husband had been killed. At the height of her grief she was visited by her long-dead father and told her husband was alive and would return.

But joy turned to grief when her father reappeared to warn of the impending death of her healthy baby son.

Both predictions came true.

And Doris Stokes had to accept the fact that she possessed an amazing gift: exceptional psychic powers that over the years of her extraordinary life have brought joy and comfort to thousands of people.

FUTURA PUBLICATIONS
NON-FICTION/AUTOBIOGRAPHY
0 7088 1786 8

DR CRIPPEN'S DIARY

Emlyn Williams

Neither novel nor biography, DR CRIPPEN'S DIARY
is a dramatic mixture of true crime and inventive fiction.

Interpreting known facts through his knowledge of
criminal psychology, Emlyn Williams has created the
journal Crippen *could* have kept, from his twenty-first
birthday to his last hours. Following the fate of his
monstrous wife and his young lover, Ethel Le Neve, it
brings to life one of the most notorious murderers of the
twentieth century.

Ingenious and convincing, Crippen – seen for decades as
a vicious murderer – emerges as a tragically
misunderstood character, tried beyond endurance.

FUTURA PUBLICATIONS
CRIME/FICTION
0 7088 3929 0

THE FACE THAT MUST DIE

Ramsey Campbell

'This, the story of a psychotic, homophobic killer in Liverpool, chills our souls not with splashes of gore, but with the more terrifying feeling of sharing the thoughts of a paranoid maniac' *Publishers Weekly*

THE FACE THAT MUST DIE

Any fan of Ramsey Campbell will find this book a must. It's full to the bursting point. A new revised, expanded version of *The Face That Must Die*. A new short story whose very title, "I Am It And It Is I", compels and excites' David Morrell, author of *First Blood*

THE FACE THAT MUST DIE

'A powerful and powerfully written novel, as we expect from Campbell. It has every bit (and even a little more) of his characteristic intensity – which often seems close to paranoia, the lurid, highly-coloured vision of a being under constant threat. It is, I confess, one of my favourite horror novels' Peter Straub, author of *Ghost Story*

FUTURA PUBLICATIONS
FICTION/THRILLER
0 7088 4394 8

PENNY POST

Susan Moody

'Distinctly impure amusement . . . relax and enjoy it.'
Daily Telegraph

Lower Ingleford seems a typical rural hamlet in the sunli
uplands of northern England, complete with Village
Institute, village green and lord of the manor. But
something is seriously amiss: milking equipment
explodes; brakes are tampered with; bullets fly – someone
is trying to kill the squire. Or so it seems. And the
motives are tangled in a morass of shady property deals,
art forgeries, and various dubious business practices.

When Kendal Santain, local landowner and apparent
target, calls on Penny Wanawake for help, he gets it. And
rather more than he's bargained for. Six feet, 126 lbs,
Bovril-black, rich, beautiful and totally uninhibited –
when Penny seeks a solution, there is nowhere for a
solution, however timid and retiring, to hide.

PENNY POST
Third in the notable series starring the inimitable
Penny Wanawake

Don't miss
PENNY BLACK
'Debuts do not come more exotic and exuberant'
The Times

PENNY DREADFUL
'The successful second book in a notable series'
Financial Times

also from Futura

FUTURA PUBLICATIONS
FICTION/THRILLER
0 7088 3165 6

What horrifying secret lies within . . .

THE VIOLET CLOSET

Gary Gottesfeld

A terrified young voice cries out from the dark.

"Da hurt . . . Da kill . . . Help me!"

These are the panic-stricken words of a little girl phoning in to Dr Rena Halbrook's radio show. But who is little Alice – and where is she?

As Charles Halleran, veteran reporter, hears the child's plea over his car radio, he recalls another little girl named Alice who died in New York 18 years before. Can there possibly be a connection?

As the anniversary of that shocking death approaches, Charles teams up with Rena in a desperate search to uncover dark secrets from the past and prevent almost certain tragedy from striking again.

Their race against time will lead them on a spine-tingling chase from the placid streets of Beverly Hills to the burnt-out tenements of the South Bronx. And the more they discover, the surer they become that what they still don't know could definitely hurt them . . .

FUTURA PUBLICATIONS
FICTION
0 7088 4550 1

All Futura Books are available at your bookshop or
newsagent, or can be ordered from the following address:
Futura Books, Cash Sales Department,
P.O. Box 11, Falmouth, Cornwall TR10 9EN.

Please send cheque or postal order (no currency), and
allow 60p for postage and packing for the first book
plus 25p for the second book and 15p for each additional
book ordered up to a maximum charge of £1.90 in U.K.

B.F.P.O. customers please allow 60p for
the first book, 25p for the second book plus 15p per
copy for the next 7 books, thereafter 9p per book

Overseas customers, including Eire, please allow £1.25
for postage and packing for the first book, 75p for the
second book and 28p for each subsequent title ordered.